# HUSBANDS
## AND OTHER
# LOVERS

*Jane Elizabeth Varley*

**ORION**

First published in Great Britain in 2005 by Orion,
an imprint of the Orion Publishing Group Ltd.

1 3 5 7 9 10 8 6 4 2

A CIP catalogue record for this book is available
from the British Library.

ISBN  0 75285 279 5 (hardback); 0 75285 280 9

Printed in Great Britain

The Orion Publishing Group Ltd
Orion House
5 Upper Saint Martin's Lane
London, WC2H 9EA

www.orionbooks.co.uk

For Greg

I would like to thank the following people:

I am indebted to Jane Wood for her editorial advice. Also, Susan Lamb, Sophie Hutton-Squire and everyone at Orion. Thank you to Clare Alexander and Justin Gowers, Sarah Graham, Deborah Lloyd and Peter Ward. Special thanks to Adam Walker. Finally, thank you to my husband for his patient support, unfailing encouragement and the grilled cheese sandwiches.

*Part 1*

# WINTER

# Chapter 1

# Work

*I've always found Friday the most difficult day of the week. A couple of years ago I fell into the habit of stopping off at Corney and Barrow, a City wine bar, on my way home. I told myself and Susannah, my wife, that this was part of the social drinking required of a successful City lawyer. I would stay for an hour or so, stop at Waterloo station to buy flowers and catch the train to Oxshott. This Friday pattern, minus the purchase of the bunch of flowers, extended first to Thursdays, then to Mondays, until it occurred on all evenings of the week. In January of this year my boss, Raul, took me aside and told me to cut out my lunchtime drinking. Clients had noted my lack of concentration and my breath. I considered his intervention an impertinence. I protested that I only ever drank at lunchtime with clients or colleagues. Raul is an American and, I reasoned, unfamiliar with British business culture, which has always been steeped in alcohol. Raul drinks herbal tea and carries a bottle of Evian water into which he drops tablets of soluble vitamin C. Case closed. Nonetheless his instruction was a shock to me and I vowed to clean up my act. Susannah, of course, had been urging me to cut down for years. We had, just days earlier, held a small New Year drinks party at which my behaviour had been found wanting. But I dismissed all her complaints as an overreaction. If I stopped drinking Susannah would only find something else to complain about. However, it was clear that the net was closing in. I had to take action. I began with Susannah.*

Susannah Agnew drove up to the gates of the Chapters and pointed the electronic remote control at a discreet metal box mounted on the right-hand supporting brick pillar. The black wrought-iron gates, topped with gilt finials, swung open.

Situated on the borders of Cobham and Oxshott, the Chapters had been described in the developer's brochure as a luxury, gated development of three five-bedroom detached houses and two semi-detached flint-faced cottages. Casual access, to the despair of deliverymen and impromptu callers, was impossible. A state-of-the-art video entry-phone system allowed the residents to vet all those who sought to pass through the eight-foot-high gates. Once inside, the three main houses, fronted by expansive lawns and brick driveways, were grouped in a semi-circle around an asymmetrical lawned and planted central island. To the left of the houses stood the pair of semi-detached flint cottages, formerly a single nineteenth-century workman's dwelling, an afterthought following an acrimonious planning dispute in which the developer had been refused permission to demolish the original building and replace it with a fourth five-bedroom house. The whole development was encased by a tall brick wall separating it from Oxshott Woods and the world beyond.

James had brought the developer's brochure home. She could recall him, standing in their Fulham kitchen, reading out the text in a tone of mock pomposity. *This exclusive Surrey development will appeal to those discerning purchasers who are accustomed to homes of distinction and who demand personal security of the highest standard.* Or words to that effect. They had laughed, congratulating themselves on their metropolitan sophistication in the face of such appalling prose, unaware that they were already falling under the spell of the copywriter's flattering words and the photographer's seductive images. Now she could see how each phrase and photograph was cleverly chosen to appeal to the forty-something affluent purchasers at which the Chapters was marketed. Bedrooms, all with en suite bathrooms, were shown romantically furnished with sleigh beds and white linen and flowers. Children's rooms – immaculately tidy – featured book-lined shelves and desks neatly set with schoolwork. The dining room was laid for an elegant dinner party. The conservatory was set for morning coffee. The kitchen portrayed a laughing couple preparing Sunday brunch.

The only laughable thing, Susannah realized in retrospect, was that she had been taken in by it all – the idea that life in the Chapters would be one long round of passionate sex and convivial parties set against a backdrop of studiously silent children.

She and James had held one party, a couple of days earlier on New Year's Day. It was a small gathering for the neighbours. In addition she had invited everyone from Peter Charron & Co, the Cobham firm of estate agents where she had been employed for the last three years as a senior negotiator. She had mixed feelings about Anthony Charron's attendance – pleasure that he had accepted the invitation coupled with nervousness at how James would behave in front of her boss. Anthony was the owner and son of the firm's late founder, Peter Charron.

She did not especially want to hold a party but it was three years since they had moved in and it was important to 'reciprocate', as her mother would put it. Twenty or so people came. James, naturally, was in charge of drinks. She bought party food from Waitrose. Matthew, her fourteen-year-old son, helped hand it round. Lynda, the Charron secretary, brought her husband and a plate of choux pastries and helped her in the kitchen. Their guests, men in chinos and checked shirts, the women dressier in velvet and cashmere, stood around the drawing room, a room James and Susannah hardly used, looking out through the French windows onto the lawn beyond. For the party Susannah had filled the terracotta patio containers with winter pansies and small red cyclamen which would die off at the first frost. They were necessary to add colour, however short-lived. She had still not come to terms with the garden: evergreen shrubs in groups of three along the borders, planted by the developer.

Anthony had arrived late and apologetically. 'The dammed car wouldn't start!'

She assumed he meant the 1985 Rolls Royce Silver Spirit that he drove at weekends. James and Matthew were very rude about it. James said it made Anthony look like a used-car dealer and Matthew said the sand-coloured paintwork made him feel sick. Anthony, in cavalry twills and a V-neck Pringle sweater, presented her with a poinsettia, the pot wrapped in gold-coloured foil and tied with a red ribbon. She was used to seeing Anthony in a well-cut chalk-stripe suit and noticed

5

that a business suit was more flattering to his figure which, while not fat, could best be described as prosperous.

She led Anthony into the drawing room. James appeared with a bottle of champagne.

Anthony held up a hand. 'Orange juice for me.'

'No. We're not allowing that,' said James briskly and he handed Anthony a glass of champagne.

'Actually, I'd prefer an orange juice.'

James was good-humoured but his voice had an edge to it. 'Just as soon as you've drunk that.'

At that moment Susannah could smell the alcohol on James's breath. She looked at him and realized he was drunk. But he could be very drunk and not show it.

There was a silent stand-off.

'I'll get you one,' she said to Anthony.

'You're not at work now,' snapped James. 'No need to follow orders.' He turned to Anthony. 'I can see that my wife thinks she's in the office. Understandable. She spends enough time there.' She noted the sarcastic belligerence in his voice. No one could pretend that he was being anything other than obnoxiously rude – and it was quite obvious to Susannah that he wanted to pick an argument.

She felt the colour rise in her cheeks. She could not look at Anthony. And then Lynda appeared as if from nowhere. Susannah wondered, in retrospect, if Lynda had heard it all. She was wonderful. She grabbed James by the arm and said in a voice that brooked no nonsense, 'Susannah tells me that you're something of a gourmet . . .'

Susannah did not recall telling Lynda any such thing.

'. . . so I shall be very offended if you don't come and try my choux balls!'

There was presumably nothing that James could say to this. Susannah watched as he was led away. She turned to Anthony. 'I'm so sorry . . .' she began.

'Nothing to say,' he cut in briskly. And then, still holding the glass of champagne, he complimented her on the house and her dress – a shortish Monsoon red-beaded affair with a matching wide scarf draped across the shoulders – at which point Michael Belmont, a local solicitor and their near neighbour, came over and the three of them had a very pleasant conversation about a title-search problem on a property in Esher. James stopped handing round drinks after a while

6

and settled himself on the sofa with Martin Hollis, who was something to do with home cinema and whom Susannah had always found an awful bore. She had to do the drinks herself until Lynda instructed her husband to take over. After a couple of hours the house had emptied, Matthew had slipped out to his friend Jake's house, where he spent most of his free time these days, and James had exited from the kitchen where she was clearing up, taking with him a bottle of champagne.

'Work to do.'

She did not challenge him. There was no point. She heard the door of the study close and knew she would not see him for the rest of the afternoon until he emerged to make a pot of strong coffee. He would listen to music or watch the small television and then fall asleep in his chair.

At work the next day, Anthony had said nothing other than to tell her what a super party it was, and Lynda had been equally complimentary. She was grateful to them. Work at least was easy: no new instructions yet and few viewings. Most of Cobham was still on the ski-slopes of France.

She opened the front door, punched the code into the alarm and walked into the beechwood kitchen, kicking off her pumps so that they slid over the smooth maplewood floor. Taking a bottle of Perrier from the imported Maytag American refrigerator she pulled a glass from the dishwasher and went up the beige-carpeted stairs to the main bedroom, itching to change out of her work clothes. She pulled off the navy shift, untied her hair and carefully folded and hung up her Jaeger scarf in one of the built-in wardrobes. She pulled on a pair of jeans and a black polo neck and brushed out her hair. Her head felt suddenly heavy. She lay back on the pillow – percale and pastel-pink – testament to her undeveloped interest in interior design.

Matthew was sleeping over at Jake's, as was his habit on a Friday. She was conscious of the silence around her, the house ridiculously large, almost mocking her; they had all singularly failed to live up to the perfect life that this house had been intended to achieve. The people in the Chapters brochure did not have bitter rows. Or avoid the neighbours lest some open window had betrayed them. Or shun each other for days on end, barely exchanging a word, the tension so unbearable that frequently she would retreat to the spare bedroom and wish she could retreat further still.

Sometimes her depression would deepen and she would tell herself that they weren't even a proper family, let alone a picture-perfect brochure one. Matthew was *her* son and fourteen with it – too old for the trips to Pizza Express and Sunday mini-rugby and walks at Painshill that all the other Cobham families indulged in. Not to mention the fact that the proper families had been married for ages and only to each other.

They had packed up their misery in Fulham and unpacked it in this house.

However hard she tried she could not stop her thoughts turning to the party, replaying it in her mind. It was not that the incident had been so dramatic. In the past he had been just the same on holiday. They would go to some beautiful resort, with sun or snow or both, and James would uncannily seek out another man just like him – high-flying, hard-drinking – and she would have to drag him out of whatever beach bar or hotel lounge he had holed up in and he would complain and tell her not to be so bloody boring.

But this was worse because it was in front of their neighbours and her boss. It seemed to her to be another line that they had crossed. She deserved an apology and this time she was going to get one.

It had not always been this way.

When she had met him he hardly ever drank during the week and never at lunchtime. Susannah's friends at the time of her engagement, of whom she had many more than now, were clearly shocked and then openly envious at her news. One, Lavinia, who owned the ground-floor Wandsworth flat above Susannah's rented basement one, could not successfully disguise the fact that she felt that Susannah had in some way jumped the marriage queue. Lavinia had been single all her life, had no children and therefore considered herself to be several places ahead of Susannah who was divorced, with a seven-year-old son and no money to buy fashionable clothes or even get a decent set of blonde highlights. All these were handicaps placing Susannah, if not at the very back of the queue with the overweight single mothers, then in accordance with Lavinia's rules definitely barring her from jumping straight to the top.

Matthew's father, whose involvement with his son had been steadily declining since the divorce he instigated – he was, it turned out, not ready for family life – took her remarriage as an opportunity to disappear altogether amid mumbled comments about not wanting to 'confuse' Matthew. Her parents expressed repeated surprise that she had managed to snare a man. On her first trip home to her parents with James, her mother, washing up in the kitchen while the men drank brandies, whispered that at least she wouldn't have to worry about money any more. Which was true – it would be absurd to deny it – but lately when Susannah looked back it was the years of struggling, when it was just her and Matthew and her friends, that were actually the happiest.

Susannah had not married James for his money. She didn't hanker for a Mercedes sports car or a country club gym membership. She certainly didn't want to give up work. She liked selling houses and if other people looked down on that she had long since ceased to care. James's money promised her something more valuable than a life of leisured luxury. It offered her stability, the security of being able to open every envelope and pay every bill – something taken for granted by those who have money and an endless source of worry for those who do not.

There were other reasons. It was as if the maxim that opposites attract had been invented for them. James loved all that she feared. He liked to bet on horses, fight in court cases, take on all comers and win. She avoided confrontation and hated uncertainty. Their marriage promised a counterbalance for both of them. And sometimes it was fun to live vicariously through him. She sat in the passenger seat while he broke the speed limit; sat at his side as he debated late into the night at smart London dinner parties; sat on aeroplanes to far-flung destinations. And in return she packed the bags, kept the accounts and tied up the loose ends James left in his wake.

She had thought, after they married, that he would settle down. He had, after all, told her often enough that he yearned for marriage and the peace of a home and a wife and an end to the bars and the searching and the disappointments.

He had at least kept his promises to Matthew. Their relationship had strengthened over the years. James was 'Dad'. Of late, they had taken to watching television late at night on Fridays and Saturdays, holed up in the inaccurately-termed family room, eating Doritos and drinking – beer in James's case, Pepsi in Matthew's – and she worried about the example James was setting his stepson. James and Matthew made joshing comments to each other about her nagging, her obsession with healthy eating and her complaints about the stream of wrappers and crumbs they left in the sofas, on the floor and everywhere else besides. They imitated her, not unkindly, but it hurt enough for her to withdraw and go to bed alone and fall asleep before James came to bed.

She wondered if it would help to get someone else to talk to him. Not his mother; Estella would laugh out loud at the very idea that her elder son had a drink problem. Not his brother; James and his younger brother Robert had never been close and as they aged they seemed to delight all the more in outsmarting and outshining each other. No, there was only her.

The light was fading now. Through the bedroom window shone soft yellow light from the mock-Victorian street lamps that were placed between each house. God knew when James would get home. Fridays often meant a taxi home. About a year ago he had got into a fight on the train coming back from Waterloo. It was unbelievable but it had happened. It was just past midnight when she had heard his key in the door and then a loud thump as he hit the hardwood floor. She had sprung out of bed – she found it impossible to sleep when he was out, even after all this time – and had flown down the stairs. He was crouched on the hall floor, blood covering the lower part of his face, ugly red smears on his white shirt.

'Oh my God,' she had cried out. Her first thought was that he had injured his head.

He said something incomprehensible.

'What?'

'It's nothing . . .'

She could hardly understand him. His speech was slow and laboured. Concussion? A cold shot of fear ran through her. 'I'm calling an ambulance.'

'No!' Now he was clearer. He started to get up. She saw that he had blood on the palms of his hands and it had left handprints on the floor. He was struggling to balance and reached out to steady himself.

'Don't touch the wall,' she said, imagining bloodstains on the stark white paint. She grabbed his arm and tried to steady him. 'James, I'm calling an ambulance.'

'Don't fucking call anyone!' His tone, the fear in it, stopped her short. She began to think more clearly.

'How did you do this?' she demanded.

He was more coherent now but clearly reluctant to say much. 'A fight. On the train. Some yob . . .'

She watched him as he straightened up, blinking hard. 'You mean you were *attacked*?'

'Leave it.'

He staggered slightly and she saw that his jacket was ripped. It was a beautiful jacket, handmade by Gieves and Hawke. Since being made a partner James had used part of his bonus to buy one very good bespoke suit every year. She could see immediately that the jacket was beyond repair. He was not wearing a tie. He looked ghastly, his skin a shade of grey and his eyes bloodshot and unfocused. She reached out and touched the jacket. He looked down at it as if noticing it for the first time. She had a hundred questions in her mind.

'You *must* go to the police. You can't let him get away with this. What if it happens again to someone else?'

But he was already walking unsteadily into the guest cloakroom opposite his study. He fumbled for the light, leaned heavily on the marble vanity unit and peered at his reflection in the mirror. 'Christ!' He raised a shaking hand to his face.

She took a step towards him. 'Let me see.'

She clasped his shoulder and turned him to her. Now in the light she could see that it was a deep cut to the lip, nothing more serious, though a bruise was forming on his right cheek. It was astonishing that one cut could produce so much blood. He stank of drink and cigarettes; he had obviously spent all evening in some bar.

Now, realizing that he was less seriously hurt than she had initially feared, her concern turned quickly to exasperation. 'What have you been *doing*? Where have you *been*?'

His voice was indignant. 'Where I always am. Broadgate.' He meant a bar in Broadgate.

Her voice took on a pleading tone. 'James, you must go to the police.'

'No. I said leave it.' And this time she could tell that it was useless to try to reason with him.

Perhaps it was just as well; he was hardly in any state to give a coherent witness statement, and goodness knows what the neighbours would think of a patrol car arriving at this time of night. She forced herself to concentrate on the present and what needed to be done. She ran her eye over his jacket – what a waste. The thought of money jolted her. 'Have you got your wallet?'

He nodded and pulled it from his inner suit pocket. She shuddered.

He had a wallet full of credit cards and the cards for their bank accounts, including their current account. She took it from him, as from a child, and checked that they were all there.

He said nothing. She lifted up the edge of his cuff to confirm that he was still wearing his watch.

'Go into the kitchen.'

She had cleaned him up with antiseptic wipes. She gave him some water to drink, which he sipped reluctantly, and then he seemed to drift into a stupor. She tried to be thankful that nothing more serious had happened. He could have been beaten half to death, or worse, for nothing more than his wallet and his Tag Heuer watch. Of course he was vulnerable, the state he was in. She knew James well enough to know that he was not the type to get into fights. He was not a violent drunk, more a sarcastic one, with an original turn of phrase if she tried to stop him drinking. Generally, though, he liked to drink by himself, in his study or watching television. His drinking had the effect of isolating him from her. The rows came when he sobered up the next day.

She could see it was hopeless to get any sense out of him that night. She took his ruined jacket from him, emptied the pockets, rolled it up and took it outside to the dustbin so Matthew wouldn't see it in the morning. Then she remembered to wipe the hall floor. And then she had got James upstairs, where he had all but passed out on the bed, fully clothed. She couldn't face the smell or the snoring so she had left him there and gone to sleep in the spare room. Spare rooms, she recalled from the Chapters brochure, were described as *guest suites* and presumably not envisioned as boltholes for the disgusted wives of drunken lawyers.

She never did get a proper explanation of what had happened on the train. He muttered something about an altercation and she had asked why no one had come to help him. He had asked her if she had read a newspaper lately. And then he had told her to stop obsessing about it. She told Matthew that he'd fallen over. For a few weeks after that he came home earlier, but soon the late-night Friday routine started up again. Now he took a taxi home, which cost a fortune but was at least safe.

There was no one she could tell about the Friday nights and all the other nights. It was too embarrassing and almost too fanciful. She was actually afraid that people wouldn't believe her, that they would think she was making it up. James was such a clever and charming man, after all. In public. Like it or not, she was alone with this. She would just have to try harder to show him that he might not *want* to cut down his drinking – but he certainly needed to.

Robert Agnew was a bastard. A cold, hard, unsympathetic, judgemental, critical bastard. But right now Natasha needed him – who was she kidding? She was desperate for him – and so she said nothing as he scanned the third page of the *News of the World* spread open on his desk.

Right now he was the only thing standing between her and her collapsing career.

'You *stupid* cow. I told you. Over and over again. But no – you knew better. Why the fuck – just out of interest – do you employ me to manage what we might loosely term your career if you then go off and ignore every piece of very good advice I give you?' He leaned forward across the desk and she had to admit, even in her misery, that he was rather magnificent. 'Natasha, they're closing in. They have been for a long time. I told you months ago.' He read from the half-page report on page three.

'"Sarah Lewin, betrayed wife of Arsenal footballer Mark Lewin, speaks exclusively to the *News of the World* about the affair that rocked her marriage. . . and how she won her husband back . . ."'

For one heart-stopping moment she thought he was going to read the whole thing. Instead he pushed the paper at her. A picture of the Lewin family glared back at her: Sarah looking unbearably smug, Mark smiling weakly and the two children all posed in the enormous back garden of their Essex house.

'"I'm just glad to have him back. And the boys have got their Daddy home,"' he quoted. He folded the paper disdainfully. 'You got off lightly. This is what they could have written: "Natasha Webster, everyone's favourite girl-next-door, is a marriage-wrecker with a fast-declining reputation. And she is about to lose all the lucrative endorsements that her PR supremo worked his arse off to negotiate for her." That's the truth, honey, isn't it? And that is what they're going to write soon.'

God, this was getting heavy. When she'd first met Robert he'd seemed such a gentleman. Suave but sort of homely at the same time. Safe and middle-class and not like all the other agents and PR people she had considered to represent her. But now she realized that was just part of the deal. He *was* safe and middle-class and respectable – with all the instincts of a bare-knuckle fighter. That felt really good when he was battling for you, but distinctly uncomfortable right now.

She couldn't look at him. Instead her eyes rested on the walls of his Soho office and the display of framed covers. *PR Week* Best Agency. Three times. Profiles. *Evening Standard* Top Media PR. On his desk she could see a framed photograph of his daughter. Arabella? Arabia? Something like that.

Robert's voice cut in. Startled, she realized that he had walked round to the front of the desk and was standing in front of her.

'They're onto you. They're after you. They've built you up and now they're waiting to pull you down. You've got an image problem. Why don't you fucking deal with it?'

She felt a surge of anger. 'I have *not* got a problem. This has all just got . . . out of hand. I'm fine.' She felt him about to interrupt so she raised her voice and ran on. 'I turn up at work and I do my job. In fact, I've been working very hard. *Very* hard,' she repeated unnecessarily, giving herself time to collect her thoughts. 'I made a mistake. He told me he loved me, that he'd leave. And he did leave—'

'Before fucking going back!'

If she didn't laugh she was going to cry. He caught her eye and she began to giggle.

He raised his eyes to the ceiling. 'Darling. What were you thinking of? A *footballer*.'

She rallied. 'Don't be such a snob. He was very . . . attentive.'

'At passes and ball skills.'

She'd asked for that one.

'And playing away from home,' he continued.

She looked away. 'All right, all right.'

He sat down and leaned back in his chair. But he was not finished. 'Natasha. You are the nation's sweetheart. Sexy enough for the dads to tune in but not so vampish that the women hate you. You love kids and animals and old ladies.' He put on a fake coy voice. 'You're just so . . . natural and unaffected.' He looked at her hard and slowed his words to emphasize his point. 'That's your image – some naïve, kind-hearted girl who just happened to wander into a television studio one day and start reading from an autocue.'

She was silent. They both knew, without needing to acknowledge it,

14

that her career had been anything but accidental. It had been plotted and manipulated from childhood. She had been moulded and pack-aged as carefully as any product on a supermarket shelf.

He turned and walked over to face the window that ran from floor to ceiling, twisting the blinds open to look out on the early Friday evening, the lights appearing all over London. She was wise enough to keep quiet.

'OK. This is what we do. A piece . . .'

'No!'

'Shut up! Just fucking listen. A piece. With someone nice. We offer them the story – the stress of the last year – not that you have any real stress in your life, but we'll think of something . . .'

God, he was infuriating, but what was the point in arguing? She could see him going into action, doing what he was best at. 'We'll have to give them something . . .'

'What?' Panic gripped her. She knew the form. Head off a hostile story by cooperating with the journalist. But they'd want something in return.

'Relax.' Robert's voice was soothing. 'We'll think of something. How you cope with the pressures of your busy life: namely exercise and a healthy diet.' He looked at her amusedly. 'Walks in the country. Get you photographed in a pair of Hunters. Rent a dog for the day.'

Reassured, thoughts of Mark Lewin receding, she started to unwind. Robert's enthusiasm was catching.

'And in the meantime you keep your head down. I don't want you out in town. Not for the next few weeks. Lie low, stay at home, just go out for work. And when you do go out, dress like Doris Day. Let me hold them off. But I need you out of the way. Moores are bloody edgy.'

Her stomach turned over. *Moores*. Moores for Babies – manufactur-ers of creams and lotions and potions – everything the caring mother needs for her children. Her contract with Moores currently involved her in the most naff TV commercial conducting fake interviews with snooty middle-class mothers and their mewling precocious children about Moores' new range of organic cereal bars and juices and those chocolate-covered rice cake things. She shuddered at the memory – anyone would have deserved a shag after that day's filming. But Moores paid the mortgage on her Putney house and the Audi and lots more besides. Above all they had, after so long, given her the financial security she craved.

She hesitated, then said, 'What did you tell them?'

He paused, aware of her discomfort. 'That it's a blip. That we have it under control. I assured them that their star presenter has no immediate plans to run off with one of their customer's husbands.'

'And the interview . . .'

'Your footie friend? You can't avoid questions on Lewin. We haven't got the clout to demand a no-go on that. But we'll work something out. I'll get onto it.' He sat down at his desk and fell silent, looking at her. 'You OK?'

'Yes. It'll be fine. We'll do the interview and it'll all blow over.' Who was she trying to convince – Robert or herself?

'Well, take it easy. Lay low.'

'Definitely! No problem. I've really learned my lesson, Robert.'

His appraising look continued for a couple of seconds until he turned away, reached for a file and began making a pencilled note. She relaxed. She felt safe now that everything was under control. As he wrote she looked at him anew, noticing the shadow on the slight tan, the slightly too-long hair greying at the temples and the strong hands. He wasn't her type: too old. He must be nudging forty. But he was attractive and she knew plenty of predatory women who would go for him. And as she shifted slightly to look again at the photograph on his desk she tried to recall how long he had been divorced and whether he had ever mentioned a girlfriend.

James, she had to concede, at least retained the ability to surprise her. He was home at just past six o'clock. And he was sober. Moreover, he had just placed a small, square, pale-blue Tiffany box on the kitchen table next to his steaming cup of coffee.

'Well, aren't you going to open it?'

He spoke nonchalantly, casting off his pinstripe suit jacket, unbuttoning the top button of his white shirt, loosening the navy silk tie. His expression was impossible to read, his features composed if slightly guarded, looking exactly as she imagined he would in some late-night high-stakes legal negotiation.

She felt absurdly embarrassed at a gesture that even James must surely know was extraordinarily inappropriate? The atmosphere between them had never been worse. They had barely spoken since the party two days earlier and the more she had thought about it, the more she was determined to receive an apology from him – an apology she had no doubt he would not see any good reason to deliver. As much to delay untying the ribbon that elegantly encased the box, she pulled out a kitchen chair and felt some small sense of comfort when she saw James mirror her and pull up a chair so that he faced her across the pale-grey marble-topped table. At least they were going to speak. Beyond them the garden lay in darkness, save for a narrow corridor of light shining from their near neighbour's conservatory.

He pushed the cup of coffee away from him and sat back. His features were drawn, his dark eyes guarded.

'I come in peace,' he said dryly.

She could not help but smile. This was James in control, charming and very difficult to resist.

She was going to try. 'I think you owe me an apology.'

He raised an eyebrow. 'What for?'

She did not rise to it. 'For the party.'

'Oh, I see.' He took a very slow sip of coffee. His voice was casual, his expression a touch confused. 'What exactly do I have to apologize for?'

Her mood changed abruptly. 'What for? What do you think?' Her voice rose. 'Your behaviour!'

'My behaviour?' he said, giving the appearance of not understanding.

'Yes,' she snapped. 'Getting drunk, being rude to Anthony, embarrassing me—'

'Anything else?'

'Yes, actually. Leaving me to clear up on my own, leaving Lynda's husband to top up everyone's drinks . . .'

'OK, OK.' He lifted his head back, looked at the ceiling, then returned her gaze. 'I'm sorry. Is that all right?'

'No, it's not!' She was almost shouting now.

'You said you wanted an apology,' he said innocently.

'Yes – and a promise that it won't happen again.'

He sighed loudly. 'Anything else?'

God, he could be infuriating. He had the ability to keep his cool while provoking her to lose all control.

'James, you have a drink problem!' she shouted, leaning across the table and extending her hand in the air.

He did not move. 'Susannah, we need to look at this in a calm, sensible and logical way. Instead of overreacting. I do not have a drink problem. . .'

'Yes, you bloody do!' She forced herself to sit back.

'There's no need to swear at me. God, I get criticized enough if I say a word out of place to you—'

She wanted to defend herself but there was no opportunity.

'And frankly, I can't promise you I will never, ever get drunk again. Be reasonable. As for the party, I'm sorry I didn't help you clear up. I did suggest we had caterers but you wanted to do it all yourself.'

She felt as though she was sinking. But there was no time to gather her thoughts in defence. James's voice was relentless.

'Let's look at this sensibly. Let's say – for a moment – that you're right. That I'm some gutter alcoholic on skid row and you're right to try and save my soul—'

'That's *not* what I'm saying!' she cut in.

He raised his hand. 'Calm down. Let's say, for argument's sake, that I do have a drink problem. Where's your evidence? Let's run through the options.'

He paused. She felt completely defeated, surly and resentful. Outmanoeuvred because she knew exactly what was coming and she couldn't do anything to stop it.

'Well?' he said questioningly.

She couldn't even look at him.

His voice fell still lower. 'Susannah. You're the one who wants to discuss this. I'm offering to do just that. The least you could do is cooperate.'

She could have hit him. Screamed and shouted. And he'd have told her that she was hysterical and neurotic and how could anyone be expected to take anything she said seriously?

'OK. Do I drink in the mornings?'

She said nothing.

'No,' he continued, 'I don't drink in the mornings. I get up, make coffee and I don't add a shot of vodka to my Gold Blend.'

He paused and took a sip of his coffee. Then he paused to undo the cufflinks of his shirt and casually roll up his sleeves. He gave every appearance of being effortlessly relaxed.

'Do I drink at work? No. To summarise: no vodka in the coffee and no Scotch in the filing cabinet. Do I drink and drive?'

That was too much. 'Yes you bloody do!'

He sighed. 'I have never been stopped by the police. I have never taken a breathalyser test – let alone failed one – because my driving has never given cause for concern. If in doubt I take a taxi.'

'You *have* driven over the limit!' She felt enraged now. 'What about after the Hollises' party?'

He gave an even deeper sigh. 'The Hollises live half a mile away. It was two a.m. along a road I have driven down countless times before. If you felt unsafe why did you come in the car with me? Or why didn't you offer to drive instead?'

'Because *you* had the keys and *you* got into the driving seat and I wasn't about to make a scene in front of everyone.'

'It's very difficult to talk about this if you're going to get upset every time I defend myself.' He paused and took another sip of coffee. 'If you're going to accuse every man who's had one glass too many and got in a car of being an alcoholic then you might as well point the finger at half the population – and plenty of women, too. What about your ladies' lunches? They serve wine; you're not telling me all those girls stick to Perrier. It's drinking amongst women that's the real problem in society.'

How had they moved from discussing her husband's drinking to analysing trends in alcoholic consumption? There was no time to consider this. James had moved on.

'I hold down an extremely responsible job. I am one of the firm's most successful partners. That hardly fits with your image of me on a park bench with a can of lager and a mongrel on a string.'

She exploded. 'You drink every bloody day, twice a day! You can't have a meal without a glass of wine. The first thing you do when you walk through the door is open a bottle. And then you finish it. And then you open another—'

'You have some too,' he interrupted.

'I have a glass, James. *One* glass. And lately I don't even feel like that. And before you say, as you always do, that you need to unwind, let me tell you that it's worse on holiday. Drinks in the room and then in the bar and then at dinner and after I've gone to bed back to the bar with whatever boring cronies you've picked up. You're so hungover you don't get up until midday and when you do you're a pig to be around. It was like that in Antibes. When I tried to get you to come to bed you called me a "controlling freak" in front of the whole bar!'

She could feel herself close to hyperventilating, rage and frustration spilling out of her, an urge to shake him.

He looked at her with disdain and spelled out his words with affected slowness. 'So I have a drink – in the evening, on holiday. Is that it?'

He got up and went over to the kitchen sink, jerking the tap so that water splashed out of the glass he was filling.

She spoke to his back. 'And when you can't drink it's worse. You're so . . . edgy and miserable. Drumming your fingers waiting for the waiter to take your drinks order. Or the time we went to that restaurant, the vegetarian one in Covent Garden, and we'd ordered and you found it was unlicensed. You tried to hide it but I could see you were livid.' She rushed on. 'And I've seen you at dinner parties when your glass is empty and the host hasn't noticed. Do you realize, James, that your glass is *always* empty before everyone else's?'

'You are obsessed!' He swung round and she could see how riled he had suddenly become. 'Listen to yourself. Checking my glass.' His tone was contemptuous. 'Haven't you got anything else to do with your time?'

But she was lost in her thoughts. 'And the worst thing is that you change. It's as if there's a different person inside you – an angry, unhappy, wretched person – and when you drink that person comes out—'

'I've never heard such psychobabble in my life—'

'That person comes out and I hate that person. It's like an addiction; you just have to have that drink. And you'd rather have that than be with me or Matthew or anyone else. And that's another thing: you surround yourself with people who drink – men like you – and God help anyone who doesn't.'

'Nonsense!' He was shouting now. 'For fuck's sake. Have you any idea how hard I have to work? If you had my life, you'd drink!' He checked himself. 'Not that there's a problem. No one else thinks the way you do. For God's sake, other men go home and have a glass of wine and their wives don't give them the third degree.'

A silence fell between them. Their argument was all too predictable. Her accusations were as well worn as his responses. He sat down again at the kitchen table.

She reached out a hand across the table. 'You could go and speak to someone. What if I were to make you an appointment with Dr Palmer? It would be totally confidential. No one need know.'

He was clearly affronted. 'That idiot? I'd sooner go to the vet.

Susannah, no one is going to know because there is nothing *to* know!'

'What harm—'

'No! Look. I can see there's nothing I can say that will change your mind. So this is what we'll do. Just to show you – to demonstrate once and for all that there isn't a problem – I will give up drinking. No alcohol whatsoever. For a whole month.' He paused as if to allow her time to absorb the significance of his statement. 'And I'm sure you would agree that no one with a real problem could stop drinking for a month. It would be impossible.' He spoke with an unshakeable assurance. 'Their alcoholic cravings would take over – hands shake, that sort of thing – and inevitably they'd be driven back to the bottle.'

He reached out his hand and took hers, running his fingers softly over her wedding ring. 'Hey, look at me.'

She forced herself to raise her eyes from the table. His gaze was concentrated upon her. The unbidden thought came to her that her husband didn't look like an alcoholic. He was good-looking and lean, with the air of a man who could run five miles and swim a couple more, his features apparently unchanged in the years since their first meeting.

'Susannah. I love you. I want this to work. And I'll do whatever it takes to put your mind at rest.' He took the blue box that lay between them and pushed it towards her. 'Aren't you going to open it?'

She forced a smile. Her head was spinning from James's abrupt shift from anger to affection. His resolve to stop drinking for a month seemed to have ruled out the possibility of any further debate about his drinking. She wanted to ask him what would happen after the month was up; she needed assurances that the drinking wouldn't resume in the same old pattern of destructive excess. But to raise that point risked reopening the argument and arousing accusations of churlishness. Instead of saying more, she pulled at the bow and untied the small knot before gently easing off the close-fitting top of the box. Inside lay a small fabric pouch. As she lifted it from the box she felt the circular hardness of a ring. Despite the anxious thoughts that held her, a small wave of excitement welled up. She looked at him and read the pride in his eyes.

'Go on then.'

She took out the ring and gasped. It was gold, inset all around with blue sapphires.

'It's an eternity ring. A symbol.' He took the ring from her and held

21

her hand, easing it next to her wedding ring.

'James . . . it's beautiful.'

'A symbol of a new start. Susannah, just give this a chance. Don't kill us off. I believe in us but you have to believe in us as well. You have to trust me.'

At that moment she felt she had no alternative, in the face of his promises and his words of commitment to her and his generosity.

She spoke quietly. 'I do. I'm sorry.'

# Chapter 2

# Moral Values

*In general, I continue to resist the accusation that my drinking has resulted in any diminution of my moral values. I have been faithful to Susannah, honest with my clients; I have not committed perjury or theft or fraud. I did, however, start a fight in the first class carriage of the 23.50 train from Waterloo to Oxshott. The fight took place on a Friday night in an old-style carriage designed for eight passengers, the banquette seating arranged in two facing rows. I was alone in the carriage until a young man and his girlfriend burst in. They sat opposite me. The girl was barely able to sit up, clearly under the influence of illegal drugs, and voluble to the most irritating degree. She insisted that her companion light a cigarette. He complied. He was no more than twenty years of age, in jeans and a cheap leather jacket, his short hair gelled into spikes. I was irritated that these two people, holding second class tickets, thought that they had the right to occupy a first class carriage. I told him so. He called me something unrepeatable. I pointed to the No Smoking sign on the window. His girlfriend, a slip of a girl, dressed for winter, bared-legged in a white leather mini-skirt, laughed. He added that I should 'fuck off'.*

*I was very drunk and the idea came to me that if I hit him they would both leave and I could get some peace. It seemed a perfectly reasonable idea at the time. So I stood up and grabbed the lapels of his leather jacket. I clearly recall the look of surprise on his face. It is not often that a man in a suit commits what the police would term an unprovoked assault. He got up and for what seemed a very long time we shoved each other back and forth. It was a face-off. And then I slipped. He had hold of me. My jacket ripped as I fell hard to the floor. The side of my face hit the panel below the window and my lip split on the window edge. I was not seriously hurt but I was humiliated. I heard his girlfriend snigger. When I got to my feet I saw that he had backed off. He thought it was all over. So it* must have been a great surprise to him when I slammed my fist square into his nose. There was the crack of bone and blood spewed out, spraying us both. He was in pain and shock. I hit him again. Now his blood was on my hands. The girl was close to hysterical and I told her to shut up. She threatened to pull the communication cord and we both told her 'no'. He mumbled the word from where he was bent over holding his face. I looked at her then and I realized that she was terrified. That, more than the blood, made me stop.

The boy was holding his face – he must have been in agony – while the girl urged him to call the police on his mobile. And then I said, in a moment of adrenaline-filled clarity, 'It's your word against mine and I'm not in possession of Class A drugs.' It was a lucky guess. They looked at each other and as the train slowed for Earlsfield they left the carriage. She called me a 'psycho' as she left, and I saw them stagger onto the platform. No one came to assist them. There are rarely ticket inspectors at that time and the first class section of the train was deserted. At Oxshott I waited until the platform had cleared before making my way out of the station and home. Susannah assumed that I had been assaulted and I let her think that. The incident has played on my mind and I have been careful since then not to place myself in a similar situation.

A Sunday morning in London, cold and crisp in January, is as romantic a setting as anywhere in the world – and awfully lonely if one is single. Standing in her pyjamas in the small sitting room of her Putney house, Natasha disconsolately viewed the debris of a Saturday night spent alone. A half-smoked packet of Marlboro Lights, a dirty wine glass, a half-finished plate of Marks and Spencer's cauliflower cheese and an empty DVD case from Blockbuster. And it was only nine o'clock. Even the small pleasures that might bring respite from her solitary state were denied her. The Putney Cafe Rouge for coffee and croissants was out of bounds – she was taking seriously Robert's advice about lying low – as were the Sunday newspapers she imagined to be filled with unwelcome news: at best Mark Lewin pictured on some family outing, shopping or riding a rollercoaster. At worst there would be a slew of vindictive comment. Last week that Samantha Wood woman had written about her in tones of moral outrage – she was a spoilt single girl, intent on pursuing her selfish dream of happiness, heedless of the misery rained down on innocent children.

As if Mark Lewin had nothing to do with it.

She put the thought out of her mind and began clearing away, straightening the throws on the pair of small sofas arranged at right angles around the aged-oak coffee table, on which stood a clutter of books and scripts, candles in stained-glass votives, and her small brass ballerina figure. Noticing with dismay the dust that had gathered, she fetched the Pledge spray from the under-sink cupboard and began a serious spring-clean in the semi-gloom. She did not dare open the wood-lattice blinds in case some photographer was hanging about outside. She might risk an afternoon walk down to the river. The house was barely a couple of hundred yards from the Thames, the riverfront dominated by the ramshackle wooden buildings that housed the rowing clubs. On boat race day the area was gridlocked.

She took down the stack of invitations from the mantelpiece, dusted the books on the shelves to either side and vacuumed the oriental rugs that were scattered on the stripped wood floor. Above the fireplace hung the oil portrait of her by Toby Ansthruther, Robert's gift to her to celebrate the Moores contract. Toby had been sweet, very upper class and insouciant and filled with stories of his wife and their new baby. So the final result had been a surprise. Not the smiling girl-next-door at all. Instead a small, isolated figure sitting upright on a simple wooden chair stared out with an expression of guarded wariness. She had not known how to react but Robert had nodded approval when he had seen it.

She decanted dead flowers from her Waterford vase and wondered yet again about getting a cleaner. But always some fearful instinct prevented her from giving a key to her house to anyone. *Never let anyone get too close.* And so the state of the house alternated dramatically from pristine cleanliness to outright burglary-style chaos. Moving onto the kitchen she bleached the sink and got down on her hands and knees to wash the floor. Her mother's voice entered her head: *If you can't do it perfectly, don't do it at all.* These were the words that had come to be the motto of her childhood, from ballet class to elocution lessons, from her first day at stage school to every audition as they progressed from mail-order catalogues through glossy magazine advertisements and then the great break – television. And then it all began again. Advertisements, then silent extra roles, then the day her mother opened the white envelope printed with the BBC logo and cried as if every hope and dream in her heart had finally come true. It was the offer of a presenter's job on *Blue Peter.* There was no question of discussing it. Her planned twenty-first birthday party had been cancelled – 'you're moving on now' – a new wardrobe of funky clothes assembled and she spent her first assignment fossil-hunting on a beach near Lyme Regis.

At least her mother wouldn't call this morning; Sunday mornings were spent playing golf with Don.

While the kitchen floor dried she went upstairs and began stripping the bed, dusting the French armoire and the cherrywood bedside tables. On the Ottoman a brood of soft-toy pigs nestled together. She knew very well that stuffed toys were supposed to be top of the list of turn-offs for men but she had never known the pigs put any man off his stride. Besides, the pigs were loyal, discreet and didn't run away which was more than could be said for any of her recent lovers. So the pigs stayed.

She was on her hands and knees with her Mr Muscle spray cleaning the bath when the telephone rang. At once her instinct for self-preservation wrestled with her need to hear a human voice. Aware that it was far more likely to be a journalist than a friend she nevertheless ran into the bedroom and snatched up the receiver.

'My dear. You're awake. Congratulations!'

'Robert.' His sarcasm washed over her and the sign of their easy familiarity even pleased her, until she wondered precisely why he was telephoning her on a Sunday morning.

'Is it the papers?' she asked anxiously.

She noted the pause.

'Yes and no. Actually they're not bad. Lewin's only made it to the sports pages.'

'And the *no*?'

'A couple of the column women are sharpening their fangs. Mary Ehrhart in the *Telegraph* says you need to grow up and . . .' there was a rustling of papers in the background, '. . . and that Henderson woman has gone all psychological and thinks you've got a problem with commitment.'

'It's the men who've got the problem!' she protested.

'Not according to Ms Henderson, our Fleet Street shrink. "The root of Natasha's problems surely lies in her childhood," he quoted. His voice took on a brisker tone. 'So. What's the nation's favourite girl doing today?'

She gave a hollow laugh. 'Cleaning, actually. And then, when the excitement of that has overwhelmed me, the ironing. And if I'm really lucky, sweeping the patio.'

'Good. Just as long as you keep out of sight—'

'Robert, I need food,' she interrupted.

'Internet delivery.'

'You've got an answer for everything.'

'Seriously, darling, lay low. And if you must go out – I have no faith that you won't – for goodness' sake look presentable. This is no time for a tired and haggard pic.'

'Understood.'

Still the uncomfortable feeling persisted that Robert had called for some other unspoken reason. But it was useless to push him. Discretion was a way of life for him and no amount of clever questioning would draw him out. He infuriated the journalists; so often he stood between them and the gossip or insider information they craved. But at the same time he had their respect. He didn't lie, or leave false trails, and he was straight – or if he wasn't it could never be

27

proved otherwise. His word that a story was accurate was guarantee enough to go to print.

'Good.' His voice was businesslike now. 'Well, I've got a houseful of guests to feed and I'm required for kitchen duties.'

'You?'

'Yes, believe it or not my life is not totally subsumed in your career. I am also employed as first kitchen assistant for Sunday lunch preparations.'

At once a sharp pang of loneliness rose up inside her. If he was the assistant, who was the cook? As they said their goodbyes a montage of domestic scenes ran through her mind. First Robert with a smiling, clean-cut girlfriend, side by side in a warm kitchen; then a traditional Sunday lunch on the table, happy guests sipping wine, conversation flowing; next coffee and chocolates in the drawing room, laughing children scampering about the house. Then an afternoon walk and tea and home-made cake and then when everyone was gone a quiet Sunday evening curled up in front of the television. Until bedtime.

As she replaced the receiver a feeling of complete aloneness engulfed her. She was an outsider in a world of families. She climbed onto her stripped bed and folded the bare duvet around her. She had so much: a glittering career, money and possessions, invitations to all the best parties. She had spent her life climbing to the top of the mountain, always professional, never late, with none of the airs and graces that other presenters adopted along the way. She drank tap water and ate whatever was served and didn't care about the size of her dressing room or the angle of the camera. But now that she was at the top of the mountain, and the long, painful climb was over, she stood at the summit alone. There was no one with her to share the view.

'Just an orange juice for me.'

Jasmine and Robert looked round simultaneously and Susannah fancied that even the hamster seemed to stir briefly. Paintball, the school hamster, occupied the upper pod of his transparent tubed cage where he slept wrapped in multi-coloured shredded paper, the cage placed on layers of newspaper on the kitchen floor. Sawdust, Araminta had solemnly informed Susannah earlier, was used in the olden days to look after hamsters and was bad because it hurt their skin. For now Araminta was nowhere to be seen, though there was a good chance that she was shadowing Matthew, who was in turn undoubtedly slumped in front of Robert's outsize television watching Sunday lunchtime football on Sky Sports. James and Susannah stood in the kitchen observing Robert and his current girlfriend, Jasmine, cooking Sunday lunch.

James spoke in a resigned tone. 'I'm off alcohol. For a whole month.'

'I've only got water or apple juice,' declared Robert, emerging from the inside of the refrigerator.

'Can't you have just one glass?' offered Jasmine tentatively from her position standing at the kitchen sink rinsing broccoli.

'No.' James held up a hand dramatically. 'Apparently not.'

There was a fractional awkwardness during which Robert cast a quizzical glance in Susannah's direction and went back to the fridge where he retrieved a bottle of Badoit.

Susannah shifted. She was unsure whether to offer Robert help, certain that any offer would be refused, but at the same time she had that feeling of redundancy that so often overcame her at Agnew events. At least Estella wasn't going to be there. James and Robert's mother had always intimidated her, from the first time she had met her. James had taken her down to his parents' house in Wiltshire where Estella, elegant in tweed and pearls, had asked her questions and glanced over her clothes. She had felt inadequate in every way.

Robert's invitation had been issued yesterday by telephone and it was James who had taken the call. An impromptu invitation to Sunday lunch and all very casual. Susannah wondered at the time why it had been issued.

'I've asked my new neighbours.' Robert was chopping carrots, surprisingly quickly and dextrously, into uniform batons. 'Andrew and Louise. Just arrived from Hong Kong.' He turned to Jasmine. 'Don't cut those too small or they'll turn to mush,' and then back to Susannah. 'Wife used to be a model. Stunning.'

Susannah would have been interested to see Jasmine's reaction to this last comment but could only see the girl's back turned away from her at the kitchen sink. Jasmine had appeared six months ago, a childlike figure dressed permanently in black, apparently picked up by Robert at a fashion shoot where she was the photographer's assistant, a role it appeared to Susannah that she reprised as Robert's girlfriend.

Robert threw a handful of carrots into a shining stainless steel pan. 'Andrew Winter's a venture capitalist – as in Harrold-Winter.' He turned to Jasmine again. 'Darling, here. Like this.' Robert began cutting broccoli florets.

James raised his eyebrows. 'They instructed us on the planning application for the Docklands Pyramid.'

Susannah felt her attention beginning to wander as James launched into an explanation of the Pyramid, loosely based on the Louvre Pyramid but larger and gaudier and filled not with art but City office space.

Involuntarily, she cast a professional eye over the kitchen. Like most owners of these Wandsworth Victorian houses, a stone's throw from the common, Robert had knocked through to form a kitchen and dining room in one. But whereas most of his neighbours, she was confident, had furnished their kitchens with the south-west London chic of aged refectory tables and distressed French dressers, Robert had opted for a modern approach. It was bold and risky and not at all what she would have advised had he asked for her prior opinion, which needless to say he had not, but she was gracious enough to admit that it had worked. So the dining area flat roof had been removed and replaced with a glass cathedral ceiling, one wall had been taken out and likewise framed with glass, the floor was now sandstone and a Scandinavian birch table so pale it was almost white dominated the space. And on the opposing wall a Whitechapel Print Shop silkscreen print, some eight by six feet, provided a shocking red abstract, suggesting a blazing typhoon sweeping across the clear whiteness of the room. She had never cared for Robert but his house would sell overnight.

Jasmine was laying the table, unwrapping from its plastic laundry wrapper a white linen tablecloth.

Susannah was anxious to do something. 'Let me help.' Together they smoothed the starched cloth across and Jasmine brought out silver cutlery and white porcelain side plates.

'Robert's serving a Sancerre and a really special Bordeaux,' Jasmine informed her and even in the moment in which she felt a stab of anxiety for this challenge to James's newfound abstinence, Susannah picked up the affectedness of Jasmine's remark. Jasmine, it was clear to her – because she herself was the same – was not a girl who had grown up watching fine wine served at Sunday lunch. Susannah's father's drinking could never have been described as social.

'I think they have a little boy. Do you think they'll bring him?' Jasmine sounded anxious. 'You don't know, do you, if you invite people to Sunday lunch. They might . . .' Her voice trailed off and she began setting out glasses – three each – a huge balloon, a smaller wineglass and a water tumbler. 'And Matthew? Will he have wine?'

'No.' Susannah picked up the edge in her own voice and backtracked quickly. 'I mean, he's got homework to do this evening.'

'He's so sweet. Teenagers can be so grumpy but Matt's such a sweetie.' Susannah resisted enlightening Jasmine that Matthew's behaviour around her was entirely uncharacteristic, that his defining mood was one of unrelenting grumpiness, and that the only explanation for his charm was the gargantuan crush he had had on Jasmine since he first encountered her at Robert's summer party. 'And he's so good with Minty.'

'He is?'

'Oh, yes!' Jasmine spoke in the sincere tones of someone who never thought ill of anyone.

Susannah, on the couple of occasions they had met previously, had struggled to make conversation with Jasmine. She seemed so young, so lacking in opinions other than those she had copied from Robert.

'How's work?' Susannah settled on this as a safe subject.

'Oh, terribly busy. We've just come back from Morocco.'

'Clothes?'

'Jewellery, actually. African. It's lovely; huge pieces. So they wanted a desert backdrop.'

'How very exciting!'

'Not really,' sighed Jasmine. 'It was really, really hot and Paul can't stand the heat and the cameras had to be kept out of the sun. It was awful . . .'

Her voice trailed off again. Paul Bass, Jasmine's boss, was an ageing fashion photographer who eschewed the modern trend for quiet professionalism and upheld the traditional vices of large cigars, huge fees and an ego beyond measure.

Susannah was saved from resuscitating the conversation by Robert's intervention. 'Jazzy. You've forgotten napkins.'

'Sorry!' Jasmine dived into the kitchen and began counting from a drawer eight white linen napkins.

'No! Use the blue ones.' Robert jostled her to one side and began hunting through. 'It's lunch.'

Susannah, observing them, caught sight of James in the kitchen beyond, picking up one of several bottles of red wine that stood in the corner, reading the label before replacing it. Turning round he noticed her watching him and the flash of irritation that crossed his face was unmistakable. She looked away, conscious that their obvious discord might have been witnessed by the others, and was relieved to see that Robert's attention was still focused on the napkins.

'Just fold them, there's a good girl.' Robert sent Jasmine off into the dining area.

It was difficult, watching Jasmine arrange the napkins in their positions, not to recall the girls who had preceded her in this same role: all of them nice girls and none of them lasting more than six months.

Jasmine took a step back and surveyed the table worriedly. 'I just know I've forgotten something.'

And as if to prompt her, Robert's voice carried from the kitchen. 'Leave it. Why don't you girls go into the drawing room?'

At this, Susannah realized she was about to be marooned with Jasmine. Worse still, James would undoubtedly choose to linger in the kitchen with Robert. And more importantly the wine. A flash of fear rose up inside her. Did she think that as soon as her back was turned he would be swigging from the bottle? No, it was nothing as crude as that. It was the certainty she felt that her presence acted as a protection, a talisman, in that when she was present she acted to control his drinking and, therefore, her absence risked it beginning again.

'Actually, I'd better just check on Matthew.' Belatedly realizing that checking on a fourteen-year-old seemed overprotective in the extreme, she added, 'And Araminta.' This would allow her to nip swiftly down to the basement, make sure all was well, return upstairs via the kitchen and with luck persuade James out of the kitchen and into the safety of the drawing room.

The steep basement stairs led into what was formerly the cellar. Robert, at apparently huge expense, had had the cellars knocked into one and tanked and painted white, then furnished as some sort of games room, decoratively at odds with the rest of the house in a laddish masculine style that Susannah, with her knowledge of Robert, presumed to be ironic: black leather sofas, a Bang and Olufsen Home Cinema system, a Playstation and, taking up half of the room, a snooker table. Matthew was absorbed in some Playstation game, apparently guiding gnome-like figures through a castle dungeon, whilst Araminta was sprawled at his feet on the zebra-skin patterned rug making beaded friendship bracelets.

It was clear that neither required her supervision and that any questioning of Matthew would be met with an irritated shrug. In any case her mind was preoccupied with James. They had survived the aperitifs – no champagne had appeared, thank goodness; that was always a temptation – and she would be sitting opposite James at lunch so that would be OK. And then this evening it would be two days, or more significantly a whole weekend, which was unheard of. For James to give up drinking for a whole weekend must be a good sign, must as he said be an indication that nothing was wrong, and surely a good sign for the future.

Araminta's voice penetrated her consciousness. Startled, she realized the child had been calling her name.

'Susannah, Susannah. Look!'

She switched on a smile and pulled herself with effort out of her preoccupation.

'I've made three,' exclaimed Araminta, holding up three strands of intricately woven multi-coloured threads. 'I'm going to put some beads in this one.'

Susannah went over and sat down next to Araminta on the rug. From Matthew's direction she heard a loud sigh, the implication being that her very presence in the room distracted him from the technicalities of Playstation. She chose to ignore it. 'And who are you making them for?'

Araminta paused. 'One for Daddy. One for Jasmine. One for . . . you?'

'Thank you!'

Araminta's deft fingers wove the fourth bracelet. At eight years old she had a focus and composure beyond her years. Susannah could barely remember Araminta's mother, Tabitha, from the couple of family functions at which they had met; her entry into the Agnew family had been followed soon after by the divorce. But she remembered enough to see that Araminta had the look of her mother: tall, with blue eyes, ash blonde hair.

'You could make one for Mummy?'

Araminta frowned. There was a pause. 'No. I don't think so.' And then, almost as if the preceding sentence had never been uttered, 'Daddy wants me to wait down here while he does lunch. Then later on we'll go for a walk.'

Matthew's distracted voice cut in, 'When's lunch?' He did not look up from the television screen or cease manipulating the black plastic controller he clasped in both hands.

'I guess about half an hour,' said Susannah, rising to her feet.

'I'm starving!'

'Well, come upstairs. There'll be crisps and things.'

'Nah . . .'

Susannah grimaced. Matthew's adoption of Oik English, as James termed it, infuriated her but now was not the time to launch into the set speech in which she reminded him that he went to a good school and that speaking like a lout was a ridiculous affectation.

In any case, Araminta was running to the stairs. 'I'll bring you some crisps . . .'

As Susannah watched her shoot up the staircase she leaned towards Matthew. 'You shouldn't let her wait on you hand and foot!' she hissed.

'Nah,' Matthew replied with a grin. 'She likes it; she's a woman.'

And with that there seemed no alternative but to cuff him playfully around the ear and retreat upstairs. As she ascended the basement stairs she heard the front door slamming shut and then made out introductions, kissing, laughter. And a woman's voice, low and carrying.

When she emerged from the basement and into the hallway she found herself in the middle of what appeared to be a mêlée but which was in fact, on closer inspection, three adults and a small child. Robert was engaged in the task of removing a pale cream sheepskin coat with a fur lining, a task complicated by the fact that its owner was smoking a cigarette. Next to them a harassed-looking man was endeavouring to carry a netted bag of assorted toys, a short plastic chair designed to be affixed to a dining chair and, at the same time, restrain a small boy from racing off down the hallway. The Winters had clearly arrived and brought their toddler with them.

There are very few women of forty, or thereabouts, who can dress like a twenty-one-year-old. Louise Winter was such a woman. She wore low-slung hipster jeans, chocolate-brown suede cowboy boots and a tight white T-shirt cut low to skim her rounded cleavage. The accessories, however, were not those found on the high street. Susannah took in the Cartier tank watch, the Tiffany diamond heart pendant and a shoal of gold bangles. Then the dark, full eyes, a deep tan and pale-pink lipgloss.

Susannah stood awkwardly, unsure whether to pretend she hadn't seen them and retreat – or stand and wait to be introduced. Her dilemma was solved by Robert turning and catching sight of her.

'Ah! Susannah. Let me introduce you to Louise and Andrew and . . .' – at this point he gave a wholehearted but not entirely convincing attempt at a benign smile – 'Oliver!'

It was obvious to Susannah that the Winters were the real guests. She caught the edge of anticipation in his voice, the flurry of activity by the door, the solicitous way he was now shepherding them down the hallway and into the drawing room. The Winters, it was clear, were to be spared sight of lunch preparations in the kitchen. She would have liked to peer into the kitchen to check on James but Robert caught her elbow and steered her in after the new arrivals.

'Champagne!' he announced theatrically and disappeared.

The double-aspect room overlooked the driveway to the front and the garden to the rear and was large enough for three chintz sofas to be grouped around the marble fireplace above which hung a huge, gilt-framed mirror. The rest of the room was filled with what she imagined were some rather good antiques, a smattering of Victorian oil paintings and the china and silver that was the hallmark of the upper-middle-class English drawing room. And a Steinway. All of it a very tasteful, slightly understated but unmistakable testament to Robert's business success. And he was still only thirty-eight.

It was not a room, however, that Susannah ever felt particularly comfortable in. It was in her opinion over-designed, and now to make matters worse she stood awkwardly in the centre of the room while both Winters ignored her and each other. Louise Winter had walked directly over to the mantelpiece to inspect Robert's rich collection of thick white embossed invitations, which Susannah thought must be rude by anyone's standards, leaving Andrew to dispense a mountain of Brio wooden train tracks onto the cream carpet. She was grateful when Oliver noticed her, holding up a wooden train and announcing baldly, 'Train!'

She was saved the effort of making further conversation by the arrival of Robert grasping two bottles of Tattinger, closely followed by Jasmine carrying a tray of glasses and three small oval silver dishes filled with almonds.

Noticing him, Louise turned away from the mantelpiece, seemingly not in the least embarrassed and said, 'You don't mind if I smoke, do you?' in a tone that implied her question was naturally a formality, the effect heightened by the action of simultaneously dropping ash from her cigarette into an orchid newly in bloom on a side table.

Robert, however, was effusive. 'Not if you have a glass of champagne with it!'

Susannah caught Jasmine's eye. Robert was a fanatical anti-smoker. He reached into a drawer and pulled out a Hermès ashtray picturing an Indian elephant.

The sight of the champagne had drawn Oliver away from the train track.

'Drink!'

He lunged, with surprising speed, at one of the long-stemmed crystal champagne glasses that Jasmine had set down on the low coffee table.

He was, Susannah guessed, aged between two and three and dressed like a miniature version of his father in thick bottle-green corduroy trousers and a blue-green checked shirt of which only the collar could be seen over the neck of a cream Arran knit jersey.

'Darling, don't do that!' Louise's voice conveyed a defeated assertiveness. 'Oliver!'

Oliver succeeded in grabbing the glass.

Louise's half-hearted tone continued, 'Oliver, if you do that I will get very cross.'

Oliver began waving the glass about wildly. 'Drink!'

Jasmine stepped forward and prised the glass from Oliver's hand. 'I'll get him one.'

Louise's 'thank you' was a fraction slow, and in the offhand manner usually adopted by a preoccupied diner to a harassed waiter. Jasmine however appeared not to have noticed, disappearing at speed out of the drawing room. In any case Robert's popping of the first bottle had distracted Oliver's gaze from the glasses.

Louise's attention was now focused on Robert, leaving Oliver to grab a handful of almonds while Andrew sat absorbed on the carpet in the construction of an advanced three-track Brio junction.

Handing champagne all round, Robert settled next to Louise on one of the pair of facing sofas set at right angles to the fireplace, leaving Susannah feeling distinctly stranded on the opposite sofa. Even Oliver had disappeared off to join his father, leaving a trail of almonds in his wake, and still there was no sign of James. She listened as Louise outlined what she described as her 'latest project' to Robert.

'Jewellery,' she proclaimed. 'Inspired by Victorian jewellery, big brooches and drop earrings, but all updated with semi-precious stones. We do a fantastic fake diamond brooch, heart shaped, and we do stars. And necklaces and bracelets. The charm bracelet is our signature piece. You can have it made up with a choice of charms and add more to it . . .'

Reluctantly, Susannah had to admit to herself that Louise was a born saleswoman, able to radiate enthusiasm and a total belief in her products.

Robert was giving her his full attention. 'And how do you sell it?'

'Through my website. Next year we're planning to open a shop in Parson's Green.'

Robert ignored this. 'And what's your selling point?'

Louise looked blank.

'Your story,' he explained. 'What makes you special? Why would anyone buy from you? Where's the value? What does the Louise Winter brand represent?'

Louise lit another cigarette and used the time it afforded her to rally slightly.

'Actually, that's a very good question. So far we've marketed it on the basis that I used to model, and then I went to art college and now I'm a mother combining designing with looking after a family.'

That this was not an impressive brand strategy was evident in Robert's expression. 'Mother starts business from kitchen table. It's hardly original, is it?'

He took a sip of his champagne and Louise inhaled deeply. If she was insulted by his appraisal of her brand strategy she didn't show it. Instead she was watching him think.

'Personally,' Robert continued thoughtfully, 'I think you need to appeal to the Fulham twenty-somethings. That is late twenties, early thirties. Pre-kids. Mothers with young children haven't got money to splash around on jewellery. Ditch the mother angle. You need to place yourself as glamorous, young and upmarket. Special enough for a City boy to give to his girlfriend but not so expensive that you frighten the horses. If you start a shop it needs to be inviting. People feel intimidated by jewellers.'

She was impressed, that was obvious. Turning her body to face Robert's she asked, 'And how would I do that?'

Robert got up and solicitously refilled her glass, then looked at

Susannah. 'Drink up!' He turned back to Louise. 'Push the ex-model line. Work on your image and then build the brand around it. In terms of the market I'd work on filling the gap between fine jewellery and costume jewellery.'

He was interrupted by Jasmine returning with a glass of apple juice. She seemed to have taken for ever.

'James says he's holding the fort in the kitchen,' Jasmine announced. She went over to Oliver and with a smile went to give him the glass. His hands reached out eagerly.

'Actually he needs his beaker,' cut in Louise. 'It's in the baby bag.' It was clear she was not going to move to get it. Jasmine had little option but to open the bag and start rifling through, extract the blue plastic beaker and then decant the juice from the glass, spilling a good splash of it in the process, and earning an offhand 'Thanks so much', from Louise and then, from Robert, 'Don't leave that, Jazz. It'll mark.'

Wordlessly, Jasmine exited the drawing room yet again, presumably in search of a cloth to clear up the spilt juice.

'If you like I can sketch out a few ideas,' said Robert, apparently as an afterthought.

Louise's response was anything but offhand. 'Would you? *Thank you*. I've heard a great deal about your firm.' She raised her voice to project to her husband, who was out of sight behind the opposite sofa. 'Darling! Did you hear that? Robert says he'll work on some ideas for the shop.'

A muffled voice called out, 'Super!'

The voice was not able to see Louise's hand rest lightly on Robert's knee at precisely the moment Jasmine re-entered the room holding a roll of kitchen towel. Jasmine's mouth tightened. She did not look at Louise, who had withdrawn her hand and was downing the last of her glass. Embarrassed, Susannah could think of nothing to say to break the sudden silence that had fallen. Only Robert looked relaxed, sitting back and regarding the three women with an expression of detached amusement.

'Shall we go in to lunch?'

Jasmine surveyed the table. Everyone but Oliver had finished the rhubarb fool. Louise, to be accurate, had not touched hers and Matthew, unselfconsciously, had offered to eat it for her. His boldness had won him her passed plate and a wink of the eye. Andrew was tapping his watch and looking at his wife with raised eyebrows. His wife, in turn, was glaring back at him. 'Don't be so bloody boring.' Louise was squeezing James's shoulder as she said this to her husband. Susannah looked like thunder and Robert, could you believe it, was refilling Louise's glass.

Jasmine had listened, but not participated, as the lunchtime conversation kicked off with a discussion of the proposed extension of the local conservation area. They had gone on to analyse house prices in the south-east, moved onto holiday villas in the Garonne and restaurants in the Nightingale Triangle, then deviated from material matters to critique the Common Entrance examination and the merits of boarding versus day school. Louise had then held forth about their time in Hong Kong, their house on the Peak, their parties, their servants (who were close to tears when she left) and the strategy she had adopted in order to oversee the refurbishment of their new house in Wandsworth whilst still resident in Hong Kong. The secret, Louise disclosed, was to secure the services of Jerzy, a Polish builder and Wandsworth local legend, with his band of illegal immigrant countrymen. Cash only, naturally. There then followed twenty minutes of builder stories – it was difficult for Jasmine to participate because she had never employed a builder, let alone sued one as Robert was frequently doing, and she planned to do all the decorating in her new flat herself.

Moments earlier, however, these safe and wholly predictable subjects had been thrown overboard by Louise, who had diverted the conversation in order to take issue with James's self-imposed month of sobriety. It was a hijack and as such a dangerous and volatile situation.

Louise pushed her face towards James. 'It's not personal. Actually, I *adore* lawyers! In fact . . . you can mandate my proxy any day!'

Louise gave a scream of laughter and James raised a wry smile. Andrew was expressionless and it appeared that rather than try again to persuade Louise to leave and be rebuffed, he had decided to turn his attention to spooning rhubarb fool to Oliver.

Louise was leaning in to James now. 'Come on! You *must* try this.' She reached over for the bottle of Marsala. 'Just a snifter,' she wheedled. 'A snifter.'

James held up his hand. His voice was unruffled. 'Really. No thank you.'

'Well, I think too much clean living can be harmful,' Louise proclaimed. 'Harmful! Think about it.' She held up her hand and began counting off on her elegant red manicured fingers. 'Sugar. Coffee. Chocolate. Meat. Do you realize what that means? Do you realize? It means *everything* is harmful. Now. The answer is . . . moderation. Everything in moderation.' She adopted a mock-serious tone. 'You don't live longer if you don't drink. It just feels like it!' She gave off another peal of laughter.

Jasmine observed it all. She felt sorry for Andrew and embarrassed on his behalf. When someone was rude to you it was almost more embarrassing for the people around you. Paul, her boss, and Robert, were always being rude to her. She seemed to attract men like that.

She hated Louise. Louise was a cow – but she had to take it all and bow and scrape to her because otherwise Robert's plan wouldn't work. It was a good plan. Harrold-Winter, he'd heard through the City grapevine, were looking for a new PR. Andrew was the way in. And Louise was the way in to Andrew. Observing them for the first time at a neighbour's drinks party, Robert had spotted her dominance in the relationship, quickly deduced that she was the power behind the throne and set out to win her confidence.

That, she had now realized, was Robert's winning formula. He held to the proposition that every man, or woman, has their price. Not necessarily money; he was far more subtle than that. Perhaps the word was manipulative.

It was ironic watching Louise at the table, believing that she was the centre of Robert's attention, unaware that she was nothing more than a conduit to her husband. Robert had been careful to sit away from Louise, to talk in a casual way to Andrew about cars and horses, Andrew's two great passions, and to position James to take the brunt of Louise's flirtatious mood. It was worse because James was a really interesting man and they'd had such a fascinating conversation in the kitchen before lunch when the others had gone off to have drinks in the drawing room. Robert had left her to finish the pudding.

'So what does a photographer's assistant do?' James had asked with genuine interest.

'Everything!' she laughed. It was especially true with Paul and included doing his weekly grocery shop at Cullens. 'But that makes the job interesting. And Paul gets great jobs.' She almost added 'still' but that would have been disloyal. 'Fashion spreads, magazine advertising, portraits . . .'

'For publication?'

'For publication and private use. We just did Joe Saltzman a few weeks ago for the *Sunday Times*, actually.'

They had talked briefly about Joe and James's work for him and James had mentioned that he did copyright work, too. Copyright law was something she had covered at college but never fully grasped so James must be clever as well as charming. And then she had realized that she needed to check if Robert wanted anything. When she got back she found that James had washed up the dishes in the sink. He seemed to want to stay out of the way. The brothers were clearly not close. Robert rarely mentioned James and they made no effort to see each other. While she filled up Oliver's beaker – Louise appeared not to lift a finger herself – they had talked about her recent trip to Venice with Robert and James had said that Robert ought to have bought her a very expensive piece of Murano glass. Then she had remembered Oliver Winter waiting for his beaker and dashed back to the drawing room.

At lunch Jasmine had been placed with the children, Matthew to her right and Araminta opposite. Oliver sat to her left on his little booster chair. That was fine by her. In any case Andrew sat the other side of Oliver. Andrew seemed nice, too. Why did such nice men marry such horrible women? They had just begun to talk about her next trip with Paul – a fashion shoot in Las Vegas.

'Make sure you go out to the Grand Canyon,' Andrew had said. 'It's a shame to go all that way and stay inside.'

'I agree.' She made a mental note to consider it as a location.

'I'm sure you'll have a great time. I like to look at the paintings in the Bellagio. You'll have to give us a report when you get back.'

Andrew seemed a thoughtful and gentle man and it was obvious that he was far better at looking after Oliver than Louise was. She would have liked to talk to him for longer but next to her Araminta was fidgeting. She was playing with her napkin and wanted to go, but Jasmine knew from past experience that she would be wise to wait until everyone had finished eating. Robert was a stickler for manners. Araminta began kicking her legs against her chair.

'When are we going for our walk?'

'Soon, sweetie,' Jasmine reassured her.

'How soon?'

'Well, I expect the grown-ups will have coffee and a chat and then we'll go.'

Araminta looked unimpressed by this.

'Will we be back in time for Mummy to get me?'

'Yes.'

Jasmine felt a tightening in her stomach. Which was ridiculous. She had never met Araminta's mother. She just knew that the arrival of Tabitha at four on a Sunday afternoon for the designated handover provoked a tension in the house which was palpable. At least it was only once every three weeks; Robert was too busy to do more. And what he neglected in time he made up for in activities. Araminta weekends were quasi-military operations consisting of a carefully selected and complementary array of educational, leisure and social pursuits. This weekend had seen them visit the Titian Collection at the National Gallery, far too adult in Jasmine's opinion – but that didn't count – then lunch at Smollensky's and the latest Disney in the afternoon. Robert did not neglect spiritual matters, either. Sundays usually saw Jasmine and Araminta ordered out of bed and marched to the family service at their local church, St Luke's, a newly-invigorated hotbed of Church of England evangelism, whose middle-class professional congregation Robert networked with zeal at the après-service coffee while Jasmine stood around eating malted milk biscuits, trying to avoid talking to anyone because they all assumed she was married to Robert and Araminta was their daughter and she was too embarrassed to put them right. Which meant that she ended up lying, if only by omission, but in a church it was surely worse? Today, however, lunch had taken precedence over worship, and a Sunday walk was one activity Araminta always enjoyed, Wimbledon Common, Richmond Park or Wisley Gardens being the top three choices.

Jasmine saw Matthew check his watch. 'Arsenal kick-off in five minutes.' He slid out of his seat. 'Are you coming?'

She would have loved to come. But she needed to stay.

'Staps playing?' Andrew asked Matthew.

'Nah. Still injured.'

'Staps is the new signing,' Matthew explained to Jasmine. 'Transferred from Eindhoven. Ten million and then tore his ankle ligament on his first outing last week.'

Matthew stood up and reached over to grab a piece of bread. Araminta, seeing this, got up too. But if she had hoped to slip out unnoticed on Matthew's tail, Robert's voice stopped her in her tracks.

'Araminta! Have you asked to get down?' His tone was jovial but insistent.

Araminta recited the formula in a bored singsong. 'Please may I get down from the table.'

Robert clearly decided to ignore the tone. 'You may,' he said, smiling beneficently.

That bit always made Jasmine wince. Not the concept – she couldn't bear children running wild round tables – just the affectation. *You may.* Why couldn't he just say yes? Increasingly she had grown concerned that there was something slightly superficial about Robert's relationship with Araminta.

But she had no time to consider this. The dialogue between Robert and Araminta had provoked Louise into a new round of passionate advocacy. 'Bringing up children! That is something I feel *so strongly* about.'

Was there nothing the woman did not feel *so strongly* about?

'People don't realize that you have to have standards. Rules are there for a reason. You might not like them. But you see, that's the point of them. Children need a mummy and a daddy and they need to stay together. It isn't always easy. But you have to stick at it.'

'How long have you been married?' It was Susannah and if Jasmine was not mistaken she was getting riled. She hardly knew Susannah, so it was difficult to judge, but she hadn't seemed in a very good mood to start with. She wondered if Susannah and James had had a row that morning.

'Four years,' proclaimed Louise.

Jasmine could feel the tension. She knew from her brief experience of London dinner parties that certain topics were best avoided when drunk. And if any subject was certain to provoke furious emotion it was a debate involving a half-cut middle-class mother on the best way to bring up children.

Louise had not picked up the note of challenge in Susannah's voice. If anything she continued with greater vigour. 'So I speak from experience. Sometimes I'm prepared to admit it; it's not easy.' She paused to give effect to the insightful words to follow. 'But nothing worth doing ever is!'

'Darling.' Andrew's voice was urbane as he cut in, rising to his feet. 'We mustn't detain our host any longer.' He turned to Robert. 'I'm sure you have plans for the afternoon.'

Louise ignored him. 'But people want an easy life. As soon as the going gets tough they bail out and to hell with the effect on the children. And society is falling apart as a result. Falling apart!'

'I don't think it's quite that simple—' Susannah began but Louise cut her intervention short.

'But it is. It's about sticking with it, not taking the selfish way out and expecting the State to give you a flat and money to live on . . .'

'Plenty of single mothers work—'

'When they're not having six delinquent children by six different fathers!'

'That is a small minority—' persisted Susannah.

'Who cause most of the problems!'

Louise really was impossibly rude, talking over Susannah and it had to be admitted succeeding as the more persuasive debater precisely because of her lack of subtlety and the blunt force of her argument. Susannah's analytical approach was simply swept aside.

While Louise paused to take a drink of wine, Susannah tried again.

'I know from my own experience that choosing to leave a marriage is never an easy option. And that many mothers do a fantastic job bringing up their children afterwards.'

Louise rolled her eyes. 'I'm sure that's true,' she said in a tone that implied the complete opposite, that it was in fact irrelevant nonsense, 'but you're married now so it obviously wasn't that great, was it? Being on your own?'

Jasmine winced. Louise was getting very close to the bone. Susannah was clearly struggling for words. A fraction of a second before Louise would surely have started up again, James's voice cut in. He spoke in a low, calm voice that threw into sharp relief Louise's shrillness and Susannah's tense responses.

'This is a debate that will have to be continued another time.'

'But we've just got started,' protested Louise.

'You have; I fear so.'

'But it's only half past three!'

'It is,' James echoed. He was very impressive. Calm, authoritative but at the same time able to give Louise the impression that she was in control.

Louise was petulant. 'Don't be so bloody boring!' she said, shaking his arm.

'But I am,' James agreed. 'Terribly boring. And quite old. And very afraid of what my wife will say if I don't get home and attack the list of chores she has prepared for me.' He rose to his feet and took her hand. 'So, dear lady, I'm afraid I must with a heavy heart take my leave of you.'

James's impromptu adoption of the language of the Victorian gentry had a captivating effect on Louise. She smiled up at him.

'You,' she said, 'are a *gentleman*. You must come to dinner. You will! In fact . . .' She began rummaging around on the floor presumably in search of her handbag. 'Let me find my filofax and write down your number. You must come over.'

Susannah wore a tight-lipped expression as she watched Louise fumble first for her bag, then for her filofax, then for a pen. Eventually, numbers were exchanged.

'We were having fun. You mustn't mind me!' She stood up. 'Now we have to say goodbye properly.'

There was something compellingly awful in Louise's extended embrace of Susannah and the accompanying protestations of new friendship and the fulsome thanks to Robert. After what seemed an age James and Susannah backed out of the kitchen, Susannah calling down to Matthew to leave and Araminta solemnly handing out friendship bracelets. By the time they had rounded up Oliver and Louise had gone to the loo, and Andrew and Jasmine had picked up the toys from the living room, it was nearly four o'clock and then in the middle of it Tabitha arrived. There was no time for Jasmine to say goodbye to Araminta because Robert had instantly hustled her into the kitchen out of the way as he always did.

And that was where he found her a few minutes later, washing up the balloon glasses that couldn't be put in the dishwasher. She guessed, from the assortment of odds and ends in his hand, that he had been tidying up. His neatness, she had come to appreciate, was obsessive. He put down her scarf on the counter – from Oasis, silk with beaded tassels – and she anticipated some complaint about it being left on the hall chair or somewhere else he deemed to be wrong.

Instead he moved up behind her silently and put his hands on her hip bones, faintly leaning into her, talking to her as if only to himself.

'Quite a pantomime,' he said dryly.

She was unsure whether he felt it had gone well or badly so she said nothing. He could be very touchy about things he had organized. He continued thoughtfully, 'So, Mrs Winter is a lush and her husband's a wimp. Much as I thought.' He moved away and picked up her scarf, toying with it. 'His problem is he thinks he needs to keep her happy.

45

That just encourages her to demand more and more.'

'And what would you do?' she asked with a trace of irritation.

'I wouldn't have married the bitch in the first place.' Robert's tone was suddenly hard. 'That accent's as fake as her tan. Did you pick up the Lancashire? Delve a little deeper – I intend to – and I think you'll find Mrs Winter is a fraud.'

Jasmine felt a stirring of unease. Robert could switch like that and a bitter tone would come into his voice and then go just as quickly. In those moments she would feel on edge and say nothing. A tense silence fell between them. He was folding the scarf with care, laying it carefully on the kitchen counter. Then she felt him draw closer to her again.

'I could take you right here.'

His hands moved to the waistband of her trousers and began tugging, his fingers feeling for the fastening and finding it at the side, deftly unbuttoning and then easing down the zip.

'Not here.'

'Yes, here.'

It was not that they could be seen. It was just that she would have liked something different for a Sunday afternoon: slow sex in bed and then a cup of tea and curling up together watching some DVD. Not that anything like that had ever happened with Robert but she kept hoping that it would once they had been together for longer and got comfortable together and he relaxed a bit.

He was still behind her, one arm locked across her waist, the other pulling down her knickers.

He had not kissed her, did not touch her other than to remove her clothing, and then when she was naked his hand stretched from holding her waist to grasping her wrist. He held her hard, his grip cutting into her, and pulled her wrist down to lower her body towards the floor.

'Go on.'

She knew exactly what he wanted. 'No,' she said, imbuing her voice with as much reluctance as she could.

'Go on,' he repeated, still holding her and using his free hand to unbutton his belt and jeans, easing his hardening cock from his boxer shorts.

'In your mouth,' he said in a low, insistent voice.

'I'm not in the mood.'

He exhaled. 'Go on.'

It was as if he hadn't heard her. She felt upset and pressurized and confused. This time he was ignoring the code between them, the play that led to the games of bondage and domination which characterized their sex life. Before, when she had said no, he had backed off and she had distracted him and it had all been OK – games she enjoyed when they were games. But now she was beginning to sense that they were more than games for Robert, that they were essential to his enjoyment, and that the intimacy she kept expecting to evolve in their relationship was, after six months, as far away as ever.

Now, for the first time, he seemed angry at her failure to acquiesce. He grasped her wrist more tightly than he had ever done before, and then he pulled her down by her hair.

'You're hurting me!'

'Go on!'

He had ignored her. She had told him he was hurting her; he must know that he was causing her pain, but he had made it worse. Now she felt scared, a hot flush rushing to her cheeks.

His tone was relentless. 'Do as you're told!'

She had had enough. 'No! I mean it, Robert.'

He said nothing. A few seconds passed. They remained posed like statues. She waited for him to withdraw, for the scene to change and everything to be all right.

The slap, when it came, was as fast as it was shocking, as it was sickening. His hand hit her hard across her face, stinging her cheek. This was no game. She was too stunned to speak. Hot tears filled her eyes but her chest was so tight that no sound accompanied them.

His voice was cold. 'I don't want to hear you speak.'

Swiftly he took hold of her body and pushed her to the floor so that she was half-kneeling, half-crouching, bewildered at the unreality of what was happening. She held on to some faint hope that he would stop. The feel of his hands pushing her shoulders made it clear that he would not. She attempted to shift away from him, kicking as hard as she could.

In response she felt a vice-like grip around her waist as he pulled her back towards him. She felt a searing pain as he grabbed her hair and pulled her head back.

'You like it, darling. You like the games we play.'

They both knew that this had moved far beyond the bedroom acting of the past. She was truly frightened now, aware how her resistance excited him, conscious that he was more turned on than he had ever been before. It was as if all the games that had preceded this moment, the silk scarves and the black blindfold and the whispered language of domination and submission, were precursors of the real domination Robert desired.

His violence scared her but the potential for violence he possessed terrified her. She had read once that for prisoners the fear of violence can be worse than the violence itself and now she understood how that would be the case. Instinctively she knew that he would delight in quelling her resistance and then go on to match it blow for blow.

She surrendered – felt her body go limp, gave up thinking of how to get away, took her mind to a different place. To a place where it was over and she was safe and it would never happen again. He pushed her forward so that she was kneeling and then used his hold on her hair to push her head to the floor. Her face pressed against the cold stone. She tried to form a picture in her mind of the front door slamming shut behind her and the cold air on her face as she ran down the street, away from this place and into the late light of the afternoon. As she felt him enter her, bruising her and impatient for his own pleasure, she realized that this act had nothing to do with sex between them. He thrust deep inside her so that she ached, but some instinct of self-preservation warned her to say nothing, that it would only encourage his abuse of her.

He was close to finishing now, his movements swifter and still more forceful. But as the first inklings of some feeling of relief crept upon her she heard his voice.

'Say you're a whore.'

She would not, could not do that. There was a part of her she could not allow him to reach, would not let him defile, a small strong core of dignity that he could not touch. So she said nothing.

His voice was calm and quieter than it had been at any point. 'Say you're a whore.'

It was the cold evenness with which he spoke the words that caused shock in her heart. The sudden, awful awareness of his calculation and manipulation. It was as if he had read her mind, sensed the feeling of relief that began to fill her as she anticipated that it would all be over, and then acted to wrench her back and further exert his power over her. At this realization the fear came flooding back, only now it was worse, heightened by her appreciation of his skill at bringing them to this moment and his determination not only to dominate her but, in the final seconds, to utterly humiliate her.

'I won't tell you again.'

She waited for him to hit her. But instead she felt the soft smooth silk of her own scarf slipped across the front of her neck. Suddenly she knew without a shadow of a doubt that this was his intention all along. He had planned this moment. Slowly he began to tighten the scarf.

'Say it.'

She wanted to believe that it was impossible, that he would never do such a thing, but she had reached a place with him where the normal rules no longer applied. She knew he was capable of hurting her. She believed now that he might be capable of anything. He was pulling it tighter now so that she was beginning to struggle for breath.

'Say it!'

She had, quite simply, never known such fear. And so she said the words he wanted and in saying them felt the last traces of her power pass to him. He came a few seconds later, the scarf loosening as he finished with her.

He withdrew from her in silence and got to his feet. She eased onto her side and waited for what would happen next. It was with relief or disbelief that she heard him leave the room and go upstairs.

Tentatively she pulled on her clothes. She wanted to cry but paralysis gripped her and it was all she could do to pull her sweater on, fasten the button on her trousers and run her hands through her hair. Some sense that she was watching herself accompanied all these actions. When she reached for a glass and turned on the tap she saw how her hand was shaking so badly that the water could barely fill the glass and that when she raised it to her lips she could hardly hold it steady.

She was so focused on trying to sip the water and take away the dryness in her mouth that she did not notice him standing in the doorway. She jumped with shock. Casually he entered the room and walked over to the fridge. He pulled the door open and took out a bottle of mineral water, unscrewed the cap and took a long drink.

'Why are you drinking tap water? London water tastes foul. You should have this.'

What in God's name was he talking about?

'I don't care what water I'm drinking.'

'What's the matter now? You enjoyed it, didn't you?'

She tried to sound strong. 'No. I didn't.'

'Oh. I'm surprised to hear that.'

It was as if Robert inhabited a different reality from what was true, from what had actually happened.

'I can't believe you're saying that.' Her voice broke and hot tears welled up in her eyes and began running down her cheeks. 'It was horrible. I didn't like it and you knew that.'

He looked utterly unconcerned. He made no move to come over to her and did not react to her emotion in any way.

'Sweetheart. We had sex on the kitchen floor and played a couple of the games we always play and talked dirty.'

'You hurt me!'

He laughed. 'Well, that's rather the point. You haven't complained before. Why are you getting so upset now? You need to sort out these moods of yours; they'll get you into trouble at work. And I suspect everyone at lunch thought the same – acting like a sulky little girl when you weren't the centre of attention.'

'That isn't true!'

'Jasmine, I'm afraid it is. As soon as things don't go exactly the way you want them you throw a tantrum. Like a spoilt, selfish little girl.'

'You hit me.'

'Yes. And then we had sex. Like we have before—'

'This was different,' she cut in.

'Well, do you expect sex always to be the same? That would be rather boring. Christ, you are so limited sometimes.'

'You hit me. On my face.' But she heard no strength in her voice. It sounded as if she was pleading with him. As she grew weaker in the argument, he grew stronger.

'Go to the police, then. And they'll come racing round, lights flashing, sirens wailing, and arrest me. But before I go to the police station I'll show them our little album. Our photograph album, the one you always enjoy posing for, dressed up – or should I say dressed down – and the home movies you like to star in. And the nice policemen will see that you have absolutely no objection to being tied up and spanked. And then it will be a question of wasting police time and making a very serious, totally false accusation. Women go to prison for that sort of thing, you know. As they damn well should.'

'I want those photographs back. And I want the films.' She knew where he kept them: in the locked cupboard in his bedroom.

'Well, little girl, *I want* doesn't get.' He gave a theatrical sigh. 'Look, we really have reached the end of the road. I think the best thing is for you to get your things and go. This clearly isn't working. I've had enough of your behaviour and quite enough of your ridiculous opinions. You've exhausted my patience. Maybe there's some man out there who could put up with you but I can't do it any more.'

She had to try one more time. 'You attacked me.'

His voice was hard. 'I did not. And if you go around saying that I did then all of London will know, very quickly and very publicly, that my ex-girlfriend is an unhinged, jealous, vicious little bitch who got dumped and didn't like it. I have a long memory, Jasmine. And I have the photographs. And I have a thousand ways of spinning a story.'

She had nothing to say. Her mind was struggling to cope with the moment, let alone the scenario Robert was playing out before her. Too stunned to speak or move or even to think, she watched him search out her handbag.

'Let's make sure you take everything with you.' He picked up her mobile phone from the counter-top and tossed it in her bag before checking inside.

'Purse, keys, phone, diary. That's all you had, isn't it? If I find anything here of yours I'll send it on to the studio. I'll be calling Paul about some work next week.' He was telling her that he would not be disappearing. He reached into his back pocket and pulled out a note. 'Here. Take a cab. You'll get one if you walk to Windmill Lane.'

She watched as he pulled out the purse from her handbag and put the money in. It was as if there were no proprieties left in existence for him to observe – that he could take her body and her possessions and every aspect of her life and do with them exactly as he pleased. She put down the glass, walked over to pick up her bag and, pausing only to gather up her coat, walked for the last time towards the front door.

Sunday evening, seven o'clock: it could only be her mother calling. Natasha stubbed out her cigarette, a habit her mother believed she had given up last year, and readied herself for the blend of forthright opinion, harsh judgement and doom-laden projection that passed for a conversation between them.

It was Robert.

'Just checking in with my favourite girl.' Robert had a wonderful way of speaking to you as if you were the only person in the whole wide world who mattered to him.

She tucked her legs under her and leaned back into the squashy cushions of her Harrods sofa. 'Your favourite cleaning lady, more like. I've even got all the gunge out from the cooker knobs.'

He put on a breathy voice. 'I'm so proud of you.'

She giggled. 'And you. How was your lunch?'

'It would have been much more entertaining if you had been there and I'm afraid you would have found it a dull old affair. My brother, his family and the neighbours. And Araminta, of course.'

His daughter. But before she had a chance to make a polite enquiry and dig a little about the possibility of a girlfriend, he had moved on.

'I have a proposition to put to you.'

The seductive tone in which this was said told her that this was not a business deal. She felt a rush of excitement.

'Dinner. You need cheering up.'

'Yes, I do!' she exclaimed.

'Nowhere glitzy, mind you, so don't book a cab to the Ivy. You're still undercover.'

'Absolutely.' Having expected to be locked inside the house for an indefinite period she would have jumped at the chance of McDonald's.

'OK. Friday. La Famiglia for eight thirty. I'll pick you up at quarter past, so make sure you're ready,' he added sternly, and rang off.

She replaced the receiver slowly and stretched out her legs on the sofa. La Famiglia, her favourite Italian. He had remembered. She liked his attention to detail. And the way he had asked her. He didn't hint or prevaricate or hesitate. He got straight to the point. She knew where she stood with him, that she could rely on what he said, that he would be there at eight fifteen and she didn't have to worry about a call an hour after he was due to say that he was stuck in a production meeting or a shoot or a traffic jam on the M4 and could they take a rain check. True, he was a bit bossy. But right now that seemed just what she needed. She felt safe with him. Protected. A thought that had begun to form in her mind since their last meeting grew stronger and more hopeful.

# Chapter 3

# Family

*My mother is proud of me. She considers me to have made a success of my life, just as she is proud to have made a success of hers. My father is an army officer, now retired. They live in Wiltshire, where they have a wide circle of acquaintances. If my mother has an inner life, it has never been revealed to me. She is a practical person, not given to introspection and dismissive of therapy. In these respects she is not unlike my wife, though Susannah worries more. Perhaps my mother lacks the imaginative capacity to worry? It would be an oversimplification to say that in my mother's eyes I was the 'good' child and Robert, my younger brother, the 'bad' child, but there is some truth in those labels. My mother tells stories of how Robert screamed incessantly as a baby, and so ferociously that she was once forced to leave him in his carrycot at the bottom of the garden. One story she does not tell is how she habitually left him in the cellar, too. He was a restless baby and an inquisitive infant. I once found him tied to the bars of his playpen. My mother had tied his wrists with long ribbons. I was about eight at the time but I did not dare untie him. My father was often away from home and I did not think to tell him, either. I suppose I considered such occurrences to be normal. My recollections of this time are very faint but recently it has dawned on me that it was about this time when Mrs Tokeley came to look after us. My mother stayed in her room and Mrs Tokeley took over. Mrs Tokeley was grandmotherly. She played with us. She taught us how to make bobble balls and Christmas decorations from flour and water which we shaped into Christmas trees and painted red and green. She called me her 'little man' and she called Robert her 'little parcel' because he insisted that she carry him every-where. And then my mother got better and Mrs Tokeley left and every-thing went back to how it had been before. But this is by way of an aside . . .*

Despite the driving rain, the appalling school-run traffic and the fact that she had a nine thirty appointment with the Awful Andersons, it was still a relief to leave the weekend behind. Susannah took her place in the slow-moving line of cars waiting to exit Fairmile Lane and join the Portsmouth Road, the jam a permanent feature of the weekday morning Cobham school-run traffic. The half-mile-long queue of estates and sports and four-by-four models edged resignedly past million-pound houses to the right and the grounds of Cobham Rugby Club to the left, its green pitches remarkable for their continued survival in a town dedicated to development of each piece of available building land.

Work afforded her some respite from the anxiety she had been unable to banish even after their return home from Robert's lunch. Relief that James had got through the day without drinking was overlaid by a whole new set of negative emotions, most of them centred on that awful woman Louise. She had sat seething in the car on the way home from Robert's house, running the events of the afternoon through her mind, hearing Louise's barking voice and her own hopeless attempts to stand up for herself and wondering, yet again, why she got steamrollered by these people. First James and then Louise had defeated her in argument in the course of one weekend. Why did all her carefully reasoned points disappear in the heat of the moment, only to return hours later when there was nothing more to be said? She needed to be more assertive; perhaps she should go on one of those courses where they taught you to say the same empowered statement over and over again, although she couldn't quite see how that would work with Louise, who didn't listen to anything anyone else said at all.

'Forget it,' James had said testily as they cruised down the A3. 'Don't let her get to you.'

But it did get to her. She had stared out of the car window on the slow journey back from Wandsworth, past the rows of suburban thirties semis and the Tolworth Tower and then the open fields of Esher, feeling stupid and inadequate and unworldly. Louise, a total stranger, had made her feel utterly powerless. And when she had finished thinking about Louise, and how she was going to turn down the woman's inevitable invitation to some pretentious dinner party, there was Matthew to worry about. He had sat mute at lunch – apart from animated attempts to impress Jasmine – thus appearing socially backward and sexually precocious. There was no point discussing it with James. 'You worry too much,' would be his reply.

Perhaps she took after her mother. Her mother worried constantly. In particular, her mother's preoccupation with money, or the lack of it, had cast a dreary shadow over their family life throughout her childhood. Her mother's opinion of their financial situation veered from high anxiety, particularly around Christmas, to ongoing low-level pessimism. Susannah had never been encouraged to go to college or travel the world. She must find a 'good job' and A-levels were sufficient for that. A good job was not one which was interesting or worthwhile or even enjoyable. For her mother a good job, ideally with an insurance company, promised employment for life with an index-linked pension at the end of it. Management was preferable to sales and self-employment was all very well for risk-takers but not for their kind of people.

Susannah's elder sister, Deborah, had opted for nursing and was currently on a three-year contract in Dubai. Deborah rang home infrequently to listen to their mother urging her to save every penny, eat all her meals at the hospital and stay away from parties where people were drinking alcohol. Their mother paid into a local store's Christmas fund and cut coupons from the newspapers and allowed herself the weekly indulgence of the football pools until the National Lottery was formed. Gratefully she opted to purchase a weekly lottery ticket, removing the long-held and baseless worry that the door-to-door pools collector did not diligently forward all his takings to Littlewoods. Susannah's parents were first-generation homeowners. But home ownership had not brought them contentment. Instead, her mother tracked the Bank of England interest rate with dedication. News reports of rate rises and repossessions would send her into a further state of fear for the very roof over their heads. Boom times reliably bypassed her family. The Midlands tool-making firm at which her father spent all his working life subsisted rather than prospered and when it eventually was bought out by a German manufacturing conglomerate her father took early retirement and her mother fretted that the Germans would be raiding the pension fund. It had not happened yet.

At the time Susannah had accepted her mother's mindset without question. Many years later she found out that her parents had virtually no mortgage and substantial savings in a Post Office account. Her mother continued to work as a cook in the local primary school 'because you never know' and resisted suggestions that they might take a foreign holiday or update their original kitchen. Maybe next year. Once, when Susannah was about seven or eight, she had indulged in a secret, powerful yearning for a doll. It was advertised on television: the Palitoy Tiny Tears. The doll, almost a real baby, wore a smocked dress and cried real tears and most marvellous of all required its wet nappy to be changed. It had a perfect baby face with radiant blue eyes and red cheeks framed by the blonde, long, brushable hair of a grown woman. But she had never asked for it. The closest she had come was to approach her mother shyly in the kitchen.

'What am I getting for my birthday?'

'A surprise.'

'What surprise?'

'If I tell you that it won't be a surprise.'

It had been impossible for her to ask outright. She could already predict her mother's disapproval and the lecture. Instead she said slyly, 'Laura got a Tiny Tears.' Laura was a classmate and neighbour whose pink-painted bedroom housed a bevy of Barbies and a white laminate dressing table with a tilting mirror.

'Well, Laura's father is a builder and he makes a packet and the taxman doesn't see any of it.' The lecture came anyway. 'Money doesn't grow on trees, you know, and we have to pay for all the people who don't pay tax. We have to pay for their trips to the doctor and their operations and school for their children . . .'

On her birthday she unwrapped a Spirograph set and looked at the expectant faces of her mother and father and pretended to be pleased.

She arrived at the Andersons' house in Oxshott Way some five minutes early, parked the car three doors down and took out from her black leather document case the property particulars for number seventeen. The photograph showed a 1930s detached house with leaded lights, brick frontage and a panelled and black painted garage door. Two tubs of geraniums were placed either side of the front door and the picture had been taken in bright sunlight, an unfortunate clue to the observant purchaser that this house had been on the market since the previous May. Further enquiries would reveal that it was in fact on the market with every agent in Cobham. The particulars omitted to show internal photographs for reasons that would become obvious to purchasers when the house was viewed. The house itself was described blandly as 'a four-bedroomed Cobham family home with many original features'. The failure of their house to be sold after eight months was an increasing source of self-pitying bemusement to the Andersons, whom Susannah had been sent to soothe and, Anthony hoped, to persuade to make some changes to the presentation and marketing of the house. Anthony no longer took telephone calls from Mr Anderson.

It was unnerving to see the front door open as she walked up the path.

'We were expecting you,' Mr Anderson said unnecessarily.

She gave him her brightest smile. He was dressed in his weekday casual clothes, the uniform of the affluent Cobham retiree: beige permapress trousers, bottle-green polo neck, a half-zip fleece with *Cotton Traders* embroidered on the chest and a copper bracelet of the type worn by those with arthritis. Reading the look of hopeful anticipation in his eyes she wondered if she should put into action at once her new resolution to be more assertive. Perhaps she should come right out with it? *Your house is overpriced, the interior needs gutting and you give off a sense of desperation to anyone we manage to strong-arm through the door.*

'It's a pleasure,' she said warmly.

'Anne's waiting for us in the kitchen.'

The Andersons continued to believe, despite ever-stronger hints to the contrary, that their kitchen was the unique selling point of the house. As she stepped through the doors Anne Anderson, a fuller-fleeced version of her husband with a grey bobbed haircut, stepped forward to greet her. 'There!' she exclaimed.

Susannah looked around. Nothing appeared to have been changed. The L-shaped kitchen was still in its usual state of semi-gloom, the natural light from the small kitchen window filtered first by a thick net curtain and then by scalloped-edged red gingham curtains. The free-standing units and appliances with their plastic pale-blue door fronts, first installed in 1962 by Mr Anderson himself, were as immaculately clean and hopelessly dated as ever. On the far side was the breakfast bar, below which were stored two leatherette bar stools standing on the cork-tiled floor.

They stood for some seconds, the Andersons standing in happy expectation, Susannah looking for some change that she might comment on.

'It's the fluorescent!' exclaimed Mr Anderson.

'The fluorescent?' she repeated blankly.

'The spotlights have been removed. A fluorescent is newly installed. A forty per cent increase in wattage has been achieved! You see – we do listen.'

Mrs Anderson cut in. 'You said we needed it brighter.'

'Oh. Yes. Wonderful.'

And with that comment she realized that, yet again, she had become enmeshed in the same conspiracy as all the other Cobham agents, in which no one was able to tell the Andersons the truth about their house. Instead, they tiptoed round the subject making wholly inadequate suggestions rather than broach the subject of the wholesale refurbishment required to bring the house up to the exacting standards of the youthful and demanding Cobham purchaser.

The reasons for this, she had spent some time pondering – and indeed discussing with Justin, Mr Charron's newest negotiator – were a combination of commercial self-interest and, in Justin's opinion, based on his A-level in psychology, some syndrome called co-dependence which, although he had explained the term in some detail to Susannah, seemed to her to boil down to feeling sorry for them. The Andersons, naïve but good-natured, believed their house to be a pearl in the Cobham housing market, had priced it as such, and no one had the heart to tell them otherwise. They had lived in the house for thirty-five years, tended and maintained and by the contemporary standards improved it, and could not understand that the world had moved on. The Anderson's credo of home improvement, of make-do-and-mend, of time spent in careful maintenance and repair, was no longer the motto of the prudent householder. Indeed the prudent householder was a dying breed, destined to be replaced by a City banker, his glamorous wife and a team of East European builders. Their work was without doubt to be literally deconstructed, probably just days after the sale was completed. The kitchen units, the avocado bathroom, the shower cubicle, the gas-effect stone-clad fireplace, all the two-tone Kossett carpet – *do you remember the Kossett Cat, dear?* – the New World gas cooker and every inch of Artex and Anaglypta and each and every one of the three-cluster spotlights, would be purged.

Two lives in a couple of yellow skips. Moreover, the conspiracy of silence as to the state of the house necessarily extended to its pricing. The two offers that the Andersons had received on the house in the early days of viewing, both some twenty per cent below the asking price, had been met with uncomprehending pain and rebuffed with zeal. The Andersons took the view that some people *always try their luck* and the right person would be along soon enough.

Peering up at the fluorescent light, and seeing no improvement in the illumination of the room, Susannah was jolted out of her complacency. She had come determined to persuade the Andersons of the need for change and perhaps even to broach the subject of a reduction in the asking price. She moved further into the kitchen, towards the dining room.

'I thought we could discuss presenting this room differently,' she said briskly, seizing the dining room door handle and pushing the door open. It stopped dead at the halfway mark. She pushed harder but the door remained determinedly jammed.

'It's the *Sunday Telegraph*, dear,' called out Mr Anderson. 'Here.'

He stepped in front of her and edged sideways into the dining room, contorting himself to bend down and push into the room a cardboard box of some weight.

'Nineteen seventy-four to seventy-six. I've been having a sort-out.'

Mr Anderson, she had been informed early in their acquaintance, had been a collector of the *Sunday Telegraph* colour supplement since 1960. He also collected back copies of the *Radio Times*, *The Garden* – the magazine of the Royal Horticultural Society – and, until it ceased to be published, *Punch*. These collections, complete and in pristine condition, filled the dining room, stored in supermarket cardboard boxes marked in black felt tip pen and piled neatly against the walls. Even if the Andersons had, by some quirk, wished to entertain surrounded by cardboard walls it would first have been necessary for them to clear the dining room table, which was neatly covered with approximately twelve piles of assorted papers. Susannah had, on successive visits, stolen a look at these and noted piles for, variously, household bills, correspondence relating to a neighbour's 1989 planning application, seed and bulb catalogues, Saga motor insurance and, naturally, a thick file labelled *House Move*.

'You see,' she began, 'this room really needs to be presented as a dining room.'

'But they can see it's a dining room,' responded Mr Anderson. 'I mean, it's self-evident.'

'Well, yes, but I think people need to be able to *see* it in use as such.'

'It is in use. We use it all the time.'

'In use *as a dining room*.'

'But we eat in the kitchen.'

A change of approach was needed.

'It's also a question of making the room look as big as possible. Perhaps taking the boxes out and storing them elsewhere.'

'Where?'

'The loft?'

Mr Anderson's tone implied that this was an insane suggestion. 'But the loft space is subject to temperature fluctuations!'

She thought quickly. 'Perhaps you could put them into storage for a while. Just until the house is sold.'

'Isn't that very expensive?' asked Mrs Anderson worriedly. 'And they might get stolen.'

Mr Anderson echoed his wife's tone. 'And of course it wouldn't be possible to move our private papers. Twenty-four-hour access is needed for those. Besides which, the removal of the boxes has no effect on the room size,' Mr Anderson concluded.

'Well, I would recommend that you clear the table and move any boxes that you can out of sight,' Susannah said firmly.

Mr Anderson paused and his tone took on an unmistakably petulant turn. 'Kings said that this was a very good-sized room.'

Kings, a London chain that had arrived in Cobham eighteen months ago, were on a mission to pick up as many instructions as possible and she was not surprised to hear that their employee had flattered the Andersons to the hilt.

'Absolutely, it is.' James's strategy from the day before came to mind.

'And they sent two people round last week,' Mrs Anderson cut in.

She resisted the temptation to ask if these people had actually made an offer on the house.

'And we are going to be a featured property in the Kings magazine,' Mrs Anderson continued.

'Posted to five thousand local households,' Mr Anderson proclaimed.

Mr Anderson had already moved to the dining room door. Mrs Anderson's presence at Susannah's shoulder had the effect of edging her towards him and out of the room. As they entered the kitchen, Mr Anderson closed the dining room door firmly behind them.

'Well, I think that was very useful. There's just one other thing we wanted to ask you.'

Hope rose in her despite herself. 'Yes?'

He grasped her arm. 'The *Daily Telegraph* says house prices in the south-east have risen by three per cent – that's an average over the last two quarters. So do you think we're underpriced now?'

Natasha lay on the bed of the most luxurious suite of the newly refurbished Thetford Park Hotel and Spa and watched as Harry fiddled with the wide-angle lens and Anna sat revising the next section of script on her Psion. Alex, the sound man, was in the bathroom smoking out of the window and Clare, the production assistant, had been sent into Windsor – allegedly to do a further reccy round the castle but actually to buy Anna's mother's birthday present.

No more than six minutes were to be devoted to Thetford Park as part of an hour-long special *Holiday* programme devoted to holidaying in Britain. The Thetford was the featured weekend luxury break, its claim to fame a zoo-themed crèche, taking its inspiration from the nearby Legoland Safari Park, which provided twelve-hour nursery care. Anna, the director, had none too subtly intimated that Natasha was miscast and mentioned that Richard Waters – the winner of last year's *Pop Idol* – had been the producer's first choice because he was married and had a two-year-old, but they hadn't been able to get him because he was in rehearsals for topping the bill on the first spring sailing of the *QM2* from Southampton to New York.

And although she was currently occupying the bed, they didn't actually get to stay the night, just pretend to. Natasha's weekend break actually took place on a Tuesday. It was a tight schedule, all the filming to be completed in one day. As a child Natasha had believed that an army of film crew, assistants, scriptwriters, make-up artists and caterers were necessary to produce even the shortest film. In fact, technology and cost cutting had long since made it possible for four people and the presenter to make this type of film. Anna could probably do the whole thing herself. A fiercely efficient and yet quirkily creative director, she had emerged barely five years ago from Goldsmiths College with a first in Media Studies and had recently featured in an *Evening Standard* feature profiling the top ten rising stars in the BBC.

Natasha found her pretty scary. On a previous *Holiday* shoot, whale-watching in Norway last summer, there had been a difference of opinion over her PTCs – pieces to camera – and she had learned that it was best to do what Anna wanted.

Anna had decided to begin outside the hotel, Natasha filmed as if arriving for a weekend stay and doing an opening PTC in front of the hotel's Palladian façade. Then they'd moved to do a jacuzzi shot in the spa, which had necessitated Clare shooing from the pool a gaggle of forty-something housewives on a spa break, although Anna had later relented and allowed the thinnest housewife to stay – instructing her to swim slow, sedate and silent lengths of the pool as part of a background shot. The crèche scene had been something of a disaster because no children were actually resident in the hotel and so they had been forced to postpone filming that until the afternoon when the bar manager's wife was bringing in her twins and her sister's three children to pose as guests.

To be fair to Anna, she had taken it all in her stride, scarcely missing a beat before shepherding them up to a Junior Deluxe Suite, where they were now gathered to film Natasha about to get changed to go down to dinner.

Anna, dressed in combats and some sweater that looked as if it had been hand-knitted and subsequently retrieved from Oxfam, but probably came from Urban Outfitters and cost a fortune, stood up.

'OK, this is where you say the bit about the room and dinner and the two restaurants and the separate kids' tea. Have you got that?'

She really could be unbearably patronizing. 'Yes.'

Anna continued, consulting her Psion. 'Then we'll get you changed and go down to the hall to film the Sunday morning shot.'

Anna turned away and began scrolling down the Psion, speaking the lines quietly to herself. 'We'll head off to the castle this afternoon,' Anna continued. 'I want to leave the restaurant for last so it's dark outside.'

'Yeah, talking of restaurants . . .' Harry's voice carried across the room.

'All right,' Anna said placatingly, 'let's just get this one in the bag and then we'll eat.'

Natasha knew that crews always got grumpy about mealtimes. Carrying a camera and all the associated equipment and the boredom of sitting around made food an all-important issue and one which directors ignored at their peril. Harry and Alex had been fed a plate-ful of Danish pastries at ten o'clock but it was now quarter to one and unless they broke for lunch soon tempers would become frayed.

'OK, let's go.' Anna grabbed her filming schedule and moved across the room to Natasha. 'And then we'll get straight down to the conservatory. The lunch special is spaghetti carbonara and the chef does a mean strawberry cheesecake.'

Harry looked mollified and picked up the camera. Natasha began to warm to Anna. It was a bloody difficult job. As the director she had to write the script, rally the crew, edit the film and direct her considerable creative talent to making the reality of holidaying in Windsor look exciting. And all the while she had to keep a watchful eye on the complex Borgia politics of the BBC if her career was to progress to bigger things, the power to commission programmes, and all that went with it – an office on the sixth floor of Television Centre, a shelf full of Baftas and an address book full of famous friends.

It was a cliché that filming involved minutes of action and hours of boredom but it was true. She allowed her mind to wander and her thoughts turned to Robert and Friday's dinner. It was a date, she was pretty sure of that, and she was surprised at how excited she was. She was coming to see Robert in a different light. Not as her stern, scolding, slightly stiff PR but as someone who had always looked out for her, given her the very best counsel, always fought her corner. Her various boyfriends had come and gone, her mother had all but deserted her, her father had deserted her – but since they'd met close to five years ago Robert had been a constant reassuring presence in her life. When she came to think of it he was actually the sole constant presence in her life. As for Mark Lewin, there had been no word from him. It made it easier. She missed him, still thought about him most mornings on waking, and ached more often than she would like for his warm body and the way he made her laugh with his impersonations of his manager and the entire BBC commentary team.

Anna's voice cut into her thoughts. 'Right. We're to start on a wide shot and end on a CU.'

She meant a close-up. Anna turned to Harry. 'Hold the shot and let her walk out to the right. OK, let's go for a take. Positions, please. Is everyone happy?' They nodded back. 'Standing by, turn over . . .'

'Speed,' said Harry.

'And *action*,' said Anna.

Jasmine knew now that her world would never be quite the same again. Two days had passed since Sunday. Two days in which she had stayed in her tiny Ealing flat, kept the blinds drawn and called Paul at seven o'clock on Monday morning, when she knew he wouldn't have arrived at the studio, to leave a message on the answer machine. She told him she was sick and wouldn't be in. He hadn't called yesterday – he was not the benevolent type – and she doubted whether he would call today, but tomorrow there would be questions because he would start to panic about the preparations for the Las Vegas shoot. For now she lay in her old grey tracksuit bottoms and her favourite white Agnès B T-shirt, now so grey it could only be worn as one half of a set of pyjamas, underneath her thick duvet in the stale bedroom air.

It had taken her an hour to get home on Sunday thanks to the cars full of country weekenders returning to London. Providence had sent her a taciturn cabbie. When she had got in, she had found the flat to be chilly with no hot water for a shower. She had set the timer for Monday evening, expecting to be away at least until then. Robert had only been to the flat once, in the very early days, and called it *bijou*, which she had taken as a compliment. The truth was that six months of weekends spent at Robert's house made her own flat seem small and shabby by comparison when she returned on the Monday evening, or sometimes the Sunday night if he had had work to do.

It was a one-bedroom flat in a converted Victorian house, closer to Hangar Lane than Ealing Common. She did not mind the five-floor walk up. On his visit Robert had requested oxygen at the top and that had made her laugh. The top floor position meant that the bedroom was formerly the attic, with a sloping ceiling and a dormer window from which she could see the rooftops of West London. Her parents had helped with the deposit. The walls had been painted builder's magnolia and she had hung framed photographs from her graduation portfolio, revelling in the freedom of hammering in nails after years of renting. The kitchen, galley style with one run of units down the side, was new and the bathroom had an undersized bath but a good shower. The living room was scarcely big enough for the Ikea round beech dining table and the Ikea pale yellow corduroy sofa. The Moroccan serving plate she had carried back from Casablanca lay waiting to be mounted on the still-Magnolia wall. She had met Robert about six months after moving in and somehow the decorating plans she envisaged had been shelved, another small casualty of the demands of their relationship.

She had waited for the water to get hot. In the time this took she toyed with the idea of not showering at all. But in her heart she always knew she was not going to go to the police. So she had taken the shower and got into bed and stayed there until now, eating Special K from the packet and drinking black coffee and tap water, watching television on the portable. She had not been able to concentrate or sleep for long because of the miserable need to make sense of it all as she ran actions and events over and over in her head. And the worst times were when another piece of the puzzle slotted into place and the reasoning behind some quirk of Robert's behaviour became apparent and the reasoning was horrible and hurtful and she would begin to cry again.

There were the obvious signs, the ones she had chosen to believe would remedy themselves in time. He had never taken her to his office. He had never introduced her to his parents. He had never let her meet Tabitha. He had not introduced her because he had known, from the outset of their relationship, that she was not important.

He had not planned a trip to Venice for the two of them. The trip to Venice had been what was known in the trade as a freebie. The two first class tickets and the three nights at the hotel were a generous present from a Middle Eastern client who owned the Venice hotel and fifteen more besides throughout Europe. She had interpreted it as a romantic gesture because that was what she wanted it to be. Actually it was a business trip: Robert spent most of his time critiquing the hotel and its competitors. He took her because she happened to be his current girlfriend. And then something had happened to change all that and she had no idea what.

They had never made love and, she realized now, they never would have done. *She had told herself he needed time.*

He avoided kissing her. His touch was cursory, possessive, rough. His names for her in bed were *bitch* and *whore* and saying them turned him on. *She had told herself it was passionate, sophisticated sex.*

She was hard up and struggling just to pay the mortgage and he was a millionaire. When her car was off the road with a broken exhaust he acted as if he hadn't heard her tell him so. *She had told herself it was an independent relationship.*

He called her names. Stupid Girl and Silly Little Idiot and Fatso. *She had told herself she was oversensitive.*

He was controlling and critical and demanding. *She told herself he was successful because he had high standards.*

There was something else but she could not put her finger on it.

She knew that he insisted on being in charge. In the beginning she had liked that; it made her feel that he cared. For example, he liked to choose her clothes for her. That was one of the first things they had done together, gone shopping on a Sunday afternoon in Selfridges, and she had felt flattered and pampered. Although, now she came to think of it, there had been lots and lots of trying on by her – and comments and little asides to the assistants by him – but at the end of the day just a couple of items purchased. Yes, she realized, he was mean. All the meals were expense account and most of the gifts were freebies; the couple of items of jewellery he had given her were silver.

How could she have been so stupid?

She had liked to tell herself she was streetwise. She had even on one occasion, in her second year at art school, outstared and outrun a man in Victoria Park. The man, who was really a boy in a hooded top and ripped jeans, had stepped out in front of her on the path by the lake and said, 'Money.' Just the single word; she had noted his brevity even in the shock of the moment. She had also heard the panic, the hint of uncertainty in his voice, the telltale nervousness of the mugging *ingénue*. Later she realized that it had probably been his first time. She had heard her voice brittle in the early evening air say 'no' and she had seized the moment to dart and run. Afterwards she had thanked the gods for youth and agility and Nike trainers.

She was streetwise but only because a girl in London on a photographer's assistant's salary could not afford to live in an area where garages and porters and civilized lit streets eased a woman's path.

She was streetwise but not to the extent of being cynical. She had believed that the world was basically good, that most people were kind, that cruelty existed in other worlds but not in hers. She had trusted men. She had trusted and loved one man in particular and he had taken her love and trust and smashed it and he had enjoyed doing so.

She had once read that power is holding someone else's fear in your hand, opening your palm and showing it to them. Robert had planned how he would show her his power and taken his time in doing it. And he held that power still in the photographs and the videos and in the

66

very fact he was who he was and she was no one and nothing.

But that was not the reason she would never go to the police, never confide in her parents, only perhaps reveal a little of what had happened to anyone. The worst of her thoughts – the darkest recollections that crept on her in the small hours while the city was sleeping and no cars could be heard in the street and the hour between three and four seemed as though it would never pass – were not about Robert at all. It was then, when she felt more alone than she had ever believed possible, that she would ask herself what she had done to deserve this. She would recollect in agonizing detail how she had played and encouraged his bedroom games, deferred to him and flattered him, allowed him to dominate in every way so that by the end he was choosing her food for her in restaurants. She had known that he had kept the films and photographs, guessed where they were locked away, but suppressed her instinctive uneasiness. How had that happened? Because she had allowed it to and that meant – and here the pain inside her reached an intensity that was almost unbearable – it meant that it was her fault. A confident woman like Louise would have stood up for herself. A respectable woman like Susannah would never have attracted his attention. But she had a fault line running through her, an ugly, shameful fault that allowed a man like Robert to come in and do exactly what he wanted and walk away knowing that he had got away with it.

There was only one option for her: to carry on as if it had never happened, to bury this part of her and her life deep inside and hope that one day she would forget.

Of course he would be asleep. It must be four in the morning in Virginia. Tabitha put down her cup of coffee and switched on the computer, the post unopened and Araminta safely deposited at school. This was as much a part of her routine now as taking Araminta to school or walking Mackie, who now lay immovable, sleeping contentedly wedged under her desk and chair, his black Labrador fur smelling wet and earthy. Mackie followed her around devotedly, albeit grumpily if required to leave his favourite spot by the Aga to accompany her around the house. Now they occupied the cubbyhole under the stairs which she had made her office, if a tiny table with a computer and a corkboard full of postcards and photographs and reminders could be called an office. But it suited her and given that the cottage had only two bedrooms, situated on either side of the steep staircase, it was a blessing to have anything approaching an office at all. The cottage, built in the 1860s for a farm worker, had the small, rough-plastered rooms of its type. She had painted the sitting room white and filled it with her collection of Blue and White and with the small amount of money left over from the purchase bought two squashy claret-red sofas which stood either side of the fireplace. Araminta would have a fire all year round if allowed and this morning the scent of the woody embers lingered in the cottage from the night before. The kitchen led off from the sitting room and beyond it the bathroom, which needed an urgent overhaul, but there was no sign of that, not unless fees for editing improved dramatically. But there was money for food and the car, a ten-year old-Peugeot estate that ran as if it would last for ever, the occasional trip to Pizza Hut in Horsham and even a weekly riding lesson for Araminta, so all things considered she was very lucky.

There were two messages. The first, naturally, from him, and her heart gave a happy leap even now, after so many emails. The second made her stomach turn. It was from Robert, the subject line *Araminta*.

She was tempted to read Robert's email first as the feelings of fear and panic rose in her but she stopped herself. She could not afford to react like that. She remembered what they had taught her, the cycle of *love-hope-fear*. Well, her love for Robert died long ago – and hope that things would change had been bitterly extinguished – but the fear could still rise up even at the sight of his name on an email. They had taught her about taking control. They had taught her to act rather than react.

So she firmly placed the cursor on Theo Hall, subject line *Happy Holidays*.

Hey, how's my favourite English lady? Thanks for the flight details. Guess I better get those grits on, sweep the porch and saddle up to meet the supply train (the coming of the railroad sure has changed things round here). Don't worry about a thing, honey. Everything with Sideshow Bob will sort itself out. Love you, Theo.

She laughed despite herself. Sideshow Bob, a character in the *Simpsons*, was Theo's nickname for Robert. She could hear his deep

Virginian cadence as he held her tight. 'Hey, honey. He can't touch you now. Remember, he's Sideshow Bob . . .'

She typed back:

Hope the Virginia steam train has got proper English tea on it. And Rice Krispies (only cereal A will eat at the moment). Shall I bring my own? I know, I worry too much. Finished the O'Hare manuscript yesterday so I'll go to the post (sorry, mail) later. Then I'm going to take the day off, meet Lizzy for coffee. I can't wait for Easter. It feels like such a long time!!! A says can we go to Krispy Kreme? Love and kisses, Tabsxxx

The telephone call would come at eleven a.m. as part of a routine established for over a year now since they had met, seated next to each other at her brother's wedding. Was it really more than a year now? Her brother Patrick and Theo had hit it off as students whilst working at a Californian summer camp for rich teenagers. Patrick was the swimming teacher, Theo had explained. 'Meanwhile, I was teaching survival skills. Not the most popular option,' he had added resignedly over lunch in the wedding marquee. 'One week only one person signed up. They actually fought to sign up for Patrick's swimming lessons. All the girls had crushes on your brother and his English accent.'

Privately, she had thought that Theo's accent was heartstopping. And his weathered good looks and his strong hands. She had reined herself in. Theo almost certainly had a girlfriend back home. They had talked about his farm, which he had taken over when his parents retired a couple of years previously. 'We grow corn and soy beans. I want to grow more vegetables for sale to the public. And try some cotton. I'm working on a business plan for a farm shop.'

She sensed that he had bigger plans for the farm than his parents would ever have envisaged but before she could ask more he had switched the subject to ask her about herself: her work, Araminta and what she did in her spare time. Then the band had started up and at the first opportunity he had grabbed her hand and pulled her onto the dance floor.

'Of course, we'll have to square dance. It's the only one we know in Virginia.'

She had laughed and they had barely left the dance floor for the rest of the evening. They left the marquee at four in the morning. The day before Theo left to go back to the USA he had come to the cottage and after lunch they had gone for a walk to Devil's Dyke. At the top, overlooking the misty green beauty of the Sussex countryside, they had kissed for the first time, long and hard, both knowing without needing to say it that they were falling in love.

'I'll be back,' he had whispered, 'if that's what you want.'

She had not cared to be casual. 'Yes!'

In response, Theo had held her tight. When he spoke, it was as if he could read her troubled thoughts about the distance that lay between them. 'Don't worry, it will all work out.'

'There's just one thing, Theo.' She needed to be sure of this. 'Is there anyone I should know about? Anyone else back home?'

'No.' There was no hesitation or consideration of her question. She looked into his eyes and knew she could trust him. In that moment she knew that Theo was an honest man. 'There was someone. For several years. Everyone expected us to get married. But I held back; I didn't know why. She got tired of waiting and I don't blame her . . .' He paused. 'Tabitha. You don't have to worry about anyone else. And you never will. I'm old enough to know that when fate puts something rare and precious in your hand, only a fool would throw it away.' And he had taken her hand and there was nothing more to be said as they walked back down the hill.

She pulled herself back to the present and turned her attention to her second email. In the past she would have left Robert's email – or letter or message on the answer machine – and, sick with worry, curled up on the sofa in an agony of indecision. But now she knew better, had somehow over the years learned and changed enough to see him for what he was. So she tapped firmly on the keyboard to open it, already guessing at the content. As she scanned the first couple of lines she realized that her guess was correct.

I am writing to you regarding your proposed holiday in the USA with 'Theo'.

I have given this careful thought and I am not prepared to give my consent to Araminta leaving the country, at least not until I have more details.

In particular, I was very concerned to hear from Araminta at the weekend that you are proposing staying at this man's house. You hardly know him! I must insist on having many more details about him before I could possibly consent. I would be failing in my duties to Araminta if I did not require this from you.

What is your (latest) boyfriend's full name?

What is his occupation (assuming he is employed).

How long has this relationship been in existence? I understand that you met him at Patrick's wedding – that was scarcely one year ago and I assume you have seen very little of him since. So this is actually an internet-type relationship with all the attendant risks that go with such liaisons.

Is he of good character? In particular, does he have any criminal convictions?

Are you proposing introducing Araminta to his friends and family?

Also, I am mindful of the fact that you are proposing going to Virginia, not a place I have visited, nor would I have any cause to. I would need to be assured that you will be staying in a hotel and be supplied with the name of the hotel and your telephone number there.

This seems to me a very ill-considered venture, Tabitha. On your past record you have shown impetuosity and a failure to follow through with your stated plans. As for your relationship, that is of course entirely your own business, but it is hard to see how this current adventure will not end in tears as has happened in the past.

An alternative would be that you go alone and Araminta goes to stay with my parents or that the trip is postponed until the summer.

Yours ever,

Robert

She sat back in her seat. It was almost laughable – the idea that she would ever agree to Araminta staying with Estella. She knew that she should not be surprised by Robert's response. In the six years since she had left him, stealing away from the house with two suitcases and Araminta while he was at work, she had been reminded of his presence on an almost daily basis. The first two years had been the worst. She had been forced to go to live with her parents. The wrath of Robert had been directed at her through his immediate hiring of Masterson Ryder Jardine, an aggressive firm of London lawyers, who used every twist and turn of legal procedure to try to carry out every threat Robert had ever made – to destroy her reputation, to sue for custody of Araminta, to make sure she didn't get a penny. Somehow she had survived, with the help of her friends and her family and most of all because of Barbara, her solicitor, who knew what it was to be beaten and abused and so scared that you thought you could never escape. But Barbara had escaped and trained as a lawyer and took her case – 'My speciality is total bastards' – and taught her so much else besides. Her parents had rallied too, when she finally plucked up the courage to tell them. Her mother's first comment was that she had suspected all along that Robert hit her. Her parents had surprised her in other ways, too. Her father, a retired planning inspector, whom she had always thought of as pedestrian and unworldly, had thrown himself into the minutiae of her case, using skills acquired during a lifetime of shuffling paperwork to file each document, check each witness statement, spot each and every discrepancy and contradiction in Robert's case. Patrick, whom she had always thought of as her little brother, had turned up one day with a cheque, his end-of-year bonus, and so they had gone to a barrister and put in a set of documents to rival any that Robert had produced. Her mother had even stopped criticizing the way she brought up Araminta. And then, when the trial was just days away and her nerves were shredded and she could barely sleep at night for fear of Robert's barrister cross-examining her – just when she thought she would collapse from the strain and exhaustion – Robert capitulated. Not very gracefully, naturally. But enough to give her custody and enough capital for her to buy a little Sussex cottage and some nominal maintenance for Araminta. It was enough. He could keep the business and all his money; she had what she wanted. Her daughter.

But Robert had not gone away. He wrote to her a few days after the case settled. In his letter he talked about conciliation and how he hoped they could put the past behind them and forget their differences for Araminta's sake. She was not taken in. She knew his underlying meaning when he ended his letter by reminding her that although they were now divorced that did not alter the fact that they were still Araminta's parents and he intended to remain *fully involved* in his daughter's life. On paper he looked like a model father. He saw her every three weeks for a weekend visit, called twice a week and never missed a maintenance payment. He also criticized Tabitha mercilessly, called, emailed and when particularly malevolent sent solicitors' letters complaining about Araminta's diet, clothing, bedtime, friendships, out-of-school activities and occasional thumb sucking. He questioned his daughter about her, creating secrets between them. But occasionally Araminta had let something slip, when she was younger and more naïve. 'Daddy needs to know about your friends because we need to look after you because sometimes you choose friends who aren't very nice.'

And now there was Theo. And they were going to go on holiday. Barbara had said Robert would need a court order to stop them and it was all bluster. So she took a deep breath and resisted the compulsion she still had, when faced with some missive from Robert, to placate him and give him all the information he asked for. She set about composing a short and succinct reply saying that their flights were booked, they were staying with Theo and he would see Araminta on their return.

# Chapter 4

# Health

*I had committed myself to a period of one month without drinking and I was determined to see it through. I felt physically healthier almost immediately. My head cleared. I had more energy. Best of all I woke up in the morning ready to get out of bed. Usually I needed close on half an hour to gently come to. I began running again and Matthew came with me. At work, relations with Raul warmed. We even went to lunch, Evians all round, on a couple of occasions. He told me that he had been born in Cuba, his family escaping when he was a baby, and described his teenage years in Miami. I discovered he was not the Harvard ingénue I had imagined. My productivity improved and I spent far more time at home. Why then, if things were so much better, was I mentally counting down the days when I could start drinking again? Why did I feel permanently edgy and irritable and deprived? Why, in short, did I feel so bloody awful?*

Susannah lay in bed listening to the sounds of James taking a shower, the bedroom warm and glowing in the soft light from her Chinese blue table-lamp. The shower was a sign that he would want sex. It was after all a Saturday night. They had settled into a predictable married routine in that respect. Saturdays, the occasional Sunday (especially if followed by a Bank Holiday Monday) and then once mid-week – normally a Wednesday, the demands of work permitting – escalating to every day on holidays.

He plainly thought that stopping drinking represented an enormous concession on his part and that no further action was necessary. He barely spoke to her. And when he did he was foul. Over dinner, lasagne and salad, she had asked him about his day at work. He did not look up from the *Evening Standard*.

'Working on the Saltzman deal,' he had muttered. When she had pointed out that she could get more information than that from the newspapers – which were enthusiastically reporting Joe Saltzman's efforts to restructure his apparently limitless debt and save his failing budget airline from collapse – James had been very short. 'Well, if you can read it in the papers why are you questioning me?'

And a silence fell between them. It felt as though she was walking on eggshells, that if she pursued the point there would be another row, and she was conscious of Matthew next door watching England's cricket team get thrashed in some overseas tour.

She had optimistically imagined that the tension between them would disappear once James stopped drinking. It was depressing to admit that it existed just as palpably after just over three weeks of abstinence. It was difficult to describe the tension. It was not anger, nothing so strong, but instead some sort of latent resentment. She watched every word lest some casual comment took them into disputed territory. There were so many areas like that. It was as if each of them kept a score sheet. She would point to the long hours James worked. He would counter by detailing the money he made. She would complain about Estella. He would allude, very subtly, to the constraints that Matthew imposed upon their social life and their ability to travel. She would point out all she did around the house. He would note that they employed a cleaner. And so it went on without resolution. Sometimes she felt they could save themselves the trouble of having a row by simply tape recording the last one and playing it back over and over.

The shower had stopped now and she could imagine James drying himself. She listened as he blew his nose, particularly loudly, and then listened to the drone of the electric toothbrush.

The door opened and James emerged naked. For a man who up until this week – when he had twice been running at six a.m. – took virtually no exercise and drank like a fish he was in surprisingly good shape. She was still, after seven years sharing the marital bed, physically attracted to her husband. It was the emotional connection that seemed to have failed.

He moved over to her side of the bed and reached to put his arms around her. His breath smelt of the garlic with which she had liberally flavoured the sauce for the lasagne.

'You smell of garlic,' she complained, which she was aware was not the most romantic response to her husband's advances, but she could not stop herself.

Her rebuff did not deter him. He ran his hand over her breasts and then down between her legs as he abandoned any plans to kiss her and began instead to nuzzle her neck with his nose. He pushed his body against hers and she felt his erection in the small of her back. Then he began to climb on top of her. 'I love you,' he whispered.

That did it. If he thought he could get round her like that he was very much mistaken.

'You really are completely bloody insensitive,' she exploded. 'You think you can just get into bed and have sex as if nothing's happened.'

He retreated. His voice was bewildered. 'Nothing *has* happened!'

'What? You barely speak to me. You sit there at the kitchen table while I wait on you hand and foot. And then you expect me to perform for you in bed.'

She felt him move away and roll onto his back so that they were no longer touching. 'How could I fucking fail to notice that?' His voice was furious. 'Christ, what do I have to do to please you? Stop breaking my balls, will you? I've had a hell of a day at work—'

'So have I!' she cut in.

'It's hardly the same thing, is it? I'm dealing with millions of pounds, with people's jobs, with a whole company that's going down the pan.'

'So my job isn't important? Well, I'm the one going into work tomorrow.'

He sounded exasperated. 'You don't have to do that. That's your choice.'

'It's what the job demands.'

'Then give it up if it's too much.'

'I'm not saying it's too much.' He always said that and it infuriated her every time. She wanted some support from him, not an invitation to give up. 'I'm just saying that I work long hours, too.'

'And I'm saying that's your choice. Hell, you don't have to work. What's the problem?'

Blaming each other for assorted hurts and failings was the only thing they did well these days. They had quite lost the ability to sit down, talk and laugh and help each other until whatever had divided them instead united them.

She felt him get out of bed.

'I'm going to sleep in the spare room. I've had enough of this.'

Pride stopped her from speaking. She would not ask him to stay. She knew how it would play out from now on through the weekend: polite exchanges punctuated by cold silences. She could not remember when they had last been relaxed with each other. It felt like they were spiralling out of control and neither of them knew, or even cared very much, how to stop it.

She had dressed carefully, seeking an effect of understated glamour, finally deciding on a Diane von Furstenburg cream and navy silk wrap dress. La Famiglia, situated at the World's End niche of the Kings Road, might from the outside appear to be a neighbourhood Italian restaurant but that impression was quickly dispelled upon entering the chic interior with its white-tiled floor, walls lined with celebrity photographs and tables buzzing with the easy laughter and confident talk of its wealthy Friday-night clientele.

Robert ushered her ahead of him. He had, of course, reserved a table and, naturally enough, it was in the garden section to the rear. In the summer the garden was open to the sky. She had been here for lunch a couple of times with Mark and the sun had shone down on them on both occasions. She determinedly put the memory out of her mind – he had moved on and so would she.

For now, the evening chill required the room to be closed in by a striped blue and white awning and warmed by gas lighters. Their table to the far right, she imagined one of the best, was discreetly placed with a full view of the room and far away from the waiters' frantic trafficking between tables and kitchen. Her entrance had attracted the odd lingering glance but diners here were cosmopolitan enough not to stare.

The waiter placed a white napkin across her lap with a flourish. 'An aperitif?' he asked.

Robert replied, 'I'll see the wine list.'

She asked for a vodka martini and opened the faux-leatherbound menu.

'The baby chicken is very good,' he commented.

Actually she was bored with chicken; sometimes it seemed to be the only food she ate. She smiled politely and on seeing that there was a special dish of grilled halibut decided on that with the inevitable green salad. Robert meanwhile had ordered 'number fifty-four' from the wine list and a bottle of sparkling water.

'Actually, I'm going to try the halibut.'

'Fish on Friday. How very spiritual, my dear.' A fraction of silence fell between them, then he leaned forward. 'That dress is very good on you.'

The compliment was a surprise but a nice one – the first spoken sign that this was not, as she had continued to suppose while getting ready, a business dinner.

'Thank you.'

Robert had never before paid her an obvious compliment and the romantic effect was heightened on the arrival of the wine waiter by the bottle of champagne he was clasping. The waiter poured two glasses, another came with ciabatta and breadsticks and took their order, and finally they were left alone. She took the opportunity to light a cigarette.

Robert raised an eyebrow. 'There's a rumour going round that those cause cancer.'

'I'm going to give up.'

'Good,' he said firmly. His tone softened. 'You should take good care of yourself.' She made a mental note to make an appointment with the hypnotherapist Harry the cameraman had recommended.

He leaned forward. 'So how was Windsor?'

'Actually, it was fun. Tough to get it all done in a day but the director's a pro—'

He interrupted. 'Do I know him?'

'It's a her. Anna Millar. Bit scary but very good.'

'When's it going out?'

She gave an apologetic half-smile. 'No idea.' She stubbed out her half-smoked cigarette.

'We ought to find out. I'll get Josh onto it.'

Josh was one of several bright young men and women who worked for Robert, prepared to work punishing hours for the highest salary in PR and the best training.

Robert looked thoughtful. 'It's not a bad slot. We need to get you further afield, though. No more Brit hols or you'll look B-list.'

He was right, of course. He had weighed up the pros and cons of doing the Windsor shoot before she had accepted, finally advising her that any loss of kudos as a result of being the presenter not going to St Kitts was offset by the wholesome, family-friendly theme of the shoot.

But she did not want this to be a business dinner and was mindful of steering the subject away from work. 'You must tell me about your daughter. Araminta? How old is she now?'

'Eight. I think you two would get on.'

'I'd love to meet her!' Ouch, she had said that too quickly. But he did not seem to notice.

'I want Araminta to experience normal life when she's with me – seeing friends and family. She's had so much disruption in her life.'

Natasha ventured a question. 'How old was Araminta when you got divorced?'

Now he was looking at her intently and she could see how serious the subject was to him. 'She was two when Tabitha left. It was heart-breaking. She picked up on everything that was going on, and of course she desperately wanted us to stay together. But her mother was determined. There was absolutely nothing anyone could say to change her mind.'

She watched silently as he took a sip of champagne, wondering if he would continue.

'I think the problems really started after Araminta was born. Before that Tabitha was able to do pretty much as she pleased. She found motherhood very difficult. She wasn't a natural. There were . . .' he paused, 'mental problems. Tabitha was always highly strung. And of course I was working all hours getting the business afloat and then coming back home and doing more paperwork. I should have seen what was going on. I blame myself.' He raised his hands in a gesture of defeat. It seemed so very inappropriate, especially when she compared Robert's efforts to the behaviour of her own father.

She rushed to intervene. 'But you mustn't do that! You mustn't blame yourself!'

He looked at her as if for confirmation. 'Do you think so?' There was another pause. 'I'll always wonder if I left it too late. Of course, once Tabitha started talking about divorce I dropped everything, found us the best marriage counsellor. I even offered to have a trial separation to give her time to think it over, but she wouldn't listen. I'll never know exactly when she met Peter.'

'Peter?'

'The first boyfriend. He used to do our garden. Rather a cliché, isn't it? Anyway, there have been plenty since.'

'What's she doing now?'

'Living in Sussex. I bought her a house down there. She gets maintenance so she doesn't need to work,' he added.

She was pondering the cushy lifestyle of Araminta's mother when Robert's tone grew more serious still.

'Unfortunately, it looks as though she may be getting herself into deep water. She's met an American man – some sort of internet relationship. Now she wants to go off at Easter to spend time with him in the States – and she wants to take Araminta with her.'

'Gosh.'

Robert raised his eyebrows. 'My reaction was slightly stronger.'

'Is there anything you can do?'

'Unfortunately the British courts are totally on the mother's side. I've asked her about him but she refuses to tell me anything. And of course that sets off alarm bells. What has she got to hide? Believe me, I'm not remotely interested in her personal life. Good luck to her; I hope she finds someone and makes it last. My concern is for Araminta. Someone has to stand up for her in all this. She's only eight years old, she's seen a succession of men pass through Tabitha's bedroom and now her mother proposes taking her to the other side of the world to shack up with some man she hardly knows.'

It sounded dreadful. 'You must be terribly worried.'

'Sometimes I wonder if I should speak to my solicitor.'

'Absolutely! I think you should. Surely you have a right to know.'

She was beginning to see Robert in a new light – as a man with all the pressures of a cut-throat industry who was also battling to care for his vulnerable daughter. No wonder he hadn't rushed to remarry. Perhaps, after his experiences, he had a distrust of women?

A short silence fell between them which was broken by the waiter pouring more champagne.

Robert turned back to her. 'Enough of me. Natasha, you look absolutely terrific tonight. It's not just the dress!'

She was taken aback. The compliment was lavish, coming from Robert, and that seemed to make it all the more valuable. She was unsure of what to say.

'You mustn't worry about the footballer thing,' he continued. 'It's going to be fine. I spoke to Moores yesterday . . .'

God, the very mention of Moores made her stomach turn over.

'. . . and they're not going to do anything prematurely. You've got another six months of the contract to run and then they'll make a decision on renewal.'

'Do you think they will?' she asked anxiously.

'Provided no other skeletons fall out of your wardrobe,' he replied dryly.

'Don't worry, they won't.'

He looked her in the eye. 'So no other young suitors are camping outside your door?'

'No! Definitely not!'

He looked unmistakably pleased. Emboldened, she decided to satisfy her curiosity.

'And you? Is there someone waiting for you at home?'

He gave a slight smile and looked her straight in the eye, to her embarrassment. 'Not tonight. No, Natasha, I don't have a girlfriend. I recently parted company with a very sweet girl who was far too young for an old man like me. Unfortunately she took it rather hard. Such a pity when one can't stay friends, but that isn't always possible.'

Natasha could imagine exactly the scenario. Some girl, probably twenty-one if that, falls for the older, sophisticated – and rich – man and builds all sorts of fantasies about the future only to realize that he was never terribly serious, and he meant it when he said he just wanted to have a good time.

'Besides,' he went on, 'sitting here tonight with you it's very hard to feel any regrets about being single.'

They sat back as two waiters brought their food and served vegetables out of old-fashioned stainless steel serving dishes.

She had had no idea that he could be so charming. And gentlemanly. So many men nowadays seemed to think it was uncool to open a car door or help her with her coat or even make a restaurant reservation. Some couldn't even summon the wherewithal to invite her out on a date. Instead they would suggest *meeting up with friends* in some obscure wine bar off the Fulham Road where she was expected to stand around, starving hungry, with a lukewarm vodka and tonic until some bright spark asked if she could get them into a club. Mark's idea of a date had been to invite her round to his rented flat to watch football with his mates. She was aware that some women had better luck. These were the women whose lovers sent them flowers at work or whisked them away on surprise weekends or brought them breakfast on a tray. These were the women who woke up on their birthday to find a shiny new car parked in the driveway with a big pink ribbon tied round it. She had never been such a woman.

Of course, it was not luck. It was choice. Somehow she always went for the guy with the boyish charm, the ruffled hair and the creative temperament. The creative temperament, in her experience, rarely if ever disciplined itself enough to achieve any palpable form of worldly success. Creative was more properly defined as feckless, irresponsible and chronically untidy. These were the guys with the sports car that kept breaking down, the overdrawn bank balance and the great job/deal/script just around the corner which never actually materialized in order for them to pay back the increasingly large sums of money she lent them – first for rent, then for the credit cards and finally for the Inland Revenue final demand. Most bizarre of all, why did no less than three of her ex-boyfriends suffer dental emergencies during her time with them – necessitating extortionately expensive weekend treatment courtesy of her Harley Street dentist – because, of course, none of them had got round to registering with a dentist since they had left home some ten years earlier.

It was time for a change.

She wanted a man who employed an accountant. A cleaner. And a hygienist. And was unattached.

She toyed with her fish and half-listened as he changed the subject of conversation away from the personal to business and some City deal with Harrold-Winter, which was a name she had heard of without having any idea what it represented. But it sounded very impressive and she knew enough about men to realize that a certain amount of time had to be spent listening to their explanations of business and looking interested. She did not mind. She felt warm and safe and comfortable. It was really very nice to be looked after for a change and to know that she would not be the one picking up the bill at the end of the evening. There was something very grown up about Robert. It was rather a relief after Mark's childish antics. Just before they split up, these had included ambushing her as she walked through the front door by squirting her with String in a Can, ruining her hair in the process.

It was undeniable that Robert was, to use a dated but nonetheless accurate phrase of her mother's, *good husband material.*

And so, after they had skipped dessert and lingered over a couple of espressos each, she spoke with genuine feeling. 'Thank you for a lovely evening. I've really enjoyed myself.'

He looked pleased. 'Good. You must let me drive you home.'

If it was rather early to go home, eleven o'clock, she did not suggest otherwise. Robert was nearly forty, after all, and a businessman, and it was a Friday night after what must have been a long week. They left the warm and still crowded restaurant and stepped out into the night air which had turned sharply chilly. She pulled her cashmere wrap more tightly around her.

'You should have worn a coat,' he scolded and after that it seemed natural to take his arm and walk past the white stucco terraced houses of Chelsea to his Mercedes – a silver estate – which she supposed must be useful for things like his daughter's bicycle or stuff like that. They drove away from the restaurant, away from Central London, past Fulham Underground station and then over Putney Bridge. After barely ten minutes they were back at Putney. He stopped outside her house but kept the engine running. 'Well, sweet dreams.'

She was not about to ask him in for a coffee; she had some pride. If he wanted to come in he would have to ask. So instead she said blandly, 'And thank you for the lift.'

'My pleasure.' He looked at his watch. 'I'm afraid you must excuse me. Early start tomorrow.'

'Something nice, I hope?'

'Not at all. A client who's having kittens about a press conference on Monday needs his hand held. We're having a rehearsal at his house, eight a.m. sharp, before he flies off to Frankfurt for the weekend in order to persuade his German bankers not to close him down.'

'It sounds very exciting.'

'Not at all. It's very dull. But it pays the bills.' He leaned over her and opened the car door. 'I'll wait until you're inside.'

She reached down for her bag and at that moment his outstretched hand settled on her waist. He said nothing but she felt the brush of his lips against her cheek and then on her mouth. He kissed her, very expertly, just long enough for her to want more. 'Thank you for a lovely evening. We must do it again some time.'

She was unsure what to say. Men were never so noncommittal with her. Men always wanted to come in, invariably tried to get into her bed and straight away pestered her for the next date. Robert was very different. He had withdrawn now and it was obvious he was not going to try to kiss her again. She really wanted him to, and then to ask to sleep with her, though naturally she would say no. There seemed to be nothing she could say, so she gave a polite smile and got out of the car, swiftly ascended the three steps to her front door and turned the key in the lock. Turning, she saw that his car was already pulling away.

She stood in the doorway for a few seconds and watched as he accelerated away towards Putney High Street. She felt strangely empty. She could not remember a man ever not asking to come in, and wondered if she had perhaps said the wrong thing, worn the wrong dress, said too little or too much. Maybe it was the smoking. She was definitely going to give up; so many men hated it, not just Robert.

She kicked off her shoes and threw her keys down on the Chinese lacquer side table that stood in her small hallway. Quickly she switched on the stairway and sitting room lights to flood the darkness of the house. Then she turned up the thermostat to twenty-one degrees. It was an unfamiliar and not very comfortable feeling to be left alone at her own front door. She knew she was being melodramatic but nonetheless she could not help but feel rejected. Yes, she felt rejected. And she suddenly wanted very much for Robert to pursue her – and catch her.

'What kind of car does Theo drive?'

Araminta was sitting in the bath, washing herself in a desultory manner with a pink star-shaped bath sponge. The question signalled an abrupt change of subject from the previous five-minute-long argument about whether Araminta needed to have her hair washed at the end of which Tabitha won a Pyrrhic victory by securing a wash that night in exchange for no washing tomorrow or Sunday. This meant she would go unwashed to school on Monday morning but it seemed more important to send her to India's birthday party with shining hair.

Tabitha sat on the lavatory which was part of a pale-blue set, she guessed from the 1970s, comprising a free-standing washbasin and a bath below standard size. She had only discovered this after she bought the house and took a bath for the first time, her knees bent uncomfortably and her back jammed against the upright end. The faded chrome taps with their Perspex grooved tops were caked with years of limescale which she soon realized was unshiftable, along with the green limey trail that led from the bath taps to the plug. At least the tiles were white and the window no longer let in a bitter draft. Most important of all the new combination boiler which she had had installed during their first winter provided a reliable supply of hot water. Still, a new bathroom would be a treat.

She was nonplussed by Araminta's question. Her daughter had no interest in cars. All vehicles were referred to solely by adjectives of size and colour.

'He doesn't drive a car, darling. He drives a pick-up truck.'

'A truck. Like a lorry?'

'No. Smaller than that. It's got a front part you sit in and a flat bit at the back for carrying things in.'

'Like wood.'

'Yes. And tools. And all the things Theo needs to run the farm.'

Araminta sounded bored with the subject. 'OK.'

There was a pause. Tabitha picked up the sponge and began absently to wash Araminta's back. A small knot of anxiety had formed in her stomach. Had Robert asked Araminta about Theo's car – as a way of trying to second-guess Theo's financial position? Money was never far from Robert's heart, certainly closer than any woman had ever been.

She itched to ask Araminta what Robert had said. Of course, it might be nothing. At times like these she felt worn down by feelings of frustration and powerlessness. Robert manipulated, wheedled and forced all manner of information out of Araminta, whereas she maintained a silence as to her differences with Robert, albeit a silence more aptly described as tight-lipped rather than dignified. To do otherwise would place Araminta in the middle of a never-ending battle between her parents, which was precisely one of the outcomes she had sought to avoid by divorcing Robert. Sometimes friends told her to retaliate – to give Araminta her side of the story – but though she had often been tempted, and whilst the occasional weary retort slipped out her lips, she remained resolved to protect Araminta from the tensions and disputes that swirled around her. So she said nothing and reached instead for the shampoo and a sure-fire resumption of hair-washing hostilities.

Paul had sacked her. He hadn't said as much. But he had. And he had done it in the most cowardly, underhand and heartless way possible – in the baggage reclaim hall at Heathrow Airport.

Jasmine had just lifted the last of his three Louis Vuitton suitcases from the moving belt – he couldn't lift them himself on account of his bad back – and was about to return to look for her own case which, typically, had yet to appear.

'Jazzy. Wanted to say something.' He looked edgy but she didn't immediately pick up on the significance of this. Instead she blithely assumed after ten hours on the plane from Las Vegas that he was desperate for a cigarette. He didn't meet her eye. He fidgeted and stuck his hands in the pockets of his Quiksilver surfing shorts, which somehow he carried off despite being nearly fifty, just as he could get away with the slogan 'Lobster Rodeo' on the white T-shirt that he had bought in the Mandalay Hotel shopping mall. Maybe it was the tan or the fact he was so thin or the thick mop of silver hair that allowed him to walk around with two racing lobsters on his back. It certainly wasn't his youthful looks. Paul had the cratered rock-star face that can only be acquired by a lifelong dedication to snorting hard drugs.

'I . . . er.' He looked into the middle distance. 'Look. Really, really grateful for all you've done. Really. You're a great girl. But you see, I have to get a new assistant.'

God, looking back, she had been so dense.

She had been pleased. 'OK. We could definitely use someone. They could help with the reorganization of the studio.'

He hadn't looked enthusiastic. 'Yeah, right. But, um, you see Jazzy, I'm gonna have to let you go.'

Realization had slowly dawned. 'Let me go?'

He looked intently at the ground and then at his Birkenstocks and then shifted his gaze to stare up at the television monitor directing passengers to the correct carousel from which to retrieve their luggage.

At that moment she started having one of those *This isn't really happening to me* moments.

He seemed transfixed by the television. 'Yeah. Really sorry. I mean, don't worry about anything. A month's pay and all that and Clarry will give you a reference.'

Clarry! That would be the professional kiss of death.

She felt hot tears burst into her eyes. '*Why?* I thought it was going really well!' Unbidden the tears ran down her cheeks. She was sure this wasn't the way professional career women dealt with crises in their work lives but she couldn't help herself.

'Yeah. Yeah. It was. Look, Jazzy, nothing personal, hey.' He shook her shoulder gently but his eyes were now focused on the far distance. It was as if he wasn't there. The whole conversation was unreal.

She persisted. 'But why? Is it something I've done wrong? I can change that. I can try to do it differently.'

'No. No. You know, plans change, need a change of scene . . .' His voice trailed off.

'But why?' she persisted, her voice breaking.

He wasn't listening. Actually, he was adjusting the suitcases on his trolley. 'Well, see you around. Give Clarry a call on Monday; she'll sort you out.' And with that he started to wheel the trolley towards the customs section.

Now, in her seat on the eastbound Piccadilly Line tube train from the airport to Ealing Broadway, going over and over the events of the past week in her mind, she could almost laugh. She recognized that she was in shock. It had all happened so quickly. She had been so shocked that she had simply watched, wordless and crying, as Paul disappeared into customs. A plump, sunburned woman, in a sleeveless T-shirt and denim shorts whom she recognized from the flight, had stopped and touched her on the arm, said something stupid like, 'Lover's tiff. Don't worry love, he'll be back,' and she had wanted to shout at her and tell her that Paul wasn't her lover, though he had made several passes at her, and he definitely wouldn't be back. After that she had retrieved her case, found another trolley and struggled onto the tube.

There had been no indication during the trip that anything was amiss. Paul had seemed fine. A bit hungover maybe – he hit the bottle in first class, but that was to be expected – which didn't really matter because she was there to shepherd him through immigration and luggage reclaim and off to the Mandalay Hotel. At least he wasn't rude to any of the passengers or the cabin crew. Once, on a flight to LA, he had got blind drunk and shouted repeatedly for the 'trolley dolly', which was bad enough except the first class cabin crew was all male. She had only managed to shut him up by hissing that the pilot was on the verge of radioing ahead to the LAPD and detailing precisely what would happen to him in a communal holding cell in a Los Angeles police station.

She had arrived with Paul, drunk but docile, and he had spent the rest of the day in his room. Probably doing coke – he would have arranged his supply in advance – and definitely in paid female company. So she was left to her own devices, 5,000 miles away from home, realizing that focusing on work was the only way she was going to get through this trip. She spent the rest of the day wandering aimlessly around the hotel, which was the size of a small English town, feeling vulnerable and self-conscious amongst the greedy-eyed tourists out for a good time. Five minutes on the Strip was enough – too hot and crowded and too full of couples walking arm in arm – so she finally found some peace amongst the Renoir and Degas paintings of the Bellagio Gallery.

On Wednesday they started with the Bellagio Hotel shoot, Paul complaining about how hackneyed it was, but the client had specified that they wanted the model shot with the hotel fountains in the background so that was that.

And then out to the Grand Canyon and the heat-hazy pictures by the sightseeing helicopter with its livery of the Stars and Stripes. It had been her idea to include the pilot in the shot – standing smoking a cigarette while Suzy, the model, posed emerging from the helicopter in homage to Audrey Hepburn in a pair of white capris, a yellow linen shirt, and a white silk scarf tied in her hair. The shoot, with its theme *Las Vegas Mob Glamour*, was for an advertising campaign for a new range of handbags and so the bag had to be prominently shown, which rather spoiled the picture. They couldn't actually shoot inside a casino, much to Paul's disgust, so they had been forced to photograph the crocodile evening bag clasped by a model wearing a red silk strapless evening dress and reclining in a gondola at the Venetian hotel, with Paul muttering, 'Hackneyed, hackneyed, hackneyed,' under his breath while she assured him that it was actually all very ironic. When she was not placating Paul she was liaising with the stylist and the make-up artist and the hairdresser and the client team, who were in awe of Paul – which was a good thing because it meant they went along with whatever he said. And then there were the films to get developed and contact sheets to pore over and all the equipment to pack up and keep in good order long after Paul had gone off for dinner – and all while she was in a permanently jet-lagged state, waking up at four every morning remembering Robert and that Sunday afternoon. She would fall asleep again at six a.m., the alarm would wake her at seven and then just as she had begun to adjust to Las Vegas time it was time to come home.

The tube train jolted to a halt at Ealing Broadway station. It was a mile walk to her house, a thin sheet of rain was falling from the darkening evening sky and not a cab could be seen. She pulled out the carry handle of the case and began wheeling it towards her flat. It was incredible how her life had spiralled out of control. She had no boyfriend, no job and no prospect of a decent reference – Clarry, who had always been jealous of her, would see to that. She felt exhausted, defeated and full of fear at the implications of what had happened. As she walked, alone with her thoughts, she did not want to believe that Robert was behind this. But she knew that the most obvious explanation was the most likely. She just didn't want to accept that the last six months meant nothing at all to him. Now, as she made her way along the wet pavement, she struggled to understand why he should hate her so much that he would make her lose her job. Spite? Fear that she would say something to Paul? Or just because he could get her sacked and he wanted to make clear to her the extent of his power?

And if Robert was behind this then Paul had capitulated to him. Two years of hard work and loyalty and cleaning up after him – in every sense – had in the end counted for nothing. The betrayal disgusted her. She had lied to his girlfriend more times than she could remember, placated angry clients over every broken deadline, apologized and negotiated and occasionally begged on his behalf to hotel managers and sundry officials and so many restaurant staff she had lost count – all so he could escape the consequences of his intolerable behaviour. The only reason his teenage daughter ever got a present from overseas was because she went and bought it in the airport gift shop. And as for the photographs, Paul may have talent and a great eye but most of the time his hand was shaking so much it was a wonder he could press the shutter. She did all the technical work and for that matter, now she came to think of it, most of the composition, too.

She let herself in to the communal front door of the building, picked a pile of mail and pizza delivery flyers off the hall table and heaved the suitcase up the five flights of stairs to the top floor and let herself in. She went into the kitchen, discovered the milk had gone sour and put the kettle on to make herself a black coffee. She checked the answer machine. There were no messages, which after four days away was a pitiable situation for a single girl. Work, and the demands of a relationship with Robert, had left little time to keep up with the handful of friends she had in London. She flicked through the post. One letter stood out. It was contained in a heavy, white, typewritten envelope postmarked W1. Sitting at the kitchen table she had an uneasy feeling but forced herself to open it. It was a solicitor's letter from a firm called Masterson Ryder Jardine, the embossed initials MRJ woven around a crest in the centre of the letterhead, whose offices were located in Upper Brook Street.

*We write on behalf of our client Robert Agnew.*

*It has come to our client's attention that you have been making slanderous accusations against him. These accusations are malicious and untrue. They have caused our client considerable pain and suffering. Further, they are damaging to his personal and professional reputation.*

*Our client is hopeful that you will voluntarily cease making such accusations. Our client seeks an undertaking from you to that effect. If our client is forced to make a court application for an injunction he will seek to recover the costs of that application and those proceedings from you.*

*We advise you to seek independent legal advice.*

*We look forward to hearing from you or your legal advisers within seven days.*

She sat down. Her head was spinning. She hadn't spoken to anyone about anything to do with Robert. It was ludicrous. So why had he got these solicitors to send this letter? An injunction? Costs? She didn't have any 'legal advisers'. How could she afford to go and see a solicitor when she had just lost her job? But if she didn't give this undertaking, whatever that was, it sounded as if he would go to court and she would have to pay for it. She found she was shaking. Her mind struggled to grasp the implications of this latest turn of events. It was as if she was under siege. Attacked and abused, then fired, now threatened with some court case she had done nothing to provoke. Her mind was filled with images of a glaring barrister cross-examining her and legal bills flooding in and then her flat being sold to pay for it all.

It was as if Robert was trying to destroy her.

It was then she had a moment of clarity. Some intertwined instincts of survival and ambition, hidden beneath her eager-to-please exterior, broke through. They were the same character strengths that had brought her this far and they starting working for her now.

Robert knew her so well. He knew that the passion of her life was her work, her photography. He knew that the greatest challenge in her life was making ends meet. Therefore he understood precisely her points of vulnerability. She had no doubt now that he was behind Paul's firing of her. Perhaps he hoped that she would disappear, go back to her parents' pub in Bromley and leave London broken and defeated. At the very least the letter was designed to scare her so much that she would never dare utter his name to anyone.

She could never tell anyone about the sex. But she was damned if she was going to give up on her photography. He didn't know her that well after all if he believed that she would turn her back on her work. For a shy, unconfident girl with parents too busy running their beloved pub to notice she was there, art and her camera had been her early escape and her route to happier times. She had been ignored at home, miserable at school but at art school she had finally felt that she belonged. Paul might not have noticed the arid beauty of the desert but she had captured it on film. Paul had scarcely noticed the helicopter pilot but she had seen, in the older man's stillness and self-confidence, the perfect foil for the teenage model's airhead looks. That day she had made a good picture into a great one. She was going to continue to do that and one day she was going to have her own studio – and assistants – and she would treat them properly, too. There had to be an answer somewhere, someone who could help her. Not her parents – the letter would terrify them. Not her few neglected friends – they'd want to know what had happened and she wasn't going to talk about that. There must be someone who knew about these legal things, who could speak to Robert and get him to leave her alone.

And then it came to her in an instant, like all the best ideas.

Robert's brother James was a solicitor! Of course! James was nice and kind and they'd hit it off at the lunch. It was all coming back to her. His wife had gone off to check on the children, and Robert had disappeared to fuss over the Winters, and meanwhile she and James had stood companionably talking while she stirred the cream into the rhubarb fool. She remembered now, they had been talking about Joe Saltzman. James was working with him, trying to save his airline. And she was sure he had told her the name of his firm. If only she could remember it, then she could call him there. Anyway, she could look on the Internet.

And then she realized what a stupid idea it was. A man like James wouldn't have time to deal with her employment problems. He dealt with multinational corporations, not photographer's assistants from Ealing. What was she thinking? Not to mention the awkward fact that Robert was his brother, his flesh and blood, whereas she was a girl he barely knew. He might even think that she was a troublemaker, a jilted ex out to cause problems, just like Robert had said at the end. She sat back and re-read the letter. The easiest thing would be to write back and give the 'undertaking' they asked for.

But some obstinate instinct rebelled against the notion. It would be an admission of guilt, in essence a promise not to do it again – and she had done nothing wrong! She felt a defiant sense of injustice. She thought on, analysing what she knew of Robert and his operating methods. Even if she gave the undertaking, there was no guarantee that Robert would go away. He might seize on her admission and pursue her with even greater spite. She thought about losing the flat. She knew she had to get another job damned quickly and face this head on. But how?

She was on the outside. She had no money, no connections and no friends who were lawyers – none of the tools rich people used to get themselves out of trouble. She had seen Paul do it all the time, putting in a call to secure an airline upgrade or a restaurant table and passing on every awkward letter to his retained lawyers with never a second thought.

But she wasn't ready to believe that the rich always won. And she had an inkling that James didn't believe that either. As she went back to her original idea, something told her that he *would* help. She could approach it differently – she didn't have to go into detail at all. Perhaps there was a tactful way. She could contact James *on behalf of a friend*, which was a fib but only a small one, explain the situation and ask for some general advice.

All she had to do now was find him. She felt hopeful and invigorated. All was not lost. She switched on her computer and logged onto the Internet.

The Monday morning staff meeting at Charron's took place at eight forty-five a.m. prior to the doors being unlocked at nine thirty. There was no conference room. The ground-floor offices were constricted by their location in the middle of a late Victorian parade at the top of Cobham High Street, which allowed no room for expansion. Anthony Charron had his own office at the rear of the ground floor; the staff shared an open-plan office to the front. They met in Anthony's office, pulling in their chairs to form a group around his oversized desk. It was an ad hoc arrangement and Susannah liked it. One of the many benefits of working for Charron's was the escape from the impersonal, performance-chart pressure of a London agency. Anthony's office displayed a wall of framed photographs of properties sold by Charron's, the equally predictable certificates of local Rotary and Chamber of Commerce membership and letters thanking the firm for its generous donations to local causes. A bookcase housed a graduation photograph of his daughter from some years ago.

Anthony opened the meeting, as she knew he would, with the news that Charron's had secured the contract to market Milbourne Manor. He had told her immediately he had received the call from Cal Doyle, the developer, but sworn her to secrecy. Milbourne Manor was not a manor house at all but a formerly dilapidated Victorian pile newly converted and substantially extended into flats.

Anthony was ebullient. 'I'm delighted to say that we beat Kings into second place. We'll be dealing with the sale of twenty luxury flats in Milbourne Manor, built by Cal Doyle. Needless to say this will be our top priority.' Everyone nodded. Cal Doyle, the Irish multi-millionaire property developer, was a highly profitable and demanding client, not averse to storming into the office to have 'a few choice words' as he put it if everything was not entirely to his satisfaction. Built like a labourer, with a vocabulary to match, he terrified Lynda and Dee but Susannah had always respected him for his professionalism and attention to every detail. She knew for a fact that his houses were well built – he had built the Chapters.

Anthony ran through the layout of Milbourne Manor, the amenities – which included a communal gymnasium and six acres of landscaped gardens – and the likely marketing strategy. Then they moved on to review the list of new instructions. Anthony liked to see all the properties on the books and usually drew up the particulars himself. 'I'll take Fairmile Lane. Susannah, perhaps you could come with me.'

She saw Justin and Lynda exchange glances but Anthony was preoccupied with marking up his diary and did not notice. His voice ran on. 'Justin, where are we on Sandy Lane?' All present let out a groan. Sandy Lane was the location of a five-bedroom inoffensive house, which should have sold overnight, but for no good reason had attracted a series of failed offers. The most recent offer, from an American who worked in the software industry, had fallen through just days prior to exchange of contracts when his wife telephoned him to say that she and their two teenage children had held a family conference and decided that they were not after all prepared to relocate from California. The previous offer had come from a couple who had announced the day before the mortgage valuation that they were pulling out –Susannah suspected marital problems were at the root of that – and before that the newly divorced man with the three children had got a better job offer in Bristol.

Justin looked up. 'I am cautiously optimistic. The valuation has been done, the offer has been issued and we're hopeful for an exchange this Friday.' Susannah knew that Sandy Lane was Justin's biggest sale so far. The negotiators in the office worked on a part salary, part commission basis. There were four negotiators altogether: Susannah and Dee were seniors and Justin and Tom, both of whom had joined in the previous year, were juniors. Justin had made by far the biggest mark.

It had initially baffled Susannah that Justin had joined Charron's at all. He was, on first impressions, diffident – appearing slight and boyish though he was twenty-five years old – and not at all like the brash young men who filled the junior negotiator jobs. Tom, who was currently on holiday in Ibiza, talked of nothing but the latest BMW 3 series, golf and Manchester United. Justin liked to read, watch arthouse films and attended a conversation class at the French Institute in Kensington. It was over lunch one day that Justin had confided in her: 'Actually, it's a day job.' He had looked apprehensive. 'What I really want to do is become a broadcaster.'

'Wow!'

He had looked relieved. 'I don't generally tell people.'

'I think it's great!' She had been intrigued. 'How do you do that?'

'Kingston Hospital Radio. Of course if I had a degree I could apply to the BBC trainee programme. But I haven't and I can't afford to go back to college. This means I can do hospital radio and send out my CV. I'm hoping to break into local radio, though of course, so are thousands of other people.'

It had become their project. Once Justin told her of his plans she noticed for the first time that he had a deep, carefully articulated voice out of keeping with his youthful appearance – 'I practise by reading out the newspaper to my mother.'

After that Susannah took a close interest in Justin's career, enlisted Lynda to retype his CV and even kept the car radio tuned into Thames Radio where Justin worked on his days off, just in case he got his break on air.

Anthony made no comment on the sale of Sandy Lane. He would, Susannah knew, continue to track the situation closely. She did not mind his interest – she found that she enjoyed discussing her work with him – but she knew that some of the others found his interventions irritating and guessed it would cause Tom to move on before long. Justin's nickname for Anthony was Captain Mainwaring, after the character in *Dad's Army*, and he was now referred to as such by all the staff, though never to his face. For Susannah, years in London estate agency had taught her to value a boss who had a genuine concern for his staff and a benevolent interest in their work.

Anthony turned to Dee and she half-listened as Dee gave her report on the lettings situation. It had proved hard to warm to Dee, a wiry woman with a bad henna rinse and a wardrobe of hardwearing trouser suits. Dee's husband worked as a long-distance lorry driver, a career choice Justin speculated he had selected after he got married. Dee was the longest-serving employee at Charron's, had local knowledge second only to Anthony's and, as she frequently mentioned, had worked alongside Peter Charron, the late founder of Charron's. She treated the other staff with universal condescension. Lynda called her Queen Dee and resolutely refused to prioritize Dee's typing. 'I take them from the bottom of the tray whoever they're for.'

Justin and Susannah privately agreed that Lynda was the real reason most of the clients signed up with Charron's. Forty-something with bright blonde bobbed hair, two sons she doted on, an accountant husband and a diploma in cordon bleu cooking, Lynda was the public face of the firm. She didn't have to try to be friendly or welcoming; she was all of those things naturally. Once Lynda settled clients with a cup of coffee and a biscuit, and Anthony Charron had given them the speech he had been making for over twenty-five years since he first started working with his father, they had forgotten the sales pitch of the big chains and signed with the local firm. Charron's was 'small enough to care and big enough to succeed'.

It was a source of ongoing banter between Lynda and Justin that Anthony Charron had a crush on Susannah. It was true that he invariably asked her to go on valuations with him and sometimes they would stop off for lunch before returning to the office. And Justin had whooped at the news that Anthony had asked her to accompany him to the Surrey estate agents' annual award lunch at the Cobham Hilton last summer. But these were all business occasions and it was not surprising to Susannah that Anthony, who had lived alone since his divorce, chose to take a colleague with him. He was, at the end of the day, well past fifty and not far off sixty. Fifty-eight to be precise, Lynda had confided. Lynda did all his personal typing. Anthony had a Surrey look about him. Well-groomed, expensive-suited with a full head of silver hair which he parted at the side, and the type of looks that engendered trust in his clients.

Sometimes they would drive out to one of the surrounding villages. Anthony always drove Jaguars, acquiring the new saloon model in racing green every two years. The Rolls Royce he kept for weekends. Susannah liked him. He was no fool. No one could survive in the Cobham estate agency business without being sharp. But she sensed that the values he adhered to in business – honesty, reliability and trustworthiness – were also those he adhered to in his private life. It had always been a wonder to her that he was divorced. One expected Anthony to be married to the type of woman who dressed in Windsmoor and baked her Christmas cake in September. His ex-wife was actually a county type, Lynda had disclosed, from an old Surrey family. Her name was Kate, her great passion was horses, and she had left Anthony four years earlier for the owner of the stables where her two horses were liveried, breaking up both their marriages in the process. There were rumours, Lynda had suggested in a near whisper, in one of their morning chats over coffee before the clients came in, that it was not Kate's first affair and the marriage had never been happy. Lynda suspected that Kate had married Anthony for his money all along. When they got divorced Anthony had had to sell his house in St George's Hill and give Kate half the proceeds – which Lynda thought was bloody unfair in the circumstances. They both agreed that it was a shame and Anthony was a very nice man and they predicted Kate would, in time, probably come to regret her decision.

Before Christmas, Susannah and Anthony had stopped for lunch at a pub on the outskirts of Ripley. The Two Brewers, which retained its traditional brick and horseshoe decoration, had recently been taken over by a young Australian couple, Kimberley and Sean, who had introduced into the small Surrey village a menu of pan-Asian cuisine. Unpredictably, it had been a huge success. The bar was packed with businessmen and they had been lucky to get a table. Susannah had ordered one of the specials from the elegantly lettered chalkboard, tiger prawns with a ginger and lime glaze. It had taken for ever for their food to come. While they waited they had talked about Christmas opening hours for the office and then their respective plans for Christmas Day.

'I shall go down to my daughter's,' explained Anthony. 'She lives towards Reigate.'

'Kingswood?'

'You remembered.' He looked pleased. 'When Kate and I were together we tried to go abroad for a few days over Christmas.'

She had not known what to say. It was the first time he had ever mentioned his ex-wife. He sipped his orange juice. She liked the fact that he never drank and drove. Perhaps it was the warmth of the fire or the good food or just the fact that it was the week before Christmas that had caused them to linger.

'Kate met someone else. A man she rode with. I suppose it's understandable, a shared interest.'

Susannah hoped that she looked as though this was the first time she had heard this information. She would hate for Anthony to think that she gossiped about him behind his back. She felt suddenly guilty for speaking about his personal life with Lynda and Justin.

'The truth is I never saw it coming.' He looked up at her. 'I expect you think that's ridiculous.'

Her heart went out to him. 'No, not at all. It was the same for me, actually. When my first husband left I had no idea things had got so bad.'

'That was one of the things I found hardest: the fact that Kate never gave me any explanation. Just the usual clichés.'

'I know,' she said with feeling. 'Part of me felt such a fool.'

'No.' His voice was forceful. 'You must never think that.'

There was a pause and she felt suddenly terribly sorry for him, alone in his Esher house. She had been there once, to collect papers when he was laid low with flu, and it was exactly as one would imagine the house of a middle-aged divorced man to be. Furnished to a minimum, decorated to the builder's finish, with none of the pictures, rugs or cushions that came with a woman's touch.

When he had resumed the conversation it had been on business matters, but she had felt touched by his confidences and that Christmas she had been careful to pick out a Christmas card that she knew he would like, a Botticelli detail, and she had given him a book that accompanied the BBC2 series *Great British Country Houses* which he had mentioned he had enjoyed.

Dee had finished giving her update on the lettings situation. Susannah saw Anthony hesitate.

'How is the management brochure progressing?'

She saw Dee's mouth tighten. 'Very well, Anthony. I'm just waiting for Lynda to type up my first draft.'

Susannah felt Lynda stir next to her but before Lynda could say anything Anthony cut in. 'Good. Let's discuss it next week, then.'

Dee gave a tight little nod and Susannah turned to look at Lynda, whose cheeks had reddened. Then Anthony ran over the weekend staffing schedule and Lynda, as she always did, asked everyone to make more of an effort to keep the kitchen clean and tidy. The meeting broke up and as they left Lynda leaned towards Susannah.

'Dee gave me that typing five minutes before we closed on Friday,' she hissed. Lynda did not work on Saturdays; they employed a relief girl to man the telephones. 'So there was no way I could get it done for Monday!'

'I'm sure Anthony guessed that. He won't blame you,' Susannah assured her.

'Do you think so?'

She saw the relief in Lynda's anxious face.

'Definitely. He knows what Dee's game is – she wants things to stay the way they are.'

'Are you sure?' Lynda asked earnestly.

'Yes! Stop worrying.'

It was impossible to say more because at that moment Anthony emerged from his office to unlock the front door and Dee came back from the ladies'. Susannah sat down and glanced over at Lynda, who gave a mock angry glare to Dee's back and then winked at Susannah. Susannah was left to wonder why she was so good at dealing with people at work and so very bad at coping with everyone at home.

'Did you really think I could wait three months to see you?'

She hadn't dared to hope. Theo sprung this on her from time to time, calling her and saying casually, 'By the way, I just bought a ticket. See you tomorrow.'

They would snatch a short, precious, intense weekend together. She had collected him on Friday morning from the airport. And then things had been as they always were. Making love, cooking breakfast and then when Araminta came home from school playing Monopoly and watching television by the fire.

It was Friday night now and though it was only ten o'clock she could tell that he was heavy with jet lag. They lay, watching the embers glow, wrapped up together on the sofa.

'I love you, honey,' he whispered in her ear. 'Everything will be fine.'

Just then the memory of her conversation with Araminta came to mind and she felt uneasy. She had not mentioned her suspicions to Theo. She could not bear anything to spoil their time together.

'Will it?' she asked, almost to herself. 'Will it be fine?'

He held her tighter. 'Tabitha, everything's always good for us.' His voice was slow and sleepy. 'I always find the money for the airline ticket. We've never spent more than a few weeks apart. And US Immigration haven't taken you to one side yet. . .'

She pushed herself into his chest and relaxed. She could sense him falling asleep beside her. Tomorrow they would go to Brighton to walk along the beach and wander the shops of the Lanes. For now everything was more than fine. It was perfect.

Robert had sent her flowers the day after their dinner at La Famiglia. A Moyses Stevens cellophane bouquet of twenty-four red roses had arrived together with a card that thanked her for a wonderful evening. Her spirits had soared. It was a shame to throw them away but they were close to wilting and Natasha needed the vase for the lilies. The lilies were, in turn, to be placed in front of the fireplace. Robert had been very precise. Harriet Haig-Brown would interview Natasha at her house. The house needed to look affluent without being showy; homely without being untidy. Robert told her to buy fresh flowers, exotic fruit and ample supplies for the refrigerator.

She had tried to cajole him. 'Can't you be there with me?'

'No! It would make you look as if you've got something to hide.' Instead he had briefed her on what to say, what to wear and suggested leaving her Barbour in a prominent position. 'I've spoken to Harriet's editor,' he said reassuringly. 'He owes me a favour and he's happy to play ball. There's no problem.'

And there hadn't been. Harriet Haig-Brown had spent thirty years in the business and had carved out a niche for herself interviewing shamed celebrities and victims of major disasters. She could be relied upon to be sympathetic when required. Harriet, a short woman in a long brown jersey skirt and faded suede jacket, arrived with a staff photographer in tow and followed Natasha into the kitchen. Natasha, wearing Joseph bootleg beige trousers and an Anne Fontaine white cotton shirt with mother-of-pearl buttons, had made them coffee, grinding the beans herself, and left the fridge door open long enough for Harriet to see that it was full of lettuce, tomatoes and mineral water. Natasha had cut down to five cigarettes a day and for the past three days had smoked them all in the garden. The house did smell better for it. Nonetheless she had bought pot pourri and a very potent plug-in air freshener that made her sneeze.

Harriet, pulling out a spiral-bound notebook, had got straight down to business. 'Do you cook much?'

'I love to – when I can.'

Harriet gazed round, taking in the Smallbone white units and the copper pans hanging from the rack that Natasha had specially polished last night.

'In fact,' Natasha continued, 'I love to be at home. I do all my own housework!' What was more this was true. Harriet looked slightly dumbfounded. She observed as Natasha put a cafetière of coffee, three cups and saucers and a plate of florentines onto a tray and led them to the living room. After they sat down Harriet changed tack.

'Do you have any big projects coming up?'

In truth she didn't. 'Too many to mention,' Natasha had responded airily. 'I've just finished filming for the *Holiday* programme, actually.' She then diverted the conversation onto a description of the Thetford Park shoot and Harriet, who relied on old-school shorthand, appeared satisfied. Besides, Natasha knew what Harriet really wanted to ask. It was the next question.

'Natasha, our readers will be interested to hear your side of the story of your relationship with Mark Lewin.'

Robert's lines came effortlessly to mind. 'Mark is back with his wife and family now – and I think it's important that they are allowed time and privacy. At the same time, I want to emphasize that Mark was separated from his wife and living apart from her when I met him. Mark was a good friend of mine and I wish him every success in the future. I think many women can relate to my experience – believing that a man is unattached but subsequently finding out otherwise.'

Harriet nodded. She, like the rest of Fleet Street, had a good idea of the true state of Mark's marriage. 'Did you ever speak to his wife?'

'No.' Robert had decided that Mrs Lewin's foul-mouthed messages on her mobile could be excluded from the interview.

Harriet frowned. 'I think she's on record as saying that she called you?'

Clearly Harriet wasn't a pushover. Natasha put down her cup. 'Off the record, she did call me. But she never spoke to me. She just left messages. You can imagine the type of thing. I didn't see any point in getting into a slanging match with her.'

Harriet raised her eyebrows. 'I can. I've met her.'

'So I didn't actually speak to her.'

Harriet thought for a moment. 'OK. I'll say that you never spoke to her directly.'

Natasha decided to get back on track. She needed to put across the story as Robert had suggested it. 'This was a difficult situation for everyone involved. I admire Mark for putting his family first. As for me, I have plenty to occupy me. I'm certainly not sitting at home waiting for the phone to ring.'

Harriet took up the thread. 'So are you saying there's someone new in your life?'

'Yes.' For once she did not need to remember what to say. 'It's early days and I don't want to say too much.'

'A name?'

'I can't give his name.' She couldn't. She still wasn't absolutely sure that she was Robert's girlfriend.

Harriet smiled thinly. 'Very well.'

'But I promise you'll be the first to know.'

Harriet paused to consult her notes. 'Natasha, I need to write something about your father.'

'My father and I see each other as often as we can. He has his own family and I have my career. He's always been very supportive.'

This was fantasy, but she had told the lie so often it sounded true even to her own ears. She had sought out her father when she was eighteen and found out for herself that he was exactly the self-centred, feckless and very married man her mother had described. As a child she had chosen only to half-believe it. When she finally met him it would be different. It hadn't been. There had been none of the tight embraces and instant intimacy she had dreamed of. Instead, they had met for coffee in a dreary hotel off the M1 and she had listened to muttered excuses as to why he couldn't be more involved. It would upset his wife. It would confuse his children – his other children, he had corrected himself. After that they exchanged Christmas cards, but he never called. It had taken a long time for her to accept that there were no very complicated reasons, psychological or practical, for his lack of interest. He was simply selfish, exactly as her mother had said.

Harriet nodded, though, accepting the explanation happily enough. They went on to talk about her mother, who always appeared in interviews as the architect of her career and her best friend. The first part was true. And then Harriet closed her notebook and let the photographer take over. Robert had been keen for a picture in the kitchen and they shot off a couple of rolls there.

'We're aiming for next week's women's section,' Harriet had told her as she pulled on her coat. 'It's a twelve-page pull-out section. If the editor likes it we may get a centre spread. No promises, though.'

'Thank you,' Natasha responded. She knew that the placing of the article was outside Harriet's control.

After they left she unplugged the air freshener, lit a cigarette and stretched out on the sofa to telephone Robert.

'It went like a dream,' she announced.

'Well done! I had no doubt it would.'

She told him Harriet's questions and what she could remember of her responses. 'Robert, thank you! It was a great idea. I feel so much better. It's as if the whole Mark thing is behind me now—'

'It is behind you,' he cut in decisively. 'You need to look to the future. Which reminds me – what are you doing on Sunday?'

Her heart missed a beat. 'Not sure.'

'Well, I would be absolutely delighted if you would come with me to my mother's birthday lunch. It's in Wiltshire, so it would mean a day out of London. But that might be just what you need.'

'Robert, I'd love to!' She was overwhelmed. It wasn't exactly a formal 'meet the parents' occasion but it was pretty close.

'Good. So if it's OK with you, I'll tell them that I'm bringing my girlfriend?'

It was more than OK. She put every ounce of effort into sounding cool. 'Robert, that's fine by me.'

# Chapter 5

# Relationships

*What was I thinking? The answer is I wasn't thinking. I was feeling bored, resentful and deprived. I was a sulking guest at a dull lunch party held by my brother, Robert. The other guests were enjoying a glass of chilled Tattinger. I was permitted a tumbler of apple juice which, Jasmine let slip, had been purchased with Oliver in mind. Oliver is three. Jasmine is my brother's girlfriend. This is not, however, a sibling rivalry 'issue'. How tedious I find that word. Nowadays every quirk of human behaviour is labelled and catalogued as an 'issue'; the preciousness of an individual human experience reduced to the lazy shorthand of the self-help book. I digress.*

*To return to the narrative – Jasmine and I were standing alone in the kitchen before lunch. She was spooning rhubarb fool into glass dishes. We were discussing the law of copyright as it relates to the protection of photographic images posted on the Internet. I was wondering what it would be like to lick her fingers. She is a photographer, a very good one. I've seen her portfolio and at the time, even before seeing the photographs, I knew she was exceptional. Jasmine is very slight but when she is relaxed and free to speak her mind she has an energy and vivacity which is incredibly strong and compelling. We spoke about places we had been and people we knew and she impressed me with her engaging spontaneity and openness. She is not jaded or cynical. She sees the best in everyone – and sometimes suffers for it. She said she thought that Joe Saltzman, whom she had photographed, was an unhappy man and even though I have spent many hours with him I had never appreciated that. She was absolutely right. And then we talked about Venice. I felt as if I could fall in love with her right then. I didn't think at all. I just needed to see her and when she contacted me for my help on a quasi-legal matter I decided that fate had intervened. Fate had intervened in order to facilitate my hopes of an extra-marital affair? I admit it is not the easiest proposition to defend. At*

*the time I did not pause to consider this. She sought help for 'a friend'.*
*The small deception charmed me. To be strictly accurate, everything she*
*said intoxicated me. I don't know where love begins and delusion ends,*
*the point at which the selfish need for love evolves into true feeling for*
*another, but I do know that I am married and that is real.*

The Agnews' sandstone house, originally built for a merchant grown rich on the wool trade of the 1800s, was placed high in a still-small Wiltshire hamlet to overlook the green valley of ancient springs and streams. They had driven down that morning, Matthew moaning about having to get up early on a Sunday. It was Estella's birthday and Susannah had bought her a Wedgwood serving plate. She continued to take great care in selecting gifts for her mother-in-law even though Estella always gave the impression that nothing Susannah gave her was ever quite right. The journey had passed in silence, Matthew preoccupied with his GameBoy and James lost in thought as if in a world of his own.

The drawing room caught the low sun as it was cast over the hills beyond, falling over the fields until it filtered through the high drawing-room windows onto the faded chintz sofas, the antique polished wood and worn tapestry rugs. Susannah watched as Estella stood to pour coffee from an ornate silver coffee-pot.

'It's Persian,' Estella said to Natasha. 'The Major acquired it during his travels.'

Most of Estella's conversation at lunch had been directed at Natasha and it continued thus after they left the lunch table to have coffee in the drawing room. The presence at lunch of Natasha Webster, the ex-*Blue Peter* television presenter, had come as something of a shock. First, Susannah had been expecting Robert to bring Jasmine. Second, she was more used to seeing Natasha on a television screen. It had been years since she had watched *Blue Peter* but she knew Natasha's face from other programmes and found that all the clichés she had heard about seeing celebrities in the flesh were true – Natasha was slimmer and shorter in real life than she appeared on screen but her unaffected persona was genuine. They had had little opportunity to speak over lunch. Robert and Estella had dominated the conversation, at times in overt competition with each other for the floor.

That was the same as ever and much else besides: Estella, defiantly pin-thin, dressed in a cashmere twin-set offset by understated gold; the Major in Viyella and corduroy. Likewise the rituals: the fuss over coffee, the tray prepared by Major Agnew, then the debate as to the merits of lighting an afternoon fire – and in the background the Jack Russells yapping and the undercurrent of small talk she had grown accustomed to over the years. The garden. The weather. The farmers. The house itself was unchanged, or so it seemed in the eight or so years since she had first visited. Back then she had been overawed, desperate for approval, clinging onto James. A newcomer in every sense.

'My husband travelled very widely during his military career,' continued Estella.

Natasha was unfailingly attentive. 'Did you travel with him?'

'Oh no, my dear. Not in those days. I had the boys to look after. Things were different in those days. Mother stayed at home.'

Susannah was uncertain if this last comment was directed at her. Sometimes with Estella it was only much later that she realized she had been verbally assaulted.

'It was often just the three of us,' Estella went on, 'very cosy together.'

'And mother had her social life to attend to,' said Robert. He turned to Natasha. 'Wiltshire's social scene is dependent upon my mother's presence.'

Estella gave a small smile. 'Most of it for charitable causes, Robert.'

Next to her Susannah felt James shift. Either he was bored or hungry or still smarting from the pressure that had been brought to bear upon him at lunch when he had refused wine. Estella had prepared a birthday lunch of roast lamb followed by bread and butter pudding. Estella was an uninspired cook and, as usual, there had been barely enough to go round.

'Have a glass,' Robert had insisted, pouring one out for James. 'Don't be a killjoy.'

'No, really. Water for me.'

Robert had not let up. 'I see. You *are* taking it seriously.' He had pushed the glass to one side and smiled warmly at Susannah. 'Well, if you think it's something James needs to do we should support you.'

'It was not Susannah's idea,' James said testily.

Estella had shot Susannah a querulous glance at that point. 'What are you making James do?'

'Nothing!' interjected James. 'Let's just drop the subject.'

There had been a small, awkward silence and then Robert had asked James blandly if it was true that Lloyd-Davies had scrapped plans to open a New York office.

'I have no idea,' said James, not looking up from his plate.

'Hmm. I think it's a market for the top five players.' Robert turned to Natasha. 'Lloyd-Davies is number eight in the Legal Five-hundred.' He had glanced towards Susannah and she braced herself for the next shot. He paused. 'Could you pass the mint sauce?'

Then Estella had taken the floor, asking Natasha a stream of questions: where did she buy her clothes; who did her make-up; had she ever broadcast live? It was clear that Natasha's answers generated the interested and approving nods and smiles that Susannah's responses never did. Susannah had formed the impression that Estella would only look truly pleased if Susannah announced that she and James were getting divorced. From the start, Estella had made little effort to conceal her opinion that Susannah was not good enough for James. Susannah was divorced. She had a child. She worked as an estate agent. Any of these three handicaps would have been sufficient on their own to disqualify her as James's future wife. At the wedding Estella had sat poker-faced, snubbed Susannah's mother – 'A very nice wedding. A brave effort!' – and given them as a wedding present a porcelain figurine of a Victorian pauper mother and child which Susannah thought in retrospect might be significant.

Natasha's birthday gift to Estella – a small Waterford bowl – had been greeted with delight. 'Look, darling,' Estella exclaimed to the Major. 'Isn't that exquisite! Perfect, my dear. Thank you!'

It was exactly the reaction Susannah had anticipated but galling nonetheless. The Waterford bowl now had pride of place on the coffee table. Her Wedgwood serving plate remained in its box on the kitchen counter.

Estella went out to fetch more coffee, a task that was usually delegated to the Major, but he had slipped off with Matthew after lunch to shoot air rifles at the bottom of the garden. The Major had always been very kind to Matthew, teaching him how to shoot and fish and repair bicycles. He passed on all manner of army stories which Matthew still loved to hear. And the Major always referred to Matthew as 'my grandson', something Estella had yet to say.

Robert took Natasha's arm and led her over to the window. He pointed. 'You see that hill over there? James and I used to go sledding down that hill when it snowed. And over there, you can just see the edge of the white horse on the hillside. I'll take you there. And down, look between the trees; there's a stream. Great for tadpoles.'

Susannah could see that Natasha was charmed. Robert made their childhood sound idyllic. She was not sure that it had been. James never said much about it, though she had the impression that he had spent much of his time in his room. She took advantage of the distraction to whisper to James, 'What happened to Jasmine?'

He was very curt. 'Why do you assume I know?' He really was in a foul mood. She sat back and looked at her watch, wondering how much longer they needed to stay.

In the background Robert's voice ran on. 'Now this room is really rather special at Christmas. Father always finds the biggest tree. And Mother is the best decorator in Wiltshire.' He put his arm around Natasha's waist and turned her into the room. 'My parents invite all the neighbours in for drinks on Christmas Eve. It's a village tradition.'

Suddenly Susannah was aware of James rising abruptly to his feet.

'I'm going to get some air.' He spoke to Robert. 'I think we should leave the girls to get to know each other.'

Robert squeezed Natasha's hand and kept his gaze on her, 'I'm not sure I want to leave this beautiful girl.'

'She'll be quite safe,' said James firmly. 'And I'm sure business talk will bore her.'

'Oh, I see.' said Robert. 'Well, if you insist . . .' He lingered over letting go of Natasha's hand.

'I promise it won't take long,' said James smoothly.

But in the event Susannah did not have the opportunity to speak to Natasha because as the men left the room Estella returned with more coffee and began asking Natasha about the presenters on the *Holiday* programme and whether it was true that so-and-so had had a facelift. Natasha played it perfectly, dropping just enough inside information to satisfy Estella while never seeming indiscreet. Then Estella recounted some anecdote about Robert's time at the local prep school – 'I had to plead with the headmaster not to expel him' – and then Robert burst in, out of breath, and said boldly, 'We had a race down the lane! Just like old times!'

It was obvious that he had won because it took an age for James to appear. Perhaps losing to Robert had been the final ignominy because James's expression when he did enter the room was tense and Susannah noticed that the two of them did not speak to each other again. She imagined it might have something to do with that Harrold-Winter contract they had been discussing at Robert's lunch. Robert could be difficult like that – keen to make business contacts but reluctant to share them. In fact, James barely said a word to anyone and soon afterwards he insisted that they leave because he had papers to prepare for the next day at work.

All in all it was a thoroughly tedious day. The trip back to Cobham had taken an age because of an accident on the M25. Matthew fell asleep in the back of the car. She knew it was useless to try to make conversation with James when he was in this kind of mood, but she had asked him if everything was all right between him and Robert.

'Fine,' he said dispassionately. 'Nothing changes with Robert.'

So it was business. But he said nothing more. Abstinence had not improved his sociability one jot. So she stared out of the window at the darkness and the lights of the cars. Her mind wandered to the first time she had met Estella. It had been an icy day, a few weeks after Christmas, and when she had walked into the house it had been filled with the sweet smoky scent of applewood. She had walked into the drawing room, just as Natasha had done today, and been struck by the beauty of the view: by the ridged hillsides, the windswept trees on the far horizon and the copses of ancient beech. As if to complete the picture, in those days James's parents had appeared to her to be an example of a long-lived and contented married life. She had taken Estella's froideur to be the natural reserve of the English upper middle classes and told herself that in time their relations would grow warmer.

Now, looking back, she understood how uncritical and impressionable she had been. It was so easy to be convinced by the appearance of the perfect family because it was an illusion she wanted to believe was real. It appeared to be the settled life she had at that time so painfully failed to achieve. The end of her first marriage had left her with a chronic sense of failure. She had met Steve at school, dated him through her teens and married him in her early twenties. He had talked a good talk. He was a builder who was always on the brink of his big break, his killer deal, his pot of gold. Every week he met a man who would open doors for him, secure funding and introduce him to rich clients. In the beginning she had loved him for his enthusiasm and sense of adventure. By the end she was desperate for him to get out of bed in the morning and go to work for eight hours to pay the bills. He was good-looking, smooth-talking and totally unreliable in every way. If she thought having a baby would change him she was soon disabused. If anything, Matthew's arrival seemed to cause Steve to regress to an even greater state of immaturity. 'I need my space, Suze,' was his constant whine as he disappeared for another night out or weekend away with the boys. When he left she had vowed never to get married again. A boyfriend, maybe. A live-in lover, even. But never a husband. It had taken James's determined pursuit and obvious steadiness to begin to change her mind. She had even told him that. On their third date, a Sunday walk in Richmond Park, she had turned to James amongst the rhododendrons of the Isabella Plantation and said, 'I don't want to get married again. I'm happy as I am. And I don't like change very much.'

James had laughed. 'Then I shall have to take you on exactly the same date, to the same place, at the same time, every week. I must warn you we're going to have to break in here when the winter opening hours come in.'

And she had laughed and only much later realized that she had unwittingly thrown down an irresistible challenge to him.

Tabitha heard the tyres of Lizzy's Renault, the familiar squeak of its breaks and the sound of car doors slamming. Lizzy would let herself in at the back. Tabitha turned to put the kettle on the Aga. Lizzy, short and self-avowedly pear-shaped, in a pair of faded jeans and a loose Sloppy Joe pale pink sweatshirt, fell through the door, one hand holding a pot of closed bulbs and the other grasping a sheaf of property particulars.

'Hello, sweetie.' Lizzy's voice was hard to place: by and large solidly middle class, with the occasional hint of South London vowels.

'Hey, let me take those.' Tabitha grabbed hold of the bulbs.

'Hyacinths, as promised. Make sure you put them on a sunny window sill.'

'Thanks!'

Lizzy waved the papers she was holding. 'I cannot believe house prices round here. I can't afford a shed. Everything is unbelievable.'

'I know,' sighed Tabitha. She had been incredibly lucky to get the cottage just before Stokesham prices entered a growth spurt.

Tabitha made coffee, the precursor to them retiring to her living room as they did at least once a week. Lizzy had been her lifeline when she arrived in Stokesham, raw and battered from the fight with Robert. It was Lizzy who had been the first to speak to her at the school gates, the only other single mother over the age of thirty at the school. Just knowing that Lizzy was down the lane helped ease the pain of the loneliness which hit her every time she walked into the cottage. And Lizzy had had a tough time of it. It was hard to believe that it was four years since Tabitha and Araminta had arrived in Stokesham. Lizzy was still living in the Vicarage then, as grand and beautiful a Victorian brick house as the name evoked. Her husband, Ian, had left a few months before. Lizzy had invited her round to Sunday lunch and afterwards they had sat on the terrace of the Vicarage, looking out over Lizzy's beautiful garden while Araminta and India played with India's dressing-up box.

Lizzy had been hopeful then of reconciliation.

'Ian is having a mid-life crisis,' she had explained over a second bottle of Orvieto. 'Some little cow he picked up on a business trip to Helsinki. A waitress in the hotel coffee shop; can you believe it? Twenty-something. So I said to him, "It's her or me," and off he went. But give them enough rope to hang themselves . . .'

'So where is he now?'

'In a studio flat in South London. She's come over from Finland and started some course.'

Tabitha had wondered at Lizzy's sangfroid that day. But in truth, looking back, Lizzy had been in denial about her situation. Tabitha had been in the house once or twice to observe how Lizzy greeted Ian when he arrived to collect India for the weekend: with stiff silence and the air of a woman waiting for her day of victory when her husband, broken and humbled, would beg to be allowed through the Vicarage doors. That day had not come. Two days after the decree absolute Ian sent Lizzy an email to say that he had remarried. She seemed to go downhill after that, as if the fight had sustained her and now that it was over she had nothing else to do. Now, listening to her friend, it sounded as if the battle lines had shifted.

'India was royally bribed. Cinema, a new dress, McDonald's. Came back absolutely exhausted on the Sunday night with filthy hair and of course The Bitch hadn't washed her clothes properly.'

'Washed them?'

'Well, there was a grass stain on the jeans and she ironed them down the middle, which may be à la mode in fucking Finland . . .' Lizzy rolled her eyes.

There was a pause.

'Of course, I don't have to let India go at all.'

Tabitha was confused. 'But I thought there was a court order for access?'

'There is. But they never enforce them.'

Tabitha stood at a crossroads. The etiquette of female friendship demanded that nothing good could ever be said about a husband who had run off with another woman. But she could not say nothing. 'Lizzy, I think India needs to see Ian. It's very disruptive otherwise.'

Lizzy's mouth tightened. 'I think the whole situation is disruptive. Poor India – shunted between two homes, having to see her father with that bimbo . . .' And then she was off, on the same refrain that Tabitha had heard for the past four years. 'It's so wrong! That you can make vows to another person and then when it all gets boring or inconvenient you can just go off and fuck some bitch.'

Tabitha leaned forward. 'Hey. I know how you feel. Well, not exactly. But I know what a struggle it is, believe me.'

'It's just so bloody unfair!'

'Hey. Lizzy, you need to think about you. It's not all about Ian.'

'But he's destroyed my life! I've lost the house, everything!'

There was a pause. The same etiquette of female friendship that forbade any positive assessment of an ex-husband also prohibited any hint that the friend in question might bear any responsibility for the breakdown of a relationship. But occasionally, observing Lizzy's controlling and stubborn nature, Tabitha could get an inkling of why Ian might have left for a quieter life elsewhere.

'You'll find a house.'

'Or a bus shelter.'

'No,' persisted Tabitha. 'A *nice* house. And it will be all yours. And then you can think about getting a different job. Maybe one where you meet people?' Tabitha ventured.

'Well it has to be better than The Morgue.'

The Morgue was in fact the office of a small chartered surveying practice where Lizzy was employed to do secretarial work for three hours every afternoon.

'Anyway,' said Lizzy, 'the fact is I'm going to have to go full time. Looking at these I'll never meet the mortgage payments otherwise.' She fanned out the property particulars. 'Looks like I'm going to have to go for something modern. One of those ghastly cul-de-sacs up behind the church.'

'But they're really practical,' Tabitha pointed out. 'You don't have the maintenance you have with older houses.'

Lizzy did not look convinced. 'Well, I'll go along and have a look but I think they're horrid.'

'I'll come with you, if you like.'

'Will you?' Lizzy brightened up.

'Of course.' Tabitha reached forward and rested her hand briefly on her friend's knee. At times like these it was difficult to suppress uncomfortable, vaguely guilty feelings about their respective changes in fortune. When they first met it had been Tabitha who was struggling, fighting just to get through each day, exhausted by the aftermath of the divorce, two years spent living with her parents and now with a run-down cottage to renovate in an area where she knew next to no one. Now it was Tabitha who had a home and a job she loved. And a boyfriend.

That fact in particular was becoming increasingly difficult to handle.

'More coffee,' Tabitha said brightly, and Lizzy followed her through to the kitchen. Her kitchen was a long corridor-like space leading off from the back room with the bathroom beyond. A haphazard assortment of units and appliances were thrown together in what had to be the least-designed kitchen ever. Lizzy had been nagging at her to get it done but redoing a kitchen cost such a huge amount of money that she would have to get a loan and the fear of that made her soldier on with a four-ring cooker, only two of which worked, a 1970s Electrolux fridge and mock-wood work surface, all of it encompassed by beige kitchen tiles.

Tabitha half-listened as Lizzy chatted on about the PTA quiz night she was hoping to organize and made a mental note that their second coffee needed to be a quick one. Ros, the crime fiction editor at Ollsens, had emailed some queries about the O'Hare manuscript and she needed to get started on editing a first novel that had arrived yesterday. If she was totally honest there was another, stronger motive, too. Theo called every day at eleven thirty, half an hour after he'd got up, brewed a pot of coffee and emerged from the shower. She would picture him, at the old kitchen table of the farmhouse, feet up in his Wranglers with a mug of very strong Colombian coffee in his hand.

'So you are coming. I'm going to get a table together.'

'Oh. Sorry. When is it?'

'The Saturday before term starts.'

Tabitha peered at the calendar attached to the 'fridge door.

'Sorry. We'll still be away. We get back on the Sunday.'

Lizzy's mouth tightened a little, 'And school starts on Monday? Gosh, Araminta's going to be tired!'

That fact had occurred to Tabitha but flights to the USA at Easter had been horribly full. 'I know. It's not ideal, but I didn't have any other option.'

There was a pause in which Lizzy seemed to be considering what to say before finally settling on, 'Well. You'll be missed.'

They went out into the garden. Tabitha showed Lizzy where she planned to dig a vegetable patch and Lizzy promised to come and help her lay out a planting scheme. And then they came inside and she said she must start work but did not mention Theo's call. It seemed more tactful not to. Lizzy had been interested enough when she met Theo at Patrick's wedding. Patrick had ensured that they were seated together but omitted to tell her so in advance. Then Theo had come back to England for a long weekend, and then another when he had met Araminta. It had all started to get serious. That was the point at which Lizzy had noticeably cooled. And, though nothing explicit had been said between them, Tabitha felt awkward mentioning his name. So she waved Lizzy off, went inside and settled down on the sofa, as she did every morning, to wait for the telephone to ring. It was as if the day began again with the sound of his voice and the forgetting in those minutes of how far away he was. Then they would both go back to work and responsibilities until, at eleven p.m., she would go back to the telephone and this time call him, say goodnight and tell him all about her day.

James replied to her email the next day. They had met the following day in the Starbucks at Liverpool Street station before he started work. In the course of barely fifteen minutes James had cut to the chase. He had tactfully asked if Jasmine was her own 'friend' and she had laughed ruefully and told him almost everything. Then he had asked her pointedly what 'precisely' had provoked the break-up with Robert and then she had told him all of it. He had not reacted. He simply told her that he would take care of things and she should do nothing until he contacted her. But as he left, he had touched her shoulder and promised it would all be fine. Then she heard nothing. She had begun to think he had forgotten all about her until his call had come and he had suggested they meet over dinner.

They sat at a window table in the *Windows on the World* restaurant of the Hilton Hotel some twenty storeys above London, looking out onto a darkened skyline. Around them in the loud and glamorous atmosphere was a cosmopolitan crowd; Middle Easterners mingled with a smart Euro set, tables of Japanese and a clutch of American businessmen. James had ordered a glass of champagne for her and a mineral water for himself.

'You look very pretty. No black?' He was teasing her.

'I have one or two non-black items – for emergencies only,' she responded, touching the front of the cerise lace dress she had bought from a vintage clothing shop in Covent Garden. It had been her Christmas party staple outfit for two years. A mortgage and the lure of camera equipment left little money for additions to her wardrobe.

'It's very nice.' She saw his eye run across her bare, slim shoulders. His gaze fell. He was on the verge of saying something, so she waited for him to begin and after what seemed a very long time but was probably only thirty seconds he said, 'You won't be hearing any more from Robert. Or from Masterson Ryder Jardine. And Paul Bass is going to give you a reference.'

She didn't know what emotion struck her the hardest: relief or astonishment. She leaned towards him to confirm what she had just heard. 'A reference!'

He looked at her coolly. 'Why not? You deserve one.'

'I just thought . . .' her voice trailed off. '. . . I thought Robert had put pressure on Paul.'

'I'm sure he had. But Robert is not all-powerful. Besides, Paul has a better nature.'

'He does?'

'Some excavation is required to uncover it. But yes, I think he felt bad about what happened. He offered the reference voluntarily, as a matter of fact.'

Clearly James had advanced powers of persuasion. He would have needed them even to get past Clarry. She was aware that it would be tactless to ask James outright what had passed between him and Robert. It would have seemed an intrusively personal question. He would tell her if he wanted to and in the meantime she would just have to wonder.

James took a drink of water. 'When you told me what had happened, in truth I wasn't very surprised. I'd suspected things like that from Robert for a long time. I'd always liked Tabitha and I'd seen her change over the years with him. And then she just disappeared from view. There was something odd. Robert was always very careful to keep her away from the family after that.'

'He always told me that she ran off with another man, the gardener.'

'Yes. I never believed that. It just wasn't Tabitha's style.'

They were interrupted by the waiter bringing their order. She had chosen the fresh fish of the day, monkfish. James had ordered fillet steak.

She took advantage of the interlude to try to frame some suitable words of appreciation for all he had done. 'I'm very grateful. You have no idea how worried I was. And I know that this puts you in a difficult position—'

'No,' he cut in. 'No, please don't think that. I'm glad you came to me. Of course I remembered you from Robert's lunch. You did absolutely the right thing. You mustn't say that.'

She was taken aback by his determination. She had thought James something of a dry, academic lawyer in their first meeting, but that was not at all his character.

'What Robert did was wrong. All of it.' He continued. 'There's something else. Paul mentioned that he had heard on the grapevine that Joan Perham-Ford is looking for a new assistant.'

She put down her knife and fork. 'Really?'

'He gave me her number. If you'd like it?'

'Like it! I'd love it! James, it would be my dream job! Joan Perham-Ford is a legend. Most critics say that she's the greatest British woman photographer. Of course, she's not so active now.'

'Which could work to your advantage,' James said thoughtfully. 'You might get more opportunity to try out your own ideas.'

'I don't know how to thank you.' James didn't seem to want to take any credit for all he had done for her. 'Thank you so much,' she said. 'I just hope I haven't caused any . . . problems for you.'

'No. And it wouldn't matter if you had,' he said with surprising vigour. 'Robert is my brother, but there are principles involved. I think the word is justice.'

She must have looked slightly taken aback.

'You think I'm pompous?' He smiled.

'No. No, not at all. I would never think that!'

'City lawyers aren't supposed to talk about justice and fairness and protecting the weak.' His tone had hardened. 'Only about chargeable hours and client care and chasing new business.' He looked out of the window. 'When I was a student I used to dream about being a civil rights lawyer – helping people who couldn't help themselves. And for a while I did. Until I saw that I could make in a day what was taking me a month.'

'Is all your work like that now?'

'Almost all. A while ago I did some *pro bono* work—'

'*Pro bono?*'

'Working for nothing. I got involved in a case about a drug called Tellium.'

'I've heard of that! The mothers whose babies were born with brain damage.'

'That's it. It was a tough one. A very well-funded pharmaceutical company versus a demoralized group of parents. They'd been fighting for years but the lawyers had second-guessed them every step of the way.'

'It sounds a minefield.'

'It was. And I loved every minute of it. They formed an action group and we would meet up every couple of weeks above a pub in Marylebone. Week by week you could feel the atmosphere change.' His voice was animated now. He talked about the intricacies of the case, but it was never dull. She thought that James was a natural storyteller.

'. . . And then we got the company on the run. It was bloody fantastic. They took us right up to the wire but we held our nerve and the day before the hearing they settled.'

'And then what happened?'

'The parents got their compensation and I went back to work. There were some ruffled feathers at the office. Comments were made about the amount of time I'd been spending on it. I've had to keep my head down ever since.' He paused. 'It didn't go down very well at home, either.' He cleared his throat. 'Anyway, you need some dessert.'

Abruptly he turned his attention to the printed card that listed the selection of desserts. It was the first time he had made reference to his wife. She liked that. None of the crying-on-her-shoulder *my wife does-n't understand me* routine. James was different. But James was still married.

She chose crème brûlée and he opted for cheese. While they ate he gave her the latest update on Joe Saltzman's exploits, which made her laugh.

'He really is totally loopy. Before he starts eating he pulls out these sachets – they're antiseptic wipes – and wipes down the cutlery. At the Dorchester Grill.'

She was helpless with laughter.

'And he won't shake hands or go within ten feet of anyone with a cold. He's a total eccentric.'

'I remember. When we photographed him he made the make-up girl sterilize all her brushes. I had to run out and get that stuff they put in babies' bottles to clean them.'

'He insists he won't touch dairy or wheat or sugar and then you have lunch with him and by the end of the meal he's ordered the waiters to take away his exotic fruit plate and bring chocolate profiteroles. He's impossible.'

'And no one minds?'

'Joe's got the kind of clout that allows him to get away with it. Besides which, whatever his troubles, no one thinks he's going down. He'll fight back and be bigger and better than ever before.'

'Sounds like fun.'

'Actually, it is. Most of what I do is so dry. Joe's a live wire. Anyhow, it'll all be wrapped up soon.' He finished the last of his cheese. 'Coffee?'

'Yes, please.' She looked at her watch and saw it was eleven o'clock. She wondered what Susannah would be thinking. He must have lied to her. Then she felt depressed and a shadow fell over her.

He reached across and took her hand. 'Look. I don't know what to say. I'm a married man. I very probably shouldn't be here.' He paused and smiled. 'That's lawyer-speak for I definitely shouldn't be here – with you, looking so beautiful, in a restaurant in London on a Friday night.'

God, when he spoke like this he was irresistible.

'Maybe it was coming off the booze . . .'

She had wondered about that. Had it been his idea or his wife's? He certainly didn't seem to have a problem now.

'One month tomorrow,' he continued. 'I don't know. I feel . . . different. My head's cleared and yet somehow I feel restless. Irritable. Discontented with everything in my life. Thoughts go round and round in my mind and I don't like them.'

'What sort of thoughts?'

'Like I've fucked up. That I'm forty-four and it's too late now. I'm married, I've got a stepson and responsibilities and bills to pay. The mortgage alone kills us. And if I'm totally honest I hate it. I wanted to do something good with my life, something significant, and I've failed.'

'But that's not true!'

'Jasmine, I make money for people. I advise them how to get out of trouble and into profit. Then I charge them huge amounts of money. That's what they should put on my tombstone. *James Agnew. He billed his hours.*'

She laughed despite herself. 'I don't think it's ever too late!'

'Maybe. All I know is that I like being with you.'

'But . . .' Her voice trailed away.

'I'm married. Yes. But perhaps we could just be friends. Meet up from time to time. Have lunch. I just . . . I just don't want to feel that I could never see you again. It seems like fate brought us together. When we talked, on that Sunday at Robert's, I wondered then when I would see you again.'

It seemed the perfect solution. To stay as friends.

'Of course. I'd like that very much.' Her heart lifted. It was exactly as James said – fated. She couldn't imagine having a boyfriend or getting close to someone again and even the thought of having sex repulsed her. But to have a friend and do nice things and be in the company of someone as intelligent and witty and fun as James . . . there couldn't be anything wrong with that. So when he asked her if she would like another coffee she said yes and in the end they didn't leave until nearly one a.m. When they emerged a steady stream of traffic was flowing down Park Lane.

He steered her towards the waiting line of black cabs. 'I'll get you a cab.'

'I'll get the night bus,' she protested.

'Are you mad?'

She was worried about the cost. She needn't have been. James hailed the cab and then spoke to the driver and she could hear them agreeing a flat rate to Ealing. He turned to where she was waiting in the back of the cab and said, 'It's all taken care of. Thank you for a lovely evening.'

He did it so tactfully and didn't make her feel poor or patronized.

He was as different from Robert as it was possible to be. If it were not for the same shade of brown eyes and the full line of the upper lip and that same expression every now and again that reminded her of Robert, it would be impossible to believe they were brothers. But Robert was gone and this was something he would never know about. As the driver whisked around Hyde Park Corner that thought gave her a shiver of pleasure which she knew was wrong, but she didn't care.

Today marked James's one month – or strictly speaking four weeks, Saturday to Saturday – without alcohol and Susannah was uncertain whether this was a cause for celebration or apprehension. James had not marked the occasion, as he had pointed out somewhat sourly as he lay in bed and she dressed for work, by leaping out of bed and cracking open a can of Stella Artois to have with his toast. She had said nothing to that. He had been in a foul mood since he got in last night, waking her up crashing around at two o'clock in the morning. Joe Saltzman, he had informed her, had wanted an offer document redrafted and only James could do it, necessitating him staying in the office with the team. He said he had eaten in the staff restaurant, which stayed open twenty-four hours a day to service the lawyers and secretaries who worked around the clock. Staff could sleep at the firm, no need even to return home before getting up, showering and beginning all over again.

They had passed the journey barely speaking. She had not asked James if he would be drinking at the Winters' dinner party that evening, because it was obvious that he intended to. The car drew up outside the address in Wandsworth and a feeling of dread filled her stomach. She hated Louise Winter, didn't much like Robert – who would presumably be bringing Natasha – and didn't understand why they had been invited at all.

James turned to her. 'Look. Just lighten up, will you? It's a dinner party. Why do you have to make such a big deal about it?'

'I don't see why we had to come at all—'

He cut across her. 'Because we were invited. It's normal to go out, Susannah. And it might be good for business.' In any case he was getting out of the car. He waited with an impatient expression while she got out, then locked the car, turned away and walked up the path ahead of her. In the driveway they passed a Mercedes four-wheel drive and an Aston Martin Vantage. She followed more slowly, wary of tripping on the cobbled path in her LK Bennett red silk kitten heels. She had gone for black, with her trusty Monsoon red silk pashmina. They stood in an uneasy silence waiting for the door to be opened. It was with some surprise, waiting by the black panelled front door, that she realized the house was detached. Robert's was a semi-detached house but this was on the opposite side of the road. She had always assumed that all these huge houses had been turned into flats. As she was considering this, the door was opened and they came face to face not, as she had expected, with Louise or Andrew Winter but instead with a uniformed Filipina maid, dressed in a black skirt and white shirt.

'Good evening.' She held the door wide. 'Mrs Winter is in the drawing room. Do you have coats?'

They did not. The maid ushered them down a hallway and into a drawing room. Susannah didn't know what shocked her most: the opulence of the room or the glamour of Louise Winter. Rapidly she was forced to recalculate the assumptions of the evening. She had, on past experiences of South-west London dinner parties, been expecting a pine kitchen table, a Le Creuset of dubious cassoulet and a few bottles of Sainsbury's burgundy. She now saw that there must be ten, even twelve people in the room, most of them as well dressed as Louise Winter. A uniformed waiter was serving champagne. The room itself was stunning. Pale aquamarine walls reflected the light from two enormous chandeliers. The furniture she recognized as Biedermeier with its simple, classical lines and motifs. She spotted a particularly good mahogany sideboard and a cherrywood sewing table simply set with a silver bowl of white roses. Louise Winter, or someone close to her, had a good eye.

James took a glass of champagne just as Louise glided up to them. Either she was expert at applying make-up and twisting her hair into a chignon, or she had been professionally made up for the evening. She was wearing a strapless cream silk sheath dress with a split up the thigh which made Susannah think of Valentino. It couldn't be.

She leaned forward and air-kissed Susannah on both cheeks before turning to James.

'So glad to see you both. Now, has Bobby looked after you?' She turned back to Susannah. 'Bernadette's brother; he helps out when we need another pair of hands.'

Bernadette? Louise may not have been born into the upper classes but she had convincingly adopted their habit of considering all explanation superfluous. It was rather overwhelming. There was no time to ask questions. Louise had already taken James's arm and led him towards a group of three positioned by the broad white marble fireplace.

'Let me introduce you to Alex and Grania De Lisle. Alex has just taken over the London office of State Express Bank. And Grania has already gained a reputation for giving the *very* best parties in London. And this is Tim Meah of the *Times*.'

Susannah could only wonder why on earth she and James had been invited. A commentary began in her head. 'To our right one of the leading figures in the largest bank in the USA. Next to him his wife, we assume an ex-model. To our left one of the leading political journalists of his generation. In the middle Susannah Agnew – estate agent and mother – whose kitten heels are scuffed because she keeps wearing them for driving, whose aged pashmina doesn't quite bear scrutiny under the chandeliers and whose black dress has a distinctly dodgy piece of hemming in school uniform grey.' To his credit, James did not miss a beat. Turning to take another glass of champagne from Bobby, he turned his attention to the conversation between the two men, which seemed to centre on exchange rate controls.

'You can't buck the market,' Tim Meah was saying confidently. 'State intervention—'

'Is appropriate to protect the individual in certain circumstances,' interrupted Alex.

Tim gave a sceptical laugh. 'Alex, your concern for the little guy is touching but not entirely convincing.'

Susannah was struggling to think of something to say when Grania turned, her gaze focused somewhere over Susannah's right shoulder. 'Excuse me. I must just go and say hello to someone.'

And with that she was gone. Clearly Susannah didn't even rate the pretence of a couple of minutes' small talk. She was stranded. James was now weighing in with some explanation of proposed City of London regulatory procedures regarding cross-border currency transfers. She had no option but to stand, clutching a glass of orange juice, pretending to look interested. She looked out across the room. Grania was talking to Natasha, Andrew Winter was talking to Robert and in the corner an elderly lady was seated between a couple Susannah recognized but couldn't quite place, though she was sure the woman had something to do with newspapers. Seeing Andrew Winter reminded her of Oliver, Louise and Andrew's little boy, but he was nowhere to be seen. Presumably he was contained on an upstairs floor.

As she stood next to her husband, surrounded by guests, she was overcome by a yearning for the quiet, solitary peace of her own living room, for a cup of coffee and a television mystery. James, once he had a drink in his hand, loved a party. But she spent all day at work meeting strangers, being pleasant and saying all the right things, and the last thing she wanted to do when she got home was to go out and start all over again. At least she was appreciated at work. Come to think of it, work was her sanctuary and home was the battleground. She thought back to that afternoon. Justin had bought a lemon and almond *citronnier* cake from Maison Blanc to celebrate the sale of Sandy Lane and she had sat with him and Anthony after the office had closed for the day, just the three of them, sharing a slice of cake and a cup of tea, feeling more part of a family at that moment than she did in her own home.

Natasha realized that when you have been alone for too long, or more accurately lived alone with short interludes of ever more unsatisfactory relationships, there is nothing quite so nice as being at a party with your boyfriend on a Saturday night.

She had spent too many Saturday nights alone in London. Industry events – parties and premières and launches – all took place in the week. And after them, on a Friday, all the people who went to them left London and went to the country to stay with friends or parents.

Now, sitting next to Robert in the dark-panelled dining room, the tall silver candlesticks casting a glowing light across the white linen tablecloth and the antique silver cutlery and the crystal glasses, she felt included. Warm and safe and somehow part of a life that hitherto she had observed as if she was standing on the cold pavement looking in. Celebrity was no defence against loneliness – rather the opposite. It was as if she had finally been admitted to the club of people who knew lots of other people and who never spent weekends alone. Married people, of course, dominated the club, but membership also extended to those with steady boyfriends and Robert felt very like a boyfriend. They hadn't slept together. Maybe tonight?

She was seated in the middle of the table, which was the best place to be. Opposite her sat Robert's brother James, who was in turn sitting next to Louise. On her other side sat Alex De Lisle, who was much funnier than she would have imagined an American banker to be. They were talking about holidays.

'I absolutely refuse to fly the nanny in first class,' insisted Louise.

'Louise is a firm believer in the English caste system,' cut in her husband, who was seated two chairs down.

Louise did not see the funny side of this. 'It's a question of over-familiarity,' she pressed on. 'You have to set boundaries.'

Alex put down his knife and fork. 'There is actually a very good reason for travelling first class.' He paused to take a sip of wine. 'It is my heart's desire that I will one day be on a plane where all three pilots mistakenly eat the same bacteria-infected meal, so that when the in-flight announcement comes over – is there anyone on board who can fly the plane – I will be first out of my seat.'

'So you've got a pilot's licence?' enquired Natasha.

'No! I don't need one. Air traffic control will talk me down.' He sat back in his seat and mimed pulling back a steering wheel. Even Louise looked amused. 'Then I shall emerge to the banks of television cameras, fire engines and people waving flags at the airport. "It was nothing," I shall say.'

They were momentarily interrupted by Bobby clearing away the plates from the main course, comprising venison, sweet potato mash and green beans with sesame dressing.

'Don't bring in pudding yet,' instructed Louise. She tapped the side of her glass. 'Wine first.'

Natasha saw that Louise's glass and also James's were empty. She'd hardly touched hers.

Alex and Louise began discussing caterers. He wanted to employ new caterers for the bank's in-house lunches. 'If I see another lamb noisette I'm going to shout *Baa*!' Alex proclaimed. In response Louise succinctly appraised the top three London firms.

'I've used them all but Boucher are the best,' she concluded authoritatively.

'You must give me their number.'

This was how business was really done – by people who knew people and recommended them to each other. Meanwhile, on her other side, Robert was deep in conversation with Alex's wife. Then she became conscious of James giving her an appraising look across the table.

'So. How did you meet Robert?'

'Through business. I needed an agent with some get up and go and

Robert was recommended to me.'

'My brother is a very good PR,' he said carefully.

'Brilliant!' she enthused. 'He knows everyone.' She faltered for a moment, not quite sure what to say next. 'Do you live locally?' she settled on, which was horribly boring but the only thing that came to mind. James had seemed aloof at lunch in Wiltshire, and he didn't seem any happier now that he had a glass of wine in his hand.

'Cobham. We used to live in Fulham but my wife wanted to move further out.'

She had noticed that Susannah was seated at the end of the table opposite an old lady whom she supposed was Andrew's mother.

'I'd love to live in the country,' she said enthusiastically.

'I'm afraid you'd be disillusioned then if you came to Cobham. Bumper to bumper four by fours and not a tractor in sight.' He gave her a dry smile. 'We grow designer shops.'

She began to warm to him. It was strange that he and Robert seemed to have so little rapport. Beyond cursory hellos over drinks they had barely acknowledged each other all evening. Robert said little about his family. On the way back from Wiltshire he had alluded to the fact that James and Susannah were going through a rough patch. It was hard to form an impression of Susannah – she had said little at lunch and they had barely had the chance to exchange a few words tonight – but on both occasions Susannah had appeared friendly if ill at ease. However, nothing had dimmed Natasha's pleasure at going to Wiltshire, meeting Robert's parents and feeling part of such a wonderfully real and old-fashioned family.

In passing, she had also noticed that Robert was tight-lipped about his ex-girlfriends. Men were always cagey about exes but Robert was more so than most. He would say nice things – *you're the only girl for me* – to head off her questions and he always said those things in a slightly distracted tone.

She was saved from further efforts at conversation with James by the distraction afforded by Bobby, who was carrying in a towering pyramid of what looked like hundreds of tiny profiteroles encircled with swirling strands of glazed sugar. It must have been three feet high.

'Croque-en-bouche!' announced Louise as Bobby struggled to reach between Alex and Natasha in order to place the pyramid of puffs and sugar in the middle of the table.

'I shall serve the croque!' announced Louise.

'Bravo!' called out Alex and then added, very quietly to Natasha, 'I read that Queen Marie Antoinette used to feed the chickens. Same kind of thing, hey?'

Fortunately, Louise appeared not have heard this. Bobby returned with plates and Louise began apportioning balls of pastry and cream and sugar.

'Andrew, pass that to your mother.'

A faint, cultured voice could be heard saying that it didn't want pudding and weren't they serving cheese first, but this did not stop the progress of the plate to the end of the table.

In the interval caused by the somewhat chaotic serving of pudding, Louise issuing orders to Bobby regarding dessert wine, Robert turned back to her. Quietly, under his breath, he said, 'I have just had a very interesting conversation with Marcia Harrison.'

A blank look must have registered on Natasha's face because he continued. 'Marcia's just been appointed as the new editor of the showbiz page of the *Sunday Mirror*. A *very* useful lady to know.'

She could see his mind churning over his conversation and was itching to ask more but knew that would look overly enthusiastic. She had learned early on that whilst one could, and usually did, discuss business at social events it was a mistake to look too keen.

Besides, Robert's mind had clearly moved on. He whispered still more quietly, 'What did James say to you?'

'Nothing. Just small talk.'

'Good. Keep it that way, will you?'


They had retired, as Louise put it, to the drawing room at least two hours ago. It was a ridiculous situation. Robert and Natasha left at midnight and Tim Meah followed soon after. The woman in the red dress whose name she still couldn't recall, and her husband, stayed for an hour. That left her and James and Louise and Andrew sitting together at two o'clock in the morning. James was smoking a Cohiba cigar and drinking brandy, or should she say Armagnac. There had been an enormous fuss about that.

'This is really rather special,' Louise had announced, cradling the bottle in her hand as she displayed the label to James, who had peered at it and nodded appreciatively. Susannah had been ready to scream then and that was two hours ago.

'Marquis of Montdidier,' enthused Louise. 'Naturally it's a Bas Armagnac. I think it's fab!' Bobby was instructed to pour the brandy into huge balloon glasses. Susannah had pointedly asked for another coffee and a glass of water and said they could not stay for much longer. There had followed some incredibly boring conversation about Bas Armagnacs of the Bordeaux region, methods of Californian wine production and where to buy absinthe in London. Now, two hours later, Louise was drawing on a Marlboro Light and knocking back the Marquis of Montdidier with very little reverence for its special qualities. Andrew had fallen asleep an hour ago in the corner. Susannah was sitting in front of a cold cup of coffee. Presumably Bobby had gone to bed.

They were talking about politics. Or was it religion now? It was impossible to get a word in edgeways so Susannah had all but given up following the conversation. It almost made her nostalgic for dinner where, although she had been exiled at the end of the table with Andrew's octogenarian mother, the conversation had been surprisingly interesting; they had talked about pre-war travel. Mrs Winter had spent her honeymoon with the late Mr Winter travelling through Europe in an open-topped two-seater sports car.

'It was a Jaguar XK 120,' she had recalled. 'We drove down through France, spent a night in Genoa, then down to Naples. My husband wanted to see Malta so we loaded the car onto the ferry – they hoisted the car up in a cargo net in those days – and we stayed at the Phoenicia. Blazer and tie compulsory and it was a hundred degrees.'

Mrs Winter was as sharp as a needle. Tim Meah, the journalist, had been sweet; he had told her some very racy gossip about the leader of the opposition, but most of the time Tim had been talking to Grania De Lisle. Who could blame him? And she had only managed a few words with Natasha before dinner because Robert had whisked her away to speak to Louise about some charity lunch.

Now James and Louise were talking in the loud, defiant way people have when they are drunk but not so drunk as to be incoherent.

'Religion is an opiate,' Louise was insisting. 'It's about controlling people.'

'Absolutely,' agreed James. 'All societies need to believe that a system exists for them to exert control over their environment.'

'Whereas the cold hard truth – which most people haven't got the balls to face up to – is that there is no God. No afterlife, no nothing.'

'Like Stonehenge. Primitive peoples believed that making sacrifices to the sun would save the crop,' said James.

They were like peas in a pod. But it could not be described as a conversation – more two intersecting monologues on the same subject.

Louise was unstoppable. 'You see, you have to take control of your own life. You have to take every situation and say to yourself, "How can I control this? How can I get the outcome I desire?"'

James leaned forward and tipped his cigar ash into the ashtray. 'In fact all societies share forms of worship and sacrifice.'

Louise continued. 'What's the alternative? Drifting along like some human doormat – mouthing "let God's will be done" whilst your life crashes about your ears. It's just laziness, actually. For people who are too lazy or too weak to take charge of their own lives.'

Susannah had noticed in the past that it was often the women who had enormous amounts of domestic help who most enjoyed holding forth on the evils of laziness and the ease of domestic management.

James started on about the Inca civilization, which sent Louise spiralling off into an anecdote about a Brazilian au pair she had been forced to sack for eating too much. Was this the type of woman James needed, Susannah wondered? Someone forthright and opinionated and in control. Perhaps she should be firmer with James and Matthew; she had had a client once who said that men and dogs needed regular feeding and long walks.

She recalled the day that her first husband had told her he was leaving. Steve had been leaving slowly for months, spending more and more time at friends' houses and making excuses to go away for most of the weekend. Once reality had dawned on her that Steve's big break existed only in his dreams – and stories – she had opened her own separate bank account into which she paid her salary and paid out for most of the bills. When he told her there was someone else he was amazed that she was so angry.

'I thought you knew! I mean, things have been awful for so long.'

But even as he spoke she was planning her next move. He had looked shocked when she had told him to pack his bags that day and leave the furniture. He had asked about the joint account. It had been gratifying to tell him that it was empty; she had not paid anything into it for months.

'I know you'll be fine.' Those had been his parting words, said to ease his conscience, but also true. She would not allow herself to fall apart. Matthew needed her and so long as he did she would never let him down. People told her how marvellous she was. Lavinia, her new neighbour, kept saying darkly that it would 'hit' her soon but it never did. It was painful and lonely but at some deeper level it was not unexpected. Her mother had told her that every woman should be able to earn her own living and Susannah had from an early age absorbed the implication that it was foolish to rely on any man. Still, she had thought that James was different from the rest.

She roused herself. 'Darling.' She tapped her watch. 'We ought to be going.'

The resentment in his eyes was palpable but his voice was reasonable. 'Five minutes, OK?'

There seemed little alternative but to agree. 'OK.'

Robert was dismissive. 'Of course, they bought the house at a knockdown price.'

Natasha had been talking about the Winters' house and how beautifully designed it was and how stunning the garden was – lit up with hundreds of tiny blue lights that shone into borders lined with shrubs and across the lawn.

Robert continued thoughtfully. 'When his mother dies Andrew Winter will come into some serious money.'

'Gosh. It seems pretty serious already.'

Robert gave a snort. 'Louise Winter has only just begun to spend. As soon as he inherits they'll sell that house and decamp to Belgravia. And that's before she starts looking at villas in Cap Ferrat.'

He took off his tie and rolled it carefully before placing it on the table to the side of the sofa.

How could Robert be so sure? But Natasha had a feeling he was right. He seemed to her to have an unusually fine-tuned ability to analyse the motivations and aspirations of everyone around him.

She leaned into him. 'Well, old Mrs Winter seemed sprightly enough.'

'Yes, she did, didn't she? Long may she continue. Clever of Louise to get Susannah to babysit her.'

He sat forward and poured more coffee into his cup. It was one o'clock in the morning but he seemed in no particular hurry to move from the drawing room sofa. She felt slightly unnerved by his reticence. Except it wasn't reticence, exactly. She was never quite sure where she stood with Robert. He would draw her in, then back away, and she would be left constantly wanting more. It was very different from the experience of unrelenting pursuit she had enjoyed with other men. She had imagined, when they left the Winters and made the short walk to Robert's house, that he would suggest going straight to the bedroom. Instead he had bypassed any suggestive lingering at the foot of the stairs by marching straight to the kitchen and making coffee. Now, in his drawing room, he seemed curiously energized, almost thinking aloud.

'Andrew's weaker than I thought. And I didn't give Louise enough credit first time round. I suspect she will make her presence felt at Harrold-Winter before too long.'

'But what would she do there? And hasn't she got her own business to run?'

'Her bauble factory? She'll get bored with it. She can only expand that sort of business so far. It's possible she'll get sidelined by the London social scene. She's hacking into the charity side – that's why Grania De Lisle was invited; she's got the biggest charity chequebook. Louise isn't charming enough to make friends easily.'

Now that Robert had said it, it seemed obvious. Louise hadn't mentioned any friends of hers all evening. Everyone there was an acquaintance – or more accurately a useful contact.

'There'll be plenty more dinner parties,' Robert continued. 'Louise is positioning them on the London social radar.'

Natasha didn't know what to say to this. It sounded so calculated, somehow.

'I liked Alex De Lisle,' she said.

'The American banker? Yes, so did I. I had a quick chat with him before dinner. Into horse-racing, so I'll get them down to Ascot.'

She noticed the 'I' and didn't much like it. She had hoped for 'we' by now. 'Ascot?' she repeated guilelessly.

'I have a box. I generally go for the week – not Friday of course. Clients love it. I expect Grania's his third wife. Actually, he's American. Make that his fourth.'

It would be *very* nice to be at Ascot. She decided to try to steer the conversation towards the personal. 'I liked your brother.'

There was a pause. 'James is very impulsive.'

It seemed an odd choice of word. She hadn't gathered that impression at all. 'Do you see much of each other?'

Robert poured more coffee. 'No. He works pretty long hours and so do I.'

'Did you get on when you were younger?'

'He spent all his time in his room studying. And there's a six-year age gap. James has never found his niche in life. From time to time he goes off on some crusade – saving the weak and needy – usually with some very ill-considered consequences.' His voice took on a harder edge and she had the feeling that there had been some personal animosity. Robert cleared his throat. 'Lately he seems to think he'll find the answer at the bottom of a bottle.'

She knew all about that. It was impossible to work in the media and remain ignorant of heavy drinking. 'Does he have a problem?'

'He was knocking it back tonight. But whether he thinks so is a different matter entirely.'

She was unsure if Robert's willingness to speak so frankly about his brother indicated deep-seated sibling rivalry or, more positively, a desire to let his guard down and let her into his life. It was certainly the first time he had spoken about his family. All in all she decided it was a good thing, a sign of greater intimacy between them.

'I shouldn't be at all surprised if James and Louise are still hitting the bottle.' He looked at his watch for effect. 'One thirty.'

She decided to say nothing. She was starting to feel slightly uncomfortable; she had never known a man take so long to make a pass at her.

'You looked very beautiful tonight.' He reached over and began to toy with a strand of her hair. 'You were the most beautiful woman in the room.'

At last! 'Thank you.'

She began to relax, allowing her weight to fall more heavily into the softness of the sofa back. She could smell his aftershave and the smoothness of his cotton shirt against her bare arm. Anticipating him leaning into her and kissing her she half-closed her eyes. He took her hand and began twisting the Russian ring, three intertwined bands of gold, that she wore on her little finger. With his other hand he took a twist of her hair, pushing it back behind her ear and smoothing it. After what seemed an age he leaned forward and kissed her very lightly on the lips. She felt a surge of longing for him. His voice, when he spoke after a few seconds, was decisive. 'I think you should stay the night.'

She lost all reticence. 'Yes.' And she could not keep the enthusiasm from her voice. She had begun to think that he would never ask, even that he did not find her attractive. Since she had started seeing Robert she had resumed an old habit of weighing herself every day and adding up the pounds she had lost, which now totalled five. He stood up and walked out of the room, turning out the lights as he left. She followed him upstairs, both of them silent, and she felt a surge of nervous excitement in her stomach which heightened as they went into his bedroom, furnished in the style of a playboy with classic English good taste, the furniture dark wood and the bed an oversized double in mahogany. She stood expectantly as he drew the curtains and turned on the bedside light. Then he took her hand and led her to the bed.

Once there, it was as if a switch had been turned on. He laid her across the white sheets and at once his hands were on her, her skirt riding up and his hands quickly unfastening the tie of her dress. His roughness excited her. He kissed her, very hard, and when she began to break away he continued regardless, all the while his hand pulling at her knickers. His touch was expert. Somehow she had known that this was how he would be: dominating, in control and very skilled. He put her hand on his belt and she followed the hint.

'Good girl.'

The undercurrent of domination and submission stirred her, the more so when he caught hold of her wrist and gently but insistently pulled her arm behind her head.

It felt wild and passionate and very adult. She was ready for it. She was tired of men who were as lazy as they were good-looking. She felt him inside her now, hard and satisfying, his other hand holding the small of her back as if to draw her even closer to him.

She pulled her legs up to encase him and he went still deeper. She felt herself come but she did not want it to stop. His style was not a surprise. But the strength of his sexuality, in a man she had hitherto always seen as naturally sophisticated, was a revelation. Robert had a raw, hungry – almost angry – passion that swept her along. She knew, as he finished, that she would want more. It was like a drug. And somehow, as with everything about him, she could never get quite enough.

It was seven o'clock in the morning. It was Sunday and she had had four hours' sleep but Susannah had to get up. Within moments of waking she was planning the day. Matthew needed collecting from Jake's house and delivering to the rugby ground at Fairmile Lane for the last game of the season before they broke for Easter. First she needed to retrieve his kit from the laundry basket. Then there was a pile of ironing to do and she wanted to get to Waitrose to stock up for the week because all the signs were that it was going to be a hellishly busy week at Charron's. Cal Doyle, their most important client, wanted to meet to discuss the marketing of Milbourne Manor. Last but not least, she had to write a thank you letter to Louise Winter.

Slowly, as these thoughts ran through her mind, she became aware that she was sleeping alone in the bed. Was James up? She looked across at his side of the bed and saw that the pillows were stacked as they had been the night before and that the covers were straight. A sense of foreboding overcame her. Thoughts of the day ahead dissipated and the events of the night before took their place. They'd left Louise's at two o'clock after much cajoling on her part and with ill temper on James's. She had driven, naturally, and they had got back here at two thirty. Then James had taken a bottle of brandy from the kitchen and gone into his office. She knew the routine. In the old days she used to try to persuade him to come to bed, but one too many rows stopped that. He would sit in his office chair, his headphones plugged into the stereo, listening to opera and steadily drinking as he gazed out into the night until eventually he would come to bed in the early hours and sleep until midday.

It was hopeless now to stay in bed a moment longer. Anxiety flooded over her and it was all she could do to slip into the bathroom and pull on her dressing gown before gliding silently down the stairs to take care of things. The study door was closed. She hesitated, looking at the white painted six-panel door. She was afraid, she realized, that James might be awake. Slowly she turned the brass doorknob and eased the door ajar. He wasn't there. The smell, however, that greeted her was as powerful as any sight. It was not so much a smell as a stench of vomit, filling the warm air, causing her to feel ill herself. She tried to hold her breath. Looking past the fitted oak veneer bookshelves filled with legal textbooks and law reports to his desk she saw an empty brandy bottle placed next to a lead crystal tumbler on the reproduction leather topped desk. She could hear music, so faint it was barely audible, the sound drawing her in.

She found him behind the desk. James lay comatose between his desk and his heavy office chair which had been pushed back, she presumed, as he fell to the ground. He had been sick over himself and the carpet and over a set of legal documents in serge blue covers and bound with thin pink ribbon, which had been placed on the floor to the side of his desk, awaiting his attention. The sound of music was slightly louder now and she worked out that it was coming from the headphones lying by his side. The CD must be on replay. She reached over to the stereo and turned it off, catching sight of the cover of *Eugene Onegin*.

It looked as though he had been sick after he passed out on the floor. He could have choked to death. Involuntarily, a twinge of guilt rose up inside her that she had not come downstairs and checked on him in the night. The thought went through her mind of how she would be feeling now if he had died.

He lay on his side, fully dressed, in his dark suit trousers and cream cotton shirt, the double cuffs undone and his gold engraved cufflinks hanging loose. Passed out on the floor in the morning light, dressed for an elegant evening party, he seemed to be a parody of himself. A man once so elegant and urbane and still handsome, reduced to this. He shifted and his breathing grew heavier. Whether it was the realization that he was alive or the second bout of nausea that welled up inside her, a surge of brittle anger overcame her as she looked at him on the floor. How could he do this to her – to them – after all the promises and the fine talk about having it 'under control'? This was as bad as ever; worse, in fact. He had drunk himself stupid at the Winters', humiliated her in front of that bloody Louise woman and then made this mess for her to clear up. And that wasn't all. Her thoughts ran on – the rest of the weekend would be ruined now. He would spend the day nursing a hangover, then the evening catching up on office paperwork, and she would be left to run the house and spend the day alone. If she was lucky he might manage a little light television viewing in the afternoon. It made her want to scream with frustration. Why wouldn't he control his drinking? She wasn't asking him to stop altogether. Just to drink like a normal person.

She could feel herself getting angrier. She wasn't being unreasonable. It wasn't much to ask at all. He had stopped for a month, therefore he *couldn't* have a problem. If he could stop for a month, logically, he could stop after a few drinks. Why did he have to go on as if he was powerless to stop? He wasn't powerless; that was precisely the point. He just lacked the willpower to do something about it.

It made her so furious she could have kicked him. Yes – kicked him really hard as he lay there on the floor, oblivious to all the hurt and misery and chaos he caused around him.

This was the private face of a man whose public persona was effortlessly erudite and urbane. James could be the most charming and witty companion when he chose to be, and it made it all the more maddening. None of the women Susannah had observed gazing at her husband so admiringly, at all the dinner parties over the years, had any idea of the reality of the man.

She forced herself to calm down. For now she had to focus on the task in hand, which was to get James upstairs, and this mess cleared up, before going to get Matthew. She stepped over James's sleeping form to open the leaded window and breathe in the fresh air from the garden.

Bitterly, as she surveyed the mess he had made on the beautiful claret-coloured carpet, an ironic choice of colour in the circumstances, she reflected that she could not see Louise Winter doing this. Whatever James was like the night before – drunk, loud and ebullient – it was his wife that he needed in the morning to clear up after him. Her anger was subsiding – at least she could take control of the situation now. First she needed to get him up. She began shaking his shoulder. It had no effect. Finally, she shook him so hard that his head hit the leg of the desk and jolted him awake. Good! Let him suffer for once.

His expression, as he squinted up at her, was uncomprehending. 'What?'

'You need to get up.'

He was looking at her as if he had never seen her before. 'What?'

'Just get up.'

'What?'

God, he was hopeless.

'Get up!' she hissed. 'You need to get to the bedroom.' She pointed at the front of his shirt. 'Look at you.' She made no effort to keep the contempt from her voice.

Confused, he looked down at his stained shirt. The sight that met his eyes at least had the effect of moving him into action. Wordlessly, he rolled onto his side and then onto all fours and somehow she got him to his feet. As she held him tight by the arm he staggered across the hallway and slowly they inched up the stairs. He stank. As they reached the bedroom she realized that she couldn't put him into bed like that. She steered him into the bathroom. Never had their en suite white-tiled and marble topped bathroom mocked her more than it did at that moment. On one side was a floor-to-ceiling mirror and she could not bear to look round lest she catch sight of their pathetic reflections. This was no image for the show-home brochure.

'Just take off your trousers and sit down in the bath.'

He took an age to undo his trousers and then nearly fell over taking them off.

'Just leave the rest,' she said impatiently. The main thing was to get him clean. She got him sitting down in the bath, still wearing his boxer shorts and socks and shirt, then took the faux-Victorian brass hand-held shower and resisted the temptation to spray him with cold water. She waited while the water turned to warm. Then he sat silently, with his eyes closed, as she unpicked his shirt from him, washed him and shampooed his hair. Lastly she pulled his wet black cashmere socks from his feet.

His voice was hoarse. 'I need some water.'

'OK. I'll get you some. Just wait there.'

After she had fetched the water he sat in the bath and drank it, then she held the shower as he held his head back and the warm water ran over him. Minutes passed in the silence and some calm seemed to descend, enough for her to take the trouble to fetch a warm towel from the airing cupboard and use it to dry his hair. Her movement was slow and gentle and she fell into massaging him. As she did so she felt his head rest against her thigh. It was then that she felt the last of her anger subside; he looked so helpless and subdued and vulnerable. They did not speak.

It would all be OK. Later they would talk and he would be forced to admit that she had been right. Together they would work out a solution. And most importantly of all Matthew would never know that any of this had happened. She ran through the plan in her mind – close up the study, take Matthew to rugby, and while he was safely out of the way return home to clean up the mess. It was a shame she wouldn't be there to watch him play but he wouldn't miss her and she needed to prioritize. Ideally she would need to keep him out of the study for the rest of the day. But even if he did go in it would be simple enough to say that James had suffered from a bout of food poisoning. It was a plausible enough story after a long dinner party. She let out a sigh. The crisis was over. It was under control. There might even be time to get to Waitrose.

And then there was nothing left to do except get James into bed, pull the covers over him and head downstairs to go and collect Matthew.

*Part 2*

# SPRING

# Chapter 6

# Family

*I waited until after lunch to speak to Robert. In retrospect my timing was ill judged. It would have been more prudent to see him by arrangement in London. The occasion was my mother's birthday, for which she had organized a small family lunch party. Robert brought with him his new girlfriend. Robert is never without a girlfriend. It was nauseating, watching him weave his tangled web, in the knowledge of what he had done to Jasmine and, I suspected, Tabitha. Never was there a character less suited to marriage and family life than my brother. Though socially confident, Robert is at heart an introvert. From an early age Robert set about building a wall around himself and no one has ever come close to loosening a single brick. As each year goes by I see the wall that encircles him grow taller and stronger. In that respect he is very like my mother: the public face is charming and controlled, the private behaviour often appalling and the true person is locked away out of sight. Neither of them has a friend to their name. I grew more restless as the lunch continued and I decided to implement there and then the plan that had been forming in my mind to confront Robert.*

*I suggested that the two of us go for a walk after lunch. We set off up the lane that runs to the side of the house, the hedgerows bare and the sun casting little warmth. When we were safely out of earshot of the house I warned him off Jasmine. I told him that Paul Bass had wronged her and that I intended to secure a glowing reference for her. I forbade him to have any further contact with her. He looked surprised at my intervention but swiftly recovered his composure. He did not make any attempt to deny his wrongdoing. Instead, he asked pointedly if Susannah knew about my new 'charity case', as he termed it. I told him that if he said anything to Susannah I would personally represent Jasmine in an action for unfair dismissal against Paul Bass and I would call him as a witness. It was a bluff but he backed off. Robert has always been sensitive about maintaining a good public image. I went further. I told him that in my opinion he needed to seek professional help from a psychiatrist. I tried to sound compassionate when I told him that I believed him to suffer from some form of personality disorder. I even offered to recommend a good psychiatrist; I knew several from my work in the field of medical negligence. It was as if I had put a flame to the fuse. He was furious. He said that if he needed help with how to drink, cheat and under-perform at work he would call me. The gloves were off. I retaliated childishly by telling him that his new girlfriend was no fool and would soon see through him. He swore he would prove me wrong. And then his reaction became more disturbing. He was angrier than I had ever seen him. He lost control. It was by now hard to follow his line of thought but in essence there followed a litany of blame against the world. Thus Jasmine was a lying bitch, Tabitha was a disloyal slut (bizarrely he insisted that morally she remained his wife) and naturally I was a failure. He said that I was jealous of his money, his women and the fact that he had had the balls to go out and do what he really wanted in life. The first two were untrue but the third hurt. He sensed that and went in for the kill. He said my lifetime's work would one day be packed up, stored in cardboard boxes and left to rot in the archived files section of Lloyd-Davies. Robert wields the thin, sharp knife of invective with precision. I had intended to put him in his place but he had bested me. He continued with some tedious jibes about the value of an Oxford degree in the real world. I had had enough and began to walk away, hearing him laugh behind me. He called out, 'Give my regards to Jasmine – I enjoyed her.' I turned round and I went back. God knows, I could have killed him. He was never good in a fight. At least not against a man. I was close to him, circling him and I could see the fear in his eyes. So he ran. He literally ran, heading for home. I took a few moments to compose myself and then I returned to the house.*

The row did not come until Tuesday. Sunday was taken up with rugby. On Monday James didn't get in from work until nearly nine o'clock and Matthew was up until nearly midnight working on a religious education project that entailed her trailing the Internet on his behalf for information on Presbyterianism and the English Civil War.

So the row was on Tuesday, after Matthew had gone to bed. James was working his way through a bottle of white wine, the day's newspapers scattered across the sofa in the conservatory.

'We need to talk.'

James continued to look at the newspaper. 'About what?'

Already she could hear her voice rising. 'About Saturday night!'

'Calm down.' James put the newspaper to one side. 'Look, I've had a hell of a day at work. Can't we talk about this some other time?'

'No!' She felt herself getting angry already. 'It's always some other time. Always next week or next month or when you're less "busy" at work. *When* are we going to talk?'

She intended to return to the subject of his working hours. She was not so foolish to believe that James's workload had increased at precisely the same time he had started drinking again.

He sighed dramatically. 'Susannah, I had a drink on Saturday night.' He held up his hand to indicate that she should remain silent. It was an infuriating gesture. 'All right. I admit it: I had too much to drink.' He paused. 'Happy now?'

She was determined not to rise to the bait. He continued. 'But I didn't have a drink on Sunday or Monday—'

'Yes you did! You had wine.'

'Wine with dinner doesn't count. Be reasonable. And now it's Tuesday.'

She could feel the argument slipping away from her. 'James. Let's talk about Saturday.'

He powered past her. 'I didn't drink at my mother's birthday lunch despite the fact that you put me in a very embarrassing situation—'

'What? I put you in no such—'

'Nonetheless I kept to your edict of one month.'

'*Edict*! We agreed that you needed to do something. And at the end of it things are worse than ever.' She regained some ground. 'And that is what we are going to talk about: Saturday.'

'I miscalculated,' he said defensively. 'I hadn't drunk for a month – which was your idea – and so I lost the plot. Temporarily.'

Was he implying it was her fault?

'And I think the venison they served wasn't quite right. The sauce was very rich and I wouldn't be surprised if the meat was slightly on the turn.'

'I didn't think there was anything wrong with it.'

'I'm sure yours was fine. It's mine I'm referring to.'

No wonder he was a top lawyer.

'James,' she persisted, 'it's not normal to pass out on the floor having been sick.'

He picked up the paper again as if to indicate that the discussion was drawing to a close. 'If you think that's strange then you've lived a very sheltered life. Go down to any rugby club on a Saturday night. You're the one who wants Matthew to go to university. What do you think a college bar is like on a Saturday night?'

She was still standing. It was all she could do not to snatch the newspaper from his hands. 'We're not talking about Matthew. We're talking about you! What about the Saltzman papers?'

'That's all under control. They're all cleaned up.'

She noticed his choice of words. It would be more accurate to say that she had cleaned them up, not entirely successfully, because an unmistakable smell permeated the blue folder covers. In the end she had resorted to spraying them with her perfume – Chanel Cristalle – and putting them out in the garden for the afternoon.

'So everything was all right at the office?'

'Yes!' he exploded. 'Will you drop it? Everything at work is under control.' His voice was shaking. 'I've got it all under control,' he echoed more calmly.

She was getting nowhere by discussing work. Besides, it was hardly the real issue. James had no problems at work. She knew he was expert at his job, charming to clients and respected by his colleagues. She was far more concerned about his behaviour off-duty.

She tried a different approach. 'I was embarrassed on Saturday night by the way you flirted with Louise.'

He rolled his eyes. 'Oh God, not this again. Won't you ever give it a rest? Susannah, not everyone lives their lives like a spinster schoolmistress. Loosen up a bit. We were just talking and laughing—'

'You were flirting with her. I was totally left out.'

'I was not flirting with her. For God's sake, her husband was there all the time. And you were there, too. Remember? Louise and I are hardly likely to carry out some nascent affair under the noses of our respective spouses. And if you felt left out, I'm sorry.' He didn't sound very sorry. 'You didn't need to be. You could have joined in the conversation.' His tone changed to be dismissive. 'You need to relax. Why do you have to be so bloody uptight about everything?' He leaned forward. 'Susannah, I just don't know what more I can do. We've got a lovely house, Matthew is doing well at school, and we're not short of money. But it's never enough. Things are never right between us. What do you want? Do you want me to go?'

Panic flooded over her as it did whenever he hinted at such an outcome. In her own mind she could run through the scenario of separation and divorce but when it came to James presenting that option to her she instinctively recoiled from it. A second divorce was unthinkable.

'No. Of course not. I just want things to be better between us. Maybe you could talk to someone—'

'Don't be bloody ridiculous!'

'You could speak to Dr Palmer. Or a person trained to deal with this type of thing.'

'Absolutely not. I've never heard of anything so ludicrous—'

'It would be private. No one need know about it.' She was aware of her own feelings on this point; she had no desire for their private problems to be made public, either.

'Just let go, will you? Stop talking all the time about how much I supposedly drink. That's what causes the rows. Everything will be fine once things are quieter at work; I'll have more time to spend at home.'

She wanted to point out that he always promised things would be better at some undefined time in the future, but James had turned to the television listings and reached for the television remote control. The late-evening news had come on. She considered reopening the argument – and the issue of the nights at the office which she knew damned well were sessions in some City wine bar drinking with his cronies – but he was wound up and half-cut. Tempting though it was to continue, long and hard experience had taught her that when he was in this mood she was the one who would end up getting the worst of it.

She got up and went into the kitchen to load the dinner plates into the dishwasher. She felt like her mother: isolated, misunderstood and responsible for keeping the whole family show on the road. As a child she had seen her mother's way of life as stifling and controlled: the way she accounted for every penny spent, in a small spiralbound notebook; the way she cleaned obsessively; the household rules about taking their shoes off and feet off the settee and no drinks in the lounge. Now she realized that these were the actions of a woman who was trying to keep life normal. At least James came home. Her father spent every weekend down at the social club and a couple of weekday nights, too. He had a second job, she had realized as a teenager, respraying cars, the work undertaken in a remote barn at the weekends for reasons she did not guess at the time. The cash from that was his. She understood now that it was his drinking money. Now as she took the placemats from the table and replaced them in the upper kitchen drawer, she felt a momentary ache of sympathy for her mother, a woman she had spent most of her life inwardly criticizing. It would pass. It was easy to feel loving to her mother when not in her company. The time they spent together was no more than companionable, standing washing up together or hanging out the washing; though she was solicitous of her daughter's welfare, her mother's fatalism gave all her observations a pessimistic quality. She would advise Susannah to 'stick it out' because there weren't many men like James out there. Not that Susannah would ever confide in her mother. Her mother needed to believe that her marriage to James was successful and Susannah colluded, as she did with so much else in her parents' life, in pretending that it was.

She poured dishwasher liquid into the Miele and set it to run, then went to find Matthew. He did spend an awful lot of time in his bedroom. He was in bed, wearing a Gap T-shirt, his hair still wet from his evening shower. It needed cutting, but she resisted pointing that out. She also held back on saying that the room needed tidying up – curtains half-closed as they were day and night, the only light the small Laura Ashley bedside lamp which sat incongruously amid the heaps of clothes, school papers, magazines, and piles of unidentifiable parts of music systems. The walls – once covered with football posters, Arsenal interspersed with the odd England team photograph – now included what she thought of as 'Page Three' posters. Except she insisted on Athena posters where the girls were at least photographed wearing underwear.

She decided to start again. 'Did you get the science revision done?'

'Yes.'

'And the history project?'

'Yes.'

His class had been set an essay question entitled 'My hero is . . .' designed to explore the qualities of a hero. It was specified on the class handout that the hero must be a character in history judged to have made a significant contribution to his or her nation. There had been some argument about Matthew's friend Jake's choice of Bono and he had been forced to do his second choice, Nelson Mandela, instead.

'Dad came up with some really good lines. He said I should write, "Did you know that heroes can come from dysfunctional families?" Dad went on the Internet and found this letter from Churchill's dad slagging him off.'

'What?'

'I've quoted from it. Churchill's dad goes on in this letter about how he wasn't clever and didn't work hard enough at school.'

It was typical. James could be relied upon to find the perfect quote or anecdote. Her homework research was pedestrian; James's – undertaken in a tenth of the time – was inspired.

Their brief conversation seemed to have petered out. Matthew was openly reading a book now. She got up.

'Well. Goodnight.'

'Goodnight,' he said absently, not taking his eyes off the page. It seemed inappropriate to lean forward and kiss him. She knew that teenagers were supposed to be moody, distant and self-obsessed but even so Matthew's withdrawal from her hurt. It was pointless to say anything; the response would be a roll of the eyes, a shrug of the shoulders and 'Mum!' said in such a way as to imply that she was the most tedious human being he had ever encountered. So, wordlessly, she left the room, closing the bedroom door behind her. For a few seconds she stood at the top of the stairs, fighting the feeling of loneliness, considering whether to rejoin James downstairs if only for some human company. Then she heard the sound of his footsteps on the kitchen floor. She made out the noise of the refrigerator door opening, the clink of glass and the sound of a cork being pulled from a bottle – the second of the night. If one added the half bottle already open that made two and a half if he finished it and she thought he probably would. He had had something before he got home, too. It was not even ten o'clock. There was no doubt that nothing about his drinking had changed and it might even be getting worse. The thought prompted a sharp pang of fear.

Images of the Winters' dinner party and the scene the morning after flashed unbidden through her mind. She had the feeling of being caught up in something that was growing more powerful and unpredictable. A grim premonition came upon her that something horrible was about to happen. Her chest tightened. At that she stopped herself short. She knew what to do but she needed to concentrate. She forced herself to think calmly and logically. As if to steady herself she took hold of the landing rail with both hands, knowing that she could stop the feelings from overwhelming her. As a child she had wakened to her father stumbling and swearing when he came home in the early hours and then she had heard her mother's voice. She had been afraid that they would argue louder and louder until finally they burst into her room, but they never did. In time she learned that all she had to do to block out the angry voices and her frightened feelings was to take her toys, her bears and her old blue rabbit, and line them up against the head of the bed and tell them in a whisper about all the nice things they were going to do the next day. It became second nature. So now she reminded herself that although James drank he always went to work and he always came home. He wasn't having an affair. He wasn't about to get the sack. She needed to stay focused and tell herself, over and over again until she believed it, that the situation was far from out of control. She began to feel better. Next she thought about Milbourne Manor and the Andersons and she made a mental list of all the things she had to do at work the next day. She breathed slowly and felt the panic subside until it was safe to move. All the same, she wasn't about to go down and watch James drink himself to sleep. There was no alternative but to turn away from the stairs and go into their bedroom to watch television in bed alone.

They doorstepped him at six o'clock, just as he was locking up the studio. For a moment Paul thought they were police officers which, all things considered, was an understandable mistake. The woman did the talking.

She finished by fractionally softening her tone. 'Paul, we want your side of the story.'

He had said nothing. He had been too horrified to speak. The word 'paedophile' was still reverberating in his head.

The woman, in a black trouser suit with close-cropped red hair, began speaking again. 'Sex with a minor; Serena was fifteen at the time wasn't she, Paul? It's a serious allegation. A paedophile offence.'

The repetition of the word weakened him physically, his legs faltering beneath him. He wanted to run before he collapsed. The implication was that he was some dirty old man preying on young girls. How could he explain that it wasn't like that at all? Serena had been a month away from her sixteenth birthday; she had flirted relentlessly with him – and actually they'd had a great time for a few weeks before she dumped him for an older, wealthier man.

Oh God, but how could he say all of that, all of it the well-worn clichés of the abuser in denial of his wrongdoing. So he had said nothing and felt the waves of nausea ride up inside him, shuddered as sweat broke out on his brow.

He needed to move, so he had begun walking, away from the studio and out onto the Old Brompton Road, the street filled with near-stationary traffic. They followed him. As he walked, with no destination in mind, he was frantically trying to recollect events. Christ, it was years ago. Ten, maybe even fifteen years. Serena had gone from strength to strength – she was a *Vogue* cover-girl, a racing driver's girlfriend, and the owner of an apartment in Manhattan and a place in the South of France. Their paths had crossed at fashion shows and charity galas and she'd always been friendly. Stoned, but friendly.

They were on either side of him now. He should have taken the Range Rover parked outside the studio but driving had been beyond him. He pushed through them. He needed to get to a tube station and he was now conscious of his mistake in walking away from Earls Court. The panic was rising. 'Speak to my PR.'

'Robert Agnew?'

At last, a break. 'Yes. Robert Agnew. The best bloody PR in London. Speak to him.'

The woman spoke. 'We have done. He says you are no longer a client with his agency.'

Paul broke into a run. He heard no footsteps now, only the shutter of an automatic camera.

Natasha sat with Anna in what was colloquially known as the 'Doughnut' in BBC parlance – the open-air circle at BBC Television

Centre, laid out with cafe seating and trees in pots, surrounded by studios and offices. Anna had secured a table by the stage-door windows, affording them a people-watching view of chauffeur-driven arrivals, while Natasha purchased two lattes from the coffee stand. They had just come out of a planning meeting for *Expat* – a series following the lives of six families recently located to southern Spain. Natasha was doing the voiceover and interviews. It was the biggest job she'd had for a long time: six episodes and the possibility of a follow-up series if the first was well received. She was grateful to Anna for putting her in the frame.

'I'm still worried that it's all been done before,' said Natasha. 'The emigrating-adventure format, I mean.'

'Not by me!' exclaimed Anna. She was wearing Diesel jeans and a Fat Face faux-faded pink sweatshirt. 'It has been done before, but this is different. For a start it's much more in depth. We're following the families for over a year. And we're covering their pasts. Lots of juicy bits there! Plus we're filming the family and friends they've left behind. It's soap opera meets reality TV.' She paused. 'Naturally, the editing will be superb.'

It was impossible not to be convinced by Anna's confidence. Natasha laughed. 'So when are they making you Director General?'

'As soon as they wake up to the fact that people who make programmes need to run this place,' said Anna gloomily. She hesitated and lowered her voice. 'Actually, I'm thinking about going freelance.'

Natasha was astonished. 'What? You're the only person here still with a job!' More and more production staff were employed on short-term contracts and lived in a perpetual state of anxiety as to whether they were to be renewed. 'And you're earmarked for the top—'

'Me and a hundred others. It's not professional, Natasha. It's personal.'

'Oh?'

'I don't have a life! I have a job. I'm either filming or stuck in an editing suite at midnight or in a bloody BBC meeting. I haven't had a boyfriend for nearly a year. And when I do get one I never see them.'

Natasha shook her head. 'All the same, it's no fun living on contracts.'

Anna shrugged. 'I should have been a presenter – with a cushy line in baby food work.'

Natasha grimaced. The Moores renewal was weeks away. Robert

said he had it all under control and she hoped he did because apart from *Expat* there was nothing else in the pipeline. 'No! You should be glad you're a director and you don't have to worry every time you look in the mirror.'

'You look great!'

'Yeah, me and a hundred others. . . And the others are young and fresh and don't mind getting up at four in the morning to go and abseil down a cliff in Wales. This is great. But long term I need some decent studio work. Something regular.'

Anna looked thoughtful. 'I think you need to put yourself around a bit more. That piece in the *Sunday Mirror* was great, by the way.'

'The mention of the *Holiday* programme? Thanks.' Robert's handiwork, naturally.

'You need to be seen,' Anna emphasized. 'You need to hang out here, invite the bigwigs out to lunch.'

Natasha knew Anna was right. She had to make more effort. Somehow in the last few weeks all her time and attention had been diverted into being Robert's girlfriend. They went out almost every night, to some party, product launch or dinner with clients, and entertained every weekend. Some days she just went home on a Sunday night and crashed out. She literally couldn't afford to look tired.

She pulled herself back to the moment. 'Anna, you've got a great job here. Don't make any quick decisions. Maybe you'll meet someone in the business.'

Anna looked disconsolate. 'Yeah, like Harry the cameraman. Two ex-wives, a pregnant girlfriend and a BBC Two researcher on the side.'

'Really?'

'Oh yes. And he's started smoking again.'

'Probably the stress of his love life,' commented Natasha, deleting from her mind Harry's hypnotherapist as a possible source of help. She reached into her bag for her Marlboro Lights and settled down to listen as Anna related the current BBC gossip.

James had secured them a table at the prow. The restaurant Putney Bridge was designed in the shape of a ship sailing in the direction of Greenwich, with views over the Thames. Below them, on the shingle waterfront, a few stray rowers were carrying their blades to the boathouses while beyond, as far as Jasmine could see, the riverside was crowded with the lights of new blocks of expensive flats, or apartments as they were called now. She was talking to James about her first week working with Joan Perham-Ford, the purpose of the dinner. Or was it a pretext? There seemed to be a reason to meet every week. They had also had dinner on the evening of her interview with Joan, at a small Vietnamese restaurant on Lavender Hill. On that occasion she had made him laugh, recounting how Joan had begun by tossing aside her CV. Instead they had had a conversation about photographs and at the end of an hour, when Jasmine expected the interview to start, Joan had offered her the job.

James had come straight from work. He was dressed in a dark pin-stripe suit and as they sat down she had caught a faint but heady scent of his aftershave. She wondered if people imagined them to be a couple on a date. It must look like that. But of course it couldn't be. Whatever the status of their meal together, it had been the perfect end to the most thrilling week.

'Joan's got the most gorgeous studio in Hampstead,' Jasmine enthused. 'And she knows everyone. There are signed photographs on the walls from prime ministers and American presidents. And she wants me to do everything: help on shoots, liaise with clients, help her with cataloguing . . .'

'And what about the location?' James said carefully.

'Hampstead? Yes, it's a rotten journey. But I don't care!'

James had been genuinely pleased for her in a way she had rarely found with men. So many of them, when one got down to it, wanted her to be successful but not so successful that they felt overshadowed.

'And you?' she asked, aware that the conversation up to that point had been all about her.

James put down his fork. 'Interesting times,' he said slowly. Jasmine was not sure whether he was alluding to his work or to his home life. She waited for him to say more. Eventually he said, 'I envy you.'

'Me!'

'Yes,' he smiled. 'Why on earth not? You have a job you love doing, something that will last. It throws my work into relief.' His tone became more serious. 'Once this Saltzman deal is out of the way I need to take a long, hard look at my future with Lloyd-Davies. Jasmine, it's not working. I need to do something else.'

'Do you mean leave the firm?'

'Possibly. Or change to a different department. I just can't keep pretending everything's OK and having a drink to drown my sorrows.'

She had noticed he was not drinking that night.

'How's that going?' she asked tentatively.

'Periodically it's going well,' he said with a disarming smile. 'Frankly, it would be a damned sight simpler if I just stopped altogether.' He shrugged and looked out to the river, then returned his gaze to her. 'But that's not what we're here to talk about.' And then he changed the subject to ask her about Joan's work schedule for the coming week.

The sign on the Two Brewers had been repainted. The Two Brewers still wore belted smocks and stood either side of a wooden barrel but they now had tails, one short and stubby, the other long and coiling, and their faces had been newly painted beneath their cloth caps so that now there was a kangaroo brewer and a koala brewer.

It was early for lunch but Anthony said that was all the better to get a corner table and they deserved it after an hour with Cal Doyle. Kimberley was wearing a sweatshirt depicting the new animal brewers. She greeted them like the regulars they had become and remembered that Anthony drank orange juice and Susannah had tonic water. Drinking at lunchtime had always made her sleepy in the afternoons.

She felt tired and tense but if Anthony noticed he did not mention anything. She was glad. She had never been one to bring her personal problems to work. It was a relief to go into an ordered world, a world where people behaved rationally and events were predictable and people, on the whole, did what they said they were going to do. In the working world people also appreciated her. Justin's reference came to mind. He had asked her to supply him with a reference for his application to do a ten-week evening class at the City Lit: *Introduction to Broadcast Journalism*. She was senior to Justin and so, technically, he reasoned, could be described as his boss. She had been pleased to do it; it was no problem at all, and he had been genuinely grateful. The next day he had brought her an Azalea with a card that thanked her for the time and care she had taken. Lynda had told her sternly not to overwater it. In the office, with the telephones ringing, clients calling in and Lynda's ongoing account of her home life, Susannah forgot her marriage altogether. It was when she was alone, in the car caught in traffic, that her mind would return to James, whose drinking in the last few weeks had returned to the old familiar patterns. She would turn over his words and actions, analysing what she had done to cause his behaviour and what she could do to change it. On occasions she would have to slam on the brakes to avoid hitting the car in front, so distracted was she by her anxieties. But then she would arrive at her appointment, pick up her papers and it was as if these thoughts were pushed into a box.

They ordered the special, pan-fried red snapper with a tomato and chervil salsa, and ran through the sales list. She tried gently to persuade Anthony to visit the Andersons but he repelled the suggestion and said she should just keep going with them. He could be stubborn like that sometimes. A few days ago she had suggested that Tom be given more responsibility but Anthony had frowned and said, 'In time. Not now.' It came from being the owner's son, she supposed, and now the sole owner himself. Charron's was still a private company owned one hundred per cent by Anthony.

She expected Anthony would want to use the time over lunch to discuss their meeting that morning with Cal Doyle. They had met him at Milbourne Manor and walked through the show apartment. The living room, she thought privately, was not as good as it could be. The best feature was the curtains, beautifully made and elegantly draped, in cream silk offset by a gold rope trim. The furnishings were less inspired: two facing peach sofas, an oak coffee table and an array of lamps, rugs and pastoral oil paintings that did not entirely succeed in lifting the room from the feel of a hotel suite.

Cal, who seemed to take less care with his appearance the more money he made, was dressed in jeans and a dust-stained sweatshirt.

'Just come from Kingston,' he said by way of explanation. Susannah presumed he was referring to the waterfront flats he was building between Kingston-upon-Thames and Hampton Court. She knew that he was a hands-on developer, who had started from humble beginnings, and was not above going on site himself for a few days if he thought a project was running adrift. Cal had turned to Anthony. 'Three architects, two surveyors and one big bloody mess. Wouldn't be surprised if the whole building falls into the river.'

She knew that was unlikely. Cal Doyle's buildings were expensive because they were built with an old-fashioned attention to detail.

Then he had talked them through the kitchen. 'Solid wood units. Granite worktops. All with those ranges you ladies like. Not that they ever get bloody used; we should just put in a microwave for your fancy Marks and Spencer stuff.'

'These aren't family properties,' she commented. 'I think the most likely purchaser is an older, possibly divorced person, who needs the extra bedrooms but doesn't want the maintenance of a house.'

Cal gave an appreciative nod. 'That was my thinking.'

Anthony cut in. 'And advertising? I assume you want national press?'

'No,' said Cal and she had to stop herself from echoing Cal's prohibition. Sometimes she felt that Anthony needed to let the client take the lead.

'I think it's a local market, isn't it?' she said quickly. 'People who live in this area but for some reason or other need to downsize.'

'Yes.' Cal nodded his agreement. 'And I don't want Sunday day-trippers. Folk with nothing better to do than read the *Sunday Times* then drive out to nosy round one of my flats.'

'Good,' she said decisively. 'Local press, a full campaign, starting ASAP.'

They had talked about pricing, which was unnecessary because Cal had already decided exactly what he wanted, and Anthony had assured him of the firm's best efforts. Then Cal had looked at his watch and hurried to pull on his weatherworn black leather jacket.

'The missus is expecting me.' He turned to Susannah. 'One of those adenoidal appointments.' Or at least that was what she thought he said. It was difficult to tell sometimes, with his accent. And then she remembered that Cal's wife was expecting their first baby. Maybe it would soften him. But probably not.

At the Two Brewers the lunch crowd was arriving, the noise level was rising and their food took an age to arrive. For a while they ate in a comfortable silence. Then Anthony put down his fork. 'There's something I need to run past you,' he said.

She pre-empted him. 'The Milbourne marketing plan?' She already had an idea for an open day one Sunday, which she was hoping Anthony would endorse.

He shook his head. 'No. It's the office, actually.' He broke off as Kimberley went by to order another round of drinks. Then he continued. 'Dee has indicated that she wants to take early retirement.'

'Gosh!' It was a shock and not just because it was not the conversation she had expected. Susannah had always thought that Dee was devoted to her job.

He carried on purposefully. 'Which creates a vacancy for someone to run the lettings department.'

Her first thought was that Anthony was going to get Justin trained up. But he went on. 'Actually, it's much more than just running the present department. God, I should have done this years ago . . .'

She was bemused. 'Done what?'

'Opened up a lettings office!' He sounded energized. 'We're losing out, Susannah! We're ticking over. We need to have a separate lettings office and to offer clients a full management service with a dedicated maintenance team.' He downed what was left of his orange juice. 'Repairs, gardening. The lot.'

She was confused. 'We do that already.'

'Yes, but we don't present it as a package – from cleaning through to check-out. Dee's heart isn't in it. She's great at letting the properties but she hates the day-to-day management. We could do so much more. Or rather, you could.'

'Me?'

'Of course.' He looked surprised. 'It's obvious. It would be your department; you'd choose the staff. Not that you could have Lynda: we'd sink without her.'

She was caught off guard. Dee was a fixture in the office, Susannah had never even considered that she must be close to retirement. Now that Anthony was outlining his plan it all seemed obvious and she felt slightly foolish for not having foreseen these developments.

'But we don't have the space.'

Anthony gave her a knowing smile, 'We do – on the first floor. The lease renewal for the tenant upstairs is coming up. We could take possession and open up the back staircase. Just like the old days.'

'The old days?'

'My parents used to live over the shop.'

She said nothing as she took in the information that Anthony owned the freehold of the entire building.

'We would continue with sales on the ground floor; lettings would be on the first floor. We'd carry on letting out the top floor for the time being. Who knows, we might need it before long!'

His enthusiasm was appealing. So was the fact that he was saying 'we', not 'I'.

He continued more thoughtfully. 'It would be easy to blame it on Dee. But in truth my heart hasn't been in it either. What with the last years with Kate . . . I feel differently now. I don't know why. I think it coincided with your arrival!'

She felt a rush of happiness. Anthony could have brought in some-one from outside, a person with experience of running a department or at least being second in command. But from the way he was talking he had never even considered doing that. She was his first choice. It was more than flattering; it was almost intoxicating. She would be running her own department, hardly a little job, and even James would have to sit up and notice that he was not the only one capable of running the show. Of course it would be stressful – and there was a huge amount of work to be done – but that did not concern her now. Now was the time to relish the moment.

Anthony was continuing animatedly. 'I want to cover Cobham, Esher – and Weybridge. We've hardly touched the market there. Maybe even look at going into Kingston at some point.'

His enthusiasm caught her imagination. 'I've always thought there was potential there!'

'Of course, you'd need staff. A secretary. And at least one assistant. Maybe Justin?'

'Definitely.' She resisted adding that he might be otherwise occu-pied broadcasting on Radio Two. She did not want anything to spoil the moment. Lettings had always appealed to her. It was somehow more controlled and formulaic than sales. A letting property in Cobham had to be presented in a certain way: immaculately clean and as impersonal as possible, a shell into which the new tenant could imagine moving effortlessly. There was no room for the foibles and tastes of the owner. She liked that.

Anthony talked about the new offices and his plans for advertising and they discussed marketing. The business lunchtime customers began to drift away and Kimberley came over to clear away their plates. Anthony reached for the dessert menu. 'Seeing as we're cele-brating . . .'

He ordered a sticky fig and macadamia nut pudding. With two spoons.

'No arguing!' he insisted. 'You don't need to watch your figure.'

And so they shared one pudding and talked about their plans for the future as the pub emptied. They were the last two remaining and Kimberley finally edged them out of the door into the bright after-noon sunshine.

It was possible, Tabitha had discovered, to travel 4,000 miles across the Atlantic Ocean and into the heart of America and feel once there that she had come home. She had believed that place, or the sense of belonging to a place, was something formulated in childhood and never forgotten, to which one would return in adulthood with a sense of comfort and familiarity.

Now, sitting on the back porch of Theo's farmhouse, she wondered at how quickly she had come to feel at peace in a place she had barely thought of a year ago. Virginia.

He returned with a jug of iced tea. She wasn't entirely sure about iced tea but she was trying.

'I've put less sugar in this time.' He put the jug down on the worn wood table and settled next to her in one of the faded garden chairs that graced the white decking of the porch.

'No sound from upstairs,' he added. Araminta had never slept so well, a combination of the air, running around with Theo's many nephews and nieces and the food she devoured with abandon.

Tabitha complained that everything she ate in Virginia tasted of too much sugar. Even the bread tasted sweet. She had searched in vain for sugar-free muesli – her breakfast staple – and substituted Theo's home-made French toast, though she drew the line at the lake of maple syrup he poured over his. Araminta did not resist, any more than she refused Theo's peanut butter and Jell-O sandwiches or his fried egg muffins or his mother's cherry cobbler.

He stretched out his legs and lit a small cigar. He did not smoke cigarettes but on these evenings, just warm enough to sit outside in a thick sweater, he would take out a small Virginian and smoke it slowly, claiming as he did so that he was only doing it to keep the bugs away from her.

'There are no bugs,' she would protest, and then he would look away and say that there would be in the summer. Then the question hung in the air. She knew she would have to tell him; she could not go on unless she did. He had to know her, to hear her history and having heard the worst tell her that he still wanted her. If he didn't, she would rather know now before it was too late and the pain would be unbearable. Except that she wasn't sure that it was not too late already.

'I need to get you a rocking chair.' It was said in a tone that made her uncertain as to whether he was entirely serious. 'A white one,' he continued. 'Of course, that's not the only thing.' He paused. 'You'll be needing a truck. And a pair of dungarees. And a dog we can keep on a chain – yep, tied to that tree.' He pointed to the yew tree in the middle of the garden. She began to laugh. This was one of Theo's favourite themes – how he was going to turn his sophisticated English girlfriend into a hick, or a hillbilly, or a redneck woman.

She never tired of looking at him. His dark blond hair with the faintest trace of red, the features that had the mark of an outdoor life, the dark tan and the firm muscle of his arms which came not from any holiday or gym but from a lifetime of hard work in all weathers.

Today he wore a checked shirt with the sleeves rolled up, a pair of Wranglers and working boots so hard and heavy she wondered he could walk in them.

He reached over and stroked her hand, gazing out across the garden and beyond to the fields of newly planted corn, the seedlings just a few inches high. 'I like having you with me,' he said.

'And I like being here.'

She loved that about him. There were no games, no pretences; he said it straight and as a result she had become the same way, the old London mores of playing hard to get or her cards close to her chest forgotten.

'So, are you going to be here for Thanksgiving?'

This was a new question. 'We haven't had summer yet.'

'My mother starts cooking early. You need to be here for that; it's quite something. Everyone comes back—'

'So I'd meet everyone?'

'Yep. My oldest brother comes in from Atlanta and my sister comes with her family. We don't know about Jack.'

Jack, Theo's youngest brother, was a marine serving overseas. In this part of the USA, she had come to realize, serving in the military, like flying the flag, was woven into the fabric of small-town life. The sense of isolation from the rest of the world, the very self-sufficiency and security of small-town life, were also its limitations. She felt at home here but it was a home with closely defined boundaries. After she met Theo she had taken to reading, in women's magazines, stories of women who had given up their London city life to follow love, or usually holiday romance, to far-flung places. Huts in Sri Lanka or Kenya, apartments in Cyprus or Egypt, even a tent in Tibet. And she had come to consider for herself the question of how it would feel to give everything up for the man you love. To leave your home, your friends and your family, to leave all that was familiar in your life. And to do all of that to your child as well.

So the question about Thanksgiving was left hanging for the time being. But she knew she would be back for the summer.

After a week they had fallen into a routine. Theo would come in from the farm at around four and they would eat early, as people did around here, seldom after six. It had taken some getting used to when she realized that even the smartest restaurants took reservations from six p.m. Then they would watch television – Tabitha arguing for the History Channel, Theo and Araminta lobbying for cartoons – then Araminta would go to bed and they'd go out onto the porch.

Bedtime, like mealtimes, was taken early. Sometimes she would catch herself, in the middle of the day, falling into a daydream in which she was in Theo's arms. Sex with Theo had been a slow and gentle revelation.

They had first made love on her first USA trip, which had in turn followed Theo's two visits to see her in England. She had been testing him, keeping him at arm's length, but it had not deterred him. She had announced that she would be staying in a hotel and he had not tried to dissuade her. Lizzy had been adamant that on no account must she stay with Theo, which, in the circumstances, was sensible enough advice. So she had booked into the Holiday Inn and for the first three nights returned there every night. Then, on the fourth day, they had not gone out to eat. He had announced that he would cook her dinner. Veal parmesan and green salad and chilled California Sauvignon and then Key Lime pie, which he later admitted had been baked by his sister. They had taken coffee into the main room, he had piled logs onto the fire and it had seemed the most natural thing in the world to lie in his arms and watch the fire and say very little. It was not that she decided to sleep with him that night. Choice never came into it. It was simply that the thought of leaving was impossible.

She had stopped him as his hand moved to touch her breast. 'I . . . This is a big step for me. I . . .'

'We don't have to do anything you don't want to.' The gentleness of his response, and the way he moved his hand from her, told her he was genuine.

'I'm sorry.'

'You don't have to say you're sorry,' he cut in. He held her firm against his chest.

'It's been a long time.'

'It's OK.' He smoothed her hair and all the things that she wanted to say ran through her mind, but she was powerless to reveal them. How could he understand? She thought about the last six years, since Robert, and the way she had avoided any form of intimacy. A coffee, even a glass of wine, but never more than that. Peter had eventually tired of her refusal to sleep with him – *I can't help you if you won't help yourself.* And then the counselling sessions when finally she realized that it wasn't her fault. How could she be sure it wouldn't happen again? she had asked. How could she know that she wasn't one of those women who kept going back to the same type of relationships? 'Because you've looked at yourself, because you've done the work,' the counsellor had assured her.

She had met Theo when she was ready to, at a time she least expected it, in that rain-soaked marquee at an English wedding she had been dreading for months because she would be a single woman in a sea of couples.

Theo hadn't questioned her or asked her if there was anything he could do, or strained to be sympathetic in an unconvincing effort to get her into bed. Instead he just held her and after a while she began to trace the outline of his skin along his neck and down the front of his shirt and then it seemed natural to unbutton it so that she could press her face against the warm brown skin. She loved the smell of him, of his neck and now of this new part of his body.

She pulled the shirt from his shoulders, felt the hard muscles of his arms and he flexed them and made her laugh. And then they kissed. A long, deep, slow kiss as she felt his arms trace her back – and then down.

'You have a great ass,' he murmured.

She burst out laughing. 'Ass? That's a donkey in English.'

'Well, you're in America. Where it means butt. And it's *really* great.'

His hands ran over her and he eased off her polo neck. With a slightly disarming deftness he undid her bra. The pleasure of his touch was so intense that at that moment she knew she would sleep with him. His body against hers, the touch of skin on skin, was beyond resisting.

'And you have beautiful breasts.'

'They're so small,' she protested. Her breast size had always been her despair.

'No,' he insisted, 'they're perfect.' And if he thought otherwise he was so convincing that she no longer cared.

'We could go to bed . . . or stay here.'

'Stay here,' she said unhesitatingly. It was too warm, the light on the walls too perfect, to think of moving.

And so they undressed and he caressed her stomach and – so slowly she thought she ached – felt deeply with his hand. He was experienced and unselfish enough a lover to make her come. Then he shifted so that he was above her and pressed himself into her. Absurdly, she had been too shy to touch him and so his hardness was a pleasurable shock.

And then he was more forceful, slipping one hand under the small of her back so that he was holding her fast as he thrust deep inside her. She pulled up her legs around his back and allowed him to thrust harder and deeper. She was lost, her face buried in the scent of his neck, her arms holding him tight with every bit of her strength. They moved together with a quick, hard passion and then he came and they lay still together until he eased away and held her and there was nothing more to say.

That time seemed an age away. It was their last night, late at night and she knew the time had come. Whatever the agonies of telling Theo, to return with so much left unsaid would be worse still.

'Theo, let's go inside.'

She saw that he had heard the seriousness in her voice. Without a word he stood and they moved inside. They sat on the old sofa, two hurricane lamps lighting the living room, and she rested her back against him. He did not question her. Instead they sat in silence for a few minutes. Then she began.

'I know you must be curious about Robert.'

'I didn't mean to pry.'

'You haven't. Not at all. I'm the one who's been secretive and afraid to tell you.'

'Afraid!' He seemed genuinely dismayed.

'Theo, I feel . . .'

'Why don't you just tell me?'

She had known for the past year that this must happen between them. The simplicity of his suggestion emboldened her to do something she had delayed for too long. 'I met Robert at a publishing party. I'd just started at Ollsens as a graduate trainee. That meant in practice that I was the general dogsbody in whichever department I was attached to. I didn't mind; I was so pleased to be working in publishing at all. At the time I was working in publicity. We had just published the autobiography of a British politician – he was well known and a bit of an old roué and so there was plenty of press interest. The party was at Hatchards – it's a beautiful old bookshop on Piccadilly – and I was sent with the boxes of books in a taxi. Robert was doing the PR. He hadn't been in business on his own for long. He was already there.'

She could see Robert in her mind's eye as she told Theo. Robert had looked immaculate as he always did, in a sober business suit, plain tie and highly polished shoes, moving around the room, double-checking every detail, issuing instructions to the caterers and getting the staff to rearrange the shop so that there was more room for the guests. She had taken such care with the book display but he had come over and rearranged them.

'You need a few showing the back cover with the author photograph,' he had told her as he deftly moved them around.

She had to admit to herself that he was right. Then all the guests seemed to arrive at once. It was a September evening with the sun coming through the leaded windows. The shop was crowded but Robert found the time to return to her as she was directing guests to the table where the author sat signing books. In between telling her all the gossip about the high command at Ollsens he asked her a host of questions about herself. It was captivating. Robert focused on her so that she felt she was the only person in the room. He didn't look over her shoulder or make an excuse to go off and talk to someone more important.

'You must think I was very naïve,' she said to Theo. 'To be taken in so easily.'

He sounded shocked. 'I don't think that at all.'

She hesitated. 'But you see, I wasn't thinking. I was new to London. I hardly knew anyone. And I'd just split up with my university boyfriend—'

'He must have been a fool to let you go!' interrupted Theo.

Tabitha laughed. 'Actually he ran off with his thesis supervisor. He was a postgrad. It doesn't matter; we were never very well-suited, but I took it hard. I was susceptible to meeting someone who would come along and sweep me off my feet and tell me what to do with my life.'

Privately she had often wondered to herself what would have happened if she had met Robert a year later, when she was stronger. She hoped that she would have seen through him. Certainly the signs were there from the start. Robert could never admit to a mistake or take responsibility for a failure. It was always someone else's fault and as time went on, usually hers. Robert had to win. A deal, an argument, a bet. He rarely gambled but when he did he hated to lose. And most of all he needed to be in control.

She doubted if she could ever convey accurately to Theo the way that things had been between her and Robert. 'In the beginning I liked it. Robert would choose what restaurant we went to, what films we saw, what holidays we had, what books I should read. And I worked in publishing! He made good choices. He has an eye for beautiful things, for the best in life. But it always had to be the "right" thing to do. So we held dinner parties for people we didn't like, serving food we didn't want to eat.'

Soon she had found that she didn't have time to keep up with her old friends. Robert was very demanding. He wanted to see her every night and she thought it meant he cared. What a fool she had been! Soon he suggested that she move in. That was her fatal mistake. Within weeks she had started to think and act like Robert. She cooked the meals he liked, wore the clothes he chose and somehow her friends never called her at his place. Instead the two of them would jet off for the weekend to stay with clients. His life became her life.

'So when he asked me to marry him I said yes. He didn't force me. I said yes willingly and happily and that is the part I find the hardest to recall. I turned the key on my own prison door.'

After she said yes everything had gone haywire. Robert found a house in Wandsworth, a total wreck, and before she knew it, quite literally, he'd made an offer on it. Then there was the wedding. She'd envisioned a few friends on a beach in Goa. That, needless to say, was not Robert's game plan. There were a hundred and fifty guests, a reception at the Savoy and a honeymoon in New York which turned out to be a business trip for Robert – he was pitching for the Ashby Hotel account. He got it.

'While he was out doing business I sat in the Ashby Central Park watching television,' she said ruefully to Theo. 'Eighteen months after I met Robert I was pregnant, living in a building site. It was all too much. Robert insisted on us living in the house, which was ridiculous – any sane person would have moved out. He wanted to save money and keep an eye on the builders. He was still complaining about the cost of the wedding, as I recall.'

It was a boiling hot summer, dust everywhere and the noise of a kanga drill reverberated throughout the house for hours on end. She went out to the common, sitting in the shade of a tree, just to get some peace. She had felt as though she was cracking up. *You either have to pull yourself together or pack in your job*, had been Robert's response. So she had handed in her notice. In retrospect, she realized it was the job that was keeping her sane.

Finally, two weeks late at the end of August, Araminta was born. It should have been such a happy time. 'It was a nightmare. I just couldn't get her to feed. I felt so inept. Robert found fault constantly. I was "fucking useless". A fucking useless wife and mother and . . . I can't say it. I began to realize that he hated me. And after the rows he would always say that I could leave but never with Araminta. It sounds like something out of the nineteenth century, doesn't it?'

Theo held her close. 'It doesn't matter what it sounds like. Or what anyone thinks.'

But it had mattered for such a long time. The hardest thing, in the last few years, had been the fear that people wouldn't believe her. Sometimes she couldn't believe it herself.

Robert did not hit her until after they got married. Certain things triggered him: for example, if they went out and he thought she was getting too much attention. If she told a story at a dinner party and everyone laughed it would antagonize him. Often he would say something to chip at her – some undermining comment – then he would go berserk when they got home. Once, they went to a wedding and bumped into a professor who had taught her at university. She had chatted happily to him about the university and people they knew in common, then the professor had made some innocent comment to Robert about how proud he must be to have such a clever wife. When they got home Robert went crazy. He started an argument about money and shouted that she could do without any housekeeping that week if she thought academic life was so attractive and his business acumen was so unimportant. She told him not to be so silly – those were the days when she answered back – and he slapped her hard across the face. She burst into tears and ran upstairs, locking herself in the bathroom. He broke the door down, held her by the hair and said she was never, ever to lock him out of any room in his house again.

It was always Robert's house. He was terribly odd about money. She had access to a joint account into which he put a small amount of money every month. But he would happily spend money on her to impress other people. So he bought her a few items of good jewellery and a couple of designer handbags, but it was all for show.

He would say that she was a nobody. That she was pathetic. That she was stupid. He would say that her degree counted for nothing in the real world. He was vicious about her family. He described her father as a failure and her mother as a madwoman – because her father wasn't rich and her mother had long ago been treated for depression. Every family secret, every nugget of information, was stored away in Robert's mind and never forgotten.

'He said that I couldn't cook or clean or look after Araminta properly. It was as if he wanted to *own* Araminta. He called her Daddy's Girl – but not in a nice way. He said it possessively as he held her.'

She had started to believe the things he said. Now when she heard the familiar refrain – *why don't women leave?* – she knew that people who said such things could not understand how quickly and pervasively it became a normal part of one's life. She would tiptoe around trying not to provoke him. 'It was the classic pattern – when he did react I would blame myself for having antagonized him. Most people know this in theory but it is another thing to have lived it.'

For a while she had thought that if she only tried harder then everything would be OK. She lost weight, exercised compulsively and cleaned that damned house as if her life depended on it, but it made no difference. Now she knew why. There was something very significant about Robert's violence that she did not understand for years afterwards. Robert could control his behaviour. Robert wasn't a man who got drunk, came home in a rage and then woke up the next morning full of remorse and promises that it would never happen again. There were such men but Robert wasn't one of them. He could switch the violence on and off. He was never out of control. And that was what made it so frightening. It was just another weapon in his armoury to control her. It went side by side with the criticism and the belittling and the way he isolated her from her family and friends. He was determined to stop her leaving.

'But I did leave. He underestimated me, I'm glad to say. One day I came to my senses.'

They had held a Sunday lunch party at the house in Wandsworth. Araminta was two by then and they had almost finished the work on the house. Almost, because Robert was never satisfied and was forever getting into arguments with the builders and finding any excuse not to pay their final bills. There were just a few people there – James, Susannah, Matthew and some neighbours. Robert had been in a foul mood all morning. He came into the kitchen while she was making a blueberry cheesecake. She could tell immediately that he was spoiling for a fight. 'Christ, why is it always the same fucking thing?' He had pointed to the row of cookbooks on the shelf. 'Is it too much to open one of those from time to time?'

'Be quiet, will you!' she had hissed. 'Araminta will hear you. This is delicious. Everyone likes it.'

'You're just bloody lazy.'

She ignored him, suspecting he just wanted a reaction. In response he started pushing her around the kitchen, shoving her, and then he put his hand up her skirt. He took hold of the flesh at the top of her leg and squeezed it really hard. She winced with the pain. His voice was contemptuous. 'You've still not lost the weight from having Araminta. You'll end up looking like your mother.' It hurt so much that she started to cry. That placated him; it often did.

The guests arrived and lunch passed without incident until the end when James, who had had quite a bit to drink, started flirting with her. It was nothing serious; he was just playing. In her opinion James was a nice man but he drank too much. He said something silly, something about *coveting thy brother's wife*. Robert said nothing and the party went on as if nothing untoward had happened. It was after everyone had left that it happened.

She was upstairs putting Araminta to bed. Robert followed her upstairs and said that he was going to run a bath. 'I remember think- ing at the time that it was unusual because he only ever took showers. And then he called out my name. Very casually. "Tabitha." And that was another warning because he very rarely called me by my name and only when he was angry. But I didn't think anything of it so I walked unsuspectingly into the bathroom. And then Robert leaped on me. Literally. He got one arm around my body and with the other hand he grabbed my hair. Then he pushed me onto the floor. I still didn't understand, even when I saw the water in the bath and the tap running. Then I saw that only the cold tap was running. It was too late

167

then. Everything happened so quickly. He had his knee in my back and I tried to scream but that was when he pushed me under.

'I thought I was going to die, Theo. And the last thought I had was that Robert would say it was an accident and the marks were where he tried to save me. I don't know how long he kept me under. It hurt so much, Theo. The pain – in my throat and in my chest and then in my head . . . And then he pulled me up and spoke to me. He said, "You just don't get it, do you? You are too stupid to get it. I am in control here." He was like a man possessed. He kept repeating that line – "I am in control" – over and over again.

'I told him I would do whatever he wanted. I said yes, yes, yes – he was in charge. I was just so scared that he would push me under again. It worked because eventually he let go and left me on the bathroom floor. He told me to wipe up the spilt water. I knew then that he was mad, that one day he would kill me and he was clever enough to get away with it. I would fall from a balcony or drown in a boat or just disappear and never be found. And he would get Araminta.

'I think, at that time, I didn't value my own life enough to get out. But I was damned if I would leave Araminta to him. I had reached a stage where I believed what Robert said about me. I would love to tell you that my sense of self was stronger but it wasn't. Robert and I were together for nearly four years in total and by the end I believed him when he said I was worth nothing. But I couldn't abandon Araminta to him or have her grow up influenced by a man like that.'

It had not been possible to leave straight away. She needed a plan, because she knew Robert would come after her. She had to go somewhere that he wouldn't find her. That's where Peter came to her rescue. Peter was the gardener. They had hit it off from the start and before long Peter's visit was the highlight of her week. By the end he hardly did any gardening – she would make coffee and they'd sit in the garden and talk. She didn't think Robert could find out. Peter was a zoology graduate who'd started gardening while he decided what to do with his life. He was still doing it ten years later. He was a very kind man. And brave – she had shown him what Robert was capable of doing. Peter had a cottage in Sussex which he used at the weekends and he said she could stay there.

She waited until Robert was away on a business trip. Peter came in his van and she packed what she could. With Araminta in her arms she left. All the time she was packing the van, even though she knew

Robert was in Brussels, she was terrified that he would somehow magically appear. 'I had reached this point of slight insanity where I believed that Robert was all-powerful and inside I doubted that I would ever get away. But I had to try.'

Robert found them after a couple of weeks. Later, she guessed that he had gone through her mobile phone bill, called everyone and worked it out from that. She had only used it once to call Peter, in the early days. She thought she had been so careful. She believed she had a guardian angel looking down on her because Peter was with her at the cottage when Robert turned up unannounced. There was an awful row. Robert said he would win custody of Araminta and ruin her in the process, but eventually he left.

She knew it was time to turn the tables. Barbara, her solicitor, called him and played him at his own game. Barbara said that she was going to apply for a restraining order to keep him away – but she wasn't sure whether to leak it to the *Evening Standard* or the *Daily Mail*. Which did he prefer? He never came back to the cottage after that. Instead he fought her over Araminta. And when he lost that battle he fought her over every penny of maintenance.

'Peter and I didn't live happily ever after. I wasn't ready to be with anyone. Robert went around telling people that I'd run off with Peter and that we were "shacked up together" but that wasn't true at all. We were friends. Peter wanted more, but I had nothing to give. I think Robert said other things about Peter because he lost some of his Wandsworth customers in the weeks that followed. Rumours started going around that he'd been in prison. Peter ended up meeting a New Zealand girl in a bar in Southfields and they live out there now. He was a good man and my friend. He risked a lot to help me. In time I came to see that it was about Robert, not me, and that there is something terribly wrong with Robert. I've spent hours wondering if it was something in his childhood but I've never found an answer. And now I've stopped thinking about why things happened. I don't want to think about it any more.'

Instead she relaxed and felt sweet relief wash over her. Theo said nothing – there was nothing to be said, as his arms tightened around her and his lips brushed her neck. He did not comment or offer advice or platitudes. He simply sat with her in the warm darkness, speaking only to tell her that it was time to go to bed.

*Part 3*

# SUMMER

# Chapter 7

# Marriage

*I knew that Susannah would never let me go over the edge. I knew that she would hold firm, a barrier against my worst excesses, saving me from my own nature. I did not consciously understand this at the time of our marriage. I know it now. Nor did I set out to hurt her. But I did. My drinking, and my behaviour when drunk and sober, has had a possibly fatal impact on our marriage. It is laughable, were it not so shameful, that I believed that my period of one month's abstinence would mark a turning point in my relationship with Susannah. I cast myself in the role of the magnanimous peacemaker. In return, I expected her to throw open the front door, thank me for coming home on time and present me with a three-course home-cooked meal. It is a wonder I did not expect her to serve it wearing a negligee. No element of my fantasy came to pass. Years of late nights, flirting, spoiled holidays, missed appointments, all the times I should have been there, and sometimes all the times I was there, have created an open wound in my marriage.*

*On one occasion I left Susannah sitting in the restaurant of the Cannizaro hotel in Wimbledon, where I was due to meet her to celebrate our fifth wedding anniversary. I forgot, went to the pub and then I lied and said I had had to work late and that I had called the hotel. I even feigned anger that the hotel hadn't given her the message. At the time I considered my story to be a necessary excuse rather than a lie. When I was telling it I almost believed it myself. The next day I went out and bought her a gold rope necklace and after that I didn't expect it to be discussed again. I thought that as long as I kept my job and didn't sleep with other women she didn't have much to complain about. So when I arranged to have dinner with Jasmine and subsequently told Susannah that I was working late, I didn't feel I was lying. To me it was just another necessary excuse. Clearly, I have a lot to learn about honesty. Did I say dinner? Every couple of weeks I endeavoured to see Jasmine. I never* drank with her. I knew that once I had that first drink, I was powerless over the others that would inevitably follow. I knew it – but I was not ready to admit it. Besides, I made up for it later. I still believed that to be an alcoholic one had to be located under a railway bridge in a permanent state of inebriation. As for my month of abstinence, it did nothing to reform my drinking. Oddly, my drinking actually got worse in the weeks and months that followed. I was nearing the end. I had crossed the line but I was too blind to see it.

It was stifling in the studio, the floor-to-ceiling windows the culprit, and although Jasmine had opened every window as soon as she arrived, the August heat had built up by nine o'clock.

Joan had abandoned work and England throughout July when she departed for her annual visit to friends on Long Island, leaving Jasmine to work a shortened day. Winters were spent in the Florida Keys where Joan owned an apartment in Key West. Today Joan had set her heart on cataloguing a box of slides from the 1970s, a series of photographs taken in South Africa. Her stated subject had been the people of Cape Town, but she had ventured into the townships and her photographs from that period were still requested today.

Joan had arrived back from Long Island tanned and renewed. Aged seventy-four, she could pass for sixty despite the fact that she refused to dye her long white hair, today tied back in a lose ponytail. She abhorred the notion of plastic surgery, smoked twenty a day and had done since she was a teenager. Today Joan, in a white T-shirt and khaki shorts, sat smoking a menthol cigarette and drinking a cup of organic redbush tea. Jasmine could never quite understand how someone so devoted to the cause of organic produce carried on smoking.

Joan had been asking her about her 'admirer', as Joan insisted on calling James.

'He's not my admirer,' Jasmine protested.

Joan tipped her ash and took a sip of tea, her legs outstretched on an ancient ottoman. 'He calls you, sends you flowers and takes you out to dinner. How does he differ from an admirer?'

'For a start he's married.'

'Aha. Yes. Wifey.'

Joan had taken a keen interest in Jasmine's friendship with James ever since she had caught Jasmine changing in the studio on her way to meet him for dinner at Putney Bridge.

'The bridge?' Joan had exclaimed. 'Are you having a picnic?'

'It's a restaurant,' Jasmine had laughingly explained.

It seemed an age away. Joan had been stern – instructing Jasmine to explain to James that she would love to see more of him and just as soon as he moved into his own place (or pad as Joan called it) he must promise to call her and they could go out for drinks. Jasmine had kept to the spirit if not the letter of Joan's declaration. She had seen James virtually every couple of weeks and they were due to meet up the following evening. But they had not slept together. She was unsure how long her resolve would last.

She became aware that Joan was talking. 'Men don't buy the house if they can live rent-free. Why do these girls think that the way to get a man to marry them is to move in? What foolishness! Has he given you anything?'

Joan was extraordinarily nosy but her interest was well-meaning and her comments surprisingly contemporary for someone well into her seventies.

'A bracelet. For my birthday. Tiffany.'

'Gold or silver?'

'Silver,' Jasmine sighed, knowing the reaction this would provoke.

'Cheapskate!' Joan was also extraordinarily rude but it was impossible to take offence.

Tonight she and James were going to Motcombs and she was going to wear the yellow dress he had liked so much when she had worn it for a walk in Hyde Park. This had become a favourite activity, circumnavigating both Hyde Park and Kensington Gardens and ending up on a bench – their bench – by the Serpentine near the bridge. They had been talking about travel. It was a game they played – planning itineraries for trips they could not take.

'I had the idea,' Jasmine had begun, 'when I was in Las Vegas that it would be huge fun to take a motor home and set off across the States, coast to coast, for six months.'

James was animated. 'I had exactly the same idea!' He began reeling off places on his fingers. 'West Coast, not too long in LA . . .'

'Definitely not.' They had agreed they both hated cities.

'Then the Rockies and out to the desert – Las Vegas and Reno and the Grand Canyon . . .'

'And Lake Tahoe. There's an open-air Shakespeare festival in the summer by the lakeside. Joan went a few summers ago.'

'Shakespeare it is, then. That reminds me, I got the tickets for *La Boheme*.'

'But they're impossible to get hold of!'

He gave a theatrical shrug of his shoulders. 'Anything for the lady . . .'

So they were off to the Royal Opera.

'Then on to the South?'

'Definitely. Nashville on the way and the Smoky Mountains and Memphis . . .'

'And New Orleans.'

'Of course, I would do all the driving,' insisted James.

'No way!'

'Yes,' he persisted. 'You'll be cooking me pancakes in the back. And in the evening we'll pull up and grill shrimp and drink wine and watch the fire-flies.'

James had a way of inspiring her to join with him in creating these visions of them together and she didn't resist. It was a delightful fantasy in which he wasn't married and she wasn't tied to her work, however happily. It was a vague, imaginary time in the future. James made everything sound like fun. He had the knack of turning the most mundane activities into adventures. And when they had done the States, he had concluded, they would embark upon Australia . . .

Susannah was momentarily confused. The doorbell rang, which was in itself unusual because anyone visiting from outside the development would need to use the entryphone. It must be a neighbour. But why then, a few seconds earlier, had she noticed the sound of a car pulling into the drive? James never came home in the middle of the day. She peered through the spy-hole in the door. First she made out the figure of James, then two other suited men, one of whom was pressing the doorbell. Had he forgotten some papers? And his key? And how to press the bell?

There was no time to think. She opened the door and vaguely recognized the man pushing the bell: Raul, James's boss. Next to him stood James and behind them another man she had never seen before. James did not look his usual self at all. Had he been taken ill? In fact James looked dreadful and the stranger standing behind him rather uncomfortable. Only Raul seemed at ease. James did not step forward to make introductions.

'Mrs Agnew.' Raul greeted her warmly. She recalled now that he was American. 'May we come in?'

She was flustered. 'Of course.'

She gave James an enquiring look as they stepped inside but he did not reply and his eyes flicked away from hers, towards the floor.

It began to dawn on her that something was very wrong, but the anxiety that had started to rise in her was cut short by Raul who, despite the fact he had never before been to their house, took charge effortlessly and gestured beyond the hallway to the conservatory.

'Mrs Agnew. We need to speak with you.' He turned to the stranger at his side. 'This is our human resources director . . .'

'I'm going to change.' It was James. He had turned on his heel and disappeared upstairs.

Now she felt seriously alarmed. 'What—'

Raul seemed to think there was nothing unusual in her husband bolting upstairs like a five-year-old in disgrace. 'I can explain everything.'

Perhaps realizing that she wasn't capable of independent thought, Raul abandoned further gesturing and walked into the conservatory, leaving her no option but to follow, the unnamed man bringing up the rear.

Raul indicated that they should sit down. He seemed very at home in their house. There was an air about him of being well-travelled, as though he would be at home in an airport lounge anywhere in the world, the effect augmented by the very slight Spanish tinge to his American accent. He was her height but thickset and, though polite, there was steeliness to his manner. She reluctantly sat down and he followed suit.

Almost at once she made to get up. 'Would you like a drink? Tea?'

He held up his hand. 'No, thank you.'

Perhaps he wanted something stronger. 'A glass of wine? Scotch.' She remembered then that James had finished the last of the Glenfiddich two nights ago, but fortunately Raul shook his head.

'Not for me.'

She had no choice but to sit back. It was damned hard to sit still; she wanted to know what James was doing upstairs, for one thing. She could hear various muffled thuds and the sound of doors opening and closing.

Raul took control. 'We've been aware now for some time that your husband has been falling short of the benchmark we set at Lloyd-Davies. James is an excellent lawyer. However, we are a results-driven firm. We can accommodate the occasional dip in employee performance, but your husband's condition goes beyond that—'

'His condition?'

'Your husband's addiction issues.'

'Addiction issues?'

'I'm not a doctor, Mrs Agnew. It's not for me to diagnose your husband.'

'Then—'

Raul seemed to shift up a gear. 'The bottom line is that your husband has a problem with alcohol.'

For the first time the HR director – she still had no idea of his name – spoke. 'It's our policy to assist employees. We operate a proactive not a reactive policy.'

She had no idea what he meant by that.

Raul picked up the thread. 'In particular we've had very good results with Grange House.'

The name was vaguely familiar but, as she struggled to place it, Raul ran on. 'It's a treatment facility. The programme they offer is twelve step-based for a period of approximately twenty-eight days. They focus primarily on alcohol and drug-related addictions and related behaviours. It's a beautiful place, very comfortable, down in Devon.'

Her first thought was that she knew damned well James was an alcoholic. But as for the rest she had no clue what they were talking about. What exactly were 'related behaviours'?

'Wouldn't it be more sensible to get him some help nearer to home?'

'It's the best inpatient programme in the country,' Raul said gently.

'Inpatient,' she murmured. 'Isn't there any alternative?'

'You mean outpatient counselling? Our experience shows that outpatient counselling while the employee remains at his or her desk has limited effectiveness in cases such as your husband's. The bottom line is that inpatient treatment offers the best outcome for James. We'd keep his job open, continue with his salary and benefits package. If he wanted to return—'

'Wanted!'

'Then we could revisit the issue of his position within the firm.'

She thought about her past efforts to persuade James to seek help. 'I don't think he'll go.'

There was a silence. 'James has indicated that he's prepared to go along with this.'

So the decision was already made. It was strange, after so long, that the end had come in this way. She had expected an accident, or a drink-driving conviction, or some sort of melodramatic event at a party. But never an intervention of this sort. She was struggling to accept the reality of it.

Raul spoke in the silence. 'Grange House have indicated that they are willing to accept James, subject to an assessment.'

Raul made it sound like Grange House was doing James a favour. 'When?'

'Tonight.'

It was too much. The rising disbelief burst out. 'That's completely impossible! How can he go to work like normal in the morning and then go into some sort of clinic or hospital or whatever it is? What is this place? How do we know he'll be safe there, that these people know what they're doing?'

'Grange House has the highest standards. There is a full medical staff there and a team of counsellors, all of whom are in recovery themselves.'

'In recovery themselves? You mean these counsellors used to drink – and take drugs?'

'They work on the philosophy that those with experience of addiction can best help others who are suffering.'

He had certainly read the brochure. She felt shocked and unable to continue the conversation. Privately she thought to herself that it would be much better for James to stay at home and go and see Dr Palmer, their GP, in the morning and get a referral to someone whose credentials could be verified. She was also reminded that James had yet to make an appearance.

'And what does James think about all this?' she asked.

'He sees the logic of accepting our suggestion of treatment.'

Some consciousness of the seriousness of James's position dawned. 'What's the alternative?'

For the first time in their conversation Raul faltered. He seemed to be considering what to say next.

'Well?' she persisted.

'Given James's record we would have no option but to dismiss him from the firm.'

She was stunned. 'For doing what, exactly? He's an excellent lawyer!'

Raul shifted uncomfortably. 'You would need to discuss the background with your husband.'

She would welcome the chance to do just that. That required his presence, however. *Where was James?* Raul got up and looked out to the garden.

'You have a great place here.'

She did not reply. This was no time for small talk. After what seemed an eternity, James appeared. Bizarrely he had changed – into jeans and an old Gap sweatshirt he hadn't worn for ages. It needed to be ironed. He lingered in the double doorway of the conservatory and when he spoke his words were directed not at Susannah but at Raul.

'I'm packed.'

'Packed!' She looked between the two men. 'Aren't you even going to discuss it with me?'

She felt excluded in the most humiliating way. Everything had clearly been decided before they even arrived at the house.

Raul looked across at James. 'I'll leave you alone.' He looked at his watch. 'We'll wait in the car.'

They left the room and she had the strong impression that James would like to have gone with them. Reluctantly, he sat down. 'I know this must be a shock. Believe me, it is for me.'

'Do you want to go?'

She had expected anger – some sort of a fight – but James's reaction was more complicated than that. If anything, his voice betrayed an emotion bordering on relief.

'I . . . Of course I don't want to go. I want to be back at my desk.' This last statement was delivered with no conviction whatsoever. 'But I don't have any option. The decision's been taken out of my hands—'

She interrupted him. 'I thought you two didn't get along.' She could not believe he was being so passive.

'Raul? I . . . I can see on some things he makes sense.'

It was extraordinary. Raul, about whom James had never had a good word to say – and who was escorting him to Grange House – now appeared to be regarded with an awed respect. Perhaps she should have got tough and shipped James off years before.

'But why? Why now? What on earth has been going on?'

James shifted. 'There's been a lot of pressure at work.' He seemed unwilling to say any more.

'Well surely there's more to it than that?'

James stared at the floor. 'I . . . Let's leave it for now. It's been a long day.'

'And you're just going to leave it like that? Disappear off with no explanation at all? I'm not a complete fool, James. Something must have happened for Raul to think you need to go into this place.'

James said nothing. It was infuriating. Didn't he think he owed her any explanation at all? Clearly her assumptions about James's performance at work had been naïve to say the least. And frankly it was the worst possible time. The second-floor office space at Charron's was falling vacant that week. She and Anthony had a huge list of tasks to work through. They were due to meet with the builder and the planning inspector that week, and next week she had meetings with the graphic designer and the printer for the brochure. Not to mention all her sales clients to attend to.

'Tell me what's going on!' she shouted.

In the silence she heard the front door swing open and Raul's footsteps across the hall floor. He appeared in the conservatory doorway.

'We ought to get going, Mrs Agnew. They are expecting us.'

She noted that James wasted no time in rising to his feet. 'I'll call you as soon as I get there,' he said with forced brightness, his gaze directed at the far end of the garden.

'As soon as you get there,' she repeated. 'James, you're not going on your own. I'm coming with you.'

Raul coughed. 'In the circumstances, perhaps it would be better if you stayed here.'

She rounded on him. 'I'm coming with you.'

Raul and James exchanged resigned glances. 'As you wish,' Raul concluded.

'That is what I wish,' she said firmly. 'And you'll just have to wait while I make arrangements for my son.'

She saw a flicker of surprise in Raul's eyes. He spoke with a new tinge of respect to his voice. 'Please, take as long as you need.'

The journey to Grange House took over three hours, with one break in a service station for coffee and, in the HR director's case, a cigarette. It was undertaken in complete silence. The HR director drove, Raul sat in the front seat and she and James were allocated the back seats. As they drove into the heart of the Devon countryside her mind was full of questions that she wanted to ask James but was precluded from doing so by the presence of Raul – who remained affable and unflappable and for whom she had developed an intense dislike.

She couldn't imagine what this place would be like. James hadn't said a word about how this was going to affect her and Matthew. Or her work. They left the main roads and diverted down a series of narrow country lanes and when they did finally arrive it was with no forewarning. Abruptly they turned into an unmarked driveway which continued for another half mile before coming to an end at two wrought iron gates. Raul, naturally, stepped out to speak into the intercom and, after a few seconds, the gates swung open.

'Stops them escaping,' quipped Raul.

No one laughed, though James raised a wry smile. 'No evening visits to the pub, then.'

They drove up the remainder of the driveway, the last two hundred yards lined with horse chestnuts. To the left a lake shimmered in the evening sun and to the right open farmland ran to the horizon. Grange House itself was a huge, gothic Victorian house with small stone-mullion windows and a centrepiece broad black front door. A woman emerged as the car drew up and they got out. Somehow Susannah had rather hoped the staff would be mainly men.

'I'm Gina. I'm the head counsellor.'

A counsellor. So according to Raul that meant she was an alcoholic or a drug addict. It was hard not to stare.

'Susannah . . .'

James's voice cut into her jumbled thoughts. They must have been speaking and she had missed the conversation, her mind wandering and her eye caught by a pagoda-style structure that stood to the side of the house, visible through the break in a circle of conifer trees.

Gina followed her gaze. 'It's our new meditation space. A present from an ex-patient.'

Susannah was uncertain how to respond. She couldn't imagine James wasting any time in there. He would be too busy in between lectures calling the office to check on his cases.

Gina smiled at her. 'This must be rather a shock. Raul's filled me in. Sometimes events move very quickly.'

She nodded. Irritatingly, Gina was patronizing in her manner but correct in her observation. How did Gina know Raul? Perhaps it was a tactic of his – to ship all his difficult employees down to the countryside, safely out of the way, while he reassigned their jobs. They were walking into the house now, the still mute HR director left behind in the car. Reassuringly, the hallway was indistinguishable from the reception of a country hotel: wood-panelled walls, a rather impressive stone fireplace filled with a dried flower arrangement and a reproduction antique desk on which stood a computer – but no papers. That, she observed, was the difference between Grange House and a hotel – there was no sign to announce its presence, no indication of its purpose, no indication in fact that this was anything other than a private house.

Gina was matter-of-fact as she opened a manila file and began taking out papers. 'James. We need you to fill in a medical questionnaire and permission to release details of your stay to your GP—'

'I don't think so!' It was her own voice. She wasn't at all sure that a twenty-eight-day stay was something that James would want on his medical records for ever.

Gina nodded, unperturbed. 'We can leave that for now. We'll just do the medical questionnaire. But why don't we start by showing you to your room? Later we need to do a medical exam and a search – Raul explained that, I think?'

James didn't turn a hair. 'Yes.'

A search? 'What for?'

'Alcohol, drugs and prohibited items,' Gina said smoothly.

'Well, James doesn't have anything like that!' It was so humiliating.

Gina, however, did not miss a beat. 'I understand. It is standard policy – nothing to do with James personally.'

There was nothing she could say to that – and Gina hadn't backed down. Before she had a chance to ask if an exception could be made for James, she continued. 'I'll show you your room. Then we can deal with the formalities while we go through our family policy with Susannah.'

It was all first-name terms here, whether you liked it or not. But there was nothing to be done because Gina was already leading them from the hallway, up the broad red-carpeted stairway, through interminable sets of fire doors and then up a further staircase. At the top Gina opened a door and Susannah saw that the top floor had been knocked through to form a white-walled room capable of comfortably housing the four single divan beds which were arranged between the sloping ceilings and dormer windows.

'Your room. We've got a great group in at the moment. A couple of the other men are nearing the end of their stay so you'll have plenty of help.'

Gazing around the room the word that came to mind was *dormi-*

*tory*. To the side of each bed stood a bedside cabinet cluttered with books and magazines, toiletries and greetings cards, and a single chair on which were arranged jeans and T-shirts and dressing gowns, with not a shirt or tie in sight. One bed was all but occupied by a giant Womble.

'Uncle Bulgaria,' said Gina, wryly catching her gaze. 'He has some compulsive cleaning issues.'

'They share?' Susannah said weakly.

'Yes. It breaks down the sense of isolation that often accompanies the later phases of using.'

What in God's name was she talking about? Whatever James did it wasn't *using*.

Gina went over to the vacant bed. 'You have a bedside table, chair and half of the wardrobe. The bathroom is to the left on the landing.'

Susannah and James exchanged glances for the first time since they had entered the building. She knew he wouldn't like sharing a bathroom.

Gina said briskly, 'Why don't you get settled in? I'll send Howard up; he's the nurse today. You can go through your bag together.'

James lifted his holdall onto the spare bed. 'Fine.'

She had expected James to object but he was strangely subdued. And that was how she left him as Howard, who looked about sixteen in a white half-smock, arrived. She had no option but to descend the stairs with Gina to her small ground-floor office.

'It's very quiet right now. There's a yoga session in the hall. That's where the lectures and some of the group sessions are held.' Gina looked at her watch. 'They'll be out in half an hour for dinner – that's at six. Then in the evening we have group activities or quiet time for the patients to work on their written assignments.'

'Written assignments?'

'We start off with what we call "seven by sevens". We look at seven areas in which drinking has affected James's life. For example his family, his work, his relationships with other people. He gives us seven examples under each heading. He'll start tomorrow,' Gina said briskly. 'We also expect him to maintain a daily journal.'

James had always been scathing of people who kept diaries – too much time on their hands. Susannah had a feeling that James may have met his match in Gina.

'James will also write his life story. Once that's completed he can go to meetings in nearby towns.'

Life story? Meetings? Did she mean business meetings – to get them back to work?

'Let me tell you something about our philosophy,' Gina continued. She had an unnervingly direct gaze. 'Grange House works on the principle that addiction is a family illness. When one family member has a problem with alcohol, all the family is affected. So our treatment of James also involves you.'

She could see that Gina was trying to be helpful but something in her rebelled at this concept of treatment whether you liked it or not. For the first time in her life she had an inkling of what it must be like to be sent away against your will to a mental institution. She would have preferred to have had some choice in the matter.

'And you have a son, Matthew?'

That was a step too far. 'Matthew doesn't need to be involved in this,' she said quickly.

Gina made no response to this. 'How old is he?'

'Fourteen.'

There was a pause. 'OK.' Gina continued in her slow, carefully moderated voice. 'This is a twenty-eight-day programme but more often than not patients choose to stay longer, to give them the very best chance of relapse prevention. For the first week we have found it easier for patients to settle in if they refrain from family contact.'

Susannah had more time to study her. Flat shoes, hair tied back, frumpy black trouser suit. Gina had missed her vocation as a prison governor.

'So we have a policy of no telephone calls or visits for the first week. You can write . . .'

It was proving very hard to concentrate. Thoughts and feelings were flooding her. After the initial shock of Raul's arrival, a creeping sense of shame at this outcome to James's drinking was overtaking her. She forced herself to be practical.

'When do I collect his laundry?' she asked distractedly.

If Gina was confused by this diversion into domestic detail she didn't show it. 'We have a washing machine, tumble dryer and iron. James will be allocated a day each week when he can do his washing. And change his sheets.'

Shrink and scorch every item, more like. He had never made a bed in his life. She wanted to argue but sensed it was fruitless. Gina had a way of baldly stating the facts – without any hint of the possibility of compromise – that precluded further debate.

'So when can I see him?' she asked sullenly. It was incredible. She was asking for permission to visit her own husband! But without pause her mind ran on to other practicalities. 'And he'll need his mobile.'

'After a week you can visit,' Gina said, 'on a Sunday. There's afternoon visiting after group on Sundays. We don't allow mobile telephones or laptops.'

'Oh. Group?'

'We encourage you to attend the family group – for friends and relatives – at two o'clock on a Sunday. It's a chance for you to ask questions and share your experiences with others in the same position. Thereafter you're free to spend time with James.'

Clearly, attendance at the group session was encouraged in the compulsory sense of the word. Susannah went on the offensive. 'But how do you know any of this works? How is locking James up in a place like this going to help him in the real world – when he isn't being kept away from alcohol?'

There was so much else that she wanted to say. *I don't want to 'share' with anyone, meditate in your garden or attend your group. And I'm damned if I'm going to disclose my private problems to complete strangers.*

'I have some reservations about this approach,' Susannah concluded.

'You may find it helpful to talk to one of the other relatives.' Gina looked thoughtful. 'There is someone I have in mind. I could ask her if she would be happy for me to release her telephone number to you.'

She could see Gina was trying to be helpful again. 'Yes. Thank you.'

'The first week will be hard for you and James. The best advice we can give you is to go home, rest and relax. Do something nice for yourself. Have a massage. See your friends. Living with an alcoholic pushes people to the brink of sanity. This can be a chance for the family to rest, too.' Gina paused. 'Also, you may want to think about telling Matthew a little about what is happening.'

She had already vowed to herself that she would keep Matthew out of this at all costs. She made no effort to conceal her disagreement. 'And why exactly do you think I should do that?'

Gina looked across at Susannah and her gaze was confident. 'Because Matthew knows everything already.'

Jasmine lasted until mid-morning before breaking down in front of Joan and confessing all. Joan's reaction was to light a cigarette, pour them each a tumbler of sloe gin and suggest that they retired to the sitting room away from the scorching heat of the studio.

'He's disappeared. James has disappeared and I can't find him. It's awful.' Jasmine broke down in huge sobs. 'I don't know if he's dead or alive.'

Joan took a deep drag. 'I think we have to consider the possibility that he's returned to Wifey.'

'He never left Wifey!' Jasmine protested. 'We were supposed to meet last night. For dinner. And I sat there, in Motcombs . . .' tears began to roll down her cheeks, 'for two hours! I felt such a fool. I called his mobile and it was switched off. I left three or four messages and then I called his office. I know I shouldn't have – I was going to pretend I was a solicitor or something if they asked – but the receptionist said he had already gone home.'

She took a gulp of the sloe gin and instantly regretted it as it scorched her throat. 'So I went home and then I tried again this morning, but it was the same thing. And then I tried his office and I got put through to someone in his department who said he was on holiday.'

Joan made a harrumphing sound.

'I don't even know where he lives!' Jasmine ran on. 'I don't know any of his friends. There's no way I can find out anything. I feel so shut out: what if he's hurt or there's something terribly wrong?'

'Or he's gone on holiday?' Joan suggested quietly.

'No. He would have told me!' She was certain of that. She knew Joan wouldn't believe her – James was a married man and therefore categorized by the world as lying, self-serving and not to be relied upon in any way.

But James was different. And then she realized that that was what every girl who was involved with a married man said to herself. They all believed that he was unhappily married, didn't sleep with his wife and only stayed for the sake of the children. Until, several years on when he still hadn't left – and his wife was pregnant again – finally the truth began to dawn that he was no different from all the others.

Thank God she hadn't slept with him. Or maybe she should have slept with him? Perhaps if she had done that he wouldn't have left her.

'It just doesn't make sense. He told me he had tickets for the opera next week.' She felt close to hysteria and light-headed from the sloe gin. 'What if he's had a terrible accident? Or a heart attack? Or been in a car crash?'

Joan exhaled. 'Give me the telephone.'

'What?'

'The telephone, dear. And the number for his firm.'

Joan was superb. Used every trick, dropped every name and before ten minutes was up she was speaking to the head of litigation who also happened to be on the committee for the building restoration fundraising campaign for the National Portrait Gallery. The head of litigation was enough of a lawyer not to divulge the circumstances of James's absence but sufficiently keen to impress Joan to indicate, off the record, that it was in the nature of paid leave.

Joan lit another cigarette. Jasmine was uncertain whether she now felt worse knowing that James was alive and well. She was no further forward in understanding what had happened to him. Joan began to speak and something in her tone made Jasmine turn away from the photographs she was pretending to study and listen more carefully than usual.

'Let him go, dear. If you can't forget him, then act as if you have. Then, if he comes back to you, you'll know that it is for the sole and simple reason that he cannot stay away.'

Before Jasmine could reply that this was impossible Joan reached down and began shuffling through a pile of papers that lay to the side of her Lloyd Loom chair. 'I think it's high time you started doing some work of your own. That should take your mind off it. The *Radio Times* have asked me to do one of their winter covers.' She began thumbing through the papers, saying distractedly, 'I haven't the patience for group shoots these days, so I'm going to suggest you do it.'

Jasmine's head was spinning from the combined effects of sloe gin, heartbreak and now an unexpected career break. 'Who is it?'

'Oh, there's more than one, dear. It's a group. The five hundredth edition, or it might be the thousandth, of some programme. Anyway it doesn't matter.'

Jasmine watched exasperated while Joan short-sightedly squinted at various pieces of paper before exclaiming, 'Here. It's the *Holiday* programme. A group shot of present and former presenters—'

'I can't do that! They want you!'

'Well they can't have me, can they? It's easy peasy. It's in the studio, dear. Just tell them to say "cheese" and press the shutter!'

Susannah walked over and switched the television off. It was ludicrously large, with a fifty-four-inch screen, which dominated one wall of the family room. James had bought the television and the two broad beige shapeless sofas and the extra-size recliner chair, egged on by Matthew. Several untidy stacks of DVDs covered the top of the television, mostly sci-fi and action titles.

'Hey, I was watching that,' Matthew protested. He continued to look at the screen as if it might burst into life again of its own accord.

'Matthew, we need to have a talk.'

He rolled his eyes. Her stomach was knotted and her head ached, it had been a frantic day at the office, and now she felt irritated. Why did he always have to be so bolshie? Her mother had never discussed anything at all with her. She went over and sat down next to him on one of the two facing sofas. He shifted away from her.

'It's about Dad,' she began.

'Yep.' He sounded totally uninterested. He reached down to pick up the newspaper from the floor and began reading the television listings.

'Matthew!'

He gave a sigh and theatrically replaced the newspaper, listings side down, on the carpet at his feet. He folded his arms and looked at her with an expression of martyred compliance.

She tried to keep her tone matter-of-fact so as not to alarm him. 'There's something you need to know. Dad has had to go away.'

He sounded bored. 'To Jersey. Yes, I know.'

'No. He's not in Jersey.'

At least that statement had caught his attention.

She continued. 'He's actually in Devon, at a place called Grange House. It's a type of . . . hospital.'

He was giving her an unnervingly hard stare. 'When did he go there?'

It was not the question she was expecting. 'A week ago.'

'So when did he go to Jersey?'

'He didn't actually go to Jersey.' She wished to God she had never told him that but at the time, in the shock of her return from Grange

House, she had needed time to think. It had seemed the right thing to do at the time.

He looked at her and she could read the annoyance in his eyes. She shifted. 'I was hoping you wouldn't have to get involved—'

'You mean you were hoping I wouldn't have to know.' He sounded more disgusted with the uncovering of her lie than surprised at the news that James was ill. 'What's wrong with him?'

'Nothing. I mean nothing physically. He's gone to discuss his . . . making some changes in his life.'

The response was predictable. 'What changes?'

She spoke in a measured voice. 'Dad has a lot of stress in his life and a lot of responsibility. Sometimes people deal with stress in ways that aren't good. He's gone to find better ways to deal with things.'

'So he's going to stop drinking?'

She could not keep the surprise out of her voice. 'Yes.'

'Why didn't you tell me?'

'Because I didn't want you to be worried.'

He flung his head back and looked at the ceiling. She tried to remember that this was a shock for him.

She leaned forward. 'Matthew, I've always tried to protect you from all this, so that you didn't know anything. Everything's going to be fine—'

But he was getting up and she knew for certain he was angry. She hated for them to be distanced. This was a time when they should pull together and rediscover the closeness between them.

Her voice reflected her exasperation and her need for him. 'Matthew, I just wanted to protect you.'

'When's Dad coming back?'

'Soon! I'm going down this weekend to see him.'

He seemed about to say something and then decided against it.

'Perhaps you could stay with Jake on Saturday, while I'm away.'

'Sure.'

He was almost by the door. She called to him, 'Matthew, we need to talk about this. About Dad and—'

'I don't want to talk about it,' he shouted. The door slammed behind him, echoed by the front door a few seconds later.

Louise Winter and Grania were waiting in the lounge of the Carlton Tower hotel drinking champagne. Each wore short, sharp sleeveless dresses – Louise in pale blue offset with white piping and pearl buttons, Grania in cream. It was unnerving, Natasha discovered, having done the voiceover on a Channel Four documentary the previous year entitled *Ladies Who Lunch,* to discover that she had become one herself. The heat of the late summer had led her to dress comfortably in a halter-neck diagonal pink and white shift dress and beaded sandals but beside Louise and Grania she looked distinctly underdressed.

'We're going to walk to Zafferano,' Louise had announced as if the hundred-yard stroll to the Italian restaurant was worthy of note.

Natasha nodded. Louise's manner was gushingly friendly as they broke the ice by discussing their summer holidays, yet she felt unaccountably ill at ease. Perhaps it was not smoking? This was Day Four following her trip to London's most expensive acupuncturist located in Notting Hill. Natasha wasn't sure if it was the needles or the thought of wasting all that money that provided the incentive.

Louise ordered a glass of champagne for Natasha before turning to her. 'Grania's been filling me in on her summer. Turns out she and Alex stayed in the same suite at Sandy Lane that Andrew and I stayed in for our honeymoon. Well, we started there, then we flew up to South Beach and then on to Andrew's uncle in New England.' This last phase of the itinerary was illustrated by a mimed yawn. The topic of travel had provoked Louise and Grania into a comparison of the relative merits of travelling British Airways First Class versus Virgin Atlantic Upper Class.

Louise put out her cigarette. 'Of course the entertainment's better on Virgin, and Oliver loves it, but the some of the people . . . Ugh!'

'I blame Air Miles,' concluded Grania. 'They ought to be made illegal.'

Then it was time to decamp to Zafferano, where there was a brief debate as to the merits of sitting in the front or back room. Louise decided on the front. They were seated to the side. Natasha, who had not been there before, took in the terracotta interior.

'Of course,' Louise said as they sat down, 'London's still empty. Once the schools go back it will fill up.'

Natasha was not surprised when Louise and Grania opted to order two starters, both salads. She chose a broad bean and parmesan roquette salad followed by linguine with prawns.

'And a bottle of Saran,' concluded Louise.

Then it was down to business.

Louise's tone was no-nonsense. 'Our committee is planning a

lunch. It's a charity lunch, naturally. For about two hundred. It's in aid of the Blue Baby Fund.'

Louise clearly did not feel the need to elaborate further about the ultra-fashionable premature baby charity. The cause, Natasha presumed, was incidental.

'The point is that we want to do a fashion show – I've got lots of designers lined up – and we would need you to act as the hostess.'

'I'm sure I can do that.' She took out her filofax to double-check.

'Next January, the thirtieth. It's a Wednesday. Just when everyone's bored after Christmas and ready to go out again.'

'Wouldn't it be better to do it in the evening?' suggested Grania.

Louise was curt. 'No. There's something big on every night. This way I know I can get the press there. Robert's working on it,' she added to Natasha.

That was news to Natasha. But a bigger issue was the date. She realized that she was already committed to *Expats*. 'Actually, I don't think I'm going to be in the country. I've been asked to do some filming overseas.'

Louise looked put out. 'Can't you change it?'

Natasha resisted pointing out that there was a crew involved, not to mention a BBC programme schedule.

'I'll check the dates,' she said lightly.

Louise looked thoughtful. 'Robert didn't seem to think there would be a problem.'

Fortunately the slight frisson that Natasha's announcement had brought about was broken by the arrival of their first course. Grania immediately sent hers back. 'I forgot I'm not supposed to have soft cheese. I'm pregnant,' she added conspiratorially to Natasha.

'Congratulations!'

'Only two months and fortunately it's not showing.'

Louise cut in, 'Have you decided where you're having it?'

Grania rolled her eyes. 'Alex wants me to have it in New York. That's where his wife had their daughter. I think that's a good reason to stay here.'

'Has he told his daughter?' interjected Louise. Clearly this was a subject that had been discussed on previous occasions.

'No. He keeps putting it off. She's coming over next week and he's promised to tell her then.'

'He's scared,' commented Louise.

Grania turned to Natasha and gave a theatrical sigh. 'Gabriella is a daddy's girl. She's eighteen and she cannot accept that her father has got remarried. He panders to her, always buying her things, paying for trips. It drives me crazy.'

'It'll be better once the baby arrives,' said Louise with confidence. 'It makes you a permanent fixture.'

Natasha wondered if Grania had broken up Alex's marriage. Grania struck her as unsuited to the role of stepmother. As for her own feelings towards Araminta, they were never alone together for long enough to allow her to make a judgement about their relationship. Robert was always chivvying them along to some exhibition or nature walk or church service. As she pondered this, the idea came to her that she should make an effort to do something alone with Araminta.

The conversation had moved on to the choice of obstetrician and maternity nurse and she was happy enough to listen, mainly to Louise, who seemed to know everything there was to know about having a baby in London. Louise finished debating the merits of Australian nannies – overrated in her opinion and expensive compared to East European girls – and moved onto the vexed question of whether the nanny should be allowed to go home at Christmas. 'Of course not! That's exactly when you need her.' She lit up a cigarette and turned her attention back to Natasha, who had been silent during this discussion. 'Are you and Robert going to get married?'

It was an unexpectedly personal question. 'I really don't know. We haven't been going out for that long.'

'How old are you?'

'Thirty-two.'

Louise raised her eyebrows. 'I would have thought Robert was quite a catch. It's not every man who wants a woman in her thirties, you know. Especially the divorced ones. Most of them go for someone twenty years younger.'

Before Natasha had a chance to work out whether she was offended by this turn in the conversation, let alone how to respond to Louise's last comment, Grania picked up the theme. 'The older you get, the harder it is to find a man. I was so lucky to meet Alex; I'd almost given up hope. And I think it's worse in London.'

'Definitely,' agreed Louise. 'When it comes to men the decent ones are married and the rest are mad. I was always suspicious of these forty-something too-good-to-be-true bachelors. They *were* too good to be true, I can tell you. Generally obsessive compulsive.'

'Or workaholic,' added Grania.

'Or underendowed,' concluded Louise. Clearly some thought-association took place in her mind because she went on, 'How many children has Robert got?'

'One. Araminta. She's eight. She lives with her mother.'

'Good!' responded Louise. 'The last thing you want is too much baggage. You end up sharing your man with a house full of foul teenagers who only agree on one thing – they all hate you.'

'You don't get any privacy,' added Grania. 'The kids tell the ex-wife everything . . .'

'And go through your things when you're not there,' continued Louise.

'And then you're pregnant cooking huge meals for them and doing their washing and you can't get any sleep because of the music. I had a friend who had to go into the Priory because of her stepchildren.'

'The strategy,' Louise continued, exhaling smoke, 'is to have a baby of your own as soon as possible. Then you establish control.'

'Control?'

'Over Robert. Once you've had a couple of kids he can't get rid of you. The divorce would be too expensive.'

This was a whole new take on marriage.

Louise must have read her expression. 'Don't look so shocked. When you get into your forties and you've got married girlfriends then you'll realize what marriage is really all about. I know at least three couples who are just hanging on until the kids finish A-levels so they can get divorced and go off with their respective lovers. Personally, I think most couples in London stay together because they can't bear the thought of selling the house.'

They were interrupted by the waiter bringing dessert menus, which all three of them waved away.

Louise leaned forward. 'Natasha, what's the alternative? Being on your own. No! Marriage is far preferable to that. Oh, don't get me wrong. I loved the single life – I had a ball. There is a time and a place for everything. Hanging out in the fifth-floor bar of Harvey Nicks is all well and good. But you don't want to be doing that when you're forty. You don't want to be on your own when all your friends have got married and had babies and London's deserted at the weekend because they're all at their Gloucestershire cottages.'

'Or sharing villas with other couples for holidays,' Grania chipped in.

'Or meeting up for coffee with the other mothers. The golden rule is that *marrieds stick with marrieds*. And if you're not in that club then you're out in the cold.'

Natasha had long been aware of the disadvantages of the single state but Louise made singledom in later life seem terrifying.

Louise gathered steam. 'Whereas if you have a husband you're included. You belong! Life is much easier and simpler. But you have to take your chance. Seize the moment!'

'Does Robert have other girlfriends?' asked Grania.

'No.'

'Don't be so sure,' commented Louise. 'A lot of women would give their right arm to be with a man like Robert. He's good-looking, charming and rich.' She reached over and topped up her own wine glass. 'I think too many women over-analyse everything. They wouldn't recognize a good thing if it came and bopped them on the nose. It's actually very simple, Natasha. Get a ring on your finger as quickly as you can – before someone else pinches Robert.'

Susannah was left to wait in the lecture room alone. She had left home far too early, with the result that she arrived two hours ahead of schedule. She was expected at two o'clock. The intervening time had mostly been spent in the nearby village nursing a cup of stewed coffee at the Gardener's Arms. The barman had asked her where she was heading and she had said Salcombe, but she thought he probably guessed the truth.

She had brought clean clothes, chocolate, books, toiletries, magazines and the post. And that week's copy of *Solicitor's Journal*. It had been a long week. There had been no news from Grange House. She had hoped that James would find some way to circumvent the rules and call her but clearly that had been impossible. Raul had called a couple of times but she found it hard to sustain any conversation with him and he had rung off after a few moments.

A problem shared may be a problem halved – and also a problem halved again and again until all of Cobham knew about it. Lynda had asked if she was all right, and at lunch Justin said bluntly that he knew something was wrong and he would like to help. She said nothing to either of them beyond alluding to James driving her mad. Lynda had rolled her eyes, said don't they all and advised leaving him to stew. She had not contacted her own family. Her mother would panic and say nothing of any value; most of the conversation would be taken up explaining to her what a treatment centre was, and her sister Deborah, ever the nurse, would advise letting the professionals take over.

As for Anthony, it had to be remembered that he was her boss.

At least in this 'family group' she could expect some answers to the questions that went round her head. She was no closer to understanding the events that had brought James to the unspecified crisis and the unexplained intervention of Raul. The patients, Howard had informed her, were having lunch. From behind a fire door she could smell a Sunday roast and pick up a hum of conversation.

After five minutes a couple arrived and nodded at her. Together they made small talk about the traffic. Then a very pretty girl in jeans and a pink corduroy jacket came and took a seat. Maybe her boyfriend was in? For drugs?

The uneasy silence of the waiting room prevailed.

And then a woman accompanied by two girls, both teenagers, sat down next to her.

'Maggie,' the woman said, holding out her hand. Susannah felt an uncomfortable pang. It was Maggie's telephone number that Gina had given her on the day of James's admittance. She had still not called but if this offended Maggie she did not give any indication. Instead she gestured to the two girls sitting to either side.

'This is Sacha – she's twelve – and this is Emma. She's fifteen.'

'Susannah.'

'Oh, you're James's wife.'

This was most unnerving.

'Ed mentioned him,' Maggie added.

Susannah's voice was a little too sharp. 'How?'

Maggie did not seem to notice the tone. 'Ed's been here three weeks, so he can make telephone calls. They've got a payphone in the hallway; only one. It causes some awful rows when the young ones get on it for hours.'

She wanted to ask how James was but it was too disconcerting to ask for details of her own husband from a total stranger. In the event she did not need to ask. Maggie zoomed on. 'James is becoming quite a star. He's really shaken things up. He's volunteered to direct the Reunion Revue. And he's smashed the dinner washing-up record!' She leaned towards Susannah and lowered her voice. 'Between you and me I think James was just what they needed. Too many women in the group. Now it's evened up.'

Revue? Washing up? Too many women?

'Women?' she asked.

'Yep. Up until last week they had six women and four men. Now it's even stevens. Four of each.' She lowered her voice. 'Most of them are alkies, which I prefer, personally. Not that I've got anything against the druggies but you know where you are with an alcoholic, don't you?'

Do you? That had not been her experience. But Maggie had turned away to speak to one of her daughters. It was nearly two o'clock. Susannah wondered if Maggie was leaving it rather late to organize some sort of childcare for her children. And then she realized that the children must stay.

The room was filling up now, twenty-five or so relatives, and she was discomforted to see that she was the only one on her own. Some people seemed to regard it as an excuse for a family outing. Her mood did not improve as Gina opened the door and led in an ambling group which she presumed must be the patients.

James was the last to come in. His features were guarded and he was wearing a sweatshirt she did not recognize with *'Lonsdale'* emblazoned across the front.

At that moment she would have given anything to be alone with him. Not to be on show, like an animal in a zoo, in a room full of people she did not know in a place she hated. But that was impossible. James kissed her on the cheek, sat next to her and before they could say anything to each other Gina started speaking.

'Welcome to Grange House Sunday afternoon family group. A special welcome to any newcomers. This group lasts for one hour. Please switch off mobile telephones. Gary is going to read the preamble.'

A young man in a black tracksuit and a pair of the slip-on sandals usually worn at swimming pools, began. 'I'm Gary. I'm an addict—'

Before Gary could continue further he was interrupted by a low moaning chorus. 'Hello, Gary.'

Clearly Gary was used to this because he ignored the interruption and began to read from the plasticized card he was holding. 'This is a safe place for all to share. All participants undertake to hold in confidence anything they hear in this group. By participating in this group we agree to leave in this room all that we see and hear here.'

Gina smiled. 'Thank you, Gary. And now we'll go round the room.'

Susannah did not know what was more unnerving – the fact that you had to introduce yourself in public, or the observation that Sacha and Emma were indeed staying for the session.

A red-haired girl, possibly no more than twenty-one, in sweatpants and a tight white T-shirt began. 'I'm Alice. I'm a patient here.'

Then the pretty girl in the corduroy jacket: 'I'm Helena. I'm a visitor and Alice's partner.'

On it went around the circle, each person defining themselves by some variety of addiction or by their relationship to a drug addict or an alcoholic. If Susannah was honest, it was the most depressing roll-call she had ever heard. They were moving on, more names and faces, and her turn was rapidly approaching.

'I'm Ed. I'm an alcoholic.'

'I'm Maggie. I'm married to Ed and I'm mum to Emma and Sacha.'

'I'm Emma. My dad's a patient here.'

'I'm Sacha. I'm visiting my dad.'

There was no choice but to join in.

'I'm Susannah. I'm James's wife.' She said this with her eyes fixed firmly on James.

In contrast he seemed to have no problem looking round the room. 'I'm James. I'm an alcoholic.'

She could not believe he had said it. As she breathed harder she saw Gina's eyes on her. 'A special welcome to our newcomers, Susannah and James. And Tom, whose mother has come today.'

'He arrived a day after me,' James whispered. 'My roomie.'

She saw James and Tom exchange glances. Perhaps James had taken Tom under his wing? Tom could not be much more than eighteen or nineteen with a shock of blond hair, a pair of baggy trousers and a T-shirt with some sort of surfer logo emblazoned on it. He reminded her of Matthew. Matthew had calmed down slightly – not enough for them to talk much, but at least enough for her to understand that he knew a great deal more than she had ever realized.

Gina was speaking, inviting them to ask questions. The mood in the room was strained and hushed and few people ventured any comment beyond asking about practicalities. Susannah was struck by Gina's stillness. Personally, she hated silences, and the silences at Grange House were particularly long and heavy. But Gina seemed content for them all to sit. After one such silence, to Susannah's relief, Tom's mother spoke. Susannah admired her courage. Her voice was quavering.

'I just want to say how glad I am that Tom's here, and grateful that you accepted him, and I'd be grateful to hear from any of the patients who've been here a little while if they could tell me how they have found it here. I worry . . .' Her voice trailed off and Susannah could feel the effort that it had taken Tom's mother to speak. She expected Gina to take control and allocate one of the patients to speak but she did not. Instead there was another long pause. She saw out of the corner of her eye that Maggie nudged Ed but he stayed silent. Eventually a woman spoke. Her voice was low, her accent confidently middle class, and she was the only patient wearing make-up and jewellery. She had on a classic-cut brown suede skirt, cream cashmere polo neck and low-heeled leather boots.

'I guess you think this is a catastrophe?'

Tom's mother nodded.

The woman leaned forward. She was striking, her auburn hair pulled back, her green eyes focused on Tom and his mother.

'It's not. I would give my right arm to have another chance at life, to sit where Tom is, aged nineteen, with the chance to do it all again – with what I know now. I came here five years ago. My husband gave me an ultimatum: dry out or he'd leave. So I came in. I thought of it as a holiday away from him and the children and the business and all the things I thought made me drink. And it worked for a while. I stopped for nearly a year. Then we went skiing. One night, in a bar, I decided that I could have a glass of champagne. I thought I was cured, that I could drink normally, that the whole rehab, AA deal was a massive overreaction to a problem that had just got a little bit out of hand. People kept asking me at parties – *Still not drinking, Sandra*? And I thought yes, still not drinking. Poor me. I just didn't get it, you see. That if you are a real alcoholic, if you need to drink, if it's in your blood, then you can never, ever drink like a normal person.

'So I had one glass of champagne. And then another. One is never enough, is it? Of course my husband was worried. I told him that I had it under control, that everyone drinks a bit more on holiday and when we got home I'd scale it down. I tried. I made sure I didn't touch spirits. I never drank before six in the evening. Well, what does that say? If you need to make rules about your drinking then you've probably got a problem. I was obsessed with trying to control it. I was impossible to be around. Especially just before six o'clock, when the kids came home and wanted help with homework and sports kit washed and homework diaries signed and I was just watching the clock waiting for the first drink.

'Someone who isn't an alcoholic can never understand the depth of that craving. Anyhow, this isn't my life story. One day, driving to the off-licence, I had an accident. The supreme irony in all this is that it wasn't actually my fault. Someone ploughed into the back of me. We got out and he smelt my breath and that was it. He called the police and they breathalysed me and took me in. And that was when I had to tell them the kids were at home alone. Aged four, six and eight. So they called social services.

'It went to court and I lost my licence. The other mothers shunned me. After that my drinking took off. And it carried on until my husband filed for divorce. And custody. I lost my husband and my children and my home.

'All I want now is to get a job and a place of my own and to have my kids to stay. At the moment I have supervised access every other weekend. I live with my parents, which is bad enough when you're Tom's age. But I'm forty-four. My husband has a new girlfriend now; they're getting married at Christmas. And she's taking care of my kids.'

Sandra stopped abruptly and her voice broke. Susannah found herself disarmed by Sandra's account. It was strange to hear it from the other side. She knew all about drinking on holiday and dashes to the off-licence and the evening drink timed for mid-afternoon. She knew all about the promises and the assurances that it could be controlled and the heartfelt apologies of the morning after. In spite of the fact that Sandra had self-confessedly brought about her own downfall, in spite of the fact she could have killed someone in her car, Susannah almost felt sorry for her. If nothing else it was impossible not to be impressed by her honesty.

Sandra's speech had the effect of energizing the room. Alice, who it emerged was scheduled to leave that week, began talking about her plans with Helena, which seemed to involve moving to Wales, growing organic vegetables and going to NA meetings. Tom's mother broke down talking about his marijuana habit. Ed and Maggie had a frosty moment when Ed suggested leaving early and Maggie made it clear that they were managing very well without him thank you very much.

And then the hour was up and everyone began leaving the room.

She felt a tightening in her chest as she turned to James, but before she had a chance to speak Ed tapped him on the shoulder. 'Rehearsal six p.m., mate.'

'I'll be there.'

God, more than anything she wanted them to be on their own, just the two of them. 'Can we go somewhere private? Your room?'

They stood awkwardly in the panelled reception hall. James shrugged apologetically. 'We're not allowed up to the bedrooms during the day. Let's go for a walk.' She followed him out into the grounds and they began to walk down the driveway, past the avenue of horse chestnuts and the lake.

'Don't let me forget your laundry.'

'It's done.'

'You did it?'

'Yes.'

It was hard to take this in. James never lifted a finger at home.

'The food?'

'School dinners with a healthy slant.'

There was a pause. 'How are you sleeping?'

'Better than I have for ages.'

'The bathroom?'

'One adapts.'

They continued in this vein, incorporating brief exchanges about her work and Matthew's school, until they reached the gate and turned to the right to walk the perimeter fence of the lawned grounds. Now they were at the furthest possible point from the house and the distance emboldened her.

'James, I want some answers. I think I'm entitled to that!'

'Yes.'

'I mean, what happened? Because it must have been pretty serious for Lloyd-Davies to pay for this.' She gestured towards the Grange House building.

He would not meet her eye. 'Everything is fine now,' he said testily. 'I made a mistake with some papers but fortunately we caught it in time.' She wanted to know more but before she could press him he added, 'Look, I'm not exactly proud of it, OK?'

She could tell from the tone of James's voice that it was useless to continue.

'OK.' It was becoming clear to her that James still required the careful handling and reserves of patience that had been needed when he was drinking.

She could not think of anything further to say. The distance between them appeared to be greater than ever. Sandra's comment in the family group came back to her – that only an alcoholic can understand the cravings. It was true. There was a part of her that could not comprehend precisely why he had been unable to stop – and why he could not drink like a normal person. This line of thinking brought the prospect of AA to mind.

'Have they taken you to an AA meeting?'

'No. I have to wait until after I've written my life story.'

'Will you go?'

'Of course I'll go.' He seemed to pull himself up and cast her an apologetic glance. 'I'm sorry. Look, I'm not exactly thrilled about it myself. It's not something you brag about, is it?'

'I guess not.'

An awkward silence fell between them. They began walking back to the house. A part of her wanted him to walk through the doors, pack his bags and come home with her. The rational part knew that he needed to stay, but she knew it rather than felt it. In truth she didn't understand his drinking or Tom's drug-taking or Sandra's self-destruction. Susannah drank moderately, had never smoked and thought anyone who took drugs was insanely stupid. She couldn't, in a phrase used by Gina that afternoon, 'identify with it'. She decided to try one more time.

'It's very hard for me to understand this, James . . .'

It was an appeal. For a few seconds he was silent. When he spoke it was almost as if to himself and not to her. 'I thought I'd been holding it all together so cleverly – didn't think anyone knew – but the truth was it was obvious to anyone with an ounce of common sense. Raul told me he was taking me off the Saltzman deal. And that was the curious part: I didn't care. I thought I would feel angry and fight. But Raul – the way he confronted me, the things he told me about his own life . . . Anyway, I felt this sense of relief. It was as if he told my story. He said it wasn't going to get any better and I believed him. I think I had been waiting for someone to say that to me. In some way, I had been waiting for that moment for twenty years. He brought me face to face with the consequences of my drinking. No second chances. That's what Sandra was talking about, really – she only stopped when it got too bad.'

'And there's no alternative to this? To leaving your home and your family? And your work? It just seems so . . . extreme.'

James grinned. 'To take a month off? To eat well and rest and not drink? To talk honestly about one's life – to take some responsibility instead of blaming everyone and everything for the way things are? Actually, I think everyone would benefit from a spell in rehab.'

Susannah could think of nothing to say to that. It seemed to sum up some sense that had been growing in her since the day Raul arrived on their doorstep – that she was losing him to these people and soon he would be like them and nothing in their lives would ever be the same again.

# Chapter 8

Grange House
Saturday 1 September

My dear Jasmine,
This is a letter I had never imagined that I would be compelled to write.
It is a letter of apology and, I hope, also a letter by which I may offer you
some explanation of my recent behaviour. I do not, in offering that explanation,
seek your forgiveness. I have no right to ask that of you. I would,
however, like to make it very clear to you that the events of the past week
do not reflect upon you or my feelings for you.

There is no easy way to break the news to you that I am currently an
inpatient at Grange House participating in a twenty-eight-day programme
for addicts and alcoholics. There. I've written the word I have
spent so long denying to myself and others. It is a word, alcoholic, which
fills me with shame and a sense of bewilderment that this has happened
to me.

It is, however, surprising what one can become used to. After one week
I am beginning to feel quite at home. You will be amused to learn that I
can now make my own bed, clean the inmates' kitchen and operate a
washing machine. Other parts of the regime I find less acceptable – the
appalling food, the snoring of my roommates and the compulsory
evening reading of AA literature.

But this is not a letter about me.

I hope to be honest with you. Honesty, it has been impressed upon me,
is a commodity I possess in short supply and apparently have lacked all
my life. I do not like that analysis but I am forced, the longer I spend here,
to accept its veracity.

I am sorry that I left you alone in the restaurant. Events last Monday
moved extremely quickly and it was not possible for me to telephone or

send a message. It must have been extremely upsetting for you and I am truly sorry. My incarceration was suggested by my boss, Raul, of whom I have spoken in the past. It appears that I misjudged the apparently clean-living Raul. He had been aware for some time of the truth about my drinking and had been waiting for the right time to present me with an offer I couldn't refuse – sobriety or the sack.

My shock at his intervention was tempered by a grudging acceptance of the truth of his observations and, most surprising of all, a sense of relief that my secret was up.

There are other secrets, too Jasmine. I did not tell you the unvarnished truth about my work, my home life or, most significant of all, the extent of my drinking. Instead, I presented myself to you as your true friend and diligent helpmate. I was also secretly hopeful of becoming your lover in spite of the fact that I am a married man. That was, quite simply, wrong of me. I put my own selfish desires ahead of your needs and your vulnerable emotional state in the wake of the events with Robert. I was heedless of your best interests and those of my family.

I do not know what the future holds. Lifetime abstinence, albeit presented in the mantra of one day at a time, remains an unappealing prospect. I am not entirely convinced of the universal efficacy of the twelve-step programme. Nor do I see myself attending AA meetings for the rest of my life.

I do accept, however, that I must make changes in my life. I realize that I must place my relationships with other people on a different footing – one based on the principles of honesty, respect and unselfishness.

Jasmine, now I am brought to the part that is so hard to write. I see now that I owe Susannah and Matthew my best shot at becoming the husband and stepfather I always wanted to be. I do know that it would be wrong of me to continue to see you. It is not a question of what I want to do, rather a question of what I need to do for the good of all concerned. I shall always treasure the many happy memories I have of our short time together. In my mind's eye I recall you now, in your yellow dress, your straw hat askew, sitting on the bench by the Serpentine as the sun went down . . .

You are a beautiful, brave and brilliant girl. I wish you well in all your endeavours. Our paths, it seems, were destined to cross only for a brief, sweet time. I am grateful to have known you at all.

With my best wishes,
James

It was an abandonment, albeit of a very modern variety, whereby a married man who might be described as a boyfriend disappears into a rehab centre to be treated for alcoholism. The feeling of loss and confusion was achingly real, however, in that James was gone and she had no means of talking to him or seeing him. Jasmine did not think she would ever see him again and that conclusion was close to being unbearable. She had considered writing back in response to his letter, thought about little else in fact, but she was sensible enough to admit that his did not invite a reply. It was undeniably conclusive in its stated purpose of ending their friendship.

She did not think of it as a friendship. Despite the short time they had known each other, the fact they had not slept together and James's status as a married man, nonetheless their time together bore all the hallmarks of a love affair. A friendship, after all, did not cause one to lie awake night after night trying to frame his face in her mind's eye or capture his voice in her head or hug her pillow, like a teenager, imagining it was his body against hers. A friendship did not cause one to seek out information in a manner that left her slightly embarrassed at her own actions but unable to stop. She had gone to the firm's website and found his listing under partners and had been thrilled to find the short biographical passage accompanied by a corporate photograph. She had put his name into Internet search engines, discarded the thousands of other Agnews, refined her search with the addition of Tellium and been delighted to read him quoted in the national press. She had wondered about the women's names that appeared alongside him. About his secretary, his female clients, his wife. She had realized that she knew so much about his life and so little about his circumstances. How was it possible to know so much about someone's childhood, the unhappiness of their family life – and not know where he lived? How could she have shared his disappointments and dreams and not be able to telephone him on a sunny Sunday afternoon and say, 'Let's go for a walk.'

'I'm here for you,' he had said on more than one occasion. But he wasn't. He was there for her in the short periods they were able to spend together and for as long as his mobile was switched on. Not between Friday evening and Monday morning. She could be run over, desperate in hospital, with no way of speaking to him.

It was baffling. How could she feel so strongly in such a short time? In the end she showed the letter to Joan. Joan put on her half-moon reading spectacles, held it at arm's length and read it with agonizing slowness. They were in the studio. Eventually Joan handed the letter back to her and removed her glasses.

'I don't want to get your hopes up,' she began.

'Don't worry about that,' Jasmine replied morosely.

'My reading of this is that he's had a lot of pressure put on him. By the people at this firm of lawyers. And by his own conscience. James, my dear, is a guilty man. By which I mean he is overcome by feelings of guilt. Now he's trying to atone for his sins by doing what he knows is right. It's a very formal letter, isn't it? Almost as if he felt he had to write it.'

'How can it be right to stay—'

Joan interrupted her. 'Because he's married and like it or not that means Wifey is ahead of you in the queue.'

'Should I write back?'

'Do you want him?'

'Yes!'

'Even though he's a self-confessed alcoholic.'

'I thought about that. And yes, I do. He's admitted he's got a problem and he's doing something about it. I think it's very brave.'

'Did you know about this?'

Jasmine paused. Had she known but not wanted to admit any fact that might spoil the fantasy? 'I noticed he didn't drink when he was with me. I thought that was rather odd, like he was trying too hard. And . . .' She hesitated. 'There were a couple of telephone calls late at night. James had obviously been drinking. He rambled on and on, about all sorts of things – it was very difficult to get any sense out of him – about how much he loved me and how he hated his work and how his life was a—' She stopped short.

'A what?' Joan said impatiently.

'A fuck-up,' Jasmine concluded reluctantly.

'Good Lord!' Joan lit another cigarette. 'Every middle-aged man thinks that.'

'He never mentioned the calls afterwards and neither did I. It was almost as if he didn't remember having called me.'

'I knew an alcoholic once who dried out,' mused Joan. 'Never the same again. Used to be the life and soul of the party, a real hoot. Turned into a dreadful bore and started going to the Brompton Oratory.'

'I do want him,' Jasmine insisted. 'Whatever happens.'

After a few seconds silent thought Joan came back to the matter in hand. 'I would stick to your course: do nothing. I can see that my advice is falling on stony ground. If you absolutely must, write something short. Don't burden him with too much detail! Men can't cope with all that at the best of times and our James is hardly in top form right now. Say that you were sorry to hear of his troubles and you hope he feels much better soon.'

'Shouldn't I say how I feel?'

'No! Saying what you feel all the time is precisely why today's young women get into such a tangle with men. *Letting it all hang out.* No, no, no. Say as little as possible. Let him come to you.'

'He might not.'

'True, he might not. But if that is the case you would never have persuaded him to in any event. He might have come for a roll in the hay but he wouldn't have stayed. Besides, my guess is that Wifey is going to be giving him a hard enough time as it is. He's hardly effusive about her, is he? Your best bet is to stand well back, get on with your life . . . and see how this little drama unfolds.'

The summer with Theo had been planned as a three-week trip and lasted for two months. The deadline for Tabitha and Araminta's return home had been extended so often that the girl on the airline desk knew her by the time she left. They had passed the last days of August shaded from the evening heat on the back porch, watching the sun go down and trying not to count down the days that remained. On the day of her departure she had concentrated on packing and tidying and when Araminta had asked her why they couldn't stay here with Theo she had been unable to answer. It had been left to Theo to say that their house in England was waiting for them and Araminta's friends were expecting her back at school, slipping his hand round Tabitha's waist and pulling her to him as he said confidently that they would be back in no time at all.

She looked out from the kitchen sink over the garden. The end of summer could be detected in the fading of her container plants, which she was amazed to find alive on her return. Lizzy had taken care of that. Somehow, much as she loved her little house, it had lost some of its attraction. It felt lonely. She reached down for Mackie, pressed against her side. Even he seemed to have lost some of his bounce, probably the result of two months being spoilt rotten by her parents.

She took her coffee and went over to the below-stairs office. Mechanically she switched on the computer and waited for the precious Internet connection to be made.

In the emptiness of the house a sense of desolation filled her. She had grown used to being at Theo's side, with his friends and his family, as he introduced her to his world. One weekend they had stolen away, just the two of them, riding his Harley-Davidson up into the Virginian mountains, through the morning mist to the deserted trails. At home they had fallen into a routine. Their bodies had become accustomed to each other in the high wooden bed that stood in the back bedroom of the farmhouse. They had lived as a husband and wife. And by the end of the summer they had known that that was how they were meant to live.

'Marry me,' he had said on their last night, the sun setting as they leaned on the porch rail, the warm, dry air blowing across the fields. 'Marry me,' he repeated softly and earnestly, his hand holding hers. There was an easy inevitability about her answer. 'Yes.' And then they had gone inside to the house that already felt like home.

There was one email, from Theo, sent at ten o'clock his time. The subject line was 'Missing You.'

Hey, you should be here. The corn is as high as an elephant's eye. Actually the soy is about twelve inches. Honey, it's really hard to get away right now. I'll do everything I can to get there for October.

She stopped reading. *October.* She knew he was a farmer and it was harvest time and he had to be there . . . but all the same. At least a month until she would see him again. She read on.

Hey, good luck with your meeting. Let me know what the lawyer says. Everything will be fine. I love you, Theo.
    PS – sorry it's short but I'm falling asleep at the wheel here.

She lowered her head to the desk and felt the hot tears come to her

eyes. In the time since she had met Theo, and in discussions with anyone she could find who had conducted – or was the word endured? –
a long-distance relationship, she had discovered that three weeks apart
was bearable but any longer than that was utterly miserable. If she had
had any idea that her feelings for Theo would weaken when she
returned home then she was confounded to find that they had intensified. She wanted to be by his side in his farmhouse. She wanted to be
his wife.

When she thought of that she could not escape the clench of fear in
her chest that accompanied any thoughts of marrying Theo, moving
to America and taking Araminta with her.

Because she could not take Araminta without Robert's permission.
A solicitor's letter had arrived days before her departure for the sum-
mer making it clear that Robert Agnew's permission would be
required before Araminta could live permanently in America. The let-
ter went on to say, in none too subtle terms, that if she remained with
Araminta in the USA he would launch proceedings under the Hague
Convention for child abduction. Barbara had confirmed he could.
And so today they were to meet to find out what could be done.

She typed a brief reply.

I miss you so much it hurts. We both miss you. Minty went back
to school today and she took her new American school satchel –
the one we got from JC Penney – and she said that she wished
you were there to see her. I took a pic on the camera – I'll email it
later. I'm dashing now to get the train and go and see Barbara.
Fingers crossed. Will call you when I get home. All my love,
Txxxxx

For now she left out the rest. She could have added that she already
knew what Barbara's response would be: that they would have to go to
court, and Robert would fight it every step of the way, and it would
cost her a fortune.

And would Robert win? Could he force her to remain here, for years
to come, kept apart from the man she loved?

She felt bereft without Theo, alone in Stokesham, added to which
she'd had a row with Lizzy that had left her bruised and stunned. It
had come from out of the blue. She had rushed around to see Lizzy on
her first day back, taking presents and chocolate. She had brought her

a small Amish quilt of red, white and blue gingham. As she went round to the back door of the Vicarage she noticed that the tomato plants had wilted. The lawn was in need of cutting and the borders looked as if they hadn't been touched for weeks. Lizzy had let the garden go and Tabitha supposed she could not blame her for that. The new owners were due to move in in just a few days and she imagined it was hard to tend a garden she had loved and was now forced to leave. She felt guilty. Lizzy had spent the summer alone, her time occupied with preparing to leave, most of the village deserted as its well-heeled residents left en masse for European sunshine. Lizzy had not gone on holiday, she had explained.

'Frankly, I couldn't face going on my own.'

Araminta and India were quickly playing upstairs amid the packing cases and suitcases and labelled cardboard boxes, delighted to rummage in the attic contents that Lizzy had decanted onto the landing.

Lizzy brought out coffee.

'So, as I was saying. I've got a box in a cul-de-sac and I'm going to have to give half of this away,' she gestured at the house to imply its contents, 'if we're going to have any hope of fitting in.'

Tabitha did her best to sound positive. 'Whatever happens you'll handle it.'

Lizzy did not respond. There was a distinct pause. 'Well,' Lizzy said severely, 'I have to say I was getting quite worried about you.'

'I sent emails,' Tabitha said, slightly confused by Lizzy's tone.

Lizzy put down her coffee cup. 'That's not the same, is it? I mean, he could be typing those.'

'What?'

'He could write them. On his computer. So it looked as though you were sending them?'

Tabitha's consideration of the bizarre notion of Theo forging emails to Lizzy was overtaken by the realization that Lizzy's tone belied a simmering resentment. Tabitha's instinct was to diffuse the situation. 'I'm sorry. I should have phoned. It was just that my plans changed when I was out there.'

'I was worried!' There was a pause and then a brighter tone. 'Anyhow, the good thing is you're back now. And Araminta's back at school and everything's fine.'

Tabitha was so tempted to say nothing. To let the coolness thaw. But she would have to tell Lizzy sooner or later. Why was it that breaking her good news filled her with trepidation?

'Actually, Theo's asked me to marry him.'

To her credit, Lizzy was not a hypocrite. She made no effort to look pleased – not even to the extent of a faked smile or a forced *congratulations*. Her expression, and her voice, conveyed cold disapproval. 'Oh. Well, it's very sudden isn't it?'

'Not really . . .'

'Tabitha! You hardly know the man. He could be anyone!'

'He's not anyone. He's Theo. I know him very well.'

Lizzy's voice was irritated. 'Tabitha. It's a holiday romance. You've been out there for a holiday. How can you possibly know him?'

Why was she justifying herself? Whatever the reason she felt an urge to persuade Lizzy to change her mind. 'We've spent a lot of time together. And talked. And emailed . . .'

'Emails!' Lizzy snorted. 'That's hardly meaningful communication. Look at these Internet dating sites. Half the men on there are married. But they don't say that, do they? They create a . . . a *persona*, that's the word. To lure you in!'

'I don't think this is the same thing at all. I met Theo here, at Patrick's wedding, remember?'

'Then he went back and you've seen each other for a few days at a time since then. I'm not denying he's very charming, but he could be anyone. He could be putting on an act. And,' she added darkly, 'it could all change once he's got you out there.'

'Out there?'

'In America. In this small town. Cut off.'

'It's really not like that,' protested Tabitha faintly.

'How do you know?' Lizzy seemed to be getting into her stride now and Tabitha had the sense of being overwhelmed. 'A few weeks . . . how can you get an idea of a place – or a person – from that? What do you know about him?' Lizzy immediately went on to answer her own question. 'What he's told you! He's single. He lives on a farm.' Somehow Lizzy's tone indicated that both of these attributes were somehow undesirable. 'Of course he wants you! You're quite a catch. Young, good job, your own house. I dare say he's worked out that you'd sell that when you went over or rent it out; either way that would be a tidy sum.'

It crossed Tabitha's mind that Lizzy seemed to have given far more thought to her financial circumstances than Theo had ever done. She felt riled. 'He's never asked for a penny.'

'Of course not. That's to be expected. He's not going to show his hand until you're over there. And it will be too late then!'

Tabitha began to rally. Lizzy had stepped over the line of friendly concern into territory that was altogether more personal. 'I understand that you're concerned for me. But I know Theo and I know everything will be fine.'

Lizzy's face darkened. 'How can you possibly know that? How much time have you actually spent together? A couple of months?'

'It's much more—'

'It's not real, Tabitha. I'm not blaming you. I can understand why you feel drawn to him. You're vulnerable, it's all very flattering and I'm sure he's very attractive. But you have to keep your feet on the ground. What about Araminta? Uprooting her, taking her halfway round the world – it would be one thing if you were single, but you're a mother.'

'I know that!'

'Besides, what's Robert going to say?'

'I have to ask for his permission—'

'Which he won't give.'

'And if he refuses, which I agree he probably will, I'll go to court and get the court to give permission instead.'

'A court case!' Lizzy seized on the point. 'Think about the stress of that, and the cost – Araminta caught up in the middle of it, a little innocent!'

Privately Tabitha shared these gloomy thoughts but she was not about to admit that to Lizzy.

'And frankly,' Lizzy continued belligerently, 'you can't blame Robert. He's bound to be concerned.'

That was too much. Tabitha felt the colour rise in her cheeks. 'Robert's only concern is to keep me here under his thumb! He sees Araminta once every three weeks. He treats her like a . . . like an accessory, not a child: parading her to church and social events and dragging her round the latest exhibitions lecturing her. I can't let Robert govern my life.'

'Are you sure you're not doing this to get away from him? It wouldn't be surprising, would it? Escaping Robert's clutches to go to the other side of the world.'

'No! And it is not the other side of the world. It's an eight-hour plane journey!'

Lizzy sat back. 'Well, I can see you're very determined. I just worry about you. I worry that in a year's time you're going to turn up here, Araminta in tow, all your money gone and I'm going to be picking you up off the floor.'

'Lizzy—'

'Maybe you want friends around you who tell you what you want to hear. I'm not one of those. I think you're making a mistake, Tabitha. A big mistake. And it's not just your life you'll be ruining – it's Araminta's as well.'

It really was intolerable. She could feel a white heat rising inside her and she was perilously close to saying things she might very well regret in the morning. There was something wrong here but she couldn't tell what. Lizzy's concern was understandable, her observations not without justification and her stated intention one of friendly concern. So why did she feel so assaulted?

She struggled to stay in control of her emotions. 'Look. I can understand your point of view—'

'Not enough for it to make any difference.'

Tabitha was determined to keep to the point. 'I can understand your point of view. But really, I know what I'm doing. I know Theo. And I love him. And soon he'll be coming over and you'll have a chance to see that for yourself.'

'That's another thing. I've never had the opportunity to say more than hello to him. When he comes over the two of you are holed up in your cottage together . . .'

Tabitha saw the expression on Lizzy's face change from belligerence to one that could be best described as petulant. And then it dawned on her that Lizzy was jealous.

It wasn't supposed to be that way. One's girlfriends were supposed to share the secrets of relationships, unite in the face of the vagaries of men, and provide uncritical, unlimited emotional support. In Lizzy's eyes Theo was undoubtedly the enemy. It was hard to know what to say.

'We could have a dinner party . . .' Tabitha ventured.

'I'm the gooseberry fool?'

'No! A nice dinner party. I can invite Patrick and his wife and one of his friends and you'll get a chance to talk to Theo and see that he's terribly nice and kind.'

Lizzy sniffed. 'I hope so. I really do.'

Tabitha picked up her handbag. 'We ought to get home. Araminta will be jet-lagged.' She looked down and saw that she had not touched her coffee, but she was in no mood to stay. She had heard quite enough. She called out to Araminta that they were leaving and, as soon as she had changed her out of her dressing-up clothes, drove home to the peace and quiet of the cottage.

It was all Paul could do not to throw the telephone against the wall. This was becoming a daily call and as such a habit, unlike his many others, that he was anxious to break. Elaine, at Sears Finer, London's largest photographic agency, did not sound any more optimistic today than she had in the weeks and months since the story had broken.

'There's nothing I can do, Paul,' she said. 'Soundwave don't feel it's the right time to have you on the project.'

Paul lit a cigarette and sat forward on his dark-brown Bill Amberg leather couch. The flat in Shad Thames overlooked Tower Bridge but today the view of the river and the City of London did nothing to inspire him. The white walls were covered in Hockneys and Brandts and his very good collection of later Beatons but right now it felt like a cell. He was desperate to get out.

'Jesus! Can't you persuade them, Elaine? Doesn't twenty years at the top of the business count for anything?'

'Paul . . .' Her voice was hesitant. 'It's an image thing. The whole shoot is based around names. And yours, at the moment—'

'Fuck them and fuck their lousy shoot! Soundwave. Who are they to lay down the law?'

'They're—'

'All right! It was a rhetorical question, darling.'

He knew full well who Soundwave were – Europe's largest mobile telephone company, with an advertising budget to match. Soundwave had originally commissioned him to photograph the top names in English football for a series of advertisements to be run in magazines and on billboards across Europe. That was until the *News of the World* had put paid to that job, and a shoot in Dubai for *GQ*, and the three-year contract that he had been about to sign with the English National Ballet.

'Paul.' Elaine's voice was cajoling. 'You've just got to sit it out. Is there any news?'

'There is no news because there is no story!' He felt as though he would explode with frustration. 'The police say, off the record, that they'll take no action. Serena says she won't press charges. Not that she bloody denied it. Saving the story for her autobiography, no doubt.'

From the pause that followed he deduced that Elaine was taken aback by this analysis. 'So how did the story get out?' she enquired.

'I have my suspicions.'

He wasn't going to go into the details with Elaine. He made his excuses and rang off. More than likely he would sound paranoid. Even to his own ears it sounded an unlikely scenario – *Robert Agnew, my own PR, exposed me to the* News of the World *because I gave a reference to his ex-girlfriend.* Robert hadn't even troubled himself to deny it. Worst of all it had been Paul himself who had told Robert the whole Serena story. Paul had been one of Robert's first clients more than ten years ago, when Robert left to start his own agency, taking half of his employer's clients with him. Back then, Robert had been full of gratitude for Paul's valuable business. They had had a drunken dinner at Blake's and the subject had turned to girls. But Robert, Paul now realized on reflection, had not been so very drunk. Robert had not talked about girls. It was only much later that Paul realized he was the one who had talked. Robert had listened.

Susannah's breakdown, as she thought of it subsequently, came when she was least expecting it: at work, on a Friday afternoon. It was not a breakdown in the classic, medical sense. She did not collapse in a state of incapacitated exhaustion. She fell just short of that. Maybe it was the thought of the long drive to Grange House that weekend, or overwork from setting up the lettings department, or the tension of living with Matthew's unremitting surliness. Whatever the reason, her natural restraint deserted her and she could not contain her wretchedness any longer.

It was triggered by something so inconsequential. Anthony had just spread out a row of carpet swatches, two-inch squares of various shades, on her desk. It was the end of the day and they were alone in the office.

He pointed to the darkest of the six squares. 'I think the green would be perfect. I'll get the downstairs done at the same time.' He gestured towards the floor which, now she came to notice it, was worn and faded. But her mind was not on the subject. She had been reminded of the last time she had chosen carpet, for the Cobham house. She had spread out the swatches on the kitchen table. They were still living in Fulham, still in love with the idea of moving. Cal Doyle offered purchasers a full interior design service. You chose the finish of your house – not just the carpet but all the paint colours and tiles, kitchen units and countertops, right down to window catches and door handles. James had wanted cream carpet; she had argued that it was totally impractical and they had settled on oatmeal beige which, when it was laid, neither of them liked very much. James said from time to time that they should have chosen the cream and employed a man to steam clean it.

As she thought back it seemed such a very long time ago, in a different world with a different man – a man, her husband, who was gone from her in every sense, whom she now saw once a week or spoke to in short, awkward telephone calls, his words sporadically drowned out by the footsteps and loud laughter of those passing him on the public telephone in the corridor.

Misery overwhelmed her and she was powerless against the feelings that flooded through her: shock and bewilderment, grief and loneliness. She cried for the lost life she had known, a life that was far from perfect but was at least, for all its flaws, predictable and private.

She cried with unselfconscious abandon and she thought maybe she was shaking and right then she didn't care that she was in the office, with Anthony, because there was nothing whatsoever she could do to halt the tide of emotion.

'Susannah.' His voice was full of concern.

'I'm fine . . .'

'What on earth is it?'

'I can't tell you . . .' she began to say and then it seemed so ridiculous to try to keep the secret any more, at least not from Anthony, who was utterly discreet and whom, she suddenly understood, was the one person she could trust.

'It's James . . .' she managed to say.

He nodded and held up a hand. 'One moment.' He pulled Lynda's chair over to her desk and sat down beside her.

'Now, tell me all about it from the start,' he said authoritatively.

'It's James,' she began. 'He's in a treatment centre for alcohol abuse.' Her voice broke.

To his credit, Anthony, whom she had always thought of as being unworldly in his outlook, did not look surprised. 'I see.'

His steady demeanour began to calm her. It was rather like talking to the old family doctor, who one realizes, in the course of an intimate conversation, is not the naïve innocent one had imagined him to be.

She told him everything, beginning with Raul's surprise arrival, the ultimatum to James, the trip to Grange House and her subsequent visit.

Anthony frowned at points but did not interrupt.

She talked on and on, sometimes jumping from one event to another out of sequence, adding recollections of James drinking, her narrative interspersed with irrelevant detail – the ghastly watery cappuccino supplied by the Grange House coffee machine, the kind gardener there who paused to chat to her – and then she unburdened her misgivings about the Grange House regime and their advice to involve Matthew. Emboldened, she told him that James was expected to go to AA.

'For ever. For the rest of his life. Maybe I should be more broad-minded but it's bloody hard to take it all in. And I did call one of the other wives, Maggie, but it was impossible to get a word in edgeways.'

He nodded. His voice, when she finally finished and he spoke, contained an unmistakable note of hurt in it. He looked at her intently. 'Why didn't you tell me this before? I feel dreadful, burdening you with this extra project. I would never have dreamed . . .' He held his hands up.

'No.' She rushed to reassure him. 'I'm glad. Really. If I didn't have my job I don't know what I'd do.'

And in that statement there existed the implicit admission that she did not have her marriage and she began to cry again.

Anthony reached out and squeezed her shoulder. 'There, there.' It was a wonderfully old-fashioned and strangely comforting thing to say and it made her want to laugh.

He smiled too. 'Well, I'm glad I've brought a smile to your face.' He continued to hold her shoulder. 'Susannah, I think you are a marvel. God knows how you've put up with it! My heart goes out to you. James is a very lucky man, even if he doesn't realize it. As for these people he's got tangled up with . . . I've no doubt that they're very well-intentioned, but I think you're right to be cautious.'

'Do you?'

'Absolutely. Who are they? What are their qualifications?'

She blew her nose.

Anthony continued steadily. 'At the end of the day – and I have every sympathy for James – at the end of the day, one can make a mountain out of a molehill.'

She felt a surge of relief derived from listening to someone normal, who spoke like a real person, using ordinary sentences and not in strung-together therapy clichés.

Anthony continued. 'There was a man who worked for me once, couldn't get a stroke of work out of him after lunchtime. I tried to help him. In the end he lost his driver's licence and I had to let him go. He tried AA—'

'Did he drink again?'

Anthony seemed lost in his recollection. 'It was a sad story. He gassed himself in his car in Oxshott Woods.' He saw her expression and quickly returned to the present. 'Years ago,' he said hastily. 'I think he had other problems. The point is,' he added rapidly, 'James clearly needs help of some variety. Personally, I've always stuck by the motto *everything in moderation*—'

'So have I!' she cut in.

'But what James needs at the moment is his business.' He rubbed her forearm for a moment. 'Susannah, you need to look after yourself. For better or worse the fact is James has disappeared and left you to get on with it. I think you should take a few days off.'

'No! Really,' she protested, 'I'll be fine.'

He looked at her doubtfully. 'This is what we'll do.' She could tell from his tone that there was no point arguing. 'You're going to take tomorrow off. Do you have to go to this Grange place on Sunday?'

'Yes,' she said dutifully.

'Then you need to have a rest. It's a long drive.' He stood up. 'I'm going to take you home.'

'I'm fine . . .' she began to protest.

He held up his hand. 'No. I'm going to drive you home. You're in no state to drive. I'll pick you up tomorrow and we'll come and get your car.'

She began to wonder what Lynda and Justin would say.

As though he had read her thoughts, he said, 'As far as the others are concerned, you had a flat battery.'

He thought of everything. It was such a relief not to have to think at all.

'You need to have an early night,' he went on.

They went out to the car and Anthony opened the passenger door for her as he always did and in the smooth quietness of the car she sat back, feeling eased by her disclosures to Anthony and restored by his quiet attentiveness.

When he pulled into the driveway, she could see the glimmer of the kitchen light through the glass panel of the front door. Matthew must be home.

He turned in his seat. 'I'm very glad you told me this. I hate to think of you soldiering on by yourself.'

She turned to him, feeling suddenly vulnerable. 'I . . . I'm sorry . . .'

'Don't say another word,' he cut in, his tone mock-stern. 'I think it's a miracle you've kept going this long. Susannah, when my father died I bottled everything up, kept it all in, concentrated on running the business. I can tell you it wasn't the right thing to do.' He stopped and in the silence she understood that there had been no one to talk to. 'That's why I keep the car.' He seemed lost in thought.

'The Rolls?' she asked.

'Yes.' He gave a self-conscious smile. 'You probably think I have delusions of grandeur. But it was my father's and every time I think about selling it I just can't do it. When I drive it I feel the old man's sitting there next to me.'

She was moved to reach out and touch his hand. 'I think you're right to keep it.'

He looked out of the side window and up at the house, then back at her. His voice was serious. 'I think you're a marvellous woman.' He paused. 'And I can tell you that if I had a beautiful wife like you, I certainly wouldn't leave her alone. Not for a single day.'

They were late on account of having sex ten minutes before their cab was due. Months together had not dimmed Robert's sex drive. He wanted sex every day and with an ever-greater intensity. He had just taken a shower and approached Natasha in the bedroom as she was zipping up her skirt, placing his hand over hers as she was about to fasten the top hook and eye.

'No! We haven't got time,' she protested.

He ignored her, leading her across the room, and pushed her onto the bed. 'You know you want it,' he insisted. He was already pulling off his bathrobe. For a man nudging forty he had a natural muscularity and a relentless libido. It still turned her on to know the strength of the desires that remained well hidden. Robert was not the type to flirt with waitresses or read *Playboy* magazine. His sexuality had a very private, secret quality to it. She was not complaining. It made her feel especially wanted.

He took the tie from his bathrobe and looped it quickly and dextrously around her wrists. He liked to tie her up. This penchant had been revealed a couple of weeks after they had begun to have sex. As he tied her up he said that it was time for her to do as she was told. He liked her to remain quiet. Sometimes he would tie her up and leave her for a few minutes. Once he had returned with a camera.

'No!' she had protested. She hated the thought of compromising pictures falling into the wrong hands. Wordlessly, he had put the camera down and left it on the bedside table. A few nights later they had got drunk and she had picked it up and snapped him. He had given her a dry smile and taken it from her.

'Natasha, you look very seductive.'

Her speech was slightly slurred. 'You can't get them processed! I'll be recognized!'

He had sighed. 'Darling, it's a digital camera. I can develop the pictures at home on a print maker. No one will ever see them.'

That had reassured her.

'You look great.' He took a picture.

'Where do you keep them?' she asked drunkenly.

'Behind lock and key. In the cupboard.' He indicated the bedroom cupboard. She felt reassured. It wasn't a big deal. What did it matter anyway? They were private pictures. Robert had no interest in parading his girlfriend's naked pictures in public. He wasn't the type.

Besides, she liked the feeling that he was in control. She liked the unpredictability, the excitement of not knowing what he was going to do next. Sex with Robert was like going up a level. Everything else seemed pedestrian. Admittedly, there were other things she was less sure about: his predilection for oral sex, though that was hardly unusual, and his desire to cane her. She had drawn the line at that.

'It bloody hurts!' she protested.

He had stopped. 'I'll just have to persuade you of its merits.'

None of it mattered when he was inside her. He fucked her so well, with an energy and a strength that took her breath away, that she was in thrall to him. He was difficult, prone to flares of temper, intent on having the last word and controlling to a degree that could be exasperating. But he was never dull, always capable of surprising her, and without exception he always left her wanting more.

They did not have time to speak properly until they were in the cab. They were expected at six thirty at a client's Dover Street gallery for the opening of a new exhibition and it was six fifteen already.

'How was work?' she asked.

'Bloody awful. Those idiots can't do anything unsupervised.'

*Those idiots* was the way Robert habitually referred to his staff.

He sat back in his seat as the cab whizzed across Wandsworth Bridge. 'I need to watch them every second of the day. Then I've had my mother on the telephone three times. It seems James has booked himself into rehab. She wants to know if I can rescue him.'

She was shocked. 'Rescue him?'

'I pointed out that he's in rehab, not prison, and we don't need a helicopter to spring him out.'

The cab driver did a sharp right turn and picked up speed past the entrance to the Harbour Club.

'Is he OK?'

'Perfectly fine. To placate my mother I spoke to the head counsellor, who seems to have it all under control. I'm only surprised it hasn't happened earlier.'

Clearly Robert's assessment of James's drinking had been spot on. 'Are you going to visit him?' she enquired. She had not much liked James but even so it must be an awful situation to find oneself in.

Robert gave her a surprised glance. 'I'm not holding my breath for an invitation. Meanwhile my accountant's hounding me for the figures for my tax return. And that bloody Winter woman has been on the phone twice today bending my ear about her baby lunch.'

The cab had now ground to an abrupt halt in Townmead Road amid the high-rise blocks of luxury riverside housing. Robert looked forward to try to make out the obstruction but as was so often the case there was no obvious reason for the jam.

Natasha shifted uncomfortably. 'Oh, I meant to tell you. I can't do it.'

He looked at her sharply. 'What do you mean, you can't do it?'

'Robert, I'm working. In Marbella.'

'You didn't say anything about that.'

'Yes, I did! I told you it was in the diary and I'd try to change it. But I can't.'

He clearly wasn't happy about it. 'The programme sounds very hackneyed. I think you should drop it.'

'Drop it! It's a good opportunity,' she protested.

Robert sighed. 'All those decamp disaster programmes have had their day. Next you'll be doing a daytime interior design programme. *How we transformed this Croydon bungalow into a Maharajah's Temple on a budget of ten pence.* Think, Natasha. You need to wait for something more cutting-edge. And if you could do that damned lunch it would be an enormous help to me. Darling, I know it's a bore but I'm an inch away from getting the Harrold-Winter contract. The money would be a help.'

She did feel guilty about not helping him – he always did so much to help her – but she wasn't going to give way. For once, she didn't agree with Robert's judgement. It *was* a good job. 'I'm sorry. I can't. Tell Louise I'll help her the next time.'

He looked as if he was about to say more. She could tell he was cross. But then he turned to her resignedly. 'Very well. As you wish. I only hope it's worth it.'

The débâcle at Lizzy's had prepared Tabitha for the possibility that her parents would not be unequivocally pleased at the news that she was going to marry Theo. Appropriately, the sky was darkening in the mid-afternoon as dark rainclouds gathered. They sat outside, on the small back patio of her parents' house, eating a tea of egg and cress sandwiches and chocolate marshmallow teacakes. She had not yet broached the subject of her engagement. She had left her engagement ring at home, which was stupid because at least it would have brought the subject straight to her mother's attention, but after the fracas with Lizzy she had decided to stay in control and raise the topic at the time of her choosing.

The garden of her parents' 1930s semi-detached brick house in Dartford was immaculate, stretching back some 120 feet to where her father's greenhouse and the compost heap marked the boundary. When these houses came to be sold it was the back gardens that attracted buyers, families who wanted space for their children to play now that the streets were no longer safe. Her parents had been talking about selling the house since her father's retirement three years ago but nothing had come of their discussions. Dartford, it had transpired, held a stronger attachment for her mother than the rose-covered cottage by the coast of her father's dreams. Her mother liked the shops and the neighbours and often said that they had too many possessions to be able to move anywhere at all.

Finally, Tabitha had put her cup down and plunged into a slightly garbled but determinedly upbeat explanation of the wonderful summer with Theo, his excellent prospects and his carefully considered proposal of marriage.

'We thought this was coming,' sniffed her mother in response. 'You might have told us sooner.'

Her mother, in Marks and Spencer jeans with an elasticated waist, and a yellow T-shirt embroidered with a lemon tree motif, leaned forward, took the lid off the Portmeirion teapot and gave the murky remains a stir. Her father had always insisted that tea should be strong enough to stand the spoon up in.

'I've only been back a week!' Tabitha protested. 'And I wanted to tell you myself.'

Her mother threw her a petulant look. 'I don't see why you couldn't have come sooner! And we would have liked to see Minty. It's been all summer, after all. Not that we shall be seeing much of her from now on.'

Tabitha sighed inwardly. 'Yes you will! You can come over – and we'll come back.'

'You say you will,' said her mother darkly. 'Why didn't you bring her?'

Tabitha felt herself getting irritated. 'I *had* to let her go to Robert for the weekend. And the last week of the holidays. He hasn't seen her all summer.'

Her mother was about to respond when her father cut in, 'And what does he say about all this?'

'I have to ask him formally for permission to take Araminta. Barbara wrote to him last week.'

'You have been busy,' sniffed her mother.

'We haven't heard back,' Tabitha continued, determined not to be sidetracked. Privately, she always found that the most difficult time – the period of waiting to see what Robert would do next. She decided not to mention the possibility of a court case.

'He might agree,' said her father. 'It's a wonderful opportunity for Minty, whatever he says.'

Tabitha exchanged glances with her father. She guessed that he had thought ahead to Robert's inevitable opposition. Her father betrayed no trace of his deduction. Instead, he asked brightly, 'And where will Araminta go to school?' Education had always been the cause closest to her father's heart.

Tabitha was glad of the change of subject. 'To the local school. It's very close. There's a school bus and it's got a great reputation.'

Her mother sighed. 'But what about the gangs? And the drugs? And the shootings?'

'Mum. It's an elementary school for little children. And it's the Virginian countryside. They don't have gangs.'

'Well, just make sure it's safe before you send Minty there.'

'She's a clever girl; she'll be fine,' assured her father in something of a non sequitur, given that the issue at hand was drug-related homicide.

True to form, her mother asked the inevitable next question. 'And what about the wedding?'

That was the question Tabitha had been dreading. She began her prepared explanation, the one she had been rehearsing all the way down. 'We want to have two weddings. We thought the proper wedding here and then a blessing in the States.'

'What do you mean, a proper wedding?'

'The actual getting married.'

'You'll have to go to a registry office.'

'We were thinking about Leeds Castle.'

'That's not a registry office!'

'No, but you can get married in all sorts of places now.'

'And what does his mother think of that?'

She had no idea. 'I'm sure she'll be happy whatever we decide.'

'Hmm.'

There followed a purposeless discussion about the rules governing divorcees getting married in church. Her mother did not agree with church remarriage for divorced people but thought an exception should be made for cases like her own daughter's. They went on to discuss who would be invited and what a lot of work it would be and how second weddings should be smaller.

Her father said, 'There'll be lots of time to work out the details.' He had clearly had enough wedding talk. He looked at the dark sky. 'We need to get on with clearing out these bedding plants before it rains.' He gestured to the neat beds that bordered the close-cut lawn. 'Your mother wants winter pansies.'

'You always have winter pansies,' Tabitha protested.

'We're putting violas in the tubs,' countered her mother.

Her father gave a slight smile. 'And daffodils at the back of the beds.'

Tabitha rolled her eyes. 'No change there, then.'

Her mother's ideas of garden design remained resolutely unchanged despite the hours she spent watching home makeover programmes.

Her father gave Tabitha a hard stare. 'Do you want some cuttings?'

Tabitha took her cue. 'Love some!'

He wanted to speak to her alone. She followed him down the round zigzagged paving stones that marked a way through the lawn to the greenhouse. Amid the fading tomatoes and cucumbers and the stacks of pots and seed trays, the presence of a radio and thermos flask gave the lie that this was solely a functional room. Her father reached for his sharp knife.

'So, what's happening?'

It was now that the real conversation could begin. Tabitha composed herself. 'Barbara's written to Robert formally asking for his permission and offering contact – that's what they call access now – in the holidays.'

Her father had begun expertly to take cuttings from an assortment of fuchsias lined up in front of him.

'And if he refuses I have to go to court and get a court order.'

'He will refuse, you know,' her father said gently.

He had picked up the 'if'. Her father read her so well, could see the part of her that hoped against all experience that Robert would agree and saw that her best interests lay in facing reality.

'I'm afraid,' her father added reaching for rooting powder, 'that the best indicator of future behaviour is past behaviour.' He looked up at her. 'Tabs. Are you sure about this? If you go to court against Robert, if you want to take Minty to America, he'll fight you every step of the way. And we know he doesn't fight by the rules.'

The fear returned, rising up inside her and clenching at her chest. 'I'm trying not to think about it. I keep hoping—'

'That he'll be reasonable.' He finished her sentence for her. 'No. Robert will never be reasonable. His sort aren't.'

She looked down at the dusty floor. 'I don't have any choice, Dad.'

There was a silence while her father thought, interrupted by the sound of raindrops falling on the greenhouse roof. She looked at him, his brow furrowed in concentration, his hands still dextrous and confident. Her mother seemed to age every time she saw her but her father was unchanging. She so wanted his approval in that moment. At last he spoke.

'Theo loves you?'

'Yes.'

'He'll look after you both?' Her father put down his knife. He spoke slowly. 'It seems to me that if you have found someone who loves you and will look after you then there's really very little else to be said.'

She threw her arms around him. She was ten years old again and her father was the most important person in the world. She would have gone ahead without his blessing but life was one hundred times better with it. He was the man who had taught her to ride a bicycle and swim across the pool and master long division when she had returned home in tears from school convinced she could never understand how to carry the leftover number. It was her father who had inspired her love of reading, taken her to exhibitions and to the theatre when money allowed. Her father listened to her, took seriously her half-baked teenage view of the world, encouraged her to believe that she had a place in it. Her father had given her a strong confidence, which Robert had done his best to destroy and had certainly dented. If he felt for her leaving he would never say so. He loved her enough to want only her happiness.

'We'll do everything we can. Of course, we live on a pension—'

She interrupted him to cut off the awkwardness in his voice. 'That's no problem. I can manage.' She knew instinctively that her father was embarrassed that he could not do more for her. The truth was that paying her legal fees was in the clutch of thoughts that preoccupied her at four in the morning.

'I'll talk to your mother about the wedding,' he sighed. 'Don't worry – she'll come round. In the meantime, I'll tot up our Air Miles . . .'

She knew he wanted to say more. She could feel him struggling for the words as the rain fell more heavily onto the greenhouse roof. Eventually he said, 'Tabitha. Life is very short; the time passes so quickly. If you love each other and you can make a good life together, go to him – and don't let anyone stand in your way.' In his voice she heard regret for opportunities missed and choices made. He turned away and walked towards the greenhouse door to go back to her mother, waiting for him in the house.

The rain was falling hard on the M40 into London and the traffic even at three p.m. was backing up into London. She should have left earlier. She wanted to get back and see Araminta, if only for a few minutes, before Tabitha arrived to collect her. She wouldn't mind getting a glimpse of the ex-wife, either – Robert always made sure she was well out of the way when Tabitha came to collect Araminta.

Natasha had resolved to make more of an effort with Robert's daughter. After all, she and Robert were all but living together. He had been rather lukewarm about her initial suggestion of taking Araminta to the cinema without him – there was no reason why they shouldn't all go, he had protested – but she was determined to show Robert that she was a sensible and capable person. She next suggested that he and Araminta came with her today to her mother's birthday lunch but Robert had pointed out that it was the Sunday School autumn term picnic that day, to welcome everyone back after the summer holidays, and that as Treasurer he needed to be at St Luke's. So she had gone on her own to Gerrards Cross.

Her mother, after her marriage to Don four years ago, had moved into St Hugh's Drive, a cul-de-sac of some ten houses, characterized by perfect lawns, gleaming cars and baseball hoops for the families with children. Theirs was a four-bedroom house with white-painted wood cladding to the top floor which gave it a seventies appearance. One of her mother's first changes on moving in was to change the original horizontally grooved garage door, painted olive green by the previous owners, to an altogether more classic nine-panelled design which Don had painted white. Her mother liked the outside paintwork to be wiped down with a damp rag dipped in a bucket of soapy water every week. Her mother had always had good taste or at least the ability to copy others who possessed it. Privately, Natasha considered the house far too big for two people who never had family to stay. Don had a daughter, Susan, who lived as her mother put it 'Up North' and appeared rarely to visit.

Her mother, in a navy-blue trouser suit and cream silk blouse, had greeted her distractedly, commented approvingly that Natasha had lost a couple of pounds and led her through to the conservatory where she served the three of them coffee. The conservatory had been added the previous year and had taken up most of her mother's attention for a full six months.

'We're going to the Bull at Bisham,' her mother announced, opening her present, a Royal Worcester serving dish to add to her set. Natasha could have predicted the choice of restaurant. Actually, she rather liked the Bull at Bisham. It stood unmarked by changes in fashion of any kind. The Bull at Bisham served schooners of sherry, pâté and whitebait, roast beef and Yorkshire pudding and had not made any significant change to the menu, or the dessert trolley, for over thirty years.

'Very nice, dear. Thank you,' she said, setting the dish down. 'Isn't that nice, Don?'

'Very nice, dear.'

Don, in shirt and Royal Artillery tie – her mother had pointed that out on more than one occasion in the past – was always courteous to Natasha and complimentary about her latest programme but beyond that Natasha struggled to find very much to say to him.

Her mother was describing their recent holiday. 'Cruising in the fjords. That's Norway, dear.'

'I know; I've been.'

'And we met a very nice couple; he's a retired dentist. They live in Cuckfield – that's in Sussex – and it's their fortieth anniversary next month and we're going down for a party which is really very nice because we haven't known them for very long.' Her mother took a sip of coffee. 'Of course, I think they've got money. He was a private dentist, one of those who left the NHS and dentists don't do badly. I think she was his receptionist. So he would have been able to pay her for that too and get the tax back . . .'

And so it went on about the other people on the cruise and their friends Patrick and Jean, with whom they were supposed to go to Corfu – but Jean had called to cancel because Patrick had to have an angioplasty – but they were going to go ahead anyway and in the meantime they had just booked to go to Venice next March for Don's birthday. More followed about the Gerrards Cross Theatre Club – they'd passed up on *Journey's End* – and ballroom dancing every Sunday and the WI which her mother still wasn't sure about but went occasionally if there was a good talk. In the lull that fell while her mother searched for the local newspaper from three weeks back which showed the WI group photographed with a man whose name her mother had forgotten – he had sailed round the world despite having a wooden leg – Natasha rallied herself to involve Don.

'Are you still playing golf?' Natasha asked him politely.

'Oh, yes. Has your mother told you her news?'

She should have realized by now that all topics of conversation sooner or later took her mother as their subject and more usually it was sooner.

Her mother swelled slightly. 'I'm Ladies' Captain next year.'

'Oh. Congratulations.'

'Unopposed! Not that I was afraid of an election.'

'You would have beaten her easily,' said Don.

'Which I daresay she knew . . .'

Clearly the mysterious 'she' had been the subject of some interest.

'Who?' Natasha enquired.

'Bridget Forsyth,' sniffed her mother. 'Divorced, of course.'

It was one of the mysteries of her mother's character that she was able effortlessly to criticize others for the self-same characteristics she shared. Clearly her mother considered that her marriage to Don served to sanitize her own eventful past. As well as having more than one affair with a married man, her mother had been divorced twice. Natasha often wondered how much of her mother's history she had seen fit to share with Don.

What was clear was that her mother was not looking back. She had a natural ability to live in the present, scheme for the future and erase from her memory events that did not portray her in the best possible light. The fragments of the past that remained were then heavily edited. So it was that Natasha had overheard her mother refer to her daughter as 'naturally talented'. Natasha, her mother had taken to saying, 'loved to perform'. All the shouted instructions, the tedious rehearsals, the tense waits for results of auditions were forgotten. Natasha's rise was an effortless result of talent and good fortune in which her mother was redrawn as the happy observer of her daughter's fortuitous advancement.

It was clear to Natasha that her own childhood was a finished chapter in her mother's life. Her mother did not like to reminisce and never chose willingly to look at photographs. She changed the subject as quickly as possible if Natasha asked her about the past. Was it that her mother's new life demanded constant momentum if it was to survive? She and Don seemed never simply to sit and be with each other. Not for the first time, watching her place their coffee cups on the flowered melamine tray, she wondered if her mother actually loved Don.

When Don said he needed to change his shoes, she followed her mother out into the kitchen.

'I've met someone.'

'Oh.' Her mother was distracted, putting the cups in the dishwasher.

'His name's Robert. He works in PR.'

'Very nice, dear. Is he serious?'

'I think so. We've been going out for a few months. He's got a daughter.'

Her mother's lips pursed. Immediately she regretted mentioning that.

'She's very good. She's eight. She lives with her mother.'

'Well, I suppose you have to expect that nowadays.'

'I thought . . . I could bring him down one day. So you could meet him.'

Her mother frowned. 'Well, let me know when you want to come. We're getting very busy . . .'

It was absurd. She was thirty-two and she could feel hot tears welling up into her eyes. It wasn't supposed to be like this. Mothers were supposed to be worried about their daughters – not to mention anxious, prying and interfering. Mothers were supposed to take their daughters shopping to Peter Jones and argue over cushion covers and then go and have coffee and walnut cake in the café. She had believed, once she had achieved all that her mother set out for her to achieve, that a measure of closeness would grow between them. That had never happened. Instead, her mother had joined the golf club, married Don and set about becoming the busiest woman in Gerrards Cross.

She pushed down the tears and tried one more time. Even as she spoke the words she knew she was making a mistake. 'I thought you'd be interested! I thought you might *want* to meet him.'

It was a mistake because her mother had never yet accepted a word of criticism. The comeback was instant. 'For goodness' sake, Natasha! I've said I'd like to meet him. What more do you want? It's just that I'm very busy. Why do you always have to overreact?'

And there it was. She was a child again. The demanding, difficult child her mother had always told her she was.

'I'm sorry. I didn't mean to—'

'And on my birthday as well! Of all the days to start complaining.'

Her mother wore her martyred expression. Then she forced a tight smile. 'But we're not going to spoil things, are we? We're going to go and have a nice lunch and Don can tell you all about our trip to China. We're just about to book it. Three weeks on a group tour. Perfect!'

There was nothing Natasha could think of to say. Every time she came down she hoped against hope that it would be different. Every time it was exactly the same. Her mother remained elusive: at best coolly distant, at worst cuttingly critical, always resistant to Natasha's reaching out for intimacy between them. At most her mother would offer a stiff embrace or a touch on the shoulder. More usually there would be nothing, just a blur of small talk and anecdote, all of it a commentary on her life with Don, a newsreel in which her mother was the star and Natasha the audience of the day.

Natasha pushed down her feelings, buried the disappointment and the neglect, and returned the tight, bright smile. 'Perfect.'

Lunch had followed at the Bull at Bisham exactly as her mother had wanted and planned. Natasha could have written the script in advance. Gin and tonics in the bar, roast beef in the restaurant below the low black beams and white-painted walls, coffee and mints to conclude. She had not been invited back to the house. They had said goodbye in the car park, her mother kissing her lightly on the cheek, her eyes averted before she and Don drove off to have a 'lie down' before ballroom dancing club.

She had reached Wandsworth shortly before three thirty, which meant she could spend half an hour with Araminta. She had noted previously that Araminta's mother always rang the bell exactly on the dot of four o'clock. It struck her as rather a strange thing to do and she had wondered if it was that sort of slightly obsessive behaviour that had contributed to the breakdown of their marriage. Robert certainly wasn't giving away any clues. She let herself in. The house was silent. But they must be in because the house was only locked on the Yale and Robert was a stickler for double-locking the door, even if she was just popping round the corner for the paper. She listened for the sound of voices. Some inhibition, the knowledge that although she had all but moved in this was not her house, made her hold back from calling out to them. Listening more closely she could hear Robert's voice. It was coming from upstairs. From Araminta's room? She climbed the stairs. His voice was low and insistent and she could hear nothing from Araminta. Perhaps he was reading her a story – in which case she would wait until he was finished.

She pressed her ear to the door. She could hear Robert close by and without being able to see them she could tell that they were sitting on the floor. She caught the end of Robert's sentence. His tone was exaggeratedly encouraging.

'Very good! I don't think I've ever known *anyone* play this game so well!'

'I'm the best?' It was Araminta.

'Well . . .' Robert's voice was doubtful. 'Nearly. Let's see if we can make you the very, very, very best.'

'OK.'

'So. Is there anything else you can remember?'

'The farm?'

'No. We've already done that.'

'My bedroom. It's got a rug on the floor.'

'OK. That's another point. What colour?'

'Hmm. Purplish.'

'Purple! That's an interesting colour for a rug. How unusual. Is it a nice purple or a not nice purple?'

'Nice purple.'

What on earth were they talking about?

'I'm bored with this game.'

'Well, that's a shame. Because I was just about to tell you how many points you've got. But you're bored so I—'

'Tell me!' shouted Araminta. 'Tell me!'

There was a pause.

'I need to count them . . . Ninety nine!'

'What's the top score?'

'One hundred. That's the most anyone has *ever* got in the Holiday Memory Game.'

Natasha felt her heart begin to beat faster. She stood fixed to the spot, terrified to move lest some stray floorboard gave her away, but painfully aware that this was not a conversation to which Robert would wish her to be a party.

'Let me try! Let me try to get some more things. We had German chocolate cake at Theo's mother's house.'

'Nearly there. You're very, very, very nearly the best . . .'

'And Mummy said Theo's family would like us.'

'Really?'

'I don't want to do this any more.'

'You need one more point.'

'Theo used to be in the army.'

'Brilliant!' Robert's voice was filled with a genuine enthusiasm. 'That's my good girl. You are the number one winner of the Holiday Memory Game. And why is it a special game?'

'Because it's a secret game?'

'Yes! And who are the only people in the world who can play it?'

'Daddies and me.'

'And why can't Mummies play it?'

'Because it's only for Daddies.'

'That's right!'

'And I'm the best?'

'The best in the world!'

She could hear Robert getting to his feet.

'Now Mummy will be here soon and you have to go and I'm allowed to see you in three weeks' time. And then we'll go and do some extra special things together, just you and me.'

'And Natasha?'

'Would you like that?'

'Yes. I like it when she's there.'

'Then I'll make sure Natasha comes. Everything is going to stay exactly the same. I'm going to stay here and you're going to come to see me. And Mummy isn't going to go to America.'

Araminta did not seem to respond.

She could hear him moving to the door. Swiftly she moved away. She had just had time to reach the top of the stairs when he appeared in the doorway. She could see that he was not fooled.

His voice was low, so Araminta could not hear, and sardonic. 'Didn't your mother ever tell you that eavesdroppers never hear good of themselves?'

'I didn't want to interrupt you.'

He looked at her for a moment, as if he was appraising her and the situation, and then gave a brief smile. 'Perhaps it's just as well.'

She was emboldened by his apparent forgiveness. 'Robert, what were you doing?'

He took her arm, led her into their bedroom and closed the door abruptly. 'What do you mean, what was I doing?'

'Pumping Araminta for information!'

She had never been so bold in criticizing Robert before but something about the conversation had disturbed her enough to challenge him.

'And what is your assessment based on? Your knowledge of bringing up children?'

She refused to be put off. 'No. It's obvious to anyone. It can't be right – questioning Araminta like that.'

'I'm her father and I'm asking her about her trip to America—'

'Quizzing her, more like.'

'Araminta was not complaining. She enjoyed talking about the holiday.'

She felt frustrated. 'You made a game of it. A secret game!'

'What's wrong with that? Children like to play secret games. For God's sake Natasha, why do you have to make such a fuss?'

'But why? Why do you need to play it at all?'

He lost his patience. 'Because I need to know! Because sometimes, in the real world, the end justifies the means. Because her neurotic mother is proposing to marry this hillbilly and take my daughter to America. I had a letter from her solicitor last week.' He continued forcefully, 'I've been thinking about my daughter's future. About her being taken away from me to the other side of the world, by a woman who is mentally unstable, to live with a man she met five minutes ago. And given that Tabitha refuses to communicate with me I have no other option but to ask Araminta what is going on. What is so dreadful about choosing to do that in a way she finds entertaining?'

He was looking at her with disapproval and she found it unbearable. Some instinct within her drove her to placate him. She found his coldness too painful to endure. 'I'm sorry. It just came across as being . . . slightly manipulative,' she conceded doubtfully.

There was a pause. She could feel him leading up to something. She could read the tension in his body and the incipient anger in his face. He turned away from her and for a split second she had the notion, which she knew was absurd, that he was going to hit her. He did not. Instead he held his hands together and spoke almost to himself.

'I will do everything – use every piece of information and every remedy at my disposal – to ensure that Araminta stays here.'

She could feel his utter seriousness in every word. She saw then the raw determination, the absolute refusal to be beaten, that had propelled him to be the best in everything he set out to do. He began to regain his composure. After a few seconds he reached out and took her in his arms. 'I'm sorry. I didn't mean to alarm you. You're right – it *is* odd. The whole situation is bloody odd. And I don't like it any more than you do. But I have to protect Araminta. It's a father's instinct.' He stroked her hair. 'Any father would want to protect his daughter.'

She felt a surge of emotion. What did she know about fathers and daughters? Her own had never cared enough to even find her.

Robert's voice was calm and soothing now. 'I think you understand that better than anyone, don't you Natasha?' She felt the tears well up in her eyes now. His voice had a hypnotic quality to it. 'It's something I have to do as a father, as a good father. I have to protect my little girl.' He looked into her eyes. 'I don't think I could live with myself otherwise. But don't cry.' He kissed her warmly on the cheek. 'It will all be over soon and then we can get on with our lives.' He took a step back. 'And you, Natasha. You need to make a decision. Are you with me on this or not?'

'With you?'

'Are you going to stand by my side in this? I need your support.'

She was confused. It was not a question she had been expecting.

Clearly he read her confusion. He held her gaze with an intensity that she had never experienced before. He was giving her every part of his attention, asking for her, needing her.

It was impossible to say anything else. 'Yes. Yes, I'll support you.'

He moved forward and reached for her. 'I knew I could count on you, Natasha. I knew you'd be loyal.'

He hesitated and she felt there was more to be said, but then they heard Araminta's footsteps on the landing and her voice calling out. Robert looked at his watch.

'Tabitha will be here soon. Look, given the situation, it might be better if you popped round the corner for a few minutes. Bought a paper or something. She's pretty unstable at the moment; seeing you could push her over the edge and she'll be in the car with Araminta . . .'

'Of course!' She understood perfectly. At that moment she would have done anything to help him. 'Of course. Whatever you want.'

Tabitha was so careful, always so careful, but he had worked it out in advance and she walked into the trap he had sprung. Araminta was in the back of the car, fastening her seatbelt and Robert had stayed on the doorstep.

'She's left her bear.' His voice was casual.

She heard his voice and saw the panic on Araminta's face. But it was too late to send Araminta back up the path for her bear because she was already belted into the back of the car. He had waited for that. So like a fool she went up the path and back up the steps to where he was standing holding the bear, avoiding his gaze, never looking into his eyes, and then before she could cry out – as she reached for the bear – his hand came for her, caught her arm and she was inside, pressed up against the wall, his body against hers, his hand over her mouth. She thought she was going to die of shock. Her heart was racing as she tried to scream; his hand was pressed into her face.

'You will never win. You can go. I won't stop you going to lover boy. But you will never, ever take Araminta.'

Then he released her and pushed her out and the door slammed. She ran down the path and into the car, trying to hide her shaking hands from her daughter.

# Chapter 9

# Daily Journal

*My mother has reacted to the news of my incarceration with scandalized disbelief. No son of hers is an alcoholic! During the course of our telephone conversation today she advanced various theories to explain away my presence here. It is a plot by the partners of Lloyd-Davies to remove their most talented rival. It is a clear case of misdiagnosis by doctors, most of whom are charlatans, and a second opinion from a Harley Street physician must be obtained without delay. It is to the advantage of Susannah, who may be in cahoots with Raul, and I must be alert to the likelihood that Susannah will empty my bank accounts while I am away. Far from shunning me, as I secretly hoped, my mother has insisted on visiting me here. Gina, in turn, has rejected my suggestion of a private session and ordered that my mother be treated like any other family member. It has therefore been decided that my parents will attend family group next Sunday. So be it. At least Robert will not be there. He made one call to Grange House – ostensibly to check on my welfare but mainly I imagine to gloat over my misfortune. My mother tells me delightedly that Robert is planning to apply for custody of Araminta and to get married to Natasha. I have no doubt that the two developments are related. Robert will do anything to win. She asked if I would swear an affidavit in support of him. I said no, but I would be happy to swear one for Tabitha and to please pass on my congratulations to her for her new life in the USA. My mother rang off. In the meantime I have my first 'couples' session with Susannah this morning. Roddy had cautioned me not to expect too much but I am quietly confident that Susannah will see a real change in me.*

'I thought we could tour Australia next summer. You, me and Matthew.'

James's face as he said this wore an expression of guileless optimism. Next to him in the family room sat Roddy, James's counsellor. The family room was situated in an outbuilding of Grange House, upstairs with windows looking out over the lake, painted a soothing shade of institutional pale lilac and furnished with three small navy-blue sofas. Two plastic crates of toys were stacked up in the corner next to a bookshelf filled with oversized children's books. This was the first time Susannah had met Roddy and, despite her first impressions of his spiky hair, lurid striped shirt and Converse basketball shoes, she liked him. Walking to the outbuilding, Roddy had told Susannah that James had been caught vacuuming the patient's lounge in perfectly straight lines and did she think this was significant? It was a relief to speak to someone at Grange House who didn't take themselves too seriously.

The sofas were placed at right angles to each other. James had led the way and taken the far sofa. She had opted to sit opposite him. As a result Roddy had had no choice but to sit in the middle which was unfortunate because it immediately gave him the air of a referee. She struggled to concentrate on the session at hand. She was sleepy and somewhat distracted. First, she had had to get up at five o'clock in the morning to drive down in the middle of the working week. Second, Cal Doyle had telephoned her during the journey to bend her ear about Milbourne Manor and the first mortgage valuation scheduled for next week.

'Bloody surveyors!' Cal had ranted. 'I'm in the wrong job! Do you think I can find some eejit to pay me to walk round a house, flash a torch and run the kitchen tap?'

There was no point reasoning with him. In any event he had rung off before she had the chance to respond.

In the silence that had greeted his last remark, James ran on. 'It's something I've always wanted to do: drive through the desert; go deep into the rainforest. Not on one of those tourist trips, though. I want to go off the beaten track . . .'

It was gratifying to see that even Roddy was looking slightly confused by this twist in the conversation, which had led on from James describing his stint as the patient charged with vacuuming the communal areas. He cut across James. 'I think we need to keep focused on the purpose of this session, which is to keep Susannah involved in the process here at Grange House. Obviously your plans after you leave are something we can discuss nearer the time.'

Roddy turned to Susannah. 'How are you?'

It was a simple enough question but one that took her by surprise. She had no idea what she was supposed to say. 'Fine,' she stammered.

'Good,' said Roddy. 'How are you feeling right now?'

Oh God, she wasn't off the hook yet.

She hesitated, tried desperately to think of something suitable, and failed. 'Fine.'

Roddy, to give him his due, continued to look relaxed.

'We find that the partners of alcoholics need help, too. Maybe James has mentioned our family weekend?'

She could see exactly where this was leading. 'No,' she said firmly.

'It's a group weekend for patients and their families,' continued Roddy, undeterred. 'We would encourage you to attend—'

'I wouldn't be able to take the time off work.'

'Fair enough.' Roddy nodded in agreement.

James cut across them both. 'I think we ought to do it, Susannah. I think it would help us both.'

She was astonished to hear the resentment in her voice. 'I'm fine. And I certainly can't take any more time off work; it's been difficult enough reorganizing my appointments to get down here today.'

James sat back and Roddy cast her a solicitous glance. 'Susannah, I'm picking up your feelings about coming down here. It's perfectly normal to feel anger towards James and it would be surprising if you didn't.'

There it was again – the irritating ability of these Grange counsellors to make patronizing but eerily incisive observations. Was it normal to be angry? If it was then Roddy's observation was the most helpful comment she had heard at Grange House. It would explain the knot in her chest that appeared at the mention of the place – or the thought of coming down here to visit – or the tense, miserable feeling that intensified every time she drove through the gates.

'Perhaps you'd like to say some more?'

No, she wouldn't.

'It's OK,' added James gently.

And that was what did it. There was nothing in his voice that pro-voked her, no anger from him, not even a patronizing twinge. Perhaps it was the manifest inaccuracy of his statement.

'It is not OK!' she hissed. 'It is not OK at all—'

She felt on the edge of her control and so she stopped and held her breath, determined to keep her response in check.

Then she heard Roddy's voice. 'Why don't you let go?' He held up his hand as if to pre-empt any further comment from James, then let his words hang in the air. *Why don't you let go?* And as she sat there she asked herself *why not?*

She looked at Roddy, and at James, and in that moment everything changed. She didn't have to be polite or strong or sensible any more. To them or Gina or Raul or anyone at all. Why not let it go?

For some reason, even though they were within a few feet of her, she heard herself shouting.

'It is not OK! It's not OK for me.' She glared at James. 'Oh – I can see life is good for you. Holed up here with a bunch of people all telling you what a beautiful human being you are.' She leaned forward. 'But I'm out there, James, in the real world, and I can tell you we don't stop what we're doing every morning at eleven o'clock to troop into "group" and talk about ourselves. No, some of us are out there getting on with life.'

James, to give him his due, was regarding her with more attention than he had for years. Roddy looked utterly unfazed and, indeed, she had the impression that his expression would remain unchanged if she leaped over to James and began throttling him. Which, now she came to think about it, was not an unattractive idea. She stopped to gather her breath.

'I'm sorry,' she said to Roddy.

'Don't be.' His voice was surprisingly sharp. 'James needs to hear this.'

She began to like Roddy even more.

He continued. 'Alcoholics are very good about thinking about themselves. Self-centredness is at the heart of the condition. And yes, you're right. Some people do come in here with the "poor me's". All the excuses – if you had a life like mine you'd drink.'

It was gratifying, out of the corner of her eye, to see James shift uncomfortably.

Roddy grinned at her. 'Poor Me! Which translates into Pour Me a Drink!'

She smiled despite herself.

'James, to be fair, hasn't tried to cover up the impact of his drinking on those around him. But you need to have a voice in this, too.'

'I just want him to get better,' she said.

'And if he does? If he does succeed in getting better? Will the past be forgotten?'

It was exactly the question that had been running through her mind since their first walk in the grounds a week ago. It had irritated her then – James's assumption that he could come down here and talk about himself and everything would be forgotten. Since then her doubts had become more serious. It was something that she had kept to herself, and certainly hadn't imagined voicing today, but something in Roddy's manner encouraged her to speak.

'I don't know. First of all, who's to say that this will work? James has promised to stop drinking before. And he's sometimes managed to stop for a while. But he's always started again.'

She paused to let her thoughts catch up with her. It was nice that Roddy didn't jump in. Instead they sat in silence and he waited for her to speak.

'I think I will always be afraid that he's going to start drinking again. I'm afraid that we will always be living under a cloud . . .'

Her voice trailed off.

'And what has that been like?' asked Roddy gently. 'Living under a cloud?'

'It's the unpredictability that's the worst. Sometimes life is good and fun and I feel we have a chance. And then there'll be some crisis at work and James will drink his way through the weekend and I find myself back in the nightmare: cleaning up after him, making excuses for him . . .'

'Do you mean lying for him?'

'Yes. To people at work, or cancelling lunch arrangements because he's too hungover from the night before.'

Roddy nodded and she was encouraged to continue.

'Or watching him at dinner parties. Getting drunker and drunker and slurring his words and behaving like an idiot.'

'In what way?'

'Flirting with other women. I mean, I don't think it's serious – I know James would never betray me – but it's . . . humiliating.'

She stopped. Roddy spoke and it was curiously intimate, as if James were not in the room at all.

'All the behaviour you describe is typical of an alcoholic: lying, blaming those closest, acting as if no one else's feelings count. I don't say that to excuse it – rather the opposite. I think it's important for you to get this out, Susannah, if you and James are going to move on. Otherwise the angry feelings are going to fester and come out in the future.'

He had her attention now. 'So how do I get them out?'

'Here. Or with people you're close to. And just as there is AA for James, so you can go to—'

She cut him off. 'I'm not going to any group. I'm not discussing my problems with a group of strangers.'

Roddy backed off. 'I can see that's something you feel strongly about.'

She nodded, but she felt so stuck, and angrier now with James than she ever had done in the past. She liked Roddy but she didn't totally trust him. He was, after all, James's counsellor. There was a pause and then Roddy talked about the work that James was doing.

'Now that he's finished his seven by sevens . . .'

She still hadn't got to grips with the jargon. 'What are they?'

'I'm sorry. We give patients a list of headings – the seven ways in which drinking affects one's life – Family, Work, Health and so on. They have to write out seven examples under each heading. It's a way of examining powerlessness under the influence of alcohol and the state of those areas of their life in general.' Roddy continued. 'James has finished those and so now he's working on his life story.'

She wanted to ask about that but Roddy had moved on to explain the Grange House requirement that patients keep a daily journal.

'Yep, more navel gazing,' he said with a half-smile in her direction. It was impossible not to return it. 'Seriously,' Roddy elaborated, 'the idea is to help patients to look more closely at their actions and motives by putting everything down in black and white.' Then he talked about the gym programme and the new art class that was starting next week. At least he spoke in a series of uninterrupted sentences. The rest of them communicated in jargon punctuated by awkward silences. Roddy was the most forthcoming and least patronizing member of staff by far.

Roddy looked at the wall clock – she had noticed that every room in the place had a clock and a box of tissues – and opened his file. 'Well, we've made a good start.'

She had the suspicion that she and James could have spent the session wrestling on the floor and it would have been described as a good start.

'When will James be coming home?' she asked, determined to get an answer about that before she left.

Roddy cleared his throat. 'Well, once he's read his life story he can start going out to local AA meetings. When he leaves depends on how long Lloyd-Davies are prepared to fund him. The standard period is four weeks. He could opt to stay longer. Lloyd-Davies have indicated that James can take another two months off after that.'

She was stunned. 'Another two months? I thought he'd be going back in four weeks! Don't they want him back at work?' She looked at James. 'What about your clients? You're going to lose them all at this rate.'

James did not answer her. Instead she saw him exchange glances with Roddy.

It was Roddy who spoke. 'I think it would be more appropriate if James discussed the options with you. It's not for me or anyone else to decide how long he stays off work. It's James's decision and he should talk it over with you.'

She had the distinct feeling that James would have much preferred her to have that particular conversation with Roddy. Instead, Roddy gathered up his papers and got up. He gave them both a cheery smile. 'I think that's my cue to leave you to it.' He turned to Susannah. 'Lunch is served in half an hour. You're very welcome to join us.'

As he walked out of the door it was as if they were two children being left alone by nanny. It was ridiculous – to feel nervous in the company of her own husband – but that was exactly what had happened.

To his credit James got up, walked over to her and sat down next to her. She knew she should shift close so that they were touching. Instead she stayed where she was.

'James, what on earth is going on? Why haven't you told me any of this?'

'I haven't had a chance!' he retorted.

She wasn't sure she believed him. 'You could have phoned.'

'Susannah, it's not that easy. Be reasonable. There's one bloody payphone and ten patients. Do the maths. All the young ones hog the phone for hours.'

'James, I feel in the dark,' she said as evenly as she could.

His voice was patient. 'I do try to call. I really do. But even when I get on the phone it's not very private.'

She knew that was true.

'Well, anyway,' she said, by way of calling a truce, 'tell me now. What exactly is going on?'

'Raul's indicated that if I want to stay longer then the firm will probably fund it.'

'Why?'

James hesitated. 'To talk. To get some things straight in my mind.'

'What things?'

'About the past. About why I drank. And what I have to do to make sure I don't drink again. Susannah, I heard you. I know you don't want me to drink again. Believe me, I don't want that either.'

She sat trying to take it all in, wondering what would be in his 'life story'. At the same time, the talk of work had prompted the fears of financial insecurity that were never far from her mind. Lloyd-Davies were a City law firm and not one with a reputation for indulging their employees' problems for long. James was being paid – for now. In the meantime, while James took time off to locate his inner child, the bills had not stopped coming through the letterbox. Her chest tightened still more at the thought of it. That week alone there had been notice of an interest rate rise on the mortgage; the quarterly service charge invoice for the development; and the council tax annual statement – they had been notified that their council tax was going up by eleven per cent because of 'changes in the allocation of central government funding'. It said that every year. She pulled herself back to the present.

'What does it mean? Reading your life story?'

'It means I read it out to the group.'

'Can I have a copy?'

He looked taken aback. 'I . . . I don't think that would be a good idea.'

'But you're going to read it out to all the group in there? And all the counsellors?'

'Yes,' he conceded.

She felt a pang of hurt. 'Well, I'm your wife. Don't I have a right to read it?'

'We can talk about it. I can tell you what's in it.'

Her voice rose. 'Well, how exactly am I supposed to understand all this if I'm not even allowed to know the details of my husband's life?'

James appeared uncertain how to answer this. 'It's just part of the work here,' he said lamely.

She felt a helpless jealousy for the group: Tom and that woman who had spoken at the first meeting and Ed and all the others, some of them total strangers. They would all know what James really thought about his own life – and she wouldn't. She felt so excluded. She had heard an awful lot preached here about openness and honesty – but it didn't appear to apply to wives.

James clearly decided to take the initiative. 'Susannah. It's going to take time to make things better, to repair the damage in our marriage. That's why I need to take some time off work. To get my head straight and get established in AA.'

*AA*. She knew that it was necessary and helpful but somehow she just couldn't embrace it in the way everyone here did. She thought back to her mother and the way she lived her life, working and caring for her family, and how nowadays her mother would be labelled 'dys-functional' and in 'denial'. But it seemed to Susannah, looking out of the window and across at the Grange House meditation space, that there was some dignity in living one's life in private. She was able to appreciate that James found in such disclosure some liberation of self. She would never admit this but to her that disclosure, the revealing of one's inner self to a group of strangers, was anathema. It was so differ-ent to all that she had learned growing up.

But she nodded her assent. 'How often do you have to go?' she asked, trying to sound upbeat.

'Oh, every day to begin with,' James said casually. 'After a while about three times a week.'

She willed herself on. 'If it's what you need to do . . .'

James squeezed her hand. 'I know it's a lot to take in. Why don't you come and have lunch? Get to know everyone?'

And that was when the feelings of anxiety that had been building since she arrived overwhelmed her. She was more tired and stressed than she had realized.

Unbidden, an image came to her. She had done nothing to provoke it, she certainly didn't want to recall it, but the recollection was as clear as if she had been taken back in time. She could *feel* it. She was aged ten or eleven. She was sitting at the small, square Formica kitchen table. Her mother was standing at the sink. There was nothing unusual in that. But Laura was there. Perhaps it was the time Laura's mother was having her baby? Susannah seldom had friends home but for some reason Laura was sitting in the kitchen with her. They were waiting to have tea. They were playing *Snap* with a pack of animal cards. She could remember the cards, with the smiling zebra and the lion with its big yellow mane. She could almost imagine her mother cooking. Toad in the Hole or Shepherd's Pie, the dishes of her childhood. And then, for a treat, a bought dessert, maybe Arctic Roll. Her mother would have been listening to Radio Two, the *John Dunn Show*. Then she heard the sound of the key in the front door and her father's voice call out and she looked up and saw the anxiety cross her mother's face. And she felt it, too; she always did. Her mother made for the kitchen door, but she was too slow. Her father came in. He stood there, staggering slightly, dressed in his dirty work clothes, smelling of beer and when he spoke – *hello girls* – his voice was slurred. He was present, stinking and swaying, for only a few seconds, but the moment seemed to last for ever. She had wanted to die at that moment, literally die, so that the shame that engulfed her would end. She had seen in her friend's eyes the condemnatory and unconcealed judgement of a child. Susannah had always known that her family was different. Now she felt them to be grotesque. Her mother must have taken hold of her father because he left the room. Afterwards nothing had been said because it did not need to be. She was careful never to invite a friend home again.

The pain in her chest intensified. It was impossible for her to face the group. She thought of their curious eyes, their expectant faces and the unspoken judgements that would be made about her. 'No.' She felt for an excuse. 'I need to get back. I've got appointments.'

'Surely half an hour wouldn't make any difference?'

'No.' She was aware that it was wrong to refuse the invitation but she couldn't do it. It was baffling, the strength of her emotion, but the idea of going to lunch with the group was unbearable. It was so strong that it was almost physically pulling her out of Grange House. All she knew was that if she stayed in that room a moment longer she would cease to be able to breathe. She picked up her bag and bolted for the door, ran down the stairs, almost slipping, and out into the bright sunlight of the courtyard. James caught up with her.

'For God's sake, what's going on?'

'I don't know.' It was the truth. She got to the car, taking deep breaths.

'Susannah, are you all right?'

'Yes. Really. I have to go.'

He reached out, pulled her to him and put his arms around her. His embrace was suffocating,

'*Please*, James. I have to go.'

She found her keys and got in the car. Outside she could see his worried, puzzled face. He was tapping on the window. She put the key in the ignition and accelerated away.

They sat sipping pre-dinner champagne at what she imagined was one of the best tables in the Ritz dining room. It was called the dining room, not the restaurant, Robert had pointed out to her as they had taken their seats. Natasha had asked what the occasion was and he had teased her that it was a surprise. It was a fabulous setting. She looked around the large, high-ceilinged room, gilded and pink marbled, and out through the high windows onto a small Italianate patio overlooking Green Park.

The atmosphere was hushed and moneyed. Tailcoated waiters glided quietly between well-spaced tables beautifully laid with silver and crystal. Around them, the Thursday evening clientele was a mix of couples marking anniversaries, families celebrating birthdays, elderly couples up from the country and well-padded businessmen talking quietly over expensive claret.

'If you listen carefully,' Robert said in a low voice, 'you can sometimes hear the sharp intakes of breath as the bill is rendered.'

She gave a polite smile. It was one of Robert's slightly irritating characteristics that he could not resist pointing out how much money he was spending on her. She let it go. At least he *had* money to spend on her which was more than could be said for most of her previous boyfriends. At least he was forbidden from using his mobile phone here, another habit that could annoy her, especially the prolonged conversations over dinner when they were out. All business, of course, so again it seemed churlish to complain.

Besides which, she was not so naïve as to have no idea of what this particular evening might be about. It was not until they had nearly finished their entrees – beef for Robert, monkfish and scallops for her

– that he looked as if he was going to get to the point.

'I wanted to bring you here as a small celebration.'

She must have looked confused.

'I need to fill you in. Events have moved forward. Yesterday I found out that we got the Harrold-Winter account – all their corporate work. It's a seven-figure account. We announce it tomorrow; I'm giving an interview to the *Standard*.'

'That's wonderful!'

It was wonderful, but it was not the reason she had hoped they were at the Ritz.

'And now that that's settled, and I don't have to spend so much time at work, there's something else I need to say.'

Her stomach was churning. She put every ounce of energy into looking cool and composed.

'It looks as though Tabitha is set on this idea of moving to America. It's ridiculous, but there you are. I've been in discussions with my solicitor.' He took a sip of champagne. 'Naturally I will refuse my permission. In my reply I'm going to suggest that Araminta comes to live with me.'

'Live with you?' she repeated, surprised. This was not the announcement she had expected.

'Yes.' Robert looked at her sharply. 'What's wrong with that?'

'Nothing!' she backtracked. 'But . . . how are you going to look after her?'

'I've been putting some thought into precisely that question. I can work from home for part of the time. My parents will help out. I'll get a nanny, of course.'

'But . . . Araminta's always lived with her mother. What does she want?'

'It's a question of what she needs, Natasha,' he said testily. 'And what she definitely doesn't need is to go off and be brought up by some hop-head in the middle of nowhere.'

'Are they going to get married?'

'That is the plan. Not that it is any concern of mine.' The bitterness in Robert's tone belied his words.

They were interrupted at this point by a waiter clearing their plates.

'Will you win?'

'My solicitor says the mother nearly always wins these cases. It's the "nearly" that I'm focusing on. I intend to convert that element of doubt into a win. Tabitha is not the model mother she portrays her-self to be.'

'No?'

'Araminta would be much better off with me. If Tabitha still wants to go to America, then fine. They can see each other in the holidays.'

'Araminta's very young,' said Natasha doubtfully. 'Surely she would be better off with her mother?'

His tone was irritable. 'Natasha, I'm not trying to take Araminta away from her mother. It's Tabitha who is doing that – by her insis-tence on pursuing this ridiculous relationship. I'm just doing what any sensible father would do. I can't stand on the sidelines and watch a lit-tle girl's life ruined because of some romantic whim.'

She realized it was hopeless reasoning with him when he was like this. For herself, she had mixed emotions. She was growing close to Araminta. All her *Blue Peter* papier-mâché expertise was coming in useful on rainy weekend afternoons, and given what he had told her about Tabitha she could understand his concerns. But some sisterly concern for a woman she had never met made her instinctively uneasy at the idea of Robert gaining custody.

He continued more affably. 'The easy thing would be to let her go. Frankly, having Araminta living with me will be very awkward. But it is my duty. Maybe that sounds old-fashioned—'

'No!'

'But I have no option. I wanted you to know what's happening. Tabitha has never been the most level-headed individual.' He called over a waiter and ordered coffee. 'And the bill, too,' he added. He looked at his watch. 'I have to get back and do some reading before this interview tomorrow. The Harrold-Winter annual reports.'

At least she was successfully disguising her disappointment. Years of coaching at her mother's side had instilled in her the ability to smile gamely at the end of every contest and audition, whatever the out-come. Her mother would purse her lips in disapproval as some tearful girl stormed out – *laugh and the world laughs with you, cry and you cry alone*. It was ridiculous to feel disappointed. She forced herself to think about Robert's good news and how nice it was to bring her here. The news about Araminta she was finding more difficult to analyse. Though she would never say it, it seemed to her unlikely that he would win if these cases always went the mother's way. And Robert was hardly the most involved father. She put these observations to the back

251

of her mind. It was silly to think he might propose with all these problems on his mind. Curiously, despite her doubts, the longer he went on without asking her, the more she yearned for him to do so.

Anthony came to see her the next day at home. He did not arrive empty handed. He stood on the doorstep holding two swollen Waitrose carrier bags. She laughed light-heartedly and swung open the door to let him in. It felt like the first time she had laughed for weeks.

'Lead the way, madam!'

In the kitchen he unpacked bacon and eggs, brioche and croissants, fresh orange juice, strawberries, raspberries and a bottle of champagne.

'I thought you might need something to pep you up!'

He had insisted that she take the day off following her last trip to Grange House. And so she had. It was incredible that she could feel so utterly drained by those sessions. James had called to check that she had got back home safely but there had been a queue for the Grange House telephone and they had said nothing meaningful. So she had gone to bed early and reminded herself that things would seem clearer in the morning and indeed they had. She had got up with Matthew, managed a brief but civil conversation with him before he left for school, and then gone back to bed for an hour.

And now Anthony was popping open a bottle of champagne. Naturally, he was too much of a gentleman to turn up unannounced. She was expecting him at noon to discuss some paperwork. The breakfast, however, was a surprise. She felt like a double agent, watching him pour champagne into glasses, crossing from the sober world of Grange House to the levity of her time with Anthony. She took a sip of champagne, savouring the sweet, cold bubbles, and wondered what Gina would say if she could see her now. Probably something to do with *medicating suppressed feelings around family of origin issues*. There was only one answer to that and she took another sip.

Anthony set to work in the kitchen. She watched him take off his chalk-stripe suit jacket and place it carefully on the back of a kitchen chair. Just having another adult there was a pleasure. Her days off were as bad as the nights; no one was at home during the day because everyone worked in London. It could feel at times as though she was the only person on the development and often she was.

He reached into the lower cupboard and pulled out her Le Creuset pan.

'Don't even think about grilling this bacon,' he warned. He pulled a slab of butter out of the Waitrose bag and began melting it, then looked around and put on her apron that was hanging from the back of the kitchen door. He understood he was wearing a suit, after all.

'Bowls?' he asked.

'Bottom cupboard to your left.'

He began cracking eggs into a Pyrex bowl.

Sensing that her help wasn't wanted or needed in the kitchen, she began laying the table. He asked her about the Chapters and her neighbours and she was a little embarrassed at how little she knew about them. It was not a friendly place to live. She found herself telling him about their previous house in Fulham and the flat she had owned before that and the house she had grown up in. He asked her about her parents and she described them as best she could but she did not tell him about her father's drinking. Somehow she didn't want him to think that she was in some way defined by alcoholism. It was baffling, though, how she could grow up with alcoholism in her family and then, after all she knew, go on to marry into it. She thought about it often. At least Grange House had shown her that she wasn't alone – Maggie had done the exact same thing. Maggie's father, she had explained to Susannah during her lengthy telephone monologue, had died of cirrhosis of the liver. But no one seemed to be able to give Susannah any definitive explanation as to why this should be. It depressed her, this human propensity to seek out the familiar, for good or bad, often unconsciously. She had tried to think back to when she had met James. She certainly hadn't consciously known that he was an alcoholic in the making. At least she was very sure that Anthony didn't drink to excess: neither of them had taken more than half a glass of the champagne.

He began serving her breakfast. 'The trick is in the timing,' he said. She couldn't have cared less about the food, good though it was, if slightly rich for her liking. It did not matter; it was such a pleasure to be cooked for. James couldn't wash a strawberry.

As they ate he asked her about Grange House. It had become their shared, secret topic. She had told him all about Gina and Roddy and now she updated him on the news that James might extend his stay.

'Sounds like common sense, wrapped in fancy packaging and sold for a lot of money!' Anthony commented drolly. 'Nice work if you can get it.'

She laughed. She was surprised to find that some sense of propriety stopped her from discussing the other patients. Occasionally she might say something of the circumstances that had brought them to Grange House, but she was careful not to give their names, not that Anthony would ever meet them. Nor did she tell him about the circumstances of her departure from Grange House.

Watching him get up from the table and put a slice of brioche in the toaster, it occurred to her that Anthony was doing more cooking in the course of one meal than James had done in all the time that they had lived there. She almost said so, but some sense of loyalty to James stopped her. Then she remembered that James was even now cosseted in Devon, discussing every aspect of his life, which meant hers as well, with a group of bloody strangers. So she said it and Anthony laughed and said, 'I had to be the cook. Kate was only interested in preparing food that goes in buckets for horses.'

He stood at the kitchen counter buttering brioche. 'But Kate was a wonderful mother. She loved babies. I think if we had had more children it might have been different, but we had just the one.'

She hesitated. 'By choice?'

He returned to the table. 'No. Kate had a difficult labour. There was a medical intervention. She couldn't have any more.'

'And you,' he asked. 'Have you ever thought about having more?'

She found she could be honest with him. 'From time to time. Sometimes I thought it might bring James and me together. I know, the oldest mistake in the book. I think if James had been keen I would have. Now I think the time has passed.'

He paused. 'I think one reaches a stage in life when it is pretty tough to start all over again.'

She told him about Matthew and how she worried about him and Anthony reassured her that Matthew was just a normal teenager. Then he made coffee, strong Colombian in the cafetière they hardly ever used, and they sat in the conservatory. It would have seemed odd not to sit on the same sofa. He spoke of his daughter and grandchildren and his son-in-law who clearly did not measure up. He talked about his house, the one he had had to sell when he got divorced, and the years he had spent planting the garden there.

'I ought to make a start again.'

Suddenly she was aware of his loneliness, which she could so well understand. It was as if they were travelling the same road. She reached out and touched his hand. And then, as she caught the look in his eye, she had the distinct impression that he would like very much to kiss her. It would have been so very easy to lean towards him and feel the safety of his embrace. In his arms there would have been no more loneliness or rejection or fear. And she knew equally well that this was not the time or place – and there might never be such an occasion. So, before he could lean towards her, she smiled brightly, said that they needed more coffee and rose from her seat. Blandly, Anthony said that was a good idea, just one cup before he went back to the office, and with that the conversation turned to business.

Tabitha arrived at Barbara's South London office with minutes to spare and climbed the steep stairs to the first floor. The rain had soaked her shoes as she walked from Waterloo station. Summer was well and truly over.

She was exhausted before the working day had even begun, having left the cottage just before a quarter past seven. As she was starting the car, Araminta had announced urgently, 'I need my PE kit.'

'It's not PE today!'

'We've got a drama class. A theatre group are coming in and they're doing a play about the rainforest and we do it with them. In our PE kit.'

She had just about kept her temper but her voice was shrill. 'You need to tell me if you need something the night before!' And then Tabitha had run back into the house in the teaming rain, grabbed a knot of PE kit from the dirty laundry, searched and retrieved a pair of white plimsolls and returned to the car where Araminta was close to tears. She felt instantly guilty. She knew that she was impossibly on edge. It was the effect of dealing with Robert. Then the car had taken a heart-stopping three turns to start, the worn windscreen wipers removed barely half the water from the windscreen and she was now late getting to Lizzy's house. Lizzy, observing Tabitha's harassed state on the doorstep, had raised an eyebrow and said words to the effect that she hoped it was all worth it. Tabitha bit her lip. She needed Lizzy to take Araminta to school and collect her because she had an after-noon meeting at Ollsens to discuss her next editorial project.

Barbara's office was a functional collection of utility furniture, law books and files. Each file was marked with the case name. It always alarmed Tabitha to see how some names appeared across stacks of five or ten files or more still. Today, Barbara was wearing her court outfit of a black suit and cream blouse with a demure kitten bow at the neck which, for anyone who knew of Barbara's feminist principles, was wildly incongruous. Barbara, however, was a smart enough family lawyer to wear neither her feminist, nor her liberal credentials on her sleeve. Her family law practice, which had now grown to employ five lawyers, represented men as well as women and was rated as one of the top five family law firms in the country, the one with the highest proportion of legal-aid work.

Barbara scanned the papers. 'As we suspected, Robert has said no to our request to take Araminta with you to the USA. Masterson Ryder Jardine . . .' Barbara gave a quiver of her shoulders to demonstrate MRJ's elevated position in the legal hierarchy, 'wrote yesterday to say that their client could not give consent without knowing more about your intentions. They want more details of your plans.' She looked up. 'It's a game. They want more details of your plans so that Robert can pretend to consider them and then say no. It makes him look more reasonable than if he just said no outright.'

'So what do we do now?'

'We go to court.'

Tabitha's stomach turned over. 'What does that involve?'

'A lot of paperwork. A hearing. And a big bill at the end of it.'

'A hearing! With a jury?'

Barbara shook her head. 'No, just a judge.'

'Will I win?'

Barbara hesitated. 'Normally I would say that the mother in a case like this would almost certainly win. Araminta lives with you, Robert isn't very involved in her life and you're moving to the USA, not to Timbuktu. But . . .'

'Mine isn't an ordinary case,' Tabitha finished resignedly.

'Unfortunately we're dealing with Robert. He will search out any possible weakness in your case and capitalize on it. My guess is that he will go all out to attack your relationship with Theo and try to prove that your proposed marriage won't last.'

'But this is about Araminta,' Tabitha interrupted. 'My relationship with Theo is none of his business.'

'In theory, yes. In practice more often than not cases about children are really cases about parents. Robert will use this as an opportunity to discredit you. It's not right, it's not fair, but that's the reality of the situation.'

Tabitha slumped back in her chair. Over the years since the divorce her fear had subsided. But now it was back and as strong as ever.

'Could I just go? Without his permission?'

Barbara laughed. 'Only if you want to be charged with child abduction. Like it or not, Robert has rights. If he won't give permission for his daughter to leave the country your only option is to go to court.'

Tabitha considered what she already knew. 'He got hold of me,' she said quietly.

Barbara looked up.

She continued. 'It was last Sunday when I was collecting Araminta from his house. He pulled me into the house and pushed me up against the wall and told me he would never let me leave. Not with Araminta.'

'Did you report it?'

'No.' She looked at Barbara and saw the flash of exasperation cross her face. 'I know, I know. I had Minty in the car and I had to get back to Sussex. And he didn't actually hit me.'

Barbara's voice was uncompromising. 'It's an assault. It's not too late to report it. And if anything happens again you must report it, straight away.' Barbara rearranged the papers on her desk as if to organize her thoughts at the same time. 'OK, this is what we are going to do. I'll make an application to the court. Then we'll sort out the paperwork. Assuming you want to go ahead . . .'

'Why not?'

Barbara closed the file and held her gaze. 'Tabitha, this is going to be a tough one. And costly. You work and you own your own home so you won't get legal aid. The law is straightforward but your opponent is capable of using every trick in the book – including lying. Robert is an unpredictable opponent. And he's got nothing to lose by going to court, not really. Even if he loses he's in no worse a position than if he had given consent.' She paused. 'Are you absolutely sure about this? About Theo and getting married and moving over there? This isn't going to be pleasant.'

Tabitha heard herself. 'I'm sure. I want to be with Theo. It will be a good life for Araminta.'

But her mind was elsewhere; back in time to when she had

first realized the nature of the man she was married to. She had fled, started anew and told herself that she had come to terms with the past. Now, in Barbara's office, she doubted that she could ever come to terms with Robert. Sometimes the mere mention of his name could cause her stomach to contract into a knot of fear. She always checked the spy-hole in her front door. She never entered his house willingly. At school plays she came late to avoid sitting next to him or talking to him and afterwards, standing together, she would feel him press his body against hers and it was all she could do to keep from bolting.

Through it all, the therapy and the years of forgetting, there had been one oft-repeated assumption – *he cannot hurt you now*. That wasn't true. He could strike at the heart of all that she held dear, threaten her future with the two people she loved most in the world, walk into her new life and try to crush it and laugh while he was doing so.

She said her goodbyes to Barbara, left the office and walked back to the underground. The rain had stopped and a few glimpses of sunlight could be seen through the thick white cloud. Her step was heavy, as if Robert were behind her, holding onto her, his grip hard as it dragged her down.

TJ was a cunning bastard. He must have been waiting and when the Domino's moped came he had seized his chance and slipped the delivery boy a ten-pound note to hand over the pizza. TJ would come up in the lift and deliver it. So here TJ was, in the flat, and the pizza had been delivered onto the floor. TJ, wearing a black Armani suit and a self-satisfied expression, was now holding two Hockneys, one in each hand, and he was about to carry them out of the door.

'They're worth a fucking fortune!' Paul was shouting.

'Paul, I've got costs. And commission. And interest. I'm a business-man. You owe me for an awful lot of white powder.'

'You can't do this! It's outrageous. It's theft.'

TJ laughed. 'Call the police, then.' He opened the front door. 'And when you've done that, write to your MP.'

Paul watched impotently as TJ headed for the lift. TJ hadn't even brought one of his minders with him. Clearly he had calculated that Paul wouldn't put up any resistance.

TJ got into the lift. 'If you need anything, give me a call.'

Paul wanted to spit at him. 'Go to hell!'

TJ laughed as the lift doors closed. And Paul, watching them, began rapidly considering alternatives.

Robert had been in a foul mood for days; they hadn't had sex for a week and she found she really missed it. She had been wondering if she needed to do something differently and was planning a visit to La Perla. And then this. Robert had just eased a solitaire diamond onto the third finger of her left hand.

'You've made me a very happy man,' he whispered into her ear.

Around them, even the hardened clientele of the Ivy had caught sight of the unfolding drama and soon champagne had arrived courtesy of the restaurant. Robert had given a little flourish to the room and people were smiling indulgently at them. It was all very theatrical.

She felt relieved that he had finally asked her. Once the court case was settled and they were married and things had got back to normal then it would definitely all be fine. Robert would feel more relaxed and be able to be more affectionate. Less moody, too. Marriage would anchor them as a couple.

His voice cut into her thoughts. 'And I'm not going to waste any time, either. I want you as Mrs Agnew.'

She reached for his hand across the white tablecloth. 'But weddings take ages to organize!'

'Nonsense. We can organize a civil ceremony in two tics.'

'But I don't want—'

'And then we'll have a proper blessing at St Luke's. I've already spoken to Nick.'

She was surprised that he had spoken to the vicar. She had been thinking about St Paul's Knightsbridge, which was bigger and looked like a proper church inside. St Luke's didn't even have pews any longer. She wasn't even sure it had an organ. Did you have to have guitars?

Robert took her hand. 'Darling, the important thing is to get married. We'll sort out the blessing later. I just want you and I don't want to wait any longer.'

So she sat back on the banquette, took a sip of champagne and admired the diamond on her finger. Robert was right – the important thing was that they were getting married, and at this moment none of the detail need distract her from that.

*Part 4*

# AUTUMN

# Chapter 10

# Daily Journal

*Tom summed it up perfectly, his comment to me delivered in estuary English as he watched my parents' car leave the driveway of Grange House. 'Your mum's just like the Queen. And your dad's like Prince whatshisname.' I had been dreading my mother's visit but in the event it passed without incident. My mother was charming, polite, warmly effusive to the staff and graciously patronizing to the patients. My father was largely silent and followed two paces behind her. Everyone, my mother proclaimed, was brave, hardworking and to be applauded. She congratulated Gina on her 'sterling work'. Poor Gina, accustomed to outright defiance, had no defence against my mother's strategy of serene condescension. My mother sat in the group, her head cocked, wearing the expression of an interested spectator. Picture the Queen once again, now on the African leg of her itinerary, watching a troupe of tribal dancers. Her attitude broadcast to all present that this session was very informative but essentially nothing to do with her. I should have given her more credit than to predict crude belligerence on her part. My mother, comprehensively outnumbered by two counsellors, Howard the nurse, eight patients and some ten relatives, was not about to launch an all-out assault on the Grange House regime. Like all the best generals, my mother knows when to fight and when to retreat. It would be more accurate to say that the family group ended in a draw.*

*Gina boldly explained the disease concept of alcoholism, the impossibility of a cure and the need to embrace life-long abstinence and sober living in all one's affairs. My mother, appearing somewhat bewildered, asked if Gina thought a virus caused the disease. Was it contagious? What about the possibility of a vaccine? And did Gina herself worry about catching it? I could not help but intervene at that point, ignoring Susannah's restraining hand on my arm. I accused my mother of being deliberately obtuse. She said she was sorry but this was all very confusing* to her. I could almost feel the disapproval of the room settle on me. My mother convinced all those battle-hardened counsellors and patients present that she was an unworldly, genteel and slightly confused old lady – and a damned good mother for turning up at all. There was one dangerous moment: Tom, my protégé, asked her if she believed that alcoholism ran in families. She said she didn't have a view on that but she did believe in National Service as a way of keeping young men out of trouble. I forget what happened next. Tom reddened, my father winked at me and I think Howard started talking hurriedly about the importance of volunteering to make the coffee at AA meetings. I breathed a sigh of relief and soon my mother recovered her composure and said that she had heard that AA did wonderful work for the afflicted.

In the sunshine of the car park afterwards she was even civil to Susannah. There was no blame, no recriminations, nothing at all. My mother asked when I would be home and I told her in a couple of days. She nodded approvingly and said that everything would soon be back to normal. And that was when I realized that this whole life-changing episode of my life was destined to be erased once she left the gates. Six weeks of my life would be airbrushed from the family memory. No one would ever know. Like my mother's breakdown or her battles with Robert, this unpleasantness would be dealt with simply by not dealing with it. My mother would never accept my alcoholism, or any alcoholism, because she would not acknowledge that the condition existed. What did I expect? In retrospect, I have to say all credit to Susannah for refusing to go to the family weekend. At least she was honest. Yes, at least she was honest about it all.

The house was as quiet as if James was still away at Grange House, the silence broken only by the sound of the plates as she slipped them into the dishwasher. They had arrived back to Cobham at lunchtime, eaten bread and cheese over stilted conversation in the kitchen, until James had got up and announced that he was going to have a nap. He looked shattered. She had got up and begun rinsing the plates ready for the dishwasher and he had slipped out of the kitchen. He had not asked her to join him in their bedroom and she was relieved. There was a distance between them, an undercurrent of tension that made their conversation, though amicable, feel strained. She wondered what it would be like to share a bed with him after six weeks apart.

On the telephone he had said that he could just as well take the train home from Grange House but she had said no, she would come down. Naturally she was early and so she had found herself waiting in the deserted reception hall, perched on the small, red-checked sofa, next to the display of leaflets with titles like *The Older Addict* and *The Disease of Denial*. The silence was broken by the muffled sounds of low voices and gales of laughter from the lecture hall and then James's voice, as if he was making a speech. Then they had all emerged in a gush of bodies and piled outside to wave him off. It must be some kind of tradition, all the patients and the counsellors and even some of the domestic staff, standing at the front of the house. She got into the car and sat with the engine running, watching in her rear-view mirror as James embraced Tom, who she fancied was close to tears, and then Gina and last of all Roddy. Even the old chap who did the garden had joined them to stand and wave at the car as finally James broke away and she accelerated down the driveway, out through the gates for the very last time.

She took out the steak marinating in the refrigerator and turned it before replacing it. James had always liked that recipe. She tried to quell the gnawing feeling of disappointment that had sprung up during lunch over the changes to her carefully thought-out plans for dinner. She had been enthusiastically telling James what she had in mind for that evening.

'Matthew gets home at six – he's got football practice so he's later than normal. Then I thought we could eat; he'll need to take a shower first, and then we could all go to the cinema. Something for the three of us.'

James had looked doubtful. 'I need to go to an AA meeting.'

She had felt slightly confused. 'Why do you need to go to a meeting already?'

'I need to go every day.'

Six weeks of listening to Grange House indoctrinate the vital importance of attending AA meetings had finally persuaded her of their benefit to James. But tonight?

'Yes, but surely you could start tomorrow?' She checked herself. 'Or don't they have them at the weekends?'

James's voice was sharp. 'Of course they have them at the weekend!' He immediately pulled himself up. 'I'm sorry. Really. There's no reason why you would know that. Yes, they have meetings at the weekend – mornings, afternoons and evenings.'

'Oh. So you could go tomorrow,' she said expectantly.

She saw his eyes shift away from her and back. 'Susannah, I know this is hard to understand, but it's something I've been advised to do. It's a period of . . . transition. Being locked away down there and then suddenly being out in the world again . . .' his voice trailed off. 'There's something else.' He gestured at the wine rack built into their kitchen units. It currently held ten or so bottles of red. 'Can you get rid of those?'

'Get rid of them?'

'Yes.' His voice was utterly serious. 'I don't want to have alcohol in the house.'

'Of course.' She felt bad for not having thought of this before. 'Is it OK if I put them in the garage?'

He hesitated then said firmly, 'No. I'd like them out of the house.'

He did not say where she was supposed to dispose of ten bottles of red wine at short notice. She supposed she could give them away. Clearly James considered the subject closed because he had got up from the kitchen table and gone out into the hallway. She observed him walk over to his overnight bag. He unzipped the side pocket, pulled out a small white book and wandered back into the kitchen.

'It's the *Where to Find*.'

'Where to find what?'

'AA . . . I recall,' he said, thumbing through the pages, 'there's a meeting in Oxshott tonight. Yes. Eight p.m.'

'Oxshott! Can't you . . . wouldn't it be better to go further away?'

'Why?'

'Because you might see someone you know!' She couldn't help herself. It was just the way she felt. Thinking that reminded her of one of Gina's favourite sayings – *there's no such thing as a bad feeling.*

'Well if I do,' he shot back, amused, 'it's because they're there for the same reason. It's nothing to feel ashamed about!'

Clearly some feelings were more valid than others. She let it go.

'So what are we going to do about dinner?' she asked resignedly.

'Eat at seven?'

'And the cinema?'

'We can go tomorrow evening. I'll do a lunchtime meeting.'

His voice told her there was no point arguing further. Clearly his mind was made up. With that, James had leaned forward and squeezed her shoulder.

'Don't worry. It'll all be fine.'

But now, alone in the kitchen, she was still worried. Now that he was home she felt more anxious than when he had been at Grange House. She had imagined that this evening would be a quiet celebration, a happy reunion, and that it would mark the start, however slow, of a return to normal life, but James's plans had torpedoed that idea. Instead of the warm homecoming she had imagined, she was left with dinner to reschedule, several bottles of red wine to find a home for and, no doubt, a pile of dirty laundry sitting waiting in his overnight bag in the hallway.

She knew that she had to centre herself. At least the pain in her chest had disappeared. She worked to rationalize the situation. First, it was unrealistic to expect companionship from a man who had effectively been institutionalized for the last six weeks; second, so much had happened in such a short time – to both of them; and third, at least she had made more progress than Estella who, it was clear, had no intention of participating in James's 'recovery', as they termed it at Grange House. She had felt sorry for Gina watching Estella repel her every effort at communicating the seriousness of James's situation. And though Susannah could never see herself embracing AA and all its attendees, she could see that James needed help and it was the best that was on offer. It was just such a damned nuisance that he had to go tonight.

She closed the refrigerator door, took raspberries out of the freezer to defrost and went to get the bag. Doing something practical always made her feel better. The bag was light – he had had precious few clothes down there – and she carried it into the utility room. Unzipping it, she discovered two pairs of tracksuit bottoms, three T-shirts and assorted underwear, all clean and ironed and folded. Quickly she searched through. Only a pair of pyjamas, folded inside a tied plastic bag, appeared to need washing. For some stupid reason this was absurdly upsetting. She felt tears well into her eyes and the same feeling of redundant exclusion she felt every time she visited Grange House, only this time it was in her own home, with James upstairs, and that made it worse than ever. She took out the pyjamas and put them in the washing machine to await the rest of a load. The side pocket, where James had taken out his book, was lying open. She went to fasten it. Then she saw that there was a slim file inside. An air-force-blue paper file. She tugged at the edge to reveal the typewritten label stuck to the top right-hand corner:

*James Agnew*
*Written assignments*

She stood completely still. Around her the house was silent. Instinctively she knew that James was already asleep upstairs. She pulled out the file. Too late, she discovered that the papers were not secured inside the file and three or four sheets drifted to the floor. As she retrieved them she glanced at the headings.

### Seven by Sevens – Financial
### Seven by Sevens – Health

She already knew what she was hoping to see. She pushed the papers back in the file and began leafing through the fifty or so sheets of paper. She found it at the back, paperclipped together, handwritten in James's immaculate writing with the heading in black-inked capital letters:

JAMES AGNEW
LIFE STORY

She closed the file but retained the life story in her hands. For a few seconds she considered what she was about to do. She already knew that she was going to read it. It was beyond imagining that any woman could hold her husband's self-penned account of his life in her hands and not read it. All that remained was to quash the guilty feeling that this was a private document. She marshalled the arguments to support the view that it was all right to continue. First, James had brought it home. If it was truly confidential he would have left it at Grange House or destroyed it or put it somewhere that she wouldn't find it. Second, she was his wife. In the world of alcoholic counselling that might not count for much but in the real world it still stood for something. She had a right to know. Last, and most decisively, they had all heard it. *The group.* Maggie had explained to her, during one of her irritating but nonetheless informative monologues prior to the start of the family group one Sunday, that the life story part of the process was 'quite a palaver'. Each patient was required to write an account of their life – and drinking – which they then read out loud to the group and the counsellors. Then they got feedback from everyone. Apparently, Maggie had whispered, with eyebrows raised, the feedback part caused 'quite a bit of upset sometimes'. The important point, however, was that a public reading meant, by definition, that it couldn't be a private document. There was no good reason why she shouldn't read it too. She leaned back against the washing machine and began.

# Life Story

I have spent large parts of my life sitting as I am now, holding an ink pen, facing a blank sheet of white A4 paper. This exercise should, it follows, be a simple one to complete. As a child I wrote innumerable short stories, essays, schoolboy poetry, thank-you letters and long lists to Father Christmas. As a student I wrote copious lecture notes, crib sheets and yet more essays, this time for tutors and then for examiners. Now, as an adult, I write affidavits and witness statements; contracts and offer documents; advice to clients and briefing papers to colleagues.

I have never in all that time written truthfully about myself.

At this point, in deference to Grange House policy of proclaiming, at regular intervals, how one feels, I should report that I currently feel *uncomfortable*.

I am also afraid of being dull. I am painfully aware that my ability to be honest is still not as developed as it should be. I am pitifully anxious both to inform and entertain my audience.

First things first! I was born in Scotland. My father, a major in the Black Watch, was posted there. Shortly after I was born my parents bought a sizeable house in Wiltshire, assisted by an inheritance from my paternal grandfather. My parents live in that house today. For much of my childhood my father was away from home on tours of duty overseas. My mother tells me that mine was a difficult birth. I have the impression that my mother did not want any more children after me but six years later my brother, Robert, was born.

My father's family come from a long line of what in Victorian times would have been known as minor landed gentry, many of whom served in my father's regiment. I know much less of my mother's family. What I do know is inconsistent. My mother has told me that she grew up in Richmond, but also in Barnes, and that her father was, variously, a businessman, a serviceman and a teacher. My mother does not like to discuss her childhood or her family and as for her surviving relatives she maintains occasional contact with her sister alone.

My mother was a very beautiful young woman. The few photographs of her at that time show a woman with something of the look of Audrey Hepburn. My parents met at a dinner dance at Derry and Tom's in Kensington High Street. My father was on leave, my mother was working as a secretary in a solicitor's office in Mayfair. It is hard to detect much that they had in common even then. That my parents' marriage has endured for nearly fifty years is in no small part due to my father's tolerant nature and his foresight, soon after the purchase of their house, in constructing for himself a large detached outhouse at the end of the driveway. My father is one of a dying breed of men who place family honour and responsibility before personal fulfilment.

Outwardly, we enjoyed privileged upper middle class lives. My mother developed a flair for interior design, gardening and entertaining. My parents hosted frequent dinners, cocktail parties and every year, in the first week of July, my mother opened the garden for the annual garden party of the local branch of the NSPCC.

I attended the local prep school and at the age of twelve went away to my father's school, Selchester. Because I had been brought up with the knowledge that I would be sent away I accepted it stoically. I realize now that the shell I had been building to survive at home was fortified and hardened during those years at school. I learned to exist within myself, to hide my true feelings and to bury, deeper and deeper, any unpleasant emotion.

It is tempting to pass on here. But I have to be honest and so I must backtrack to answer the question of what precisely I was surviving at home. The answer, unfortunately, was my mother. My mother's rages. Her tendency to scream if shoes were left in the hallway or fingerprints appeared on the stairway or a piece of roast potato dropped from the fork onto the dining room floor. My mother adopted a 'quick to anger, slow to praise' philosophy of child-rearing. My father and I retreated – him to his outhouse, me to my bedroom and my books and a world of fantasy. Sometimes I would fantasize that my mother would be taken ill and have to go to hospital in the countryside and stay there. I had read about isolation units for people with TB situated on some remote Scottish island and I thought one of those would be perfect for her. I did not wish her dead, I think. I know from our learned counsellors here that children fantasize about the death of a parent more frequently than is commonly admitted but I don't think I wanted that. I just wanted some peace and quiet. My mother excelled in the role of chief critic – of her family, friends and neighbours. I quickly learned that the best time to approach her was a few minutes after six o'clock when she was invariably holding a large crystal tumbler filled with gin and tonic.

I escaped lightly compared to my brother Robert. I was six years old when he was born. Here I am shifting momentarily from the role of narrator to that of commentator. I believe that by the time of Robert's birth my mother was a more confident person than the young girl on the arm of the dashing army officer. She often said that I was her 'good little boy' and Robert was her 'naughty boy'. Robert was certainly my mother's child – strong-willed, assertive, intrepid, fearless even. And so the two of them became locked in a monumental battle of wills that lasted all of Robert's childhood and, for all I know, continues today, in which my mother set out to control a boy who was equally determined to resist her at every step.

Back to the narrative. I left Selchester with a clutch of A-levels and a knee injury from playing rugby, which continues to cause me pain to this day. I had made few friends there and none that I cared to retain. I saw university, at Oxford, as a fresh start and in many ways it was. I think those university days were the happiest of my life, a sad fact given that some twenty-five years have passed since then. I found activities – rowing, studying law, student politics – all of which I found I had some aptitude for. I enjoyed some freedom for the first time in my life. My drinking then, I believe, was no worse than any number of young men in the college bar on a Friday night. Girls? Yes, I had my first girlfriend but more by accident than design. We were tutorial partners in first-year contract law. Our eyes met over 'Treitell on Contract' – I should explain that is a textbook and an attempted joke. Clara and I went out for about a year until she ran off with a postgraduate student and married him soon afterwards. As a footnote they are still together which goes some way to soften the blow to my pride.

Was I heartbroken? No. I liked Clara very much and at the time I believed that I was in love with her. But in truth I was too afraid of women to be capable of falling in love. I approached a relationship as I approached life in general – as an intellectual challenge in which I must retain control of my emotions and actions. I was not, however, a total caricature of an English public schoolboy. I could feel very emotional about issues of injustice. It seemed to me, as it does now, very wrong that people are denied access to justice simply because they do not have the money to go to court. At university I entertained ideas of becoming a lawyer who would defend just those people. My parents meanwhile made no secret of their hope that I would follow my father into the army. The compromise reached was that I took articles with a London commercial firm in order to get a good training. Thereafter I would be free to practise in whatever field I chose. The firm I chose was Lloyd-Davies and I am still there twenty or so years later.

I became a good lawyer. I have to be honest – a very good lawyer. I have the ability to use the law in a creative way, to know when to settle and when to fight on, to differentiate between bluff and actuality. A good litigation lawyer thinks like a chess player – several moves ahead – and behaves like a poker player. I enjoyed the intellectual challenge of my job, but I hated the absence of any moral value in my work. A couple of years ago I took on a *pro bono* case – one for which I was not paid – involving a large pharmaceutical company. It was the happiest time of my career. When it finished the return to corporate work seemed duller than ever and the pressure greater still to make up the billable hours lost to the firm while I was working on the case. Also, I'm sure it was frustrating for my wife to see even less of me than usual during this period. For the majority of the time, however, I was a diligent City lawyer. As the years passed I fell into a cycle of work and drinking, punctuated by the masculine pursuits of the English middle-class man: cricket, rugby, trips to the varsity match and stag nights – my own, in passing, involved visiting a pub situated at every location on the Monopoly board. None of our party went to jail but we mislaid two articled clerks in Vine Street and the head of the firm's private client department passed out in the Angel, Islington. My marriage changed the location but not the character of my drinking which was by then, although I would never have admitted it at the time, alcoholic in nature. I *needed* to drink and I drank more, never less. If I measure the amount and frequency of my drinking at ages twenty, thirty and forty the progression is startling. But at the time it crept up unnoticed.

Latterly I have taken to blaming my wife, Susannah, for my situation at Lloyd-Davies. I have told myself, usually when drunk, that I am forced to stay there by the expenses of family life. That I see now is not true. I could have chosen to leave at any point in the last twenty years. Why have I stayed put? A combination of laziness, easy advancement and a huge salary cheque, made larger still when I was made a partner.

Time for a Grange House 'feelings check'. I am now feeling *nervous* because we have reached the point in the story when I can no longer avoid telling you about my marriage to my wife, Susannah.

273

I met Susannah eight years ago. I was looking to purchase a flat in Putney and she was the estate agent who showed me round. I did not like the flat. I was, however, attracted to the girl with great legs in the sober suit who was so very markedly uninterested in me. That was a challenge. I was in my mid thirties, unmarried and so in constant demand to make up the numbers at the dinner parties of colleagues. I wasn't short of the attention of girls who dropped heavy hints about how they loved children and cooking and opera – and was I going to Marble Hill that year? No? Well, if I wanted to go they were getting a party together . . .

Susannah was different. Susannah ignored me and never returned my calls. She continued to take very little interest in me until date number three or four. By then I had found out that she was divorced with a young son, and she was having trouble both with her landlord and with the enforcement of a child maintenance order. Saddle up the white charger! My crusade brought me into contact with Susannah's son, Matthew – a credit to her. Matthew and I have always got on well despite my drinking.

I am feeling my way in the dark here but I think it is safe to say that at that time I felt a strong desire to rescue Susannah and make her life easier and look after her. I still, at times, can feel that way. But as I review the past eight years I see that I have failed comprehensively in my intention to make my wife happy. If anything, my marriage coincided with a marked acceleration in my drinking. When all is said and done I have to face the awful possibility that actually Susannah and I are very different people.

I do not blame her for this. Susannah has led a life that has led her to value security and stability – the safety of a home, money in the bank, a job she enjoys. Those are the very things I now find stultifying. Whether we can reach a compromise remains to be seen.

The situation is, naturally, complicated by the legacy of my drinking. Susannah has endured the unpleasantness in various forms of living with an active alcoholic. I do not know if she can find her way to forgive me and put the past behind us. The omens, at present, are not encouraging, but it is early days.

I feel that I must make amends to Susannah and Matthew if I am to live with my own conscience.

There is a postscript.

Earlier this year I met a girl – Jasmine. At the time she was the girlfriend of my brother, Robert. We met at his house, at a lunch party, during my spell of self-enforced abstinence. My frame of mind on that day can be summed up as sober, resentful and bored. These feelings intensified as the afternoon wore on and those around me became progressively more drunk. Drunken people, I discovered on that day, are extremely tedious company when one is stone cold sober. Jasmine was an exception. She is exceptional – an extraordinarily beautiful and talented and kind person. We 'clicked', as you youngsters would put it, immediately. While the others went for drinks in the drawing room I endeavoured to hold her hostage in the kitchen. I was first attracted to her gentle manner and her obvious enthusiasm for her work – she is a photographer – and her generosity of spirit. It was also immediately obvious to me that Robert treated her appallingly, riding roughshod over her good nature in the most bullying and unpleasant way. I had witnessed the same story with his now ex-wife.

Shortly afterwards they split up. This is my story, not Robert's, so I will simply say that she came to me for help and I was sufficiently enthralled by her and horrified by my brother's behaviour that I did not hesitate to do everything I could to help her. It would be tempting at this point to observe the white charger plodding out of retirement to be saddled up for one last crusade. That would be tempting but also, I think, an oversimplification. There is something of the survivor in Jasmine; a tight coil of strength runs through her, which disqualifies her from the role of damsel in distress. One thing, as they say, led to another. I conspired to invent reasons for us to meet at ever more romantic locations. I was falling in love and quickly falling apart. I was a circus act, spinning plates, dashing from one to the other. I was lying to everyone – frequently to my wife, often to those at work and also to Jasmine by omission because I was choosing to reveal only the most flattering side of myself to her. I was drinking huge amounts followed by days of abstinence in which I saw Jasmine and tortured myself with thoughts of my situation.

I say I tortured myself with my thoughts. I did not, however, occupy myself with the actions that might have provided a solution to my self-created problems. I did not stop drinking. I could not stop seeing Jasmine. That would be unbearable. I did not speak openly and truth-fully to my wife. I did not ask for help at work. I was driven by self-will and pride and delusion to speed on until, inevitably, I crashed.

Jasmine was the occasion but not the cause of my downfall. It was as if she held up a mirror to me. I saw in her, with her, a life that I had always wanted but never had the courage to achieve. I saw the possibility of something that had eluded me all my life – intimacy with another human being.

The final cause? I made a mistake at work. It is an irony that work, in which I had always excelled, proved to be my final undoing. I had been working for some months with a high-profile businessman. His business strategies, like his moods, changed frequently. Often I took work home at the weekend to catch up. I had already had one close shave with a stack of papers I returned to the office in a less than pristine condition. One morning, in a hungover and thoroughly distracted condition I inadvertently placed my note of my client's latest takeover strategy in the envelope destined for a letter addressed to his business rivals. Why was I carrying out secretarial duties? Because I was running late with the papers. Why was I running late? Because I had spent the previous evening, when I was supposed to be working on them, circumnavigating the Serpentine arm in arm with Jasmine in a romantic trance.

The dominoes fell.

By the time I realized my mistake the paperwork was in a DHL van headed for the West End. I had no choice. I had to tell Raul, my boss. He did not, as I had feared, fire me on the spot. His words, as I recall, were 'first things first'.

Raul, the man towards whom I had for so long harboured the most uncharitable and resentful thoughts, proved to be my legal guardian angel. He set about retrieving the papers – a motorcycle courier was promised riches beyond his dreams to catch and mug the man from DHL – and thereby saved my skin. Next, he informed me that he had been expecting this day to come. I had been given sufficient rope and duly hung myself. Finally, the choice was put to me of dismissal from my job or transportation to Grange House.

You might conclude that I came here to save my skin. Actually, at that point in Raul's office, I couldn't have cared less about the job. I knew Susannah did not feel the same, however, and that getting myself fired might not matter to me but would be devastating to her. No, I came not to save my job but quite the opposite – to run away from work and my wife and my family.

Naturally, Grange House was not the safe haven I imagined it to be. There have been no cosy chats with sympathetic doctors. No basket weaving. Most important, there has been no truck given to the idea I still held onto when I arrived that I could be taught to drink like a normal person. In the past my efforts to control my drinking were short-lived spells of irritable abstinence after which my drinking resumed as ferociously as ever. Yet I persisted in thinking that one day – when life was easier – I would be content with a glass of champagne and half a bottle of wine. I see now that my life circumstances are actually very good, that I endure no more stress than millions of other people, many of whom live far harder lives than I do in circumstances of much greater financial hardship. In passing I will add that, despite my alcoholic medication for my self-diagnosed stress, I drank more on holiday than at any other time. The reason for my excessive drinking, I now believe, is nothing to do with my life and everything to do with the fact that I am an alcoholic. The remedy, I now see with relief rather than fear, is total abstinence. Whilst it is not a prospect that fills me with unalloyed joy it has to be preferable to the alternative, which is to drink ever greater quantities of alcohol with ever more unpredictable results.

I am grateful to all of you here who have brought me to that point with your insights, some more tactful than others, but all I know in my best interests.

I am less sure about the prospect of living sober in a world that is soaked with alcohol. I am fearful about the work ahead needed to rebuild trust and intimacy within my marriage. I am unexcited by the thought of returning to work. It is easy at my age to meet and speak only to those who move in the same circles, who share identical values to oneself, a world in which a partnership bestows identity and status. I would like to get on a surfboard in Newquay with Tom. I would like to walk in the Pyrenees with Ed. I would like to see the world today. I am tired of 'working for my retirement' – what a very depressing phrase that is.

So we reach the end. The prosecution portrays a forty-four-year-old drunk in the midst of a mid-life crisis. The defence counter with the picture of a reformed character, set for a new life of clean living. The jury, most definitely, is still out. As for me, I am looking forward to the next stage of my journey to which this life story is a passport – a night out on the town at the local AA meeting.

I am now feeling that I would like a cup of coffee and a game of pool.

She read it twice. The first time it was difficult to concentrate, such was her urge to *know* and so she scanned rather than read each word of the close handwritten pages. James's writing was never less than elegant if occasionally difficult to read. Once she reached the part about Jasmine it was hard to concentrate at all because her stomach was turning over and her mind was only partially attentive to the story. Other thoughts burst in: could this be some kind of invention of James's to impress them or entertain them or make him seem more interesting? And then, as she read on, she remembered that Sunday at Robert's and James's lengthy absence and all the other absences; she knew then that it was true. There were no crossings out or amendments, only the one footnote, and she wondered if this was a second draft. She sensed it was not – James had simply sat down and written this. The second time she read it more closely, noticing details that she had missed before. The walks by the Serpentine – she could envisage that because Matthew had loved it there and when he was eight or nine there had been a phase of trips there on summer Sunday afternoons when they would take out one of the pedaloes. By the time she finished she was shaking.

She had wanted to know and now she did. The knowledge, however, did not satisfy her, because there were details missing. He did not say if he had slept with Jasmine. He did not say if he was still in contact with her. He said that he wanted to save their marriage – but did he mean it? How could she be sure he would not go running back to this girl when he was at work? Or at an AA meeting.

Had there been other affairs?

How had they spent their time when they were not walking round the Serpentine?

The knowledge did not free her. It possessed her. She put down the life story and began thumbing through the other papers. Most of it seemed to be about drinking. She searched for a mention of Jasmine's name but could not find it. She found a typewritten sheet, *Guidelines for Your Moral Inventory*, which looked a promising title – surely a moral inventory would have to include an affair – but there was no moral inventory to be found.

Searching down through the side pocket she found his mobile telephone. It was switched off. The battery had to be flat after all that time. But her charger was in the bedroom. There was no alternative but to replace the papers, zip up the side pocket and go out to the car to use her car charger.

She started the engine, exited from the development and went to Oxshott Woods. It was a short drive and in the five minutes it took her to reach Sandy Lane she focused all her attention on driving within the speed limit and not running into the car in front. Gratefully, she swung into the small car park. It was lunchtime and the car park contained four or five other cars, two containing businessmen eating packed lunches and talking on the telephone. Perhaps to their mistresses? The others, all estate cars, were empty, probably belonging to dog-walkers. She considered walking into the woods herself but decided against it. This was no time to get lost amongst the dense oaks and beeches of the woods, which extended for miles. Instead she parked the car as far away as possible from the others and pulled out James's mobile.

Fortunately James did not have a pin number. Why had she never thought to check his telephone in the past? Other women did so regularly – and email and pockets and credit card statements. She had not checked his telephone because it had not occurred to her that there would be any reason to do so.

There were ten messages and then a voice saying that this mailbox was now full. The last five were work-related. One was from their accountant. Four were from Jasmine – they were the oldest messages, three left on the same evening and one the next morning. With each successive message her voice grew increasingly distressed.

In the first the voice was light-hearted, casual and relaxed. 'Hi! I'm at Motcombs. It's nearly eight thirty. Did we say eight or eight thirty? Maybe I got it mixed up. Or I'm in the wrong place altogether. Call me!'

So Jasmine was sufficiently intimate with James not to deem it necessary to use his name or leave hers.

The second, gratifyingly, was less confident. 'James. I'm still waiting at Motcombs. Where are you? Can you call me and let me know if you're coming? I don't know whether to order and I'm feeling a bit of a lemon sitting here. Bye.'

The third was altogether different: upset, with a definite edge of panic and confusion. 'James, I'm leaving Motcombs. It's ten o'clock. I've waited two hours. I'm really, really worried! Will you please just call me and let me know what's happening? I'm going home now.'

Finally, the last message, and in it Susannah heard plainly the anger and sense of rejection. 'James. It's Tuesday morning, I've just spoken to your office and they say you're on holiday. I can't believe this! I just can't believe you've gone off and not even told me! I didn't think you were that type of person. I thought at least we knew each other better than for something like this to happen. It's just so . . .' and here the crying began '. . . it's just so horrible. Please, please, please call me and talk to me just so I know. It's so awful not knowing what's going on.'

Susannah could concur. It was horrible not knowing what was going on. She listened again to the last message, to Jasmine's voice breaking, and heard her crying. She was pleased that this girl was crying. It soothed her own misery, which might not be an honourable or edifying or mature emotional response to the distress of another human being, but that was how she felt. She was glad that this girl who thought she could steal her husband was in pain. Never before had she experienced feelings of angry possessiveness towards James as she felt now.

James was *her* husband. But he clearly had grave doubts about whether he wanted to continue to be so.

Before she had a chance to think any further she heard a telephone ringing. She looked, confused, at James's mobile still in her hand, before realizing that it was her own mobile ringing, buried in her handbag. She began rummaging through her bag and found it just as it was about to cut out, which meant that she answered it without having the opportunity to check the number.

'Susannah?'

The voice was familiar. It was a man's voice with an Irish accent.

She could not have cared less about being polite. 'Who is this?'

The voice sounded a little put out. 'Cal Doyle!'

Her most important client. If she had checked the number she would never have answered it. 'What do you want?' she snapped. If she sounded breathtakingly rude she couldn't have cared less.

He did not miss a beat. 'I want to talk about Milbourne Manor and why we've only made one sale.'

What was there to lose? Why not just tell him? James kept rattling on about honesty – whilst practising it with a partiality – so why not give it a go?

'Because they're overpriced. And because the show flat looks cheap. You've economized and it looks lousy.'

'I know. I used a new interior design firm—'

'That's not my problem. You need to fix it. Frankly, I wouldn't waste my time showing any more purchasers around until you do. As for the sales, you need a properly planned and executed marketing strategy, which you'll never get while you keep chopping and changing agents.'

'I know—'

'And actually, for the record, given that you do nothing but complain about every agent in Cobham – and how you could do a better job yourself standing on your head – why don't you? You either need to stick with one agent or do your marketing yourself. At the moment you're getting the worst of both worlds—'

'I know.'

At last she heard him.

'Well if you know, why don't you just bloody do something about it instead of bleating to me every week?'

The silence was so long that she thought she had been cut off. Then she thought about the chances that Anthony might sack her for losing their biggest client. And then Cal Doyle spoke.

'Very well. I appreciate plain speaking. I'll redo the show flat and we'll go from there. Good day to you.' He rang off.

She was conscious of the sweat on her brow and her hands shaking. She could not believe that she had spoken to him like that. It was the worst thing she had ever done in her entire professional life and the only time she had lost her temper. She was terrified that he would call back but as she sat there, regaining her composure, the phone stayed silent. Around her the occasional dog-walker and runner went to and from their cars. A few cars passed by. In an hour or so the roads would be busy with the afternoon school-run merging into the evening commuters back from the City and the West End. She again considered getting out and walking to calm herself, but the sky through the trees was overcast and set to rain. There was nowhere else to go but home.

She was not the type of woman who would be able to keep her new-found knowledge secret. James had always said that her face was an open book. He would see her and know immediately that something was wrong and the whole story would be revealed. Her anger was now tinged with fear at the prospect of James's reaction to the news that she had read his life story and listened to his mobile telephone messages. Not only that but she was beginning to think ahead to consider the possibility of further revelations. She needed to know every detail of his relationship with Jasmine: every meeting, every intimacy, every gift. And every lie he had told her. But just as surely she knew that the details would do nothing to calm or placate her.

A second wave of shock hit her as she attempted to start the car. She would have to live with this for ever, the knowledge of what had happened and the fear that it would occur again. She began to cry. She had not believed it possible to feel still more alone and vulnerable than when James left for Grange House. She wanted to feel safe and secure, to feel solid ground beneath her feet, not to live on these shifting sands. Vindicated in her assessment of her husband's alcoholism, proved right in every respect, she had got what she had asked for. Except, as she was rapidly discovering, what she had asked for was not what she wanted at all.

# Chapter 11
# Daily Journal

*My study is unchanged. In it is everything of significance from what I think of now as my 'old' life. I feel a rawness that I could not have anticipated. In six weeks I have become institutionalized. It is so quiet here. No shouting, no telephone ringing, no running footsteps in the corridor. No laughter. It is the return to home from boarding school all over again: I miss the very people whose enforced companionship I found so irritating. I have spent six weeks craving solitude and now that I have it I am homesick for the communal life. I look at my watch and I wonder what they are doing. I can see them now on the afternoon walk. I miss all of them, very much. I even miss the arguments about the chores and the damned payphone.*

They had not been able to reach any resolution themselves. The row, acute in its bitterness and chronic in its repetition of facts and feelings, had continued through the rest of the day and into the night until eventually James had suggested that they go to see Roddy for advice. Worn down, she had agreed. Roddy was undoubtedly the best of the bunch and at the very least he could be relied upon not to let James off the hook. Roddy saw clients, mainly ex-patients, in London on a Thursday and so there was nearly a week of brittle silence between them before their appointment in Roddy's Harley Street consulting room.

It was a room of the type hired by the hour, situated in the basement of the building and therefore windowless. She could tell it was a hired room by the sparse furnishings – a round table with four low chairs and a pine-framed impressionist watercolour print on the wall, a field of poppies, and the absence of any personal effects.

Roddy had suggested a two-hour appointment, which she supposed reflected the gravity of their situation and some seriousness of purpose on Roddy's part. This was more than could be said for James, who was being far too casual about the whole affair for her liking. The appointment had necessitated her taking a half-day off work. James had announced that he would not be travelling back on the train to Oxshott with her – he was going to go to a London lunchtime AA meeting with Ed.

Roddy, in a sharply cut navy linen suit, had been listening to her account of the discovery of James's 'affair' as she termed it. She had just reached the point where she had confronted James.

'I waited until Matthew had gone to bed. And then I told James that I knew everything and there was no point in lying to me any more. James wasn't sorry at all – or only sorry a tiny bit.' She held up her finger and thumb barely separated to illustrate the point. 'He acted as though it didn't matter. That it was all in the past and could be swept away and I should just forget about it and pretend it never happened.'

'That isn't quite fair,' interjected James, but she overrode him.

'Well, that's how I *feel* it was. Or is it only your feelings that count?'

James's eyes flickered away from her and he did not answer.

'But it did happen,' she concluded, 'and now I feel as though everything is built on sand and I can't trust him any more . . .'

Her voice trailed off. She could have said more – Roddy's failure to make any immediate comment invited her to do so – but the remaining thoughts she harboured were not ones she was ready to share with either of them. To do so would be putting a light to the fuse. So she breathed hard, as if to push the feelings down.

The customary therapeutic silence continued for about ten seconds and then Roddy looked up at her and said, 'You feel angry. And betrayed and distrustful. That is perfectly normal. Those feelings will take time to process. Unfortunately I can't wave a magic wand to make you feel better. Nor can James.'

'I realize that,' she said dispiritedly.

Roddy employed another device she was familiar with. 'What would you like James to say?'

She was ready for the question. 'That's he's sorry. Really sorry. That it was a mistake and this girl turned his head, that he allowed himself to get involved in something that was wrong. I want him to admit that just because he didn't sleep with her that it's still wrong.' She looked at Roddy. 'James seems to think that because they didn't go to bed that makes it all right. But I think he had an affair in every other way. That's one point we just can't agree on. He still lied to me and deceived me and bought her things and took her to places. He did all those things behind my back. But he seems to think it's all tied up with drinking and that makes it OK.'

Roddy nodded. 'I see. It's problematic, isn't it? How does one deal with events that occurred when James was drinking, that he sees as a past episode in his life, but which are all too real to you and continue to cause you pain.'

'Exactly!' she exclaimed.

Roddy was not about to give her another opportunity to vent her frustration. She noted how he turned his attention quickly to James. 'James. How does that feel to listen to Susannah?'

James shifted. 'Obviously uncomfortable. I do understand why you feel upset. I do. Although I want to make it clear that I didn't sleep with her.'

Hearing him say that yet again exasperated her. 'That's not the point!' she hissed.

Roddy hastily intervened. 'I think we should let James finish.'

James looked up at Roddy. 'I want to rewrite the script. I am sorry about the past – genuinely.' Then his gaze shifted to her. 'We can't follow a new script, we can't change the lines of the play between us, if we are continually reciting the old lines.' It was an appeal.

She knew he was right. It was what was required. She listened to him carefully as he continued. 'But it's over. It's in the past. And as importantly it is a symptom of things that were wrong at the time – with me and with us – and those are changing now.' He held out his hands palms up. 'We have to live in today. Yes, what happened in the past matters and I'm not suggesting we sweep it under the carpet, but we have to move forward and make changes.'

She took another deep breath. Part of the difficulty of communicating with James was his adoption of the jargon of Grange House. Didn't we all 'live in today'? But she knew that the remedy was change on both their parts.

'I think you have to *want* to change,' she began slowly, thinking aloud. She knew she had Roddy to thank for the ability to speak her mind, because she had come to trust him. 'Actually, I think to achieve real, lasting, meaningful change a person has to want it very much. Funnily enough, it wasn't until I listened to Estella last Sunday that I understood that – when I saw the extent to which one can build a wall and live behind it one's whole life. It's tempting to say that Estella must be a very unhappy and troubled woman and I think she probably is. But she will never change—'

'Miracles happen,' interjected Roddy.

'It would need one,' concluded James.

'She won't change because she doesn't want to,' Susannah said thoughtfully, almost to herself. 'James wanted to, he was forced to, because his life was spiralling out of control and if he didn't do something about his drinking he was going to lose everything.' She paused. 'I'm not in that position.' She could see James sit up in his chair.

She turned to him. 'At the beginning I loathed Grange House and everyone in it, because I didn't choose it and I never wanted it.'

'You wanted me to stop drinking!' James protested.

'Yes. I did. And I still do. And for the record . . .' she felt herself begin to choke up, '. . . for the record, I am very proud of you and what you've achieved. I think perhaps I haven't made that clear before.' James made to speak but she forced herself to press on. 'But the price was very high, James. I don't think you will ever understand how I feel about the way this has exposed my life as well as yours, how we have been subjected to the total invasion of our family's privacy, how it feels to have no choice about that.'

Roddy's voice was soft. 'Susannah, I think when you went to Grange House more than any other emotion you felt shame.'

'Yes, yes I did. And before you tell me so Roddy, I know full well that that's exactly how I felt about my father's drinking. *Ashamed*. Ashamed of his drinking and determined to keep it a secret. I haven't sat in that family group for six bloody weeks and learned nothing at all. I'm well aware that some of this is about the past. But it is *my* past. Not yours or James's or anyone else's to tell me what I should do about it. And maybe I can't "deal" with it in the Grange House way – or I don't want to – or maybe I can find my own way.'

She hurried on, fearful of losing her train of thought and the ability to express it. 'I don't believe that talking is the answer to everything. I can see it helps some people. But if honest talking solved everything, righted every wrong, there would be no need for divorce. Sometimes it isn't possible to forgive and forget.'

'What makes it possible?' prompted Roddy.

'I think I *can* forgive the drinking. And I think, in time, I can forgive this friendship with Jasmine – although I'm absolutely furious about it.' She wasn't about to let James get away with it there and then. 'The point is I'm not sure I *want* to.'

She turned to James. 'I'm not a fool. I know you don't want to go back to Lloyd-Davies. I know you need AA, and I can see that things can never be the way they were. But this isn't just about you. It's about what I want, too. For the last few years my whole life has been about you: trying to change you, trying to control you, trying to cure you. I've never stopped to think what I want.'

She smiled sadly. 'It's very easy for an outsider to say "forgive and forget". But years have passed like this. Drinking leaves a legacy – of blame and bitterness and fear. I think the fear is the worst, the fear that it will happen again. I suppose it is like an affair in that way. No matter what anyone says I think I will always blame myself for not helping James to stop earlier and I will always feel a failure that strangers helped him when I couldn't.' She looked at Roddy. 'That may not be what the Grange House textbook says but that's just the way it is.' She gave him a hard stare. 'I know what you're about to ask – *What do you want, Susannah?*'

Roddy laughed. It was as if James wasn't there. She continued thoughtfully. 'OK. I know I want a relationship that isn't dependent for its survival on a team of counsellors and an audience of recovering alcoholics. I know I want stability and financial security. I want to stay in Cobham and do my job and live a normal life. I know I want to be a better mother. I know I've made mistakes with Matthew. I'm about as open with him as Estella is with James. As for the rest . . . Maybe I'm a dull, Surrey woman at heart but I don't want to grow soy beans in the Orkney Islands or sail a boat around the world or stand on my head for two months in an Indian ashram.'

James cut in to explain. 'A trip to India is Tom's latest idea for when he gets out.'

Roddy frowned. 'And not a very good one. Susannah, your life doesn't have to change in such radical ways. AA is supposed to be a bridge to normal living, a return to the normal world.'

'I'm sure it is. And I know that lots of people go back to their work and their families. But I know something else as well. I've spent years selling houses, quite a few of them for divorcing couples. You're not the only one who deals with couples in crisis. Hell, I have to get them to agree on a price and I can tell you there's usually one partner who's desperate to move and the other who would be quite happy if the house never sold.' She pulled herself back to the point. 'When I talk to the wives about their husbands what I hear is not some long list of grievances or crimes. What I hear, over and over again, is the same phrase: *We haven't got anything in common any more.* And to be frank, I'm not sure James and I have anything in common any more. Really, I wonder if we ever did.'

She looked at James and then at Roddy. She had come this far and there was no turning back. It was time to light the fuse. 'I'll be totally honest. This is my dilemma. How do I forgive the past, with no guarantees about the future, and move forward to a new life with James when I'm not at all sure I want that new life at all?'

Robert had bought all the newspapers. His secretary had placed the announcement of their engagement in the *Times* and the Saturday edition of the *Daily Telegraph*. Last week, the morning following Robert's proposal, the *Mail* and the *Express* had carried inside pictures of them leaving the Ivy accompanied by a short piece about Robert's romantic proposal over dinner.

While he measured out Colombian coffee, she sat at the kitchen table thumbing through the front pages. Two carried the same image, albeit from differing angles. It showed three women, dressed in black, walking through a churchyard. Two were arm-in-arm and the third, the most glamorous, followed two or so paces behind. It was the face of the youngest that caught Natasha's eye, because it could only be described as grief-stricken.

She was drawn to pick up the tabloid. The headline read 'Paul's Women'. The report described how yesterday the three women in the tortured life of photographer Paul Bass were united in grief. His ex-wife, daughter and girlfriend Bella attended his funeral in Mortlake with more than 200 showbusiness figures. Paul, who had battled drug addiction all his life, was found at his Thames penthouse dead from a suspected drug overdose. An inquest had been opened and adjourned the previous week.

'Didn't you know Paul Bass?' Natasha put the newspaper down. She looked at Robert, who had now moved onto the part of his morning routine that consisted of juicing oranges and grapefruit, which he did in a ratio of three large oranges to one red grapefruit. It was nice to have a man in her life who could cook, even if he was slightly pedantic about it.

'Who?'

'Paul Bass.'

Robert sounded preoccupied. 'Yes, he was an ex-client.'

'He died. It's in the papers.'

'Yes, I know that.'

An edge had crept into Robert's voice but she disregarded it. 'You didn't go to the funeral?' She was curious.

Robert put down his curved and serrated grapefruit knife and turned to face her. 'Why would I waste my time going to the funeral of a drug-addled snapper with a penchant for young flesh?'

She turned back to the report. 'Lots of people went. He was quite a figure in his time.'

'No,' Robert said deliberately, 'he was not. He was an average photographer who got lucky.'

'What about his early work? The Paris fashion shows. He was one of the first to photograph backstage. And his—'

He sounded irritated. 'Let me assure you that Paul – whom I knew rather better than you did – was a mediocre photographer who will very quickly be forgotten. Dying alone with a needle in his arm is about the most memorable thing he ever did.'

'You can't dismiss his entire body of work because of the way he died,' Natasha persisted. 'He was exhibited at the V & A!'

'Yes, so are umpteen Chinese pot-throwers and assorted women who embroider frocks.'

She felt unaccountably annoyed. 'Anyhow, I think he was talented.'

Robert was not going to allow her the last word. He sighed and then said slowly, 'He was not. He was a pencilled name in the address books of people who think of themselves as movers and shakers. That's all. A name that, as we speak, is being quietly erased all over London.' He walked over and took the newspaper from her hand. 'Those women look a bloody shower, too. Someone should have told the daughter to tie her hair back. And whoever advised them that black headscarves look chic got it all wrong. They look like they're hawking clothes pegs.'

She was silenced now. Robert could be ruthlessly cutting in his assessment of others. It was to be expected from someone in his line of business. What was more disturbing, and she had noticed it more than once, was the callousness of some of his reactions. It was a characteristic that over time she would work to ameliorate. One often read about marriage having a softening effect on men, especially high-flying men like Robert. It had already occurred to her that they should move out of London to the countryside, especially once they had children. Maybe Gloucestershire? Or Norfolk? All these places were the same, really.

Robert turned away. 'Paul is one of those people who couldn't cut it. It's not a question of feeling sorry for him or pointing out that he won the egg and spoon race when he was ten years old. Out there, in the real world, he couldn't survive. He was a loser.' He looked round at her. 'A loser. That's what they ought to put on his headstone.'

The telephone call could not have come at a worse time. Araminta was at school. Theo was upstairs sleeping off his jet lag. Tabitha had just sat down to finish editing the remaining very flawed chapters of a first novel by Jeff Hunter, who was better-known as a chef with a spot on breakfast television. She had told Ros she should be paid for rewriting it. She had planned a light lunch, then perhaps a walk on the Downs. They did not need to eat in expensive restaurants or to search out the big city lights in order to enjoy themselves. It was enough to cook breakfast together; to lie entwined on the sofa watching evening television; to go to bed together and wake up together. It was remarkable how quickly they felt at home with each other, as if the long weeks of separation had never occurred, and they were once again living comfortably side by side.

The telephone call was from Barbara. Tabitha knew immediately from the tone of Barbara's voice that there was something wrong.

'Tabitha, I'm sorry to get your Monday morning off to a bad start, but I know you wanted to hear from me straight away if there were any developments.'

She had not wasted any time. 'Of course. You've had a response from Robert?'

'Yes. In this morning's post. And I'm afraid it's rather more than a response to our application to the court. It's something of a counterattack.' She could hear Barbara leafing through papers on her desk and dread flooded through her. 'Tabitha, I'm afraid Robert has applied for full custody of Araminta. And he's getting married.'

As with all shockingly bad news, her first reaction was disbelief. She felt physically winded and her mind struggled to accept the news as it simultaneously sought to calculate the implications of Robert's actions.

She heard rather than listened to Barbara's voice continue. 'Robert's filed a residency application. He's asking for Araminta to live with him and his new wife. He wants Araminta to attend school in Wandsworth and then spend part of the holidays with you.'

'Part?'

There was a pause as Barbara consulted the paperwork. 'Up to half,' she quoted.

'What?'

As she sat in her tiny office under the stairs it felt as though Robert had invaded her house, as though he was in her office with her, enveloping her with his presence.

'Why?' Tabitha managed to ask.

Barbara sounded resigned. 'In Robert's case I would say that it's tactical. It's a means of putting pressure on you to stay in the UK rather than risk leaving without your child. Of course, some men do feel very strongly, and with good cause, that their children would be better off with them. I don't feel Robert falls into that category.'

A feeling of outrage had begun to form. 'How would he look after her? He's a workaholic! He has absolutely no idea how to look after

Minty on a day-to-day basis.' she concluded.

'That's as may be. We'll have to wait to see what he says in his affidavit. That's when he sets out the reasons why he thinks the court should give him custody. I would anticipate that he'll make much of his new status as a married man. Until then we'll send in the form to the court opposing it and you need to think about the reasons you'll give why Araminta should stay with you.'

Her head was spinning. She half-listened as Barbara gave her assurances that they would fight tooth and nail and that hers was an exceptionally strong case. She knew from her experience of the divorce that lawyers in these situations never told you the one thing you wanted to hear – *you will win*. They told you reassuringly that your case was strong; that the law was on your side; that decisions nearly always went in a way that was favourable to your situation . . . but not that you would win.

Barbara rang off and her thoughts turned to Theo upstairs. Seeing him walk through the arrivals hall at the airport she had run like a teenager into his arms, heedless of the families around her, and held him never wanting to let him go. Now she felt despondent. Her first notion was to keep the news from Theo. It was almost unbearable to have their few precious days together overshadowed by the news of Robert's legal manoeuvres. But even as she had the thought, she knew that she wasn't capable of hiding anything from Theo. Sure enough, when she took him up a cup of coffee he knew immediately that something was wrong.

'Hey, what's up?' he asked sleepily, pulling her into the bed with him.

He lay horizontally across her brass bed, his tanned body all the more attractive against the white sheets. The bedroom was tiny, barely large enough to accommodate her bed and a polished oak chest, which served as a bedside table. Light filtered through the curtained dormer windows and a shaft cut through across the red carpeted floor.

She pulled slightly away from him to lie on her back and stare at the ceiling.

'Barbara telephoned. Robert is asking for Araminta to live with him.'

Theo pulled her back towards him. His voice was relaxed. 'No judge is going to award him custody—'

'How do you know?' she said anxiously. 'And he's getting married.'

Araminta had mentioned Daddy's friend Natasha and told her that Natasha was famous. Tabitha had not paid too much attention, assuming that the relationship would go the way of all the others. Yet again, Robert had proved unpredictable. Her head felt heavy now, the pain that returned at times of stress now once more pressing down on her. She felt suddenly tired and sapped of energy.

'Honey, it's a tactic. It's obvious. No one is going to believe that the timing of this marriage is coincidental. The judge will see through it.'

'What if he doesn't?'

'He will.'

She looked at him. 'Theo, judges sometimes make terrible decisions! They set murderers free who go off the next day and kill more people – and meanwhile they send people to jail for ever who are totally innocent. Judges want everyone to think they're infallible but they're not!'

Theo held her tightly. 'Tabitha, you've got to have some faith. You've got a very strong case. You've got a great lawyer. You need to trust that this will work out. You're not doing anything wrong, here.'

But that was exactly how it felt sometimes, as though she was being in some way judged by the world – as a mother, as a wife, almost as a human being – and that the verdict on her hung in the balance.

Theo sat up and rested himself on one arm, simultaneously reaching for his coffee. 'It's a pretty obvious tactic—'

'A tactic,' she cut in angrily. 'That's what everyone says.' Theo looked at her quizzically. 'Barbara said the same thing. But saying that it's a "tactic" implies that this is all a game. This is my life we're talking about! The law seems to reduce it all to a game of strategy, each side making a carefully calculated move and then waiting for the response of the other side. Why does it have to be like this?' She felt close to tears.

'Hey.' Theo smoothed down her hair. 'Just take a deep breath. It's all going to be fine.'

'We don't know that!' she protested. 'He could win and I could have to pay costs, I could lose the house and I wouldn't have Araminta and I couldn't come to be with you because otherwise I'd only see her in the holidays—'

'Stop right there.' Theo's voice was suddenly authoritative. 'If you think like that, you're going to drive yourself crazy. Just focus on what you need to do today. Which is what?'

She felt sullen. She knew he was right but even so . . . She forced herself to reply, 'Nothing. We're going to wait to see what Robert is going to give as his reasons for Araminta living with him.'

'OK. So until then there's nothing you can do. It's normal to be worried – but if you let it take over your life then Robert's already won.'

She was confused. 'How do you mean?'

'Because he's got you on the run. You're thinking about him and what he's going to do next, but you can't determine what Robert's next move will be. You just have to wait. I know it's tough, honey. But it's all going to be fine.'

She said nothing. How could he understand? It was so easy to tell another person not to worry and so difficult to put that advice into practice oneself.

He seemed to read her thoughts. 'I know it's easy for me to say . . .'

'I feel as though Robert has come back from the past. Sometimes I think I'll never be free of him.'

He stroked her hair. 'Tabs, don't give him so much power over you. You're not married to him any longer. You're free. And I'm with you.'

'You don't know him.'

'True. But I recognize a bully when I see one. You just have to stand up to him. I'll be right by your side every step of the way and I want to prove that to you. I've been meaning to tell you: I want to give you some money to help out with your legal fees.'

'No!'

He laughed. 'Why not?'

'Because it's my battle. Robert is my ex-husband. There's no reason why you should get involved.'

'Miss Independent, huh? I *am* involved. I'm your fiancé. Remember? Your battles are my battles. I'm not going to stand back and watch you worry yourself senseless about money.'

'But—'

It was so difficult to say it – the fear she held of giving up her new-found, hard-won independence. In her memory she traced her downfall from the day she became financially dependent on Robert. She had vowed, when she left, that she would never become dependent on a man again, that she would always be able to walk away.

'Take it,' he said firmly. 'I don't want it back, either. So don't get any ideas about paying me back.' He reached over to the oak chest where his wallet lay and pulled a folded cheque from it. He handed it to her wordlessly. She gasped when she saw the amount.

'Theo . . . It's too much . . .'

'Take it.'

'This isn't your savings?'

He grinned. 'No, far worse than that. It's the Harley.'

'You sold your bike?'

'Yep.'

She felt choked. 'Theo. Thank you. I don't know what to say.'

'You don't have to say anything.' He pulled her down and began stroking her back. 'Honey, I'd do anything for you; don't you know that? Loving someone isn't about keeping score. It's wanting the very best for them, doing everything you can to make their life better.'

He pushed her onto her back and looked down at her. 'I love you. With my heart and body and soul. I don't think you really know that yet. That's OK. I'll wait for as long as it takes. Even if it takes for ever.'

Jasmine could have handled the *Radio Times* presenters' shoot. What made it close to impossible were not the demands of the A-list presenters, the tight schedule, the fact that two of the back lighters fused halfway through or even the fact that she had never in her life taken a group photograph destined for publication, let alone the cover of the *Radio Times*. What she could not handle was her indecision engendered, at the very start of shooting, when she heard Natasha Webster show a very large diamond solitaire to Fleur Gowrie and confirm that she was getting married to Robert Agnew next month. Natasha and Fleur were placed at the centre of the group. Natasha was beautiful in a no-make-up jeans-and-white-shirt kind of way. The presenters had been told to dress down and there had been long negotiations with Fleur, who must be seventy but looked twenty years younger, to persuade her to change out of a cream two-piece Dior suit and into something more in the holiday mode supplied by the team of BBC assistants who were anxiously supervising the shoot. Joan had given precise instructions as to how to organize the fifteen presenters and drafted in Rizzo, one of her ex-assistants, to lend practical and moral support. Rizzo, looking the part in Levi 569s and white T-shirt, whispered in her ear.

'As soon as I give the word, get going. Don't give them time to think how they look or we'll be here all day.'

They were to be pictured with sandcastles and buckets and spades and an assortment of tagged luggage. Natasha had got it just right, even down to her pale-blue espadrilles. She wore her hair loose with a pair of brown tortoiseshell Cartier sunglasses pushed back. And she had been charming – not at all put out that it was not Joan who would be taking the picture – and willing to be directed at every turn.

Jasmine had been using the light meter just inches from Natasha when she had heard Natasha speak under her breath to Fleur. 'We want something low-key. Just family and close friends.'

'And the honeymoon?' Fleur was checking her reflection in an ivory-encrusted compact. It was all Jasmine could do to stop herself dropping the light meter. She looked unseeing into the small device in her hand, all her attention focused on the conversation unfolding to her side.

'Venice. Not straight away. Robert has to work.'

'You'll have to get him to take you to the Cipriani.' Fleur snapped the compact shut.

'I've always wanted to go there,' enthused Natasha.

How could she not have known? But on reflection the *Guardian*, the sole paper Joan took, did not consider showbusiness marriages to be newsworthy events. She looked again at Natasha. Jasmine noticed that she held herself with elegant poise, encircled by an aura of calm authority, two characteristics that Jasmine herself had always felt she lacked.

It was impossible to concentrate. She took twice as many shots as she would normally have done. Her nerves were shredded and her sense of humour had deserted her. Without Rizzo to marshal the presenters she would have been lost.

Natasha had obviously changed Robert. It stood to reason; she wouldn't be marrying him otherwise. Natasha had tamed him, set boundaries, shown him that she was one woman who could not be pushed around. A woman like that with the pick of any man would expect to be treated like a queen.

Her thoughts ran on as she packed up the equipment. It was clear that Natasha had no idea who she was. Robert had not even seen fit to mention her name. Jasmine was an inconsequential piece of Robert's history, unworthy of a footnote.

As she was loading the final camera case she heard a voice at her shoulder. 'Thanks for the shoot.'

'Oh.' Jasmine stumbled to her feet. 'Yes. Sorry.' She had no idea why she was apologising. A flicker of confusion passed across Natasha's serene features.

Jasmine's voice sounded, to her, absurdly false. 'Um, thanks for coming.'

'It's a pleasure.' Natasha managed to be wholly professional without being aloof. She continued, 'I wondered if you could send me a print. I know we don't have pre-approval but my agent always likes to have some input.'

This was her chance. Her chance to do what? To warn Natasha that she was marrying a sexual deviant abuser? A man who got his kicks beating up women? A control freak? Who was to say that he was the same person with Natasha? It seemed impossible that he would be. And the consequences of that warning could be catastrophic. Her life was good; work was wonderful; Joan had already intimated that there were other shoots she might pass onto Jasmine if this one went well. Did she want to jeopardize that, to antagonize Robert, to have him come after her again, all for a problem that in all likelihood didn't exist any more? Wasn't this what they called 'letting go'?

Natasha was regarding her expectantly.

'I. . .' she repeated. 'I'll send you a print as soon as we have one.'

'Great. Do you have my agent's address?'

'Your agent?'

'Yes. Robert Agnew. I'll write it down.'

'I have it.'

Jasmine knew she had spoken a fraction too quickly.

Natasha sounded quizzical. 'You do?'

She hesitated. 'On file. We have the address on file.'

'Thanks. I'm sorry, I didn't catch your name.'

She thought fast. 'It's Joan Perham-Ford Photography.'

If Natasha thought it strange that Jasmine did not offer her name she did not press the point. She had turned to go. Jasmine had the impression that Natasha was a woman with a life to attend to. A woman who was more than capable of looking after herself. A woman who would no doubt dismiss any words of warning as the jealous mutterings of a discarded ex-girlfriend.

The committee of the Blue Baby Fund lunch, all weary of their chair-woman's company, had dispersed without delay from their impromptu meeting in the lounge of the Carlton Tower Hotel,

Louise's home from home in central London. She had called the meeting at short notice. Its subject was the Restaurant Tree. The Restaurant Tree was the responsibility of Edwidge, a thin and rather vague woman whose husband was attached to the Swiss Embassy and whose only contribution to the discussions so far was to compare all the restaurants of London unfavourably with those in Geneva. Louise, lacking confidence in Edwidge, had in effect removed her from command of the Tree, taken charge herself and instructed each of the committee to secure a meal for two, with wine if possible, and to obtain evidence of it in the form of a letter, a template of which she handed out. The letters were to be placed in large foil envelopes of different colours and pinned to potted trees yet to find a sponsor. Guests would bid for each envelope. It was the luck of the draw whether one drew La Gavroche or the local greasy spoon.

Grania had caught up with Natasha at the corner of Carlton Place and Sloane Street. She didn't look remotely pregnant. She was wearing high-heeled chocolate suede boots, which she had matched with brown leather jeans and a cream ski jacket. Grania turned to Natasha and said in an overly casual voice, 'I know! Why not have lunch?' And then, as if to pre-empt any refusal, she added, 'Just a quick bite. We could go to the General Trading Company?'

Natasha was more than happy to accept. 'Actually, I'd love to.' After all, she was not in a hurry. There was nothing to be done on *Expats* for another month, when she would be going out to Spain. Last week she had done the voiceover segments for the footage of the families left behind. It was much more intriguing and creative than the usual shots of leaving parties and tearful farewells. Anna had done a great job, editing the footage to subtly demonstrate that not all the relatives were sorry to see their loved ones move hundreds of miles away.

Today, there was just the post to collect from her house in Putney and more boxes to be packed in preparation for letting it. Robert was nagging her to get on with it. Going there these days made her feel sad and guilty because she was neglecting her little house.

It was almost too cold to walk but even if they had been minded to catch a cab the short distance to Sloane Square it would have been impossible. All the cabs had their yellow 'For Hire' signs switched off, which Grania had blamed on the influx of tourists visiting London for early Christmas shopping. They walked south down Sloane Street. As they crossed at the junction with Pont Street, Natasha's eye was caught by a neat crocodile of Hill House children, in brown knickerbockers and hand-knit jerseys, following their teacher. Beyond them the austere white-walled stone exterior of St Columba's, the Church of Scotland in London, rose up. Natasha and Grania walked briskly, passing Richard Ward the hairdresser on the left and Partridge's the grocers on the right. At Sloane Square they bore right into Symons Street and entered the General Trading Company. Natasha was tempted to linger in the table and glassware department, but Grania had already headed for the cafe to the rear. They passed through the Traditional Living section, with its array of gilt and bronze antique Buddha figures, Imperial chests with burnished locks, oversized balusters and an assortment of ginger jars, chrysanthemum motif-vases, candelabra, and framed fragments of antique Chinese script. Natasha could have bought everything, but Grania swiftly secured them a corner table in the minimalist stone and bamboo surroundings of the cafe.

They ordered the soup of the day, spiced squash accompanied by pumpkin bread, Natasha making a mental note to eat only half the bread and then have a salad for dinner because tomorrow was the dress fitting.

'I thought you might not come to Louise's meeting,' said Grania, 'with all your wedding preparations.'

'Oh, Robert's handling all that.' Natasha rephrased it. 'I mean, his office is. There's hardly anything to do. Just the dress, really.'

'Alex and I got married in Barbados,' said Grania sadly. 'His children wouldn't come and then some of his friends said they couldn't make it . . .' Her voice trailed off. 'It was rather awkward.'

Natasha found it difficult to know what to say to Grania in reply. 'You got married – that's the important thing.'

Grania's expression was difficult to fathom. 'I thought so at the time. I was so determined to get him and to make him mine. I don't think I thought very much about life beyond that.'

It was obvious that Grania wanted to talk. Natasha prompted her. 'Married life?'

'Yes. And all that goes with it. I married Alex but that meant I also married his work and his family and his lifestyle.'

'His daughter?'

With that the floodgates opened. Grania's voice was despairing. 'Yes. I have honestly made a *huge* effort with Gabriella and tried to be nice and involve her and actually it's worse because whatever I do it's still the same. Whenever I go shopping I buy her something and I've tried taking her out for lunch but I know that what she really wants is for me not to be there. Even if Alex didn't go back to her mother she'd still rather have him to herself. '

'What does Alex say?'

'He's never there! It's work or business dinners or bloody golf. I guess I never noticed it before because I had my own life in New York. But here it takes time to get to know people on more than a superficial level. As for Alex, every weekend he jumps in the car and heads off to some godforsaken part of Surrey and spends all day there. Then he gets home and spends the evening bitching about how much his back hurts. The only thing he begs me for is a deep-heat massage.' She leaned forward and whispered, 'As for sex, he lasts for ninety seconds. Max!' She sat back again. 'Why can't he play tennis? Or squash? Or anything that doesn't take all damned day!'

They were interrupted by the arrival of their order. As the very pretty French waitress set out soup and bread, Natasha pondered what Grania had told her. It was not at all what she would have expected. She might have speculated that Louise's marriage, for example, was not the perfect union that Louise portrayed it to be. But Grania had barely been married for a year, Alex had heaps of money and they were always going out to fabulous parties with everyone who was anyone. And Grania was having a baby. Except, of course, none of that had anything to do with being happy. Or not being lonely.

'Of course,' Grania continued, breaking off a small piece of bread, 'I don't want to put you off. It's just that . . .' She paused. 'I remember when we had lunch – you, me and Louise. We were telling you how important it is to get married *blah blah blah*. But it's also important to be *happily* married. I think there's far too much talked about "the" single life and "the" married life when what is important is the people involved.'

Natasha was rapidly reconsidering her opinion of Grania. She realized that neither of them had been able to speak candidly to date. Socialite lunches and charity committee meetings were not the places for honest or heartfelt conversation.

Grania's expression was animated now. 'I remember when I was living in New York. I'd stopped modelling then and I was working for a friend – Jay – who had a shop in Tribeca selling traditional American home furnishings. I told people that I was working as a designer but

300

really I was a shop assistant.' She took a sip of water. 'I'm sorry. Am I boring you?'

'No, not at all!' It was a further revelation that anyone like Grania could believe themselves to be boring.

'If you're sure,' Grania said doubtfully. 'Back to the point. My life was good. I'd made enough from my modelling to buy an apartment.' She had hardly touched her food. 'At Sixty-third and Lexington,' she added. 'Of course, Alex made me sell it when we got married, but before I met him I had dinner parties there. I knew so many people and I was invited to parties almost every weekend. That was how I met Alex – Jay's father had a place in the Hamptons and one weekend we went out there. His father hosted a lunch party that Sunday. It was early summer and everyone stood out on the terrace overlooking the pool. Alex had a house nearby and he was there with his wife. Of course, he had to give her the house in the divorce. And that's how it all began. Once it started all I wanted was to be married to him. I recall one Friday evening leaving the shop just before Christmas; it was dark and I was walking through Little Italy to the subway. It was snowing and the shop windows were decorated with the most fabulous Christmas decorations. All the bakeries had their windows piled high with gingerbread cookies and red and white candy canes. It was per-fect – and inside I felt so empty and incomplete and not a part of any-thing at all. I was waiting to cross the road when next to me a car stopped at the lights. It was a four-wheel drive, I think a Cadillac, headed with all the other cars out of Manhattan for the weekend to Long Island, probably Sag Harbour or North Haven where the week-enders have their houses. Inside the car was a family. The daddy was in the driver's seat, in his weekend clothes – a checked shirt and cash-mere pullover – and the mummy next to him and their two children in the back, a boy and a girl. At that moment I wanted so much to be that mummy in the car, to be that woman with her safe, secure, happy life and her adoring husband and her wonderful children . . .'

'With no worries about waking up alone on Christmas Day,' added Natasha.

'Exactly! But now,' Grania's voice lowered, 'now I *am* that woman. This is what I wanted to tell you. Last week Alex and Gabriella and I went out to dinner. We were driving along Kensington High Street on our way to the Belvedere. The atmosphere wasn't very relaxed, I can tell you. And we stopped at the lights. There was a young woman standing there waiting to cross, no more than twenty, holding a gym bag and talking on her mobile phone. She was laughing and looking at her watch and rushing to cross and she looked so free. So carefree! I realized that I have nothing to rush to now. I thought back to the couple I had seen two years ago in New York and I recollected something that I had not noticed at the time. He was driving and she was looking straight ahead and neither of them was speaking! That's how it is with Alex and me. How many married couples that you see driving around together are actually talking to each other? I've started looking. Hardly any of them! Now I wonder what it was that I *really* saw that day. Come to think of it, the husband did have a kind of distracted expression. Probably because he was thinking about his mistress! Maybe they were on the verge of spending the entire weekend in a beautiful house arguing with each other.' Grania shrugged her shoulders theatrically.

Natasha laughed. 'I love your story! It reminds me of a saying. Never judge your insides by other people's outsides.'

'Exactly! And that is what I did all the time, imagining everyone else's lives were fairytales.' Grania paused and looked away into the middle distance. 'There's another saying that comes to mind, too,' she said and now a bitter note had entered her voice. Her eyes did not meet Natasha's as she continued. 'If he'll do it *with* you, he'll do it *to* you.'

Natasha hesitated. 'You mean Alex?'

Grania pulled her gaze back to meet Natasha's. 'Yes. I think he's probably having an affair. Or if not an affair then the beginnings of one. I know his MO.'

'MO?'

'Modus operandi. When we met at the Hamptons Alex was very careful not to flirt. He was businesslike and very complimentary about his wife. At the end of the lunch, he gave me his business card and said that the bank was refurbishing its office. He gave me some bull about how the bank wanted a traditional American image and how it sounded as if the items in Jay's shop would be perfect. Of course,' she laughed, 'it would have been much more sensible for Alex to ask Jay directly – he was standing just a few feet away. But that wasn't the point and deep down I knew it; I just wasn't prepared to be that honest with myself.'

'I'm sorry,' said Natasha.

'Most people wouldn't think I deserved any sympathy. I stole him from his wife, just as she stole him from the first Mrs De Lisle – after she'd worked to fund Alex through his stock exchange examinations. I'm beginning to appreciate what they both had to put up with. I also think that his ex-wife didn't put up too much of a fight to keep him after she found out about us.'

It was nosy but impossible not to ask. 'She found out?'

'Yes. I'd packed his bag for him on a business trip. She unpacked it and realized that he would never have folded his shirts so perfectly.'

'Careless of Alex.'

'Or deliberate. I think he didn't really care. She didn't suggest counselling or give him an ultimatum. She threw him out, went to the lawyers and took him to the cleaners. I guess I was the last of a long line. Of course, Alex swears blind I was the only one who mattered and why can't I be content with that?'

'He did marry you, didn't he?'

Grania rolled her eyes. 'Alex is one of those men who need to be married, for practical reasons as much as anything. Practicality is never far from their minds. Has Robert made you sign a pre-nup?'

'No, we don't really have those in England.' It was an uncomfortable thought that if American-style pre-nups did exist then Robert would almost certainly have asked for one.

'Well, that's good anyway.'

Natasha was unsure what to say. 'What are you going to do?'

Grania gave an ironic half-smile. 'I'll probably say an awful lot and do nothing. I haven't got any proof. It's just a feeling. Besides, there is that part of me that thinks it was inevitable. I knew the type of man Alex is. Why should I have any grounds for believing that I could succeed in changing him where everyone else had failed?'

'But, if he loves you – and I'm sure he does,' Natasha added hurriedly, 'then of course you would expect him to be faithful. Perhaps the baby will bring you closer together.' Too late she realized how lame this sounded.

'Maybe,' said Grania, unconvinced. She leaned over the table and her words were slow and heavy with emphasis. 'Just be sure, Natasha, that you know the man you're marrying. Make sure you love and respect him just the way he is. Because take it from me – the chances of him changing are next to nothing.'

Lynda pulled an apologetic face, Justin smirked and Anthony disappeared into the kitchen. It was the end of the day on Friday and the call was widely anticipated. Anthony and Justin made a habit of avoiding answering the telephone after four thirty. Lynda nodded to indicate that she had transferred it to Susannah's desk telephone.

'Gerald Anderson.'

The rest of the conversation would play out as it did every week. She knew exactly what he wanted. She tried to sound positive. 'Susannah Agnew. How can I help you?'

'Just wondered if there were any viewings this weekend.' Even his voice was the same, his tone one of anxious hope.

Thus began the Friday call from the Andersons to check that she had not forgotten a weekend viewing for the house. The question and the answer were always the same. The Anderson house had now been on the market eighteen months. Justin had suggested having a wake to mark the two-year anniversary.

'No,' she said, endeavouring with every ounce of energy to sound patient, 'I'm afraid not. Nothing so far.'

'No chance a punter has slipped through the net?'

Was it his irritating phrasing? Or was it his querulous tone? Or was it the fact that he said exactly the same thing every bloody Friday?

She saw red. She had been about to sit down but decided to remain standing.

'No! There is no one. And frankly, Mr Anderson, I doubt there will be for some time.'

Lynda looked up from writing out her shopping list. Justin was already listening with his full attention. Fortunately the office was empty of clients.

'Oh? That's a pity.'

'It's a fact.'

'A fact?'

'Yes. Because your house is overpriced. Way overpriced, by about fifteen per cent. In the year since it's been on the market, whatever all the other agents may tell you, the market in Cobham for your type of unmodernized property has gone dead. If you want to sell it you need to bring the price down.'

'Oh.'

'And that's not all. If you're serious you need to change the marketing. It isn't a desirable family home. It is to you, yes. But to a purchaser it is a rare opportunity to purchase an unmodernized family home requiring refurbishment.' She stopped herself. 'Total refurbishment.'

'Yes.'

'I'm sorry. I don't want to hurt your feelings. Really, I don't. But we can't go on pretending that this strategy is working when it plainly isn't.' She paused. 'What did you say?'

She had a sense of déjà vu.

Mr Anderson's voice was curiously ebullient. 'Yes. I know. I'm not a total fool, you know!'

Given that that was exactly how she had regarded him to date she found it very difficult to think of a response to this.

She heard him sigh. 'I know. It's Anne. I'm trying to protect her. The house is Anne's pride and joy. I know what's going to happen. Downlighters and Poggenpohl kitchens and wood decking. I watch the television, you know. But Anne doesn't see it that way.'

Sympathy for Mr Anderson began to seep through. For the first time since she had met him she saw him not as a client, or more accurately a damned nuisance, but as a person.

'I'm sorry, but I have to be honest with you. What we could do is reduce the price – leave the marketing as it is – and blitz our list. If that doesn't work after a month or so then we could look at presenting it differently.'

There was a pause. 'Did you have a figure in mind?'

The policy of honesty had gathered a momentum of its own. 'Ten per cent,' she said firmly.

'Ten?' he repeated resignedly.

'At the very least. Which would mean, if the house sold, you'd be out of the house and down to Cornwall in time for Christmas.'

'I'll have to speak to my wife.'

'Mr Anderson, it's your decision. I can only give you my opinion.'

'Well, I appreciate it. There's no point living in a fool's paradise, is there?' He rang off.

Anthony emerged from the kitchen just as Justin punched the air and Lynda slid her shopping list under her keyboard.

Anthony looked as if he was about to say something.

'Is there a problem?' Susannah said efficiently.

He appeared to be at a loss for words. 'No. Not at all.' And with that he turned on his heel and hurried into his office.

## Chapter 12

# Daily Journal

*The latter years of my marriage, I now realize, were a sham. By the time we moved to Cobham Susannah and I existed under conditions of uneasy peace punctuated by periods of sustained sniper fire. We communicated in a desultory way about the house, about friends, about work to some degree, about anything except the things that really matter. Each of us was anxious to prove that we did more, contributed more, that our job was more important or stressful. I know I was guilty of being very small-minded on occasions, of leaving Susannah to clear up dinner because I was at pains to show what a high-powered day I had endured. In the beginning it was different. We wanted the very best for each other. We supported each other in every way we could, taking pleasure in the other's accomplishments and sharing each other's struggles and disappointments. I do not know if that time can be recaptured. It most certainly will not be if Susannah's friendship with Anthony Charron continues to intensify. It is eleven p.m. and she is still not home.*

The house was quiet except for the light in James's office. The curtains were only partly drawn and as she parked the car on the driveway she saw him inside working at his desk. He would be preoccupied and she would be able to slip upstairs. She was not quite ready to have a conversation about how she had spent her evening. And if he was doing some work for Lloyd-Davies she certainly didn't want to disturb him. For the first time in years, without his bonus, they were close to running an overdraft.

However, he called out to her as she entered the house and she had no option but to go to the study doorway. From there, she could see his desk covered not with papers but rather a partially folded ordnance survey map.

Its unexpected presence confused her. 'What's that?'

He did not look up. 'A map of a small part of the Welsh countryside.'

She could not stop the sharp tone that entered her voice. 'And why on earth have you got that?'

'It's for Alice and Helena. They've found a rather grand but neglected house which they want to turn into a high-class B & B. They'll grow all their own organic produce, of course. And it's much more economically viable than the original idea of the smallholding.' James spoke distractedly without looking up from the map. 'The problem is the easement that runs across most of the back garden. It may mean that Farmer Giles can take his cows across their planned kitchen garden. I have the deeds, too.'

'I hope they're paying you,' she said, knowing full well that they weren't.

'I doubt it,' he responded smoothly. 'Any more than Anthony Charron intends to pay you for your time this evening.'

Now he looked up at her and his gaze was chillingly uncomfortable. She faltered. 'Anthony Charron?'

He looked back at his map and said in an absentminded tone, 'Yes. Anthony Charron. Your boss. You did say you had a work commitment this evening.' James looked up. 'I'm not a complete idiot.'

Susannah could think of nothing to say to this because she had no idea what he was talking about.

Before she could ask him he continued, 'There's an expression – you might have heard of it. Sometimes the noun changes but the essence is the same. The sanitized version is "Don't kid a kidder".' His voice was cold. 'How long have you been sleeping with him?'

It was impossible. She reacted in the only way she could. She started to laugh.

'Sleeping with him? Are you mad?'

'Please, just tell me the truth,' he said dramatically. 'He's been after you ever since you joined that firm. And Matthew told me he was here having breakfast with you.'

She sighed. 'I *told* Matthew he was here – hardly the act of a woman trying to conceal an affair.'

It was very slightly gratifying to see him falter.

'James,' she said sternly, 'I wasn't with Anthony Charron.'

'Well . . .'

'And I didn't want to tell you where I was going until I knew more myself.'

He held his hands up in surrender. 'Fair enough. Well. Where were you, then?'

It was so tempting to let him wonder, but she didn't have the heart. Instead she turned and wandered off into the conservatory, leaving James no option but to follow her. She put on a table lamp and looked around at the stack of old magazines on the teak coffee table and realized that it was months since they had sat in here together. She sat down on the edge of the sofa.

'I was with Cal Doyle.'

James looked horrified. 'Are you having an affair with him?'

'James! I'm not having an affair with anyone. Especially not Cal Doyle. For the record he's married and his wife's expecting a baby. Cal's offered me a job.'

'A job?' She could see the surprise in his eyes.

'Actually, that's not quite true. I told him that he would be better off doing his own marketing and sales and he's asked me to set up the office. It's more like a directorship.'

James was still standing. 'And you'd leave Charron's to do that?'

'Of course. It would be my own show. I'd want a three-year contract to give me some security. But Cal's expanding—'

'Oh, it's "Cal" now, is it?' he interrupted.

She ignored this. 'There's more than enough work right now, let alone with what he's got planned. And he doesn't penny-pinch on the budget. I'd have a secretary, a decent car and a full benefits package. In time I would probably get an assistant.'

'I suppose you've already got someone in mind,' James said and the slight tone of resentment was unmistakable.

She ignored it. 'Well, it's tempting to poach Justin but I think that would be mean to Anthony. I'll just have to put the feelers out. Why don't you sit down?'

He did so reluctantly. 'And there's nothing with Anthony Charron?'

'No!' She knew this was not quite true but whatever there was did not need concern them at this point. She felt uncomfortable with the half-truth, however. 'We're friends. Anthony has been very supportive.'

James snorted.

'But there has never been anything other than friendship,' she assured him. 'I promise you.'

'He'd like more,' James said sourly.

'Maybe he would. But I'm powerless over the way he feels, aren't I?'

James gave a resigned half-smile. Then his expression turned more serious. 'I can see how excited you are, and perhaps this isn't the time to rain on your parade. But I can't help feeling that I'm being cut loose.'

She hesitated. 'I don't mean it that way.'

'Susannah, you can be honest with me. With Roddy, the other day, you said you weren't certain if you wanted to go on with our marriage. I don't want to push you into an answer . . .' His voice trailed off.

She knew the answer. She had known it when Cal had told her the salary and she had mentally worked out the mortgage she could afford. She had known when she had asked him about the hours he would require and silently calculated how they would fit in with school. She had known it because not once during dinner with Cal Doyle had she thought about James or what he would say. She had taken the job and set in place all that she needed. Maybe she had known it in her heart when she had read James's life story and recognized, past the haze of her anger over Jasmine, that James was right when he had written that they were very different people.

In the end it was the unspoken words that cast the die. In the silence that followed she did not say that she loved him, forgave him, would stand by him or follow him. He did not tell her that she was the most important thing in his life. He had not assured her that he would do anything for her. He did not proclaim them to be soulmates.

All the years that had preceded this point and all the events of the past year, had come to this defining moment. It was over between them.

She used the easiest words. 'I think we ought to separate.'

They both knew it was a euphemism.

He nodded. He put his arm around her shoulder. She had heard of couples at the end of their marriage finding a sudden passion and marking their final time together by making love. It was not that way for them. They felt like brother and sister.

Susannah was reflective. In the end it wasn't about Jasmine, or Grange House or even the fact of James getting sober. It was about all the years before. The question in her mind was not whether to leave now. It was why she had not left before. But James did not need to know that. The lies, the betrayals, the raised hopes and the broken promises had corroded their marriage until there was nothing left to save. Drink, not Jasmine, had been the other woman. And for years Susannah had fought her rival, determined to keep her husband, willing to suffer all the consequences and humiliations of James's drinking rather than lose him to her foe. She understood why she had begun by hating Grange House, Gina and Raul – because it felt as though they had succeeded where she had tried for years and failed. At least she understood now that James had been in the grip of an addiction stronger than both of them. She was genuinely proud of him for all he had achieved, but fighting a battle had left them no time to nurture a marriage. The harsh words, the loss of intimacy and all countless small ways in which they had ceased to care for each other had left them with nothing more than the shell of a marriage.

They sat in silence punctuated by the stilted discussion of details.

James stared at the floor. 'I'll move into the spare room.'

Then they talked about Matthew and she said that she would tell him.

James was clear. 'I'm not going to abandon him.'

'I know.' She believed him. 'And I'm going to take a month off before I start with Cal. I'm going to spend it with Matthew. I want to be . . .' Unbidden the Grange House phrase 'emotionally available' popped into her mind. 'I want to have some fun together,' she concluded.

'Well, I'm not disappearing.'

'Thank you.'

'You were right, by the way. I am going to hand in my notice to Lloyd-Davies. I haven't known how to tell you. And then I'm going to take some time off to decide my next move.'

'I thought you might train as a counsellor.' Once she would have made the comment sarcastically but now the suggestion was genuine.

'Apparently that's what all newly sober alcoholics fresh out of rehab want to do. I'm not sure I have the patience.'

'I think you have the insight.'

'Actually, Susannah, there's something I've been meaning to tell you.' He paused. 'I'm thinking about growing alfalfa in East Anglia.'

And despite it all she laughed and went into the kitchen to make them coffee.


Lizzy's cheeks were flushed, her glass was empty and her brown corduroy skirt had ridden too high up her thigh. It was half past midnight and the effect of the fire in the close cottage living room added to Tabitha's sleepiness. Sitting next to Theo, Lizzy occupying the easy chair to the side, it was all Tabitha could do to keep her eyes open. The evening had been a partial success. Her parents, who had departed two hours earlier, had talked easily with Theo, who had fielded her mother's questions about his family – and her father's questions about the farm – with easy charm. It had been less easy to involve Lizzy in the conversation.

'Well, it all sounds wonderful. Wonderful,' Lizzy repeated inconsequentially. 'I hope you'll invite us over. If Tabitha still wants to know her old friends.'

'You and your daughter are always welcome to visit,' Theo said smoothly. He took another sip from his coffee cup. Tabitha imagined he must be more tired than she was. He never fully got over his jet lag before it was time to go home again. Occasionally she would wake up at three or four in the morning to find him gone and hear the faint sound of the television downstairs, waking again momentarily when he returned at six or seven.

'Oh, people always say that,' said Lizzy dismissively. 'We'll stay in touch,' she mimicked. 'It soon comes down to a Christmas card.'

'No,' Theo said firmly. 'Any friend of Tabitha's is more than welcome.'

Lizzy looked up at Tabitha. 'Would you mind very *very* much if I had a cigarette?'

'No, of course not.'

Lizzy began rummaging in her handbag. 'I don't normally,' she explained, 'but sometimes after dinner I let myself have one. And you?' she looked enquiringly at Theo.

'The occasional cigar.'

'Oh, well you must have a cigarette!'

'Not for me.'

'Oh, come on!'

'No. I'm fine as I am.'

Theo reached across the table, took the box of matches they used for lighting the fire and struck one in order to light Lizzy's cigarette for her. Tabitha wished he hadn't. She knew he was only being polite but there was something about Lizzy's mood and the intimacy of the gesture that made her feel uncomfortable – might Lizzy misinterpret it?

'You should get Tabitha to buy you a nice Cuban cigar when she's up in London. Ian used to smoke them. Probably still does. At least she has to put up with the stink now—'

Theo cut her off. 'Definitely best to smoke them outside.'

'On your porch,' said Lizzy. 'Very home town.'

Tabitha caught the hint of mockery in Lizzy's tone and the flicker across Theo's face but he said nothing.

Lizzy appeared not to have noticed anything because she went on. 'I hope Tabitha's going to be happy there once the novelty has worn off. I can't quite see our London girl settling down on the farm.'

There was an uncomfortable silence. 'It's a good life and I'm sure she'll be very happy,' said Theo evenly.

'But it is hard work,' Lizzy persisted. 'Farmers here are always complaining about how they can hardly survive.'

'Living off the land is never easy. No one ever got rich being a small farmer. But there's more to it than that. We're caretakers; we don't "own" the land—'

'You don't own it?' cut in Lizzy abruptly.

'Yes, legally,' Theo said patiently. 'I'm talking in a spiritual sense.'

'Oh.' Lizzy gave a silly laugh. 'Very profound!'

Tabitha wasn't sure if she felt embarrassed on Lizzy's behalf or irritated by her continued presence. There was also the question in her mind of how Lizzy was going to get home.

There was another long silence.

Lizzy broke it. 'Well, I think you're very brave. I mean, most marriages struggle to survive at the best of times. I should know. And it's not as if it's the first time for Tabitha.'

Tabitha shot Lizzy a warning glance.

'I'm just trying to be honest. There's no need to look at me like that.' Lizzy's voice had a quarrelsome tone now. 'I wouldn't be a good friend to you if I didn't speak honestly, would I?'

Tabitha felt upset for herself and embarrassed for all of them. Goodness only knew what Theo was currently thinking about his future wife's judgement when it came to choosing friends. She looked across at him but his features were impassive.

'Tabitha will be just fine,' said Theo firmly and got up, but as he moved to the door Lizzy lunged forward in her seat and grabbed his hand.

'Oh God,' she wailed, 'I've said the wrong thing, haven't I? I didn't mean to! I'm just worried for Tabitha! And it's important, isn't it?' She was still holding onto Theo's wrist. 'I mean, how people get on with their exes. It's an indication.'

'Lizzy,' Theo said patiently, 'Tabitha and I have talked about all the things you're concerned about. In detail. Over many months.'

'Precisely,' said Lizzy, letting go of Theo and reaching for another cigarette. 'You're too involved. That's why it helps to have an impartial third party involved.'

*We don't want you involved*, Tabitha wanted to scream. She started to calculate how she was going to get Lizzy home, apologize to Theo and avoid Lizzy ever taking a trip to visit them in the USA. Imagine a week of this under the same roof.

Theo returned with his coat on and the car keys in his hand. 'I'll drive you home.'

It might not be the subtlest method but it was effective in telling Lizzy that it was time to leave. She had little option but to rise to her feet. 'I hope you'll remember which side of the road to drive on!'

Theo's tone was resigned. 'I'm sure you'll remind me.'

Lizzy turned to Tabitha. 'Thank you so much! I hope I didn't say too much.' She plunged towards her and Tabitha found herself enveloped in a soft bear hug smelling of smoke, wine and perfume.

'Of course not.'

'It's just that I want the best for you. The very best. I know how difficult marriage is and how careful you have to be and I don't want anything bad to happen to you.' Lizzy seemed unaware of the aspersion this was casting on Theo, who was standing barely two feet away. 'It's such a big step and you're so brave and I worry. That's the thing. I worry about you,' Lizzy repeated unnecessarily. She turned to Theo. 'You should have seen her when she arrived in the village. She was a broken woman. *A broken woman*, Theo. Never stopped crying. Totally lost! And then Peter abandoned her—'

At that moment Tabitha desperately wished Lizzy would abandon her, too.

'Which was another terrible blow. There were times when I didn't think she'd make it. We used to sit in the evenings and drink red wine. We were like sisters. I have always thought of Tabitha as my sister,' she declared to Theo, clutching her hands together to demonstrate the point.

Theo was buttoning up his coat. His hand rested on the door latch. 'Did you have a coat?'

Lizzy, who was looking at Tabitha in a less than focused way, did not seem offended by Theo's directness. 'No. I'm warm-blooded.' She gave a theatrical laugh. Just as they were about to set off down the path, Lizzy turned anxiously to Tabitha. 'I'll come back in the morning for the car. Oh, and India!' She gave another peal of laughter.

'No rush,' said Tabitha. 'Come as late as you like.'

Tabitha put the thought out of her mind that tomorrow's challenge would be preventing Lizzy from staying in her sitting room all afternoon. And then she felt mean because there had been times in the past when Tabitha had been very grateful for her company. Relief combined with uneasiness as Tabitha watched them get into the car. Seeing another woman sitting next to Theo was unnerving as they reversed down the driveway and out into the lane. She went inside and began clearing the table of glasses and dessert plates, wrapping the remains of a raspberry pavlova, her father's favourite even if she had used frozen raspberries, to put it in the refrigerator. She began loading the dishwasher. No matter how much she tried to clear up as she went along, she always seemed to have a heap to do at the end of the evening. It was the small items that caused the problems because they had to be handwashed. She carefully rinsed the small Limoges dishes she used for pre-dinner olives and almonds, the bone-handled dinner knives and the art deco glass bowls she used for pudding – all of them finds at local antique fairs on a Sunday afternoon. There had been plenty of wedding presents when she had been married to Robert, including a Royal Wedgwood dinner service from their list at Thomas Goode, but Robert had kept hold of all of that and everything else, even the things her friends had given her.

Abruptly the front door opened and Theo reappeared. He shot her a weary smile. 'Your friend likes to talk,' he said, slipping off his coat.

'Is everything all right?' she asked nervously.

'Of course.' There was the briefest hesitation. 'Of course.' He looked as if he was on the verge of saying more.

'What is it?'

'Nothing,' he said distractedly, picking up a piece of walnut bread from the breadbasket and breaking off a small piece.

'Did she make a pass at you?'

He started laughing. 'Don't be silly!' He picked up a tea towel and began drying the glass dishes. It was a companionable scene and yet Tabitha felt subdued. After a few minutes Theo put the cloth down, came over to her, took the silver cake slice from her hand and placed it in the kitchen sink. Then he pulled her to him. 'Don't worry. Lizzy talks a lot, that's all. It's kind of . . .'

She finished his sentence for him. 'Irritating?'

'Yep.' He kissed her on the forehead. 'Let's go to bed.'

'I haven't finished clearing up!'

'We'll do it in the morning.'

'I'll do it, you mean.'

He began kissing her neck and his hands ran down her back. 'It's bedtime. Right now.'

He took her by the hand and led her upstairs.


Jasmine stepped back and surveyed the results of hours spent stripping wallpaper on a Saturday night. Joan had warned her sternly only to approach one room at a time. Jasmine was impatient to transform the living room but common sense dictated that a girl with no decorating experience should start with the smallest room. The bathroom had been papered in Laura Ashley nautical stripes with a border at the top of blue and white sailboats. Most of the paper now lay on damp strips in the bathtub. Joan had further warned her to expect the worst of the plaster below but in fact it was in good condition with nothing that a tub of filler wouldn't cure. Jasmine had planned her paint scheme: aquamarine walls and paintwork in an off-white colour called 'Moon Rise'. Lorraine, who owned the flat beneath hers, had done something similar. They had started talking on the staircase, fallen into a routine of having coffee in the evenings and gone out to All Bar One in Ealing on a couple of occasions. It was not Jasmine's scene but Lorraine, who was newly divorced, liked to 'get out' as she put it. When the flat was finished, Jasmine planned to hold a housewarming party and use it as an excuse to get in touch with the art college crowd.

She still thought of James. No longer on waking, but still every day, wondering where he was and how he was doing and whether he had stuck it out at Grange House. Sometimes she thought about his wife. Maybe they had 'rediscovered the passion in their relationship' as it said in women's magazines. Joan, naturally, had allowed no time for moping. 'Life's short. Enjoy it while you can,' had been her directive. Joan, who had outlived two husbands and combined each of them with a string of lovers, had clearly never lingered too long over the memory of any of them.

Jasmine felt suddenly tired. Looking at her watch she was shocked to see it was nearly midnight. She began clearing the wallpaper from the bath and floor and got ready to apply the filler. That way it would dry overnight, ready to be sanded in the morning.

She did not know which would be harder – telling Anthony that she was leaving or explaining to him that she and James were divorcing. The first piece of news would disappointment him, the second she feared would raise false hope, and there was nothing she could do to comfort him on either point.

She told Anthony as soon as she could persuade him out of the office. She decided on the Two Brewers. A public venue seemed easier somehow, at least for her. She had intended to begin by telling him about Cal Doyle but somehow her carefully formulated plan unravelled as soon as they had sat down. The bar was half empty, before the lunch crowd flooded in, but she appreciated the privacy and brushed off Anthony's suggestion that they should sit outside.

They ordered shrimp salads and drinks and then she was further delayed in her announcements by Kimberley chatting at some length about her ideas for the winter menu. At last they were left alone.

Anthony clasped his hands and asked her earnestly, 'So how are things with James?'

316

She had no choice. She could hardly give him some flannel that things were great and then announce ten minutes later that they were getting divorced.

She felt a surge of nervousness. 'Actually we've decided to get a divorce.'

To his credit, Anthony was obviously genuinely concerned for her. 'I'm sorry.' He frowned. 'How awful for you. When did he announce this?'

'He didn't. We decided to go our separate ways. It was a mutual decision.'

She could see from his expression that he plainly didn't believe this explanation. 'Well, to be accurate it was my decision.'

He sounded mildly shocked. Perhaps he had imagined that James, in the throes of a relapse, had thrown her out of the house. 'Well, you must do what's right for you.'

It was so tempting to sit back and leave it at that, but she had to press on. 'I think, perhaps, that I haven't been totally straight with you, Anthony. I think that I have used you as a . . .'

'Shoulder to cry on?'

'Yes.'

'Well, I'm a very happy shoulder.'

He wasn't making it easy for her. She stammered out the sentence she had prepared in advance. 'I think I may have misled you into thinking that we could be more than that.'

'I certainly hoped so.'

She felt dreadful. 'I'm sorry.'

She could see the flicker of sorrow in his eyes but he said quickly, 'It's perfectly all right. You mustn't give it another thought. You must have a great deal on your mind.'

Anthony was being the perfect gentleman and that made it all the worse because there was more to come.

She had to be honest. It was Gina who had taught her that. Gina, whom she had never grown to like but came to respect, had spoken about honesty. It had been in one of the Sunday family groups. Speaking more quietly than usual, Gina had told them that nothing – work, family, possessions or achievements – counted for anything if they were based on dishonesty. Not brutal honesty, nor honesty as a weapon to wound, but the honesty that is an essential truthfulness and integrity in every aspect of one's life. It was when she had started to be honest with herself, to stop blaming and start looking at her part in what had happened, that everything had changed.

'I married James for some good reasons. He's bright and funny, the life and soul of the party and he's a very good lawyer. But I married him for all the wrong reasons, too. I thought Matthew needed a father and I needed a husband. After my first husband left I wanted stability and security and I think at some level I knew that James needed me to keep him on an even keel. I was his counterbalance. Of course, when he stopped drinking all that changed.'

'One imagines that things would get better.'

'They did, in some ways. But there's too much water under the bridge.' She paused. 'Can I ask you something? A personal question.'

'Ask me anything you like,' he said easily.

She hesitated. 'After Kate had her affair . . . did you ever ask her to come back?'

Anthony gave her a rueful smile. 'Ask her? I begged her. But she wasn't going to give him up. Even if she had I'm not sure we could have got past it. Superficially, maybe. It takes a very special type of person to forgive after an affair. I mean really forgive and not drag it up every time there's a row.'

She spoke with feeling. 'It takes a very special type of person to live with a recovering alcoholic.'

At that moment, in the warm companionship they shared, she almost considered going outside, calling Cal Doyle and telling him that she had changed her mind. As much to end the possibility of backing out she blurted, 'Anthony, I have to hand in my notice.'

Now he looked stunned, and rushed to reassure her.

'Susannah! Because of our friendship? There's no need.'

'No, not because of that. Because I've been offered another job.'

'Good Lord!' Clearly an alarming thought had come to mind from the expression on his face. 'Tell me it's not Kings!'

'No. It's Cal Doyle. He's asked me to do sales for him.'

He sat back. She was dreading his response now. But after a few seconds he said philosophically, 'Hmm. Well, I can't say I'm surprised.'

'You're not!'

'Susannah, you're the best. The very best I've ever worked with. I'm only surprised he hasn't asked you before.'

This was not the time to bask in the compliment. She felt the need to give him some explanation. 'The money is very good and now that

I'm going to be on my own—'

He cut her off. 'My dear, say no more.'

She was not, in any case, going to tell him that she relished the opportunity, for the first time in her life, to run her own show. Cal Doyle wanted results but he wasn't concerned with the detail of how to achieve them.

'Of course,' Anthony said, and she could tell that he was serious, 'you're not having Justin.'

'Absolutely not.' This was also not the time to tell Anthony that Justin was currently shortlisted for the job of 'Bloke on a Bike' – reporting on London traffic conditions for Buzz FM's breakfast radio show from the pillion of a Harley Davidson driven by a retired Metropolitan Police motorcyclist.

'I feel awful. I'll do whatever you need me to do for a smooth handover,' she assured him. 'What will you do about the lettings department?'

'Oh,' he said blithely, 'Dee will stay on. Ever since I said you were taking over she's been regretting her decision to leave. That's Queen Dee for you.'

'I didn't think you knew we called her that!'

He sat back and regarded her with unconcealed amusement. 'I've been in this business for a very long time. It's in my blood.' He looked her in the eye. 'Susannah, you'd be surprised what Captain Mainwaring knows.'

Anthony's reactions had been predictable. Anthony's age, background and position combined to give him a resilience and control of his emotions that allowed them to leave the Two Brewers as friends.

Susannah, as she knocked on Matthew's bedroom door the same day, had frighteningly little idea of what her own son's reaction to the news of his parents' divorce would be. They had agreed that she would break the news and James would join them later. This time she had no plan, no speech and no strategy. She found Matthew lying on his bed, headphones plugged in, eyes half-closed.

'I haven't got any homework,' he said defensively as she came in.

She sat down on the bed, causing him to start and regard her with puzzlement.

It was never going to feel right. There was never going to be a perfect set of appropriate words. So she came straight out with it.

'Matthew. There's no easy way of telling you this, so I'm not going to wrap it up or do anything other than tell you the truth.'

'Hang on.' He shifted slowly and began searching under the Arsenal duvet for his iPod. She realized that he couldn't hear a word she was saying.

She pointed at his ears. 'You need to take those out,' she said loudly. It was one of his most irritating habits, his belief that one could hold a conversation whilst watching television or listening to music and even, on occasions, doing both.

She began again, recited the same preamble, and then paused before looking him in the eye and saying slowly, 'Matthew. I'm sorry. But Dad and I are getting divorced.'

He lay back on his pillow. 'Wow.'

Her instinct was to rush in and say whatever it took to make it all better, to ease the shock and soothe the pain. Experience had taught her otherwise.

He looked back at her. 'Are you going to get married to someone else?'

She had not expected that. 'No! There's no one else involved.'

He gave her a sideways look. 'What about Anthony Charron?'

'No!'

'He fancies you.'

'Matthew!'

'He does. It's obvious.'

'Matthew, there is absolutely nothing between me and Anthony. He's my boss and a friend but nothing more.' Never had she been so glad not to have fallen into another man's arms.

'So why?'

'Your father and I have been unhappy for a very long time. His drinking has been an issue—'

'No shit!' Matthew said sarcastically.

She decided to ignore that. 'But that's not all. We've spent many years being unhappy and even now that he's sober some things haven't changed.'

'You should have told me before. It's not like I didn't know Dad drinks.'

She didn't want to believe it but she knew it had to be true. 'Did you? Did you really know about the drinking? About everything?'

He rolled his eyes. 'Duh! It's pretty obvious, you know.'

She felt despairing, 'I know. I know that now. At the time I was try-ing to protect you. I wanted you to have a childhood. I wanted us to be a family.'

'Mum, I'm fourteen!'

'Yes,' she said weakly. 'I just . . . I did it the only way I knew how, Matthew. You don't have to pass an exam when you become a parent.' She rushed on. 'I just wanted the best for you. I wanted you to have a nice life and not be worried about things and I wanted you to feel safe and secure.'

She thought about the little boy who had climbed into her bed night after night, snuggled on the sofa with her, clung to her on the school steps on that first day. She was close to tears.

'Mum, it's OK.'

'I made it up as I went along. Now I can see that I should have been a better mother, gone to classes, read books. I should have seen what was going on—'

'Mum, it's OK! Leave it!'

She looked at him uncomprehendingly. 'How can it be? How can it be OK? I've put you through two divorces, chosen two men to be fathers to you and not managed to stay married to either of them. God, you're a child from two broken homes! But I am definitely going to go to a class on how to parent teenagers.'

'Mum! *Please* don't start going to classes. You're fine. It's not all your fault. I'll still see Dad.'

'It's not the same as living together,' she protested. 'It's not the same as being a real family.'

'Mum, you need to chill. It's OK. It's not exactly a surprise. I mean it is a surprise but it's not, if you see what I mean.'

She didn't but she nodded anyway.

'Loads of kids come from divorced families.'

'That doesn't make it OK! And Jake's parents aren't divorced,' she observed.

Matthew looked confused. 'So what?'

'Are they happy?'

He shrugged his shoulders. 'I don't know. I don't think about it. What's that got to do with anything?'

Could it be possible that he actually didn't think about it, didn't compare her with other mothers and generally had very little interest in analysing Jake's family situation?

'But you must notice,' she persisted. 'Isn't that why you spend so much time there?'

'Mum. He's got a pool table. We do PlayStation. We play poker—'

'Poker!'

'For chips, not money,' he sighed. 'Everyone plays.'

'I don't!'

'OK, you don't,' he conceded. 'Mum, I don't spend my time listening to Jake's parents' conversations. I hardly speak to them.'

She could believe that.

'Have you and Dad totally decided? Have you talked about it?'

She almost smiled. It was astonishing, the coexistence of sharp insight alongside childish naïvety. There were, after all, things he didn't know and didn't need to know.

'Yes. It's not something we've taken lightly and we've talked a lot. Matthew, Dad and I want different things and now that your father has got sober the differences between us have become more obvious.'

'Like what?'

'He wants to leave Lloyd-Davies. He wants to "find himself" I suppose you'd say.'

Matthew rolled his eyes. 'Is he going to get a tambourine and dance down Cobham High Street?'

It was hopeless not to laugh. 'Stop it! You'll have to ask him yourself.'

Matthew was clearly thinking about the wider implications. 'So what's going to happen to the house?'

'Nothing. We're going to do nothing until you finish the school year. We don't want anything to interfere with your education.'

'That figures.'

'And you won't have to change school.'

But he had already moved on. 'Are we staying here?'

'Dad's going to find somewhere else to live and we'll stay here for the time being—'

'Can we afford it?'

Once again he had caught her off guard.

'Yes, but not indefinitely. I'll sell the house and find somewhere new.'

'Somewhere small, you mean.'

She ignored that. Matthew's materialism was not one of his most appealing characteristics, but then all teenagers seemed to be that way these days. 'Nothing is going to change more than it has to. Dad can come and go.'

'And you're not going to start seeing Charron?'

'Matthew, for the umpteenth time, no! Why are you so worried about that?'

'Because he's an oldie and because of that car. If you try to make me go in his car I'm going to go to court and divorce you.'

'Divorce me?'

'Yep, kids can do that now. So watch out.'

It was incredible, the change in one generation. Her parents' marriage, her father's drinking, the family finances, were all a closed book to her and even into her adulthood had largely remained so. Or was it that they had both known more than they chose to reveal? Would her son one day sit in some therapist's consulting room talking about his emotionally unavailable mother and the family secrets of his childhood? Possibly. Would he be told that he had been burdened with too much information or given too little; that his mother had distanced him or, alternatively, smothered him; that his mother had projected all manner of issues and inadequacies onto him and he needed to detach from her as a matter of urgency?

She put her arms around him. 'I love you. Everything will be fine. I promise.'

For the first time in a long while he put his arms around her in response. 'I love you too, Mum.'

# Chapter 13

# Daily Journal

*A number of people have congratulated me, in a surprised tone of voice, on hearing the news that I intend to continue to play a full role in Matthew's upbringing. They comment that I am, after all, 'only' his step-father. It is widely anticipated that I will bolt from family life into the driver's seat of a two-seater sports car. Despite the fact that I have been Matthew's de facto father since he was seven, and I have known him since he was six, even in these modern times it appears that blood will out. I did not know it at the time but over the course of the last eight years the growing closeness of my relationship with Matthew has healed me at least as much as it helped him. I did not consciously set out to correct the mistakes of my childhood but nevertheless in some way, despite my alcoholism, I forged a bond with this small boy that I did not achieve with my own father. My father's great and lifelong love is not his family but the army. As a child I accepted his absences, as a young man I fiercely resented them and now I have come full circle to acceptance again. My father is permitted to be a fallible man, just as I have discovered myself to be. I am grateful for all the burdens of step-parenthood. I will remember Matthew's first rugby try even as the high stakes deals and the court steps victories fade from my mind. I would like to think that I added some fun and mischief to the life of the rather serious and timid child I first encountered. I do have some regrets, first and foremost that I ever taught him how to tackle so damned well. We have a rugby match tomorrow, fathers and sons. I have a new set of boots and a reputation to defend.*

Jasmine had no intention of crashing the wedding, declaiming that Robert was a wife-beater and ripping Natasha's veil from her face. She had no desire even to be seen, let alone heard. And yet some impulse, masochistic or otherwise, had brought her to the Aroma cafe in a side street off Brook Street, which afforded her a partial view of the front entrance to Claridges where, in less than an hour, Robert was going to marry Natasha. The Aroma was an Italian family-run place where sandwiches were still made to order and boxes of panettone cake for Christmas lined the glass counter-top.

Why was she here like a criminal returning to the scene of the crime? She had ordered a latte and taken a seat set back from the window where the light was such that it would be unlikely for the casual passer-by to see her. There was only one other occupant of the cafe, an elderly man eating a cheese and tomato sandwich, and she was worried that they might want to close soon.

As she sat sipping the steaming hot coffee she analysed her motives. She knew that she needed to be here. She needed to show herself that she could be here, in a place and at a time that was important to Robert. She needed to be here precisely because he would not wish it so. It was a point of principle. At the beginning, in the days after the attack, it was as if he had claimed whole areas of London for himself. In the first week she could not contemplate returning to any part of South London or to Wandsworth or to Covent Garden or to numerous specific places – restaurants they had dined in, shops they had frequented, parks they had walked in. The nine o'clock news reminded her of him. So did organic decaffeinated coffee, because he had once lectured her, at length, about the chemical process used to decaffeinate ordinary coffee. The Church of England reminded her of him. So did the *Financial Times*, engraved gold cufflinks and shirts with collar bones. Lilies reminded her of him and so did brioche and smoked almonds and Taittinger champagne.

And then she had begun to buy flavoured crisps again, especially salt and vinegar. Robert only ate plain ready salted. One day at Sloane Street tube station she stopped and bought *Cosmopolitan*, just for the hell of it, really. He disliked the publication intensely. She wore her hair as she pleased, had it cut, then put a rinse through it and didn't much like the effect but realized there was no one to criticize or complain about it anyway. She ate dessert and finished it. She ordered steak and asked for it to be well done and for good measure accompanied it with a glass of cold white wine.

For now there was no sign of Rizzo. It was Rizzo, on assignment for one of the tabloids, who had told her about the wedding details. But she intended to be long gone before Rizzo arrived. She just needed to be here, to show that she could go where she wanted whenever she pleased and there was not a damn thing that Robert Agnew could do about it. Then the door swung open and James was standing looking straight at her. He wore morning dress with a white rose buttonhole and his face was unreadable. He looked just the same, as though all the months had never happened.

She would have expected to feel embarrassed and gauche, but though the moment was charged she did not feel ashamed. Without speaking James came over and pulled out a chair.

'Jasmine—'

She interrupted him. 'I needed to be here.'

He gave her a half-smile. 'It's OK. I understand. I imagined you might—'

'I just . . .'

'Felt compelled?'

'Yes.'

The waitress interrupted them and she was happy when he ordered a coffee.

She was surprised. 'Shouldn't you . . .'

He pulled in his chair. 'I'm early. It can wait. As you can imagine, it's not an occasion I'm especially looking forward to. My parents would be upset if I didn't go, though.'

There was a long silence. She began to feel self-conscious. 'James, you must think I'm a complete lunatic. Or a stalker. Or both.'

'No. I don't think that at all.'

'I just wanted to be here.' She stopped speaking and let her mind work and then she found herself speaking out loud. 'I think maybe I was fascinated to see the person who has managed to change Robert.'

James raised an eyebrow in his characteristic gesture. 'Why do you suppose that he's changed?'

'He must have done, or she wouldn't be marrying him.'

The waitress brought coffees and the bill. Jasmine had the uncomfortable feeling that she wanted to close up.

'I'm not sure I follow your reasoning. Is your proposition that women only marry kind and decent men?'

She faltered. 'But he *must* have changed.'

He took her hand and his voice softened. 'No. I don't think so.'

'How can you be so sure?'

'Because he has no reason to. Without going into any detail, I suspect that Robert has very strong reasons for wanting to get married as quickly as possible.'

She was intrigued but realized that it would appear indiscreet if she asked for more details. Besides, mention of marriage had caused her involuntarily to look at James's left hand and to see that he was not wearing a wedding ring.

He had caught her gaze. 'I came with Matthew,' he said.

'Oh.'

'Susannah and I have separated.'

'I'm sorry,' she said as sincerely as possible.

And then she could no longer deny to herself that she had come to see James as well.

He spoke hesitantly. 'No, I'm the one who should be apologizing. I am sorry – for not turning up at Motcombs and then for writing to you and not speaking to you. You deserved better than that.'

'No, I understand. You needed to get well. How's it going?'

'You mean am I still drinking?' He smiled. 'No.'

'And it's permanent? I mean, you can never drink again?'

'Yes. How did you know that? Most people think that one dries out, weaves a few baskets and then goes back to a G&T before dinner and a couple of glasses of claret.'

'I know that an al—' She stopped herself. 'I know that you mustn't drink again. Actually it was my old boss who explained it to me. Paul. He'd been in and out of rehab and he knew he could never stop at one drink or one joint. He knew it but it didn't stop him.'

'I saw that he died.'

'Yes. It's very sad.'

He looked at her and his tone was urgent. 'Jasmine. There isn't a day I haven't thought about you.' Then he faltered. 'I . . . I'm sorry. That was wrong of me. I've no right to turn your life upside down.'

There were a hundred questions she wanted to ask him. Beginning with Susannah. Who had initiated the separation and why? Jasmine sincerely hoped she wasn't implicated because she hated to have anything bad on her conscience. But James had changed the subject.

'How's Joan?'

She sensed his discomfiture and followed this new line of conversation. 'The same as ever!'

'And your decorating plans?'

'Hey, they're not plans any more! I've done the bathroom and the bedroom and started the living room.'

He pulled a face. 'Tell me it isn't going to be red.'

'Almost. The colour is called Bengal Rose, but it isn't pink, more a muted red. The painting will be easy – I'm going to line the walls to get a really good finish. Sanding the floorboards was a nightmare.'

'Dust?'

'No, getting the sander up the stairs.'

He laughed and she told him about her plans for the kitchen. He began telling her about house-hunting in Cobham but caught himself and looked at his watch. 'I really must go.'

As if to underline the point the waitress came and cleared away their cups and began piling chairs on tables.

'We close early on a Saturday,' she said pointedly.

Jasmine pulled on her coat. James left a note which provided for a generous tip and then they stepped outside onto the pavement.

They walked three or four paces towards Claridges and then he half-turned towards her. 'Oh by the way, there's a new exhibition at the V & A. You've probably heard of it. The Richard Avedon Retrospective.'

'Oh, yes. Joan and I got tickets to the first night.'

There was the merest disappointed flicker across his features. 'Of course. I was thinking of taking Matthew this Sunday. With the bribe of lunch afterwards, naturally.'

'Oh, he'll love it,' she enthused.

'Good,' he said curtly. 'Well . . .'

There was a silence that seemed as though it would never end. 'You'll be late,' she ventured.

'Yes. I must be going. Goodbye, Jasmine.'

And with that he turned and walked briskly towards Claridges.

There were to be fifty guests at the wedding ceremony in the French

Salon of Claridges Hotel and that was plenty in Robert's opinion. Robert's secretary had been instructed to compile a shortlist of five wedding venues, which Robert had cut down to a final two and after that there had been no choice at all because Claridges was the only venue available at such short notice with a licence to conduct weddings. A cancellation, the manager had informed them *sotto voce* at their appointment to decide the menu and seating arrangements and even the flowers. It was all very simple; everything could be organised by the hotel. Robert said more than once that only a woman could make organizing a wedding seem complicated. There would be time later for bells and smells as he put it, not that the evangelicals of St Luke's Wandsworth would suffer the use of incense. Natasha had invited her mother and Don and a handful of old friends, also Anna from the BBC and a couple of fellow presenters who would excite the attention of the photographers when they posed, as pre-arranged by Robert, after the ceremony.

She stood in front of the full-length mirror in the hotel room. Her Catherine Walker dress was faultlessly elegant, cut tightly in a demure long-sleeved design to produce an elongated silhouette, the soft V-neck decorated with pearl embroidery. Now, standing in the dress, she was relieved that she did feel like a bride, albeit a slightly older, sophisticated, worldly wise bride. Her mother was late and in the absence of her bridesmaid – Araminta, who was with Robert at his house – she was alone. Robert had a horror, as he put it, of a row of thirty-something spinsters dressed as Tudor serving maids.

She could not sit down in case she creased the dress. Tom at Nicky Clarke in Mount Street had earlier put her hair up and Michelle had done her make-up. Robert had taken very literally the tradition that he should not see his bride on the day of the wedding because he had not even called her. She felt slightly flat. She had always loved films where the bride was surrounded by friends and sisters and aunts on her wedding day, all fixing hair and painting nails and swapping stories of honeymoon nights and wedded realities.

There was a knock at the door. It was Grania. They mirrored each other in their expressions of surprise.

'You're alone?' Grania said, her tone midway between an exclamation and a question.

'I'm waiting for my mother,' Natasha said brightly. 'She's stuck in awful traffic.' She felt obliged to fib by way of explanation. Grania came in and there followed a minute of exclamations and compliments about her dress and tales of last-minute fittings and alterations. Grania was dressed in a shift dress with a boxy short jacket, both in pale green, which would have challenged anyone with skin that was not, like Grania's, naturally olive and flawlessly tanned. Her pregnancy was obvious now but in the neat, compact way of tall, slim women. She took off her broad-brimmed hat, in a slightly darker shade trimmed with a broad ribbon and corsage, and placed it carefully on the bed.

'I brought you this.' Grania held out a small, inexpertly wrapped package. 'It's just something from me. We got you a serving platter from the list.'

Natasha unwrapped it to reveal a tablet of stone, rough and patterned with interwoven stripes of differing brown hues.

'It's a piece of sandstone,' Grania explained. 'It's millions of years old. I have one on my desk.'

Natasha thought she knew why. 'It's timeless.'

'Exactly. It's a reminder that all that troubles me or vexes me today is really so insignificant in the scale of things.'

'How are "things"?'

Grania gave a wry smile. 'Alex appeared last night, at past midnight, with an enormous bunch of roses.'

'I see.'

'And he's been especially attentive today. He's in the bar downstairs with the Winters. Hair of the dog, as you English say.'

Natasha could think of nothing to say to this.

'But that isn't what I came to say. I wanted to apologize for the other day.'

'Why?'

'Because I don't want to put you off. What's happening in my marriage is my affair – or his – and just because I'm rather cynical doesn't mean that you should be.'

Natasha forgot about the potential creasing of the dress and sat down. 'No, not at all.' She was surprised at how good it was to see Grania. 'You did make me think about things. I mean, sometimes it's so confusing. Everyone says that marriage is hard work and you have to make compromises. And lots of people say they had doubts just before their wedding, but that's just pre-wedding nerves.'

Grania gave her a searching look. 'Are you having doubts?'

330

'No.' She corrected herself. 'Not exactly. Sometimes I think Robert is very . . . definite in what he wants, but that's precisely what makes him successful.'

'And attractive.'

'Yes, I suppose in time that will soften, that we'll be more of a team.'

Grania frowned. 'It may,' she said doubtfully.

'You don't think so? I was thinking when we have children and move house that would make a difference. Instead of living at Robert's place.'

'I think you should move house as soon as possible. Have you discussed that?'

It was embarrassing for Natasha to admit to the vague nature of these discussions. 'Well, I know Robert doesn't want to stay in Wandsworth permanently. And he definitely wants a place in the countryside.'

Grania got up and moved over to the window. 'For what it's worth I didn't have any doubts at all on my wedding day. I was going to be the third – and definitely the last – Mrs De Lisle and I was going to succeed where the other two had failed. I was going to be unfailingly glamorous, always supportive, attentive in every way – yet retaining my own outlook and interests and friends. Oh, and I was going to be best friends with his children and graciously cordial to his ex-wives. It hasn't quite worked out like that.'

Natasha could not help herself. 'Why?'

'It's simple, really.' Grania turned round to address her. 'You can't change another person. Alex is restless, ambitious . . . predatory. And that's huge fun when one is a mistress and rather uncomfortable when one is a wife.'

Natasha could not help but ask, 'What are you going to do?'

'Oh, stick it out. Probably have more babies and divert myself with yoga classes and decorating the nursery and then spend the next few years meeting up with the other mothers to bitch about the nanny.'

'You wouldn't leave?'

'No. Unfortunately, I happen to love Alex. Sometimes I wish I didn't.'

'And the . . . the things you don't like about them; do you think they get better or worse?'

Grania gave her a hard look. 'What things?'

Natasha stood as if on a precipice about to launch herself off. 'Robert likes to be in charge . . .' she began slowly. 'And I don't want to sound ungrateful or awkward – he's nearly always right.' She paused to look around at the room and glance at the enormous diamond on her finger and wonder what exactly she was complaining about – or why she was doubting the very thing she had wanted for so long. 'It's just that sometimes – not all the time – it's easier to go along with what he wants than to put up a fight.'

Grania considered this. 'What does he do if you don't agree?'

'He gets cross. Not angry, normally. It's more that he gets irritable and then he . . .'

'Sulks?'

'Yes! It's ridiculous, isn't it! Robert storms off into his office or disappears out of the house for hours and then there's an awful atmosphere when he gets back.'

'And you usually end up giving in.'

'Just to keep the peace.'

Grania sighed. 'I don't think that's unusual with that type of man. They're used to getting what they want and being as manipulative as they need to be in order to get it.'

Grania's analysis was interrupted by a knock at the door.

Natasha's mother and Don stood outside next to Robert's parents and Araminta.

And that was the end of any conversation, intimate or otherwise. Araminta came charging into the room and her mother and Don followed carrying a large wrapped parcel. Estella, in a neat navy boucle suit, gave Natasha an approving nod. 'Very good, my dear.'

Don stood awkwardly holding a gaudily wrapped parcel.

'It's a deep-fat fryer,' announced her mother, who had ignored Natasha's hints about not wearing a trouser suit. She had opted for beige with a heavy brocade coat-style jacket. Next to Estella's suit it looked distinctly unsophisticated. 'We did ring up that store but there was nothing that seemed right so we made our own choice. You'll find it's very useful.'

'For chips,' added Araminta.

'Not too many,' cut in Estella.

'Oh, you can do much more than cook chips in it,' breezed her mother. 'Fish fillets, chicken . . .'

'Doughnuts,' added Don.

'I think these lists are such a good idea,' said Estella. 'People have such awful taste.'

332

If this was a jibe at her mother it did not appear to hit the mark because she nodded in agreement.

'Robert sends you his love,' continued Estella. 'We were very pleased with Araminta's dress. Weren't we, dear?'

'Enchanting,' confirmed Major Agnew.

Araminta was twirling around the room, dressed in a classic brides-maid's dress of pale-pink raw silk, her waist encircled by a ribbon tied in a perfect symmetrical bow at the back. She looked so innocent and in that moment Natasha felt a surge of feeling for the little girl who might so soon be parted from her mother. Grania was moving to the door.

'I'm sure you have a great deal to talk about.'

Natasha knew full well that they hadn't.

But Grania was already adjusting her hat, her mother was inspecting the room-service menu and Estella had taken up a position on the sofa. 'Now, my dear, let's have a proper look at that dress.' She beckoned Natasha toward her.

'Good luck,' called out Grania.

'It's very slimming,' continued Estella, reaching for her glasses.

Her mother swung round. 'It certainly doesn't need to be. Natasha's always been very careful about her figure.'

Major Agnew caught Natasha's eye. 'Why don't we all have a nice glass of champagne?'

Susannah was utterly bewildered. She had never imagined that it would be so difficult.

They were sitting at the kitchen table, the late Saturday afternoon light already fading. Laid out on the surface were a pack of cards, a set of property particulars and the remains of a *citronnier* cake of which Matthew had eaten more than half. The cake had been supplied by Justin, who was standing at the kitchen counter making a pot of tea.

Matthew sighed. 'It's easy. You start with a pair.'

'A pair,' she repeated slowly.

'That's right,' he said encouragingly. He laid down some cards to show her. 'Here, this is a pair of clubs. This is a pair of spades.' She concentrated hard. She always got the black cards confused.

'OK. Then you have to look at how high a pair is. For example, a pair of tens beats a pair of fours.'

Justin called out to them, 'Don't forget to mention aces.'

She knew Justin was trying to be helpful but she needed to go slowly. It was the second week of her month off. She had resolved to learn poker ever since she found out that Jake's mother played. She had also decided to learn to ski. It was something she had always meant to do but never got round to. So after Christmas she and Matthew were going to the Alps for a week. And next weekend he was having a sleepover with four of his friends, the first ever at home. She had never quite had the confidence to do that before, not when James was living there.

Justin had called round after the office closed to drop off the particulars of a property that had only come on the books that morning. Since her departure from Charron's Justin had taken to calling in on an almost daily basis. He had taken on most of her clients and he was now quite at home in her kitchen. He seemed to be motivated by genuine concern for her wellbeing coupled with ongoing panic at his newfound responsibilities. In addition to his visits, Justin called approximately three times a day asking her what he should do next in the office. They had held a surprise party for her. Anthony had made a speech, Lynda had made a cake and at the end Anthony had presented her with a carriage clock. She had been reduced to tears. Even Dee had said that she would be missed.

But she was not missing Charron's. It was fun to be at home and spend time with her son doing nothing much as opposed to nagging and chivvying him. In the past she had been so preoccupied with worrying about Matthew that she had never taken the time just to *be* with him.

Matthew reached over and started to read the particulars Justin had left on the table.

'They're only rough,' warned Justin. 'I haven't even had a chance to measure up.'

'Isn't Anthony doing that?' she asked, surprised. She was trying to shuffle the pack of cards, only to see them fall in a splayed pile at every attempt.

'Nope,' said Justin, carrying over two mugs of tea, 'he's too busy bugging Dee.'

'It looks tiny,' said Matthew disparagingly.

Justin frowned at him. 'Young man! It is a character property with scope for further extension.'

'Is it?' she asked, interested despite herself.

'It's called Railway Cottages. The owner is an old lady. Must be seventy if she's a day.' He took a sip of tea.

'Going into a home?' she asked, reaching over and taking the particulars from Matthew.

'No. Getting married. So she wants a quick sale.'

'Gosh!'

'Yes, convenient isn't it!' said Justin brightly. 'Now, the stairs are steep,' he warned. 'And internally it's dated. You'd want to put in a new kitchen and bathroom, but you could put a two-storey extension on the side.' He turned to Matthew. 'Which means you could put a pool table in on the ground floor and have a spiral staircase leading up to the second floor. You could even make the second floor an open gallery. Like a bachelor suite—'

'All right!' she cut in. 'Why don't you suggest that we install a hot tub and a swimming pool while we're about it?'

'It does have a hundred-foot garden, actually,' retorted Justin, unfazed. 'And it's the owner's pride and joy. Amazing. She's got fantastic beds and a lawn like a bowling green plus a vegetable patch at the back.'

'How many bedrooms?'

'Two. But as well as the extension you could have a great attic room. So you could get it up to four or have three bedrooms and an office.'

'Will you stop selling it to me?' she exclaimed. She had taught Justin most of the lines he was now using on her.

'Cool,' said Matthew. 'I think we should see it.'

She raised her eyebrows. 'Excuse me, I'm the professional around here.'

'Exactly! That's the problem. You're involved personally. Time to get off the case.'

'I'll fix up a viewing,' said Justin. 'It's one of a pair. The other one is owned by a yuppie couple with a Porsche.' He grinned at her. 'So you'll feel perfectly at home.'

'It's a deal,' said Matthew, shuffling the pack with the dexterity of a Las Vegas croupier. 'Now, can we get back to the game?'

The car pulled away from the kerbside of Claridges. Araminta was waving and so were Anna and Grania and Louise and Oliver Winter, who was dressed in an Edwardian-style sailor-suit, and James and all the guests who had spilled out to see them off. She felt close to tears

335

but she could not have said why. Next to her Robert was issuing instructions to the driver regarding the route to Cliveden. She was Mrs Natasha Agnew, or Mrs Robert Agnew if one wanted to be formal. She was a married woman with a gold ring to prove it. She could not imagine ever taking it off. She smoothed down the skirt of her going-away suit, classic pale-pink Chanel with a pair of LK Bennett kitten heels in matching pink suede.

The wedding had been perfect, a masterpiece of good taste, consummate planning and flawless execution. She had entered the French Salon to the sound of Handel's Harp Concerto in B Flat Major, held a simple bouquet of cream and russet roses edged with a touch of hypericum, and walked slowly as much to prevent Don stepping on the small circular train of the dress as for any solemn effect. Behind her Araminta walked two paces back exactly as Robert had shown her. She had not been nervous. From the moment she entered the room and half the heads turned and Anna gave her a discreet thumbs up, she was lost to the moment, scarcely able to believe that it was really happening. The fifty guests were seated in five rows, the chairs set in a slight semicircle and widely spaced to give an impression of greater numbers. The high-corniced ceiling, the ornate blue and white panelled walls and the crystal chandeliers provided an opulently formal setting. His father had read John Donne's 'A Valediction: Forbidding Mourning':

> Such wilt thou be to me, who must
> Like th'other foot, obliquely run;
> Thy firmness makes my circle just,
> And makes me end where I begun.

The registrar, a woman in her late twenties, wore a functional royal-blue suit and addressed them in the style of a civil servant recently trained in public speaking. There were no hymns. The Westminster register office, despite Robert's repeated challenges, had refused to deviate from its policy of forbidding any religious readings or music, including Robert's choice of Blake's *Jerusalem*. He had called the lady in the office a small-minded bureaucrat. But Natasha had forgotten all that as Anna read Shakespeare's 'Let me not to the marriage of true minds':

*Let me not to the marriage of true minds*
*Admit impediment: love is not love*
*Which alters when it alteration finds,*
*Or bends with the remover to remove:*
*O, no, it is an ever-fixèd mark . . .*

Robert had eased the ring onto her finger. He had chosen not to wear one himself; he wore a signet ring and that was enough.

Before she knew it, it was all over. No one had warned her the ceremony would be over so quickly. There was no video; Robert thought they were common and wondered what sort of person sat down to watch it anyway, and now she was sorry. Afterwards everyone had said how beautiful she looked and even her mother had been tearful, which was almost shocking. She had moved to embrace her and for a few moments they had held each other close. Grania had stayed by her side and Anna had been ridiculously excited. James had kissed her lightly and told her Robert was a very lucky man; Andrew Winter had told her she was 'stunning'. Alex De Lisle had avoided her and stayed close to Grania. They drank champagne and ate exquisite canapés and then they cut the cake. The cake had been described in the example photograph as 'Victorian Grace' – three tiers with white icing, yellow roses so lifelike they could have been real and curved scrolls of fleur-de-lys piping inset with silver dragees. At the reception she spoke to everyone and there were photographs, the groups marshalled by Robert's secretary

Each detail was exactly as it should have been. Now the car had reached Chiswick. As the red-brick houses flashed past her it came to her that it was almost too perfect, too irreproachably correct, altogether flawless in every fine detail. Some small, indefinable but nagging sense of discontent settled upon her. She wondered if she was bad to think this way, to be so ungrateful when the wedding had cost so much and gone so well, and yet the feeling persisted. Perhaps a church wedding felt different. Or a summer wedding? Perhaps she should have put her foot down and insisted that they go away on a proper honeymoon, not just for one night. She turned over these thoughts in her mind until the car reached the M4. The driver settled to a steady seventy and her head felt so heavy . . . She was woken by the car making the sharp turn into the gravelled drive of Cliveden and saw the lit shell-style sculpture of the Fountain of Love ahead of her.

Natasha watched as Robert cracked open the champagne and poured it into the two flutes placed on a silver tray covered with a white linen napkin.

'It was like a fairy tale,' she mused out loud.

Robert's voice was suddenly irritated. 'No. Quite the opposite. There was no magic about today; there never is. It was the result of careful planning and precise execution.'

She was taken aback by his response. 'You make it sound like a military operation.'

'I think that's preferable to believing in Grimm's fairy tales.'

She lay on the oversize double bed of their room. It overlooked the front of Cliveden, the stone columns framing the entranceway to the stone-fronted house. Their room was enormous. The check-in clerk, on hearing they were on honeymoon, had upgraded them to a suite. There was a seating area in front of the bay window, furnished with an oversized red chintz sofa and two Queen Anne armchairs. To the side, on a walnut sideboard, another linen-covered tray held bottles of Hildon mineral water and a huge bowl of fruit. Robert was standing by the antique dressing table where he had emptied his pockets of his keys and a folded order of service and taken his wallet from his jacket pocket. She lay in her slip and the cream silk sleeveless camisole she had worn under the suit. Her Chanel suit had cost her a small fortune and she intended to look after it.

He took a deep drink of champagne, then pulled a face and examined the label.

'A good reminder why I drink Taittinger.'

'Oh, for goodness' sake. Does it matter?'

'Yes. It does matter, actually. It is precisely my attention to detail – which you now find so tedious – that ensured your day was exactly as you wanted it.'

'I didn't mean—'

He swung round. 'Well, what did you mean? Did you mean you had a perfect day by complete accident? By chance? Because of the alignment of the stars predicted in *Cosmopolitan?*'

'No. I don't want to fight.'

'Then don't say such ridiculous things.'

She was close to tears now. They were on the brink of an ugly row and she had no idea how they had even begun to argue. This had happened before and she had always diffused the situation, but why on earth should she have to placate her husband on their wedding night? It was as if he was spoiling for a fight.

Robert took off his tie and rolled it loosely.

She mustered all her energy. 'Shall we go for a walk? The grounds here are—'

'No.'

'Designed by—'

'I know. Jellicoe, amongst others. It's dark. And I have papers to prepare.'

She had been about to say that they could at least walk down to the terrace, but he had confused her. 'Papers? It's our wedding night.'

'Yes, it is. I am also – as I have told you before – very busy. That's why we've postponed the honeymoon.'

'Can't you leave them until tomorrow?'

'I could, but I'm not going to.'

A feeling of impotent frustration washed over her. She sat up on the bed. 'What could possibly be so important that you have to do it tonight?'

Robert looked at her coldly. 'Araminta's custody case. The deadline for filing my evidence is Monday. We have a nine thirty a.m. appointment with the lawyers to swear the affidavits.'

'We?'

'Yes. Obviously *we*. As my wife you will be giving evidence.'

'But it's nothing to do with me.'

Robert looked furious. 'Let me get this clear. "My husband's fight to gain custody of his eight-year-old daughter is nothing to do with me."'

'I didn't mean it like that.'

'That's what you said,' he snapped back at her.

'I meant I haven't got anything to say about it. It's between you and Tabitha.'

'No. You are wrong again. You need to give evidence as to your role as my wife and your new position as Araminta's stepmother.'

He sounded impossibly pompous and she could not contain a disbelieving laugh. 'Robert, I have no idea what to say.'

'I anticipated that. My lawyer has drawn up an affidavit. All you need to do is sign it.'

'I think I'll need to read it first.'

'As you wish. Then you'll sign it.'

'And if I don't agree with it?'

'You will.'

It took a few moments for the implications of Robert's remarks to take effect in her mind.

'Are you saying that your lawyer has already drawn this up? Without even speaking to me?'

'Technically what he has drawn up is a draft – a suggestion of what you might want to say if you had the time and capability to do it yourself. An affidavit represents your position, naturally. But lawyers write affidavits for their clients all the time. Once you see him, you will approve the draft and sign it as your statement. It's very simple.'

'How does he know what I think?'

'I told him.'

She felt very annoyed. 'Robert, you should have let me do it!'

Her flash of anger appeared to amuse him. 'Oh I should, should I? Would madam also like to deal with Moores? Would madam also like to deal with the British press? Or would you prefer to be selective in your choices, delegating the difficult situations to me and keeping the manageable ones for yourself?'

'I would like a say!'

'You don't need a say.'

She could see that their discussion, if it could be called that, was going nowhere. She forced herself to take a deep breath. 'Well, tell me what it is that I think.'

'Nothing very complex or sophisticated, I assure you. It must appear realistic. Simply that I have an excellent relationship with Araminta and that you believe her best interests would be served by living with us on a full-time basis with visiting rights, limited visiting rights, granted to her mother.' He sat down on one of the small Queen Anne chairs and gave her a hard look. 'Natasha, I do hope you're not going to become awkward about this.'

She struggled to find her voice. 'I'm not trying to be awkward. I just wish that you had asked me about this before going ahead and getting your lawyer to write things. I think you should have consulted me.'

'Oh, you think I should have consulted you, do you? And what precisely would that have achieved? Let me tell you: it would have sent you into a blind panic on the eve of our wedding at a time when you were barely coping.'

'What do you mean?'

'Getting yourself into a state about your dress, about the menus, about—'

'I did not!'

'Yes, you did. And so I took a view that the best thing for all concerned was to protect you from any unpleasantness. I took the same position with Moores. Looking at the state you are in now I was entirely right.'

'What do you mean?' The mention of Moores jolted her. 'What is going on with Moores?'

Robert's expression mirrored his matter-of-fact tone. 'Moores notified me some time ago that they were not going to renew your contract—'

'What?'

'I said Moores notified me some time ago that they were not going to renew.'

The news came as a total shock. She had just assumed that Robert was taking care of it. He had given her no reason to believe otherwise. She was incapable of keeping her voice down. 'Why?' Then her mind ran on. 'It's my only regular income!'

'Is that what you expect me to tell them? "Please don't fire Natasha; she needs the money?"'

She felt desperate. 'Why?'

He shrugged his shoulders, 'They wanted someone more family friendly. Fortunately I was able to suggest Richard Waters, the Pop Idol idiot.'

'But he's your client!'

'And so a commission is payable. Yes. What would you prefer – that another agency got the business? You really are deeply selfish, Natasha.'

'I think you should have kept the business for me!' He didn't seem to care at all. In fact, he seemed to be deriving some point-scoring pleasure from his own wife's misfortune. She couldn't believe that he was being so callous.

'Oh, poor little girl.' He was mocking her now. 'Me, me, me! Well, sadly my dear, in the real world what you want isn't what you get.'

She was furious now. 'You had no right to replace me like that! You should have let me speak to them.'

He was unrepentant. 'What do you think you would have said to

341

Daniel Moores that would have made any difference?'

'I would have liked to try!'

'For Christ's sake, this isn't kindergarten. It's not about *trying*. It's about winning, Natasha.'

A suspicion had entered her mind and it was impossible to dislodge it. 'How much are they paying Richard Waters?'

'What?' She could see from his expression that she had caught him off guard.

'How much are Moores paying Richard Waters?'

'It's not a comparable deal to yours. The work is different.'

She knew then that Waters was being paid more than her, that Robert had negotiated the increase and that his commission would be in consequence higher. What she did not want to know was whether he had arranged it that way.

Robert had recovered his composure. 'Besides, what do you expect me to do? Refuse to work with Moores because they don't want you any more?'

'Do you have to put it like that? Why don't they want me?'

His tone was caustic. The gloves were off. 'You want the truth? Christ, I'm tired of protecting you. Because your face doesn't fit. Because your presence on British TV screens, if you ignore *Bravo*, is not exactly overwhelming. You're not current or even very interesting to advertisers – or commissioning editors.'

She felt devastated. 'There's *Expats*,' she said quietly.

He paused. 'And then what, Natasha?'

She felt physically winded. 'So what are you saying? Are you telling me my career's over?'

'No,' he sighed. 'I'm not saying that at all. Your career, as you put it, which by the way was created for you by your mother and then run by me, so don't take too much credit, is something about which you have to be realistic. You can work on a freelance basis, on cable television—'

'Cable!'

'Cable is an expanding medium. Besides which, you're not a single girl any more. You're my wife – which carries with it certain obligations. Araminta will be living with us and in time we'll have our own child. There will be the London house to run and a place in the country – you might even live there full-time. I don't have a nine-to-five job. You knew that when you met me.'

She gave an empty laugh. 'So I'm supposed to give up my career and sit at home and have babies.'

'No, you are supposed to work when you can, run the house and support me in my business, which makes the substantial amounts of money you like to spend. I'm not some Victorian husband, insisting that you give up work and sign all your property over to me.'

'But—'

'No.' He waved his hand around the room. 'This all costs money. So did the wedding. I didn't see your family offering to pay. I picked up the cheque, as I always do. Most women would display some gratitude. But not you. No, what we have instead is a wedding-day tantrum about your contracts, your job and how you want all the material benefits of being married but none of the obligations.'

'That's not fair!' she protested.

'Oh for goodness' sake.' He started laughing. '*It's not fair*. Why don't you stamp your pretty little foot and throw your favourite doll out of the window?'

'You don't take me seriously at all!'

'No, I don't. When you can express yourself in a coherent and dignified manner perhaps I will. Until then, I will order things as I think fit.'

She tuned out his voice. It was impossible to try to speak to him and foolish to expect any emotional support from him. In the midst of it all, as a feeling of aloneness took hold of her, the old survival instinct took over. She began to think. 'I'm going to call Anna at the BBC on Monday and see if she can put out some feelers.'

'As you wish.'

She felt emboldened. He really was out of order speaking to her in the way he had. Enough was enough, 'And I'm not agreeing to moving anywhere until we know the outcome of the court case. We don't even know that you'll win. And I'm not even sure that you should.'

To her surprise he said nothing. She had expected a riot to break out. Instead, he got up and walked into the bathroom. She heard the sound of a tap running, the water splashing into the bath, which was odd because Robert never took a bath. In fact he had commented before about the unhygienic nature of lying in one's own dirty water.

When he returned he sat down, looked out of the window at the now dark night sky. From outside came the sound of a car pulling up and she could just make out the voices of the driver and the doorman.

Robert was holding his champagne glass, by the stem as he always did, apparently intent on studying the pattern of light falling across the cut crystal. He spoke as if to himself. 'I did hope that you weren't going to take this attitude. But I suspected you would. Women, in my experience, always do.'

'What attitude?'

'A dishonest attitude. A lying, deceitful, grasping attitude.'

She was incredulous. 'Surely you're not saying all women are the same?'

'That is precisely what I am saying because that has been my experience.'

'Robert, please don't be like that. I want to support you. I just . . . I know that Araminta is very important to you and you want the best for her. But she's only eight and she's always lived with Tabitha. It would be a huge change for her.'

'I agree. That is why Tabitha should give up her plan to move to the USA and set up home with a stranger. This is her choice, Natasha. If Araminta comes to live with us that will be a natural consequence of the choices she has made.'

'You're asking her to choose between her future husband and her child!'

He paused. 'You have no idea how much it saddens me to hear you speak like this. Whose side are you on?' He stood up and looked at her.

Then, wordlessly, he went into the bathroom and she heard the water stop running.

He called out to her. 'Will you come in here?'

Mystified, she went into the bathroom. It had been carefully renovated so that the old white porcelain basin with its broad rim and the enormous enamel bath remained. The faded, glazed tiles were original, decorated with a delicate blue willow pattern, and the stone floor was worn down by decades of use. The bath was full with water.

Did he want them to take a bath together?

He moved towards her. 'You have to understand that you are responsible for this. That's very important, Natasha.' His voice was mechanical. 'You have driven me to a point where I have no option. I have tried to reason with you. I have explained, repeatedly and in detail, why I am pursuing this course of action which is in Araminta's best interests. You have done nothing but question and complain at every turn. You have made me do this, Natasha, because you simply would not give me the loyalty and support that I have every right to expect as your husband.'

He took hold of her arm and edged her so that they were standing to the side of the bath. She was totally confused. 'Robert? Do what? What are you talking about?' Was he going to make her sign something? Perhaps he wanted her to telephone Tabitha and plead his case? God, could he be planning to kidnap Araminta and he needed her to be his accomplice? Why were they standing in the bathroom? It was baffling.

He did not answer her. His other hand reached out and smoothed out her hair. When he spoke it was as if she wasn't there. 'It is a question of consequences. I have to show you how much you frustrate me. I have to show you how much you drive me to the point of despair.' His hand had stopped smoothing her hair now. Instead he had formed it into a ponytail. He started to twist it, slowly coiling it into his hand . . .

And then the silence was shattered by a telephone ringing. She started and her jolt of surprise was mirrored by the look of confusion on Robert's face. The ring was harsh and amplified by the tiled bathroom.

'Who on earth . . . ' He reached into his pocket, pulled out his mobile and glanced at the name. She thought he was about to let the telephone go onto the answer machine when on the sixth ring he answered it. 'Louise. My dear.'

Louise? Natasha could not make out Louise's words but she could tell from the raised voice that this was not a business call.

Robert was able instantly to assume his business persona. 'My dear, calm down. I am delighted that you called.' All his attention was focused on the telephone call. 'Louise, you were quite right to—'

Louise must have interrupted. She spoke at length, Robert listening intently, her raised voice audible if not her words.

At last he was able to cut in. 'Absolutely outrageous . . . Totally understandable . . . A fact of life . . . These things are never black and white.'

He walked into the bedroom and shut the door behind him. It was clear that she was meant to stay put in the bathroom. If she followed him he would only wave her away; he could get terribly irritable when he was on the phone. She could hear him faintly through the door. There was obviously some huge problem between Louise and Andrew because she could hear talk of divorce and later Robert repeated the name of a hotel – she couldn't catch the name, but she thought she heard Robert telling Louise to stay put there for the time being until everything blew over. After that Louise must have resumed talking because she could hear nothing. She wished she had a magazine to read. The window was too high to see out of so there was no view and she didn't even have her wash bag to unpack; it was still in the suitcase along with everything else. She thought about taking a bath but guessed that the water must be cold by now. She went over and trailed her hand in.

It was cold, really freezing cold. The only explanation was that Robert must have forgotten to turn the hot tap on. So, he was fallible after all! She pulled the lever to release the plug and the water began to drain away. Then she sat down on the radiator, which was uncomfortable but better than the floor, and began reading the only printed material in the room, a copy of the hotel policy on water conservation as it related to washing towels. Finally, she was debating whether she could silently creep back into the room to retrieve *Vogue* from her suitcase, when the door opened. Robert stepped in with a jaunty expression. Clearly, whatever crisis Louise faced, he hadn't let it get to him. 'Well, well, well. Louise Winter has a problem.' He gave a false laugh. 'And she's very anxious for my advice. It seems that Mrs Winter has been a very silly girl. First she's been carrying on with Alex De Lisle. Second she's been caught out by none other than old Mrs Winter. I thought she was a sharp old bird. It turns out that old Mrs Winter has been having her followed for some weeks now. The balloon went up this evening when they got home. The photographs are now in her son's possession.'

'Gosh. What's Andrew going to do?'

'Divorce her. Not that he knows that yet. He'll be shell-shocked and Louise is promising to pursue a life of sainthood.'

'But—'

'I know. Andrew always seemed such a wimp. Not so old Mrs Winter. Louise has been exiled to the Holiday Inn on the Cromwell Road. A nice touch.'

'What does Louise want you to do?'

'Oh, call Andrew, dissuade him from doing anything rash, generally smooth things over.'

He turned and walked back into the bedroom and she took the

opportunity to escape her bathroom exile. She slid onto the bed as unobtrusively as possible. She could see that Robert was preoccupied. He started scrolling through the numbers on his mobile, pacing across the room as he did so. 'What's the child's name?' he asked her absently.

She thought for a moment. 'Oliver.'

'Oliver,' he repeated to himself. She watched as Robert called what she presumed was Andrew's number. It was answered immediately. Robert's voice exuded sincerity. They began formally enough. 'Andrew, is there anything I can do? I was once in a similar position myself . . . Sadly, yes. Louise is a wonderful woman and I hesitate to give advice . . . In fact, I should say nothing . . .'

There was then a long interlude in which Andrew spoke and Robert said very little. She could see that he was clearly absorbed in the task of listening to Andrew. Once or twice he interrupted to clarify or confirm a detail but for the most part he listened. She could never remember him listening to her with such diligence.

Then, after an age, Andrew must have come to an end because Robert began, 'Well, if pushed to proffer a word to the wise . . .' He paused. 'No. On second thoughts it would be wrong for me to offer my experience.' There was another intervention by Andrew. Robert continued. His tone remained sympathetic but had assumed a solicitous edge. 'Andrew, my only suggestion – man to man – would be to take advice. Legal advice. It's just a precaution. Anyone in business would do the same. I use Masterson Ryder Jardine. They are extremely discreet, very efficient and the very best at securing the interests of their high net-worth clients.' The subject of money clearly provoked Andrew because Robert ceased to speak while Andrew's raised voice could just be heard. Andrew Winter appeared to be pouring out both his heart and his financial concerns. At the end of it Robert pressed on with a new forcefulness. 'I'm sorry to say that I think your mother is quite right. Securing your assets is your prime concern. Whatever you feel, you have a responsibility to look after little Oliver's financial future. Seeing a lawyer doesn't commit you to anything – one hopes that everything will be resolved to your satisfaction. But if it isn't . . . Exactly! One hopes for the best and plans for the worst; there's no better way of putting it . . . Personally I wouldn't delay. They are the best and it's vital to secure them first. You're quite sure Louise wouldn't seek legal advice? . . . Well, if you can't rule it out then it's important not to wait until Monday. I'll put in a call this evening. I have the sen-

347

ior partner's home number . . . No, it's no trouble at all.' Another interlude followed. Robert, when he spoke, sounded worldly wise. 'I'm sure Louise is very sorry. And if you're totally confident, beyond any doubt, that this will *never* happen again . . . No? I'll put in that call.'

He rang off after telling Andrew Winter, yet again, how very sorry he was and inviting Oliver round to play very soon. He lost no time calling Philip Ryder at home and briefing him on Andrew Winter's situation, the likelihood of Louise taking Andrew to the cleaners and the necessity of levering Andrew into taking action as soon as possible. Then he snapped the mobile telephone shut.

He spoke to her animatedly. 'Next I'll invite Andrew to dinner. Somewhere local, not too flashy; I don't want to make it look like a set-up. Maybe Chez Max? You, me and some pretty thing from the office. Give him a blast of female attention. Someone to show him that a future exists beyond his harridan of a wife.'

She was disturbed. She could see that he had double-crossed Louise; that was predictable enough. But she couldn't understand this latest plan of action. 'Shouldn't they work at their marriage? I mean . . . isn't it his decision to make? You seem to be rushing Andrew into the arms of your lawyer, who will persuade him to start divorce proceedings.'

Robert was unabashed. 'I don't see why that's a problem. Louise is a social-climbing, adulterous bitch. I had a grudging respect for her before. Not any more. It was a stupid mistake to make and an even more idiotic error to get caught. Greedy, really. In the meantime I intend to hold Andrew's hand – and become his confidant – through this whole ugly mess. He won't have any friends he can confide in. It would be too humiliating for him and too complex an issue for their public schoolboy rugger-brains. Their idea of strategy is working out how to kick a ball between two white posts. No, this is the opportunity I've been waiting for. And I intend to maximize it.'

He wandered into the bathroom and called out quizzically, 'You let the water out.'

'Yes. It was cold. You must have forgotten to turn the hot tap on.'

He wandered back into the bedroom. 'I must have. Well, we'll just have to do something else instead.'

He moved over to the window. She felt relief. The argument was over, Robert's very odd behaviour in the bathroom was forgotten and he seemed to be in a good mood for the first time all day. She could even put his earlier horrible comments about her career behind them – maybe he was more threatened by her success than she had realized? His voice cut into her thoughts. 'Now. I think it's time you showed me what a very dutiful wife you are.'

Even though his voice was not especially playful, she decided to enter into the spirit of things. It would be nice to make love tonight, on their wedding night, and not to do any of the kinky stuff for once. One could have too much excitement.

She poured some champagne into her glass and, taking a sip, sauntered towards him. He was sitting in the armchair nearest to the window. She went to draw the curtains.

'That won't be necessary.'

'You don't want everyone looking at us!'

'That won't be necessary.'

Determined not to be disheartened she repositioned herself to the side of the window, hopefully out of view. She pulled the silk camisole over her head and the slip from her hips to reveal new, very expensive and undeniably sexy black lace La Perla brassiere and knickers. His gaze flickered over her but he made no comment. She tried to ignore the feeling of disappointment at his lack of interest.

His voice was sardonic. 'I think a wife should kneel at her husband's feet.'

She decided to humour him. Anything to avoid another row. As she slid to her knees she saw him simultaneously draw down the zip on his trousers.

'That's not very romantic!' she exclaimed.

'Oh I see,' he countered irritably. 'Now we're married it's off the menu, is it?'

'No . . . I just mean on your wedding night it's nice to be . . . romantic.'

'This is romantic. It's also nice to be generous and giving and unselfish.'

He held her face. 'Go on.'

'I don't feel in the mood.'

He persisted. 'Just do it. You'll get in the mood.'

She felt miserable and defeated. To refuse would certainly ignite another row and she couldn't bear it. She began, reluctantly, to do as he asked. She felt him move with her and go deeper and then, with no warning and after barely any time, it was over.

She felt a quiet fury. Angry misery engulfed her and now there was nothing that she could say to herself to rationalize the way she felt towards him. He said nothing to her, not a word. She felt tricked and used and disgusted, with him and with herself for letting him. He was a pig. He was selfish. And it was obvious he didn't give a damn. She was still on her knees when he got up. He spoke as if nothing untoward had occurred. 'I need some sleep.' She heard the bathroom door close. He clearly felt no obligation to excuse what had happened – and it came to her that there was no possible good or loving explanation for what had passed between them. She stayed there for a few moments, a newly married woman honeymooning in a sumptuous room in a luxurious hotel, left sitting alone on the floor.

# Chapter 14

# Daily Journal

*Tonight I was promoted to the position of coffee maker at the Tuesday night Cobham AA meeting! Have just got off the telephone to Ed, who congratulated me heartily, then dropped into the conversation that he is chairing the Thursday noon Clapham. Damn! There was one dicey moment tonight when it looked as if the post might be contested and an election held. But my challenger (two months sober) backed off in the face of my overwhelming suitability for the post (four months sober and previous form stacking chairs). I have been entrusted with the key to St Anthony's church hall, instructed as to the correct use of the urn and given free rein as to the choice of herbal tea bags. I am astounded at how nervous I am at my newfound responsibility: which biscuits; full or semi-skimmed milk; whether to offer decaffeinated (what self-respecting alcoholic drinks that anyway?) and how to get those pesky stains off the teaspoons.*

*I have now settled into a routine of attendance at three meetings a week, a fortnightly session with Roddy and too much 'consultancy work' from Lloyd-Davies than is good for me. The sale of the house moves on, the rented pad is up and running and Susannah and I have coffee once a week ostensibly to bicker half-heartedly about the terms of the divorce but really for her to show off to me about her new job. She's bought a Jaguar sports car. I'm currently in a Volvo estate. All standard stuff. Stern lectures from Roddy anticipated. He wants me to deal with the divorce and then indulge in some year-long period of 'meditation and reflection' before making any life changes. All well and good but as I told him last week if I lived my life in that thoroughly sensible manner I wouldn't be an alcoholic. He looked stumped at that. Hell, it's about living sober not existing-sensibly-and-never-having-any-fun sober. 'Suit yourself,' he said peevishly. And I told him I would. Or, to put it more eloquently: to thine own self be true.*

Natasha realized that she had hitherto lacked the resolve, rather than the means, to open the locked cupboard door of Robert's bedroom. All it required was a call to a Garrett Lane locksmith, who supplied her with a key to what was a standard lock. Even though they were married she had continued, albeit for only two days, to think of it as his bedroom, in his house. She had believed that she could not open the door. To do so, she had told herself, would be to intrude on his privacy. That, of course, was nonsense. She had no qualms about glancing through his opened post or the Christmas cards that had begun to arrive. No, it would be more accurate to say that she would not open the door for fear of leaving evidence of her actions.

Her wedding night should have been evidence enough. It was almost enough. That night she understood, lying far apart in the bed, that her new husband intended to treat her with contempt. She still believed, however, that Robert loved her in his own way and that while love existed there was hope for something better to emerge. The truth came in the offices of Masterson Ryder Jardine at nine thirty that Monday morning when she read the affidavit that Robert's solicitor had prepared for her and understood that Robert had married her because he needed a wife and he needed one quickly. She heard, in the way that Robert discussed the case, that he would do anything to win. She saw, in the eyes of his lawyer, that this was a case that should be settled, not contested. Philip Ryder, a man in his forties whose office displayed silver-framed photographs of his wife and three children next to trophies for karate and golf, had sounded pessimistic.

'It will be very difficult for you to make a case. Their side contends that Araminta will have a settled family life out there, attend a good school—'

'Not a private school,' interjected Robert.

'No, but the court system does not insist on that.'

'Well, it damned well should do in cases like these.'

Philip Ryder was unruffled. 'Unfortunately, there are precedents that apply to all children.'

Natasha wondered if Mr Ryder believed this was unfortunate at all. They went back and forth in this vein and then Philip Ryder cleared his throat and said, 'Have you considered a negotiated settlement? By which I mean giving your consent to Araminta leaving with her mother provided that certain conditions were met—'

'No.'

Mr Ryder went bravely on. 'If you lose the court may impose its own schedule of visitation rights – which may be less than you could have gained by negotiating today.'

Robert was impatient. 'I don't give a damn about visitation rights! I am not in the business of negotiating defeat. I am in the business of winning. If you can't achieve that for me then you had better stand down from the case.'

To his credit, Philip Ryder stood firm. 'No lawyer can promise you that you will win. We believe we always obtain the very best outcome for our client. I would be failing if I did not point out to you the risks of pursuing this course of action.'

It was a surprise to see Robert back off. 'We can always negotiate, but not now. I want to put in the evidence of the witnesses. See what their response is.'

Philip Ryder made a note on his lined A4 pad. 'Very well.'

Before she had a chance to think of an excuse he pulled out a typed document. In it she said that Robert was a wonderful father. She went into some detail about the time and attention he lavished on Araminta. She made sweeping promises about the perfect life Araminta would have with them should the court award him custody. She read it and by the end she felt miserable and dizzy. None of what her statement said was untrue. There was nothing concrete she could point to as a reason for not swearing it. Yet all of it was a distortion of the truth, exaggerating Robert's involvement and silent as to his motivation in pursuing the case so ruthlessly. She signed. She would have liked to have read Robert's statement but he asked her to go outside while he went over this and other papers with the lawyer, so she left the room. Robert had gone straight to the office from the meeting and she had made up some story about going shopping. Instead she had rung the locksmith and made an appointment for that morning.

Now she was home, looking at the open door of the cupboard she had speculated about for so long. There was nothing there. Nothing at all. The locksmith had looked at her with some amusement. 'Worth the wait, love?' She had paid him, in cash, shown him out and gone disconsolately back upstairs. It was just a bare room with white-painted walls. Perhaps Robert kept it locked to stop Araminta locking herself in. Or maybe the floor was unsafe. She stepped back quickly into the bedroom. As she did so her arm brushed the door frame and she knocked something over. She picked up a wooden pole, some five feet long, of the type used to open windows with catches out of reach. She looked back into the room and upwards and then she saw that there was a loft hatch.

Using the hook she pulled at the door, revealing a ladder. She wasted no time and climbed into the room above, which was carpeted and shelved in the style of an office. On one side there was a fully equipped photographic processing laboratory. She figured that from the sink and the clips and the containers of chemicals. She looked around. The other side of the room housed a desk, chair and computer. The room was windowless and lit by a safelight. The sink did not look as if it had been used recently. Of course, Robert had a digital camera now. She walked over to the floor-to-ceiling bookshelves that were installed above the desk along the length of the wall. Each shelf held identical box lever files. The labels were in Robert's careful handwriting. They were not names; they were dates. It was an archive.

The thought came to mind that perhaps it was innocent, a place to store records. For tax purposes, for example. She knew it was not. Her heart was pounding now and she wanted to run down and call Robert, any excuse, just to check he was at the office. It was absurd. She forced herself to breathe and relax.

She took down the most recent file, for the current year. There were some receipts for clothes, including the receipt for Araminta's bridesmaid dress. Next she picked up a photocopy of a letter in Robert's handwriting. It was addressed to Paul Bass's ex-wife Tina.

*I knew Paul first as a client and then, I am privileged to say, as a friend for over twenty years. The shock of his passing is . . .*

She did not bother to read on. Next were items she recognized: more receipts from shops they had visited together, a pair of gloves he had bought her in Harvey Nichols, an umbrella in the General Trading Company – and the receipt for tea there. Why did he keep all these receipts? Then a receipt for dinner at the Ritz and several from La Famiglia. She saw that in the file was the receipt for every item he had ever bought her. It was an inventory. There were theatre programmes

– *The Importance of Being Earnest*; *Waiting for Godot*; *Cirque du Soleil* – cinema tickets and stubs for entrance to museums. On the back he had written details of the day.

There were programmes from church events, local fairs and craft sales, and every event that they had ever been to. It included scraps of papers, telephone messages she had written for him, lists, inconsequential notes – *Gone to get the papers Nx* – even shopping lists, for goodness' sake. She began to feel disorientated. It was too much. It was obsessive. She found herself confronted by the physical evidence of a mind that could not be described as normal.

Then things she began not to recognize intermingled. There was a postcard from Morocco:

*Dear Robert*
*Thank you for my super brill wonderful birthday presents. They are FAB and I am going to wear them every day and think of you when I put them on in the morning and take them off at night (!!??). I hope you have a very successful trip. Love and kisses and hugs, Jazzy xox-oxoxo*

Pinned to the card was the receipt for a pair of silver drop earrings from Wilfords, a chi-chi gift shop in Southfields. She and Robert had been there on several occasions. She turned over a ticket stub from the El Greco exhibition at the National Gallery.

### 25/4 – Araminta and Jasmine

Jasmine? It was an unusual name. Between two restaurant receipts was a solicitor's letter to presumably the same Jasmine. It was from Masterson Ryder Jardine. Not from Philip Ryder, but another lawyer who described himself as the litigation partner. She read it.

*Our client is hopeful that you will voluntarily cease making such accusations. Our client seeks an undertaking from you to that effect. If our client is forced to make a court application for an injunction he will seek to recover the costs of that application and those proceedings from you . . .*

Her heart was beating faster. What had Robert done to Jasmine and why did he need to keep her quiet? She tried to steady herself and to keep her focus. She replaced the file, noticing as she did so that last year's was missing. Where were the photographs? Of course, he would not put them with other papers. He would want to keep them somewhere more protected than that. He would want to use acid-free paper. She began to look around.

There was a three-door filing cabinet behind her. She almost wanted it to be locked. Then she would have an excuse to leave and shut the door and try to forget all that she had uncovered. But the top drawer slid open. Now there were names. Each album held a name.

*Jasmine, Elizabeth . . .* She pulled open the other two drawers. Each held identical albums, each catalogued by name, the label written in Robert's bold hand. There had to be at least twenty. In the bottom drawer she found *Tabitha*. There were some films, too. Thank God she had never let him use the video camera. Quickly she began to search through the albums, looking for her own name, but she could not find it. She began to panic. What had he done with her photographs? She could not leave without them – she had no doubt to what use Robert would put compromising pictures of a woman who had dared to leave him. She forced herself to calm down. They must still be in the digital camera. She began looking and found it in the desk drawer. She switched the camera on and saw that she was right. Thank God she hadn't let him have full rein with it. There were thirty or so pictures, contained on one disk. Deftly she extracted the disk and placed it in her pocket. She thought about switching on the computer and checking the hard drive but there wasn't time. There was no phone connection, which was as she anticipated – Robert wasn't the type to share what he had with others. This was a very private obsession. The computer was for editing and printing. That, at least, was something to be thankful for.

It was hard to think straight as she struggled to keep at bay the recurring fear that Robert was going to appear. Hesitantly she opened one of the albums. *Jasmine*. Something about that name sounded familiar. She felt uncomfortably like a voyeur, a Peeping Tom, and so she did not linger. But immediately she recognized the photographer from the *Radio Times* shoot – the girl who had been so nervous and tongue-tied. Pieces of the puzzle began to fall into place. Araminta had once let slip the name *Jazzy*, earning herself a disapproving glance from Robert. Araminta had never mentioned her again.

Quickly she closed the album. She looked at another and one other – because she had to be sure. In a few minutes she was sure beyond any doubt. All the pictures were the same: the standard poses of any adult magazine, here and there the props she knew so well. The collection was differentiated from what might be called normal, or at least acceptable, by the sheer number of pictures and the care that had been taken to assemble them. The photographer did not love his subject. There was no effort made to pose or present each woman to her best effect. They were just records, flat and passionless, as emotionless as laboratory records.

By the time she finished she didn't want to look any longer, because she felt sick to the stomach. She took Jasmine's album and Tabitha's – it was hopeless to try to take them all – and patted her pocket to make sure she had the disk from the camera. She descended the ladder, pulled out her suitcase from under the bed, then had an idea and went back and took the last four years' worth of box folders. And the films. Somehow the films seemed worse than the photographs. Technically it was theft but now the normal rules didn't apply. Robert didn't fight fair, so why should she?

It was so tempting to leave the door open, but that would give him advance warning. She packed the albums and the folders and everything else that she could, moving as quickly as possible now, running down to the kitchen for black bin liners in which to throw the remainder of her belongings. This was her only chance; whatever she left she could never reclaim because it would be impossible to come back here. Curiously, she felt no sense of loss. It had never been their home; it had remained Robert's long after she had moved in, imprinted with his tastes and immune to her presence. She piled her things into the car and began to panic because it was getting dark now, past four o'clock. Even though she knew that he must be at the office she still had an awful fear that some impulse or second sense would cause him to come home. She started the car and pulled out the A–Z.

It was tempting to go straight to Ealing, to the address on the solicitor's letter to Jasmine, that very evening. It was tempting, but she knew it was wrong because she was in no control of her own emotions, let alone able to break the news to Jasmine that her ex-boyfriend was an obsessive nutter who had kept a collection of pornographic photographs of all the women he had ever slept with.

Instead, she drove to a hotel, somewhere central and safe. She was too scared to go to Putney. It was there, in her room at the Sheraton Belgravia, that Grania swept in. Natasha had discounted calling her mother, considered calling Anna but instinctively felt drawn to Grania.

'You're absolutely right not to go home. Stay here, keep holed up. Did you use a false name to check in? Yes? Good! The man is highly dysfunctional. Probably a sociopath.'

'Gosh! What is that, exactly?'

Grania admitted she was not quite sure but thought it had something to do with using other people for your own ends. Natasha found that she was not interested in psychological labels or discussing his self-esteem or his problems with intimacy. Nor was she any longer interested in how Robert had come to be the way he was. She just wanted to be free of him.

In the end she had told Grania the whole story as they worked their way through the mini-bar – Natasha taking the alcohol and Grania the chocolate – sprawled on the executive double bed.

At the conclusion, Grania's expression was sombre. 'I think Robert is dangerous.'

It was a relief to have her feelings confirmed. 'Do you really think so?'

'Yes. I do. I think he has no emotions. I always thought that and now I wish I had told you. Age has its advantages in one respect: you become a better judge of character.'

'You're not old!'

'Forty.'

It was hard not to stare.

'Good genes and an even better surgeon, dear.' Grania broke off a triangle of Toblerone. 'But back to Robert. All this stuff he keeps – it's an obsession. I think he is obsessed with keeping control, even after the women have gone. Look at the letter his lawyer sent to that poor Jemima girl.'

'Jasmine.'

'Whoever. He's doing the same thing to his ex-wife. He doesn't want Araminta. He wants to control Tabitha. That's why—' Grania stopped herself short.

Natasha gave a self-deprecating smile. 'Why he married me. It's OK, Grania, I've worked that out. I feel so stupid. You must have seen that was his game.'

'No. Robert is a very seductive man and, I imagine, very difficult to resist. One never knows the ins and outs of other people's relationships and one can be quite wrong. I was just . . . suspicious. Now I blame myself for not saying more.'

Natasha shrugged. 'Who's to say I would have listened?'

'Sometimes one has to make one's own mistakes. Take it from a pro.'

Natasha was beginning to get a headache from the stress of the day and the fear of Robert's reaction, not to mention the bottle of white wine she'd had. She rang room service and ordered hot chocolate. 'How's Alex?'

Grania frowned. 'Different. Very attentive. Whatever was going on – if there was anything – it isn't going on any more. I can feel it. And there's something else.'

'What?'

'There are rumours going round about the Winters. It's funny but I just have this odd feeling about Louise. Of course, Alex would swear blind he's never given her a second glance . . .'

And at that moment Natasha understood perfectly why Grania had not disclosed her suspicions about Robert. The truth hurts. The truth holds great power. Sometimes that power is too much for one person to exercise. Was it better to speak the truth? Or was it better to let two faltering couples have a second chance?

Natasha put on her best and blandest *Blue Peter* expression. 'I haven't heard anything.' It was almost true. She hadn't heard anything that day.

'Good. Because I would really, really hate it to have been her. She was so keen to be my friend. In fact, I don't think I could have got past that one.'

Natasha waited until Friday to go to Ealing. In the meantime she ignored Robert's messages, on the hour on her mobile, withdrew her instruction to Foxtons to let her house and found the courage to telephone Daniel Moores to ask him why exactly she had been dropped from the Moores contract. He had sounded surprised to hear from her, nervously commented that he had understood that she had decided to retire from the limelight, and let slip that Robert had suggested Richard Waters as a natural successor now that she wanted to step down.

Jasmine's entry phone was out of order, so she had had no choice but to wait until one of the residents appeared, walk in confidently behind her and ascend an awful lot of stairs to Flat E, the photograph album wrapped in a Waitrose plastic bag under her arm.

There was a moment of surprise on Jasmine's face but then it cleared and she smiled and opened the door to invite her in.

Jasmine's voice was expectant. 'I can imagine why you're here.'

Natasha felt herself choke up. The evening with Grania had been one thing but this was something else. Jasmine came up to her and held her tight. Even though Natasha was the elder of the two and the more successful in worldly terms, here it was Jasmine who was the wiser. She led Natasha through to the tiny living room, where lining paper covered three quarters of the walls. In the corner stood a stepladder and beneath it a neatly stacked pile of decorating tools, paint trays, pots and brushes.

'I'm in the middle of decorating,' Jasmine said unnecessarily. 'Would you like a drink? A cup of tea? A glass of wine?'

'No. Thank you.' Natasha sat down in the sofa that half-filled the room. She struggled to find the appropriate words to use. 'You must think this is ridiculous. I mean, I only just got married.'

'I know.' Jasmine sat down at the other end of the sofa.

'You know? Oh, the papers . . . Well, I've left Robert. I should never have married him. I feel such a fool!'

Jasmine was obviously sincere in her concern. 'No! I feel so guilty: I should have warned you when I had the chance.'

Natasha was bewildered. 'Warned me?'

'At the *Radio Times* shoot. I overheard you talking about the wedding. And I wondered if I should tell you what had happened to me, I really did, but I thought . . .' Jasmine's voice trailed away.

'You thought I wouldn't take any notice?' Natasha suggested softly. 'Sad to say, I almost certainly wouldn't have. Now I look back, all the signs were there, but I ignored them – or chose to believe that Robert would mellow in time. I guess I had to make my own mistakes.'

'I always do!' said Jasmine, grinning.

'At least you had the sense not to marry Robert,' she said positively.

'Actually, he never asked me.'

Natasha spoke with feeling. 'You had a lucky escape.'

Jasmine looked away. 'In some ways.'

Natasha hesitated. 'I came to give you this.' She pushed the package at her. 'I want you to know that no one else has seen it. No one knows it exists.'

She watched as Jasmine pulled the plastic bag away. She did not open the album.

'There are negatives at the back. I haven't checked, but I imagine that's everything. There were some films, too. Only a few that I could see.'

'Robert only got the video camera last year.'

'I got all of them. I burned them. I didn't watch them,' she added.

'Did you get any other albums?'

'Mine. And Tabitha's. I couldn't take any more. I had to get down the ladder . . .'

She recounted the story of the attic room. At the end Jasmine began to cry. 'I never thought I'd get them. I thought he would always have them and one day – if I ever got famous or had my own exhibition – Robert would sell them to some tabloid or some magazine.' Natasha pulled a tissue from her bag and slid over to put her arm round Jasmine. 'And I knew I had to try not to think about it and to carry on but it was always there. In the back of my mind. It's just such a relief! I'm going to burn the photographs; I'm going to make a bonfire and burn them.' She looked up at Natasha. 'What are you going to do?'

'Well, I think it's safe to say I no longer have an agent. But I do have a house. And some repeat fees from Moores, which should pay the mortgage for a couple of months.'

'Will Robert try to stop you getting more work? That's what he did with me.'

Natasha refrained from saying that she knew that. 'I'm sure he will, but he hasn't done anything yet. He's trying to get me to meet him.'

'Don't!'

'I never want to see him again. There's something I need to do before I can even think about work. You see – I got away. And so did you. But there's someone who hasn't. I have to get Tabitha away, too.'

It was worse than Tabitha had ever imagined. She knew that Robert's statement would be hostile. She understood that Estella, in her statement, would support her son. But Lizzy! She had never once, not for a second, imagined that her own friend would give evidence against her.

But here it was, contained in the bundle of documents that had arrived that morning from Robert's solicitor, the two-page affidavit of Elizabeth Warren of 16 School Close, Stokesham, Sussex.

*I have known Tabitha Brett for three years. I would describe us as good and close friends. We have spent many hours together socially and shared childcare obligations. I believe that I am a trusted friend. For example, I have a key to Tabitha's house for emergencies and I look after her house when she is away. I have met Tabitha's fiancé Theo Hall on several occasions and had the opportunity to form an opinion of him.*

*In my opinion Tabitha has struggled with the demands of motherhood and a career. On one occasion she described Araminta's forthcoming holiday with her father as a 'relief'. She added that she needed a 'break'. I have seen her drink alcohol in large quantities. On one occasion she drank in excess of the legal limit for driving a vehicle. She was unable to drive her car home from my house and had to call a taxi.*

*Her house is often untidy and disorganized. She has complained to me that she finds it difficult to manage all the washing, cleaning and cooking at times when her work schedule is busy. On one occasion Araminta was sent to school without her packed lunch.*

*I believe that she has entered into a relationship with Theo Hall with undue haste and insufficient consideration for her daughter's welfare. It is my opinion that Tabitha is emotionally volatile. On occasions too numerous to mention she disclosed to me her fears that she would never meet 'a good man'. I believe Mr Hall to be a well-intentioned man who fulfils Tabitha's desire to be married.*

*I know Araminta Agnew, the subject of these proceedings, very well. She has stayed overnight at my house on more than ten occasions. I know from speaking to Araminta and from my contact with other mothers at the school that Araminta is extremely popular and is great friends with my daughter, India. I believe that Araminta will suffer if this and other friendships are broken.*

*I give this evidence in the spirit of friendship and in what I believe are the long-term best interests of Tabitha and Araminta. I believe that Araminta should be resident in the UK.*

She called Theo, heedless of the time difference, waking him up. She read it out to him. By the end Theo was laughing. 'Is that it? Who is she kidding? So you sometimes find it difficult to run the house and work.'

'It makes me sound so terrible!' Tabitha interrupted him. She felt close to hysteria.

She could hear him getting up and going to the kitchen to make coffee. 'It's *supposed* to make you sound terrible. That's the attorney's job. It doesn't mean anyone is going to believe it. Read that out to every other single working mother in Great Britain. What do you think they would say? *I work full-time, my house is immaculate and my child has never once in the last three years forgotten any school item.* C'mon. It's the way it's written. Tabs, you're a saint and the judge will see that. Anyway,' he added thoughtfully, 'Araminta's going to lose all her friends at Stokesham if she goes to live in Wandsworth.'

Theo's words did nothing to lift Tabitha. The shock of the betrayal was too great. Someone she had trusted, at the most vulnerable time in her life, had taken her confidences and used them against her.

'Theo, I feel such a fool. I had no idea. I just cannot believe it!'

She heard the hesitation in his response. 'Actually, I'm not totally surprised.'

'You're not?'

'Do you remember the dinner we had together? Lizzy talked a load of bull. But she also asked too many questions. I noticed that in the car when we were driving back.'

'You mean . . . you think Robert approached her ages ago?'

'Who knows? Tabitha, who cares? If she wants to sell out her friend, it says more about her than you.'

She knew he was right but she could not seem to pull herself together.

'What about Robert? What does he say?'

She sighed. 'Oh, it's all the usual. Twenty-eight pages of everything that's wrong with you and me. Nothing new.' She paused. She had expected to be shocked and wounded by Robert's affidavit. Actually, she now realized, she was close to being immune to it. She began to read. "I am extremely perturbed by the prospect of Tabitha uprooting Araminta from her environment, taking her away from all that is familiar to her and taking such a grave risk with Araminta's future—"'

'Nothing new there, then,' observed Theo.

At some level Tabitha knew he was right. But on another his very confidence about the case made her feel more alone than ever. He could not share her anxiety and fear because he did not feel it. It was her battle and he was on the sidelines – rooting for her, but on the sidelines nonetheless.

A feeling of despondency came over her. 'What if we lose, Theo?'

'You have to hold your nerve. That's exactly his strategy. He's a bully, remember.' Theo repeated all the confident assurances that he had told her so many times before. Then, as he always did, he told her he loved her and she told him that she loved him. As Theo rang off the doubt persisted in her mind. She got up and looked at herself in the bathroom mirror. To her own eyes she had aged. The weight had fallen away from her. Circles, grey and purple, were permanent under her eyes. If she was like this now, how would she stand up in the witness box? The case was about Araminta but she was the one on trial, as was every aspect of her life and character. It was so unfair. How many people could go into court and answer to everything they had ever done in their lives, every decision, every break-up and feel good about it all?

She forced herself to focus; Barbara wanted her comments on the paperwork. She went back to her study, sat down and picked up the papers. She could not face reading Lizzy's affidavit again. Or Robert's. She turned to that of Natasha Agnew. How bad could it be? By the second paragraph she had read enough.

*Robert is a devoted father and, in my opinion, would provide a stable and loving home for Araminta. As Robert's wife I am committed to supporting Robert in his duties as a father. I work on a freelance basis and would tailor my work commitments in order to help him care for Araminta . . .*

Tabitha put the paper down and thought about what kind of woman could marry Robert and be persuaded to support him in this. Was she deluded? Money-grabbing? Emotionless? She felt a surge of hot fury towards this Natasha. Did she believe what she was writing? Or, worse still, did she know it was false but swear it to be true? Images came to mind of this strange woman welcoming Araminta home from school, playing with her, bathing her at night. It was an intolerable prospect. Tabitha looked at the stack of papers on her desk. At stake was the one thing she could not afford to lose: Araminta. Her mind ran on. Perhaps true love and happy endings only happened to other people. Was she foolish to hope that she could ever get away? Was the price of freedom too high?

She picked up the telephone and dialled.

'Barbara. Don't say anything. I want to talk about settling with Robert.'

Justin handed her the keys to the house. He looked nervously at his watch. 'Are you sure?' he said for at least the third time.

She couldn't keep the exasperation from her voice. 'Go on! Pick up the keys from me later.'

He hurried to his car. 'You're a star!' he shouted, opening the driver's door.

In truth she was pleased. She knew as soon as she had driven up to the front door of Railway Cottages that this could be the one. And if Justin's one-week stint reading the evening traffic news on Thames Radio gave her a chance to spend time there alone so much the better. He had failed to secure the position of Bloke on a Bike at Buzz FM. It was now Babe on a Bike because the job had gone to an ex-Page Three girl. But he was broadcasting this week at Thames while the traffic man was on holiday. Goodness knows how long Justin could hold out before Anthony discovered.

The owner was on honeymoon, which was even better. She hated being trailed round a property by a nervous seller pointing out to her what was self-evident. She knew which room was the bathroom, which was the kitchen and she could identify a shower unit without assistance. Susannah had spent her working life dealing in floor plans and measurements, not to mention location and still more precise location, but for her it had always been about feel: the feel of a house when she walked through the door, sensed its aura and tested whether or not it was a happy house.

She took in the ivy covering the front of the red brick, looked up to the quaint gables and down again to the tubs of winter pansies. She noted the care with which the front door had been sanded and varnished and the original stained-glass panel. She let herself in. The hallway was as she expected: narrow, rather dark and hung with a collection of watercolour paintings of English landscapes. All easily remedied by antique white paint – her perennial favourite and the colour she recommended to solve all problems – and better lighting. The banisters were original. Slowly she walked from room to room. It was exactly as she had anticipated. The clean and worn carpet. The linoleum in the bathroom. The dark wood picture railings and original cornices and the small tiled fireplace in the front room. It was perfect. It was perfect because it felt right. It felt warm and good. None of the detail mattered in the end. She looked out of the back window and saw that the garden was, as Justin had reported, immaculate. She could see that the neighbours had installed a gazebo, decking and a brick barbeque. Justin was right about them, too.

She saw immediately that the kitchen needed to be knocked through to form a kitchen dining room. She would have to take care to find a kitchen in keeping with the cottage. Definitely not white, possibly wood, but most likely hand-painted units and a dark marble counter-top. Perhaps she knew more about interior design than she had given herself credit – or was it confidence – for? She looked at the room, ostensibly working out the dimensions, but really thinking about people.

She needed to invite her mother; they should spend time together without her father. Her mother would enjoy the garden. They could go shopping or visit Wisley or Windsor. She had spent so many years criticizing her mother for the things she didn't do – but she had never thought to do them with her. And she needed to invite Deborah, the sister to whom she hardly spoke. She would have dinner parties and she would begin with the Charron's crowd. Not immediately – she did not want to give Anthony false hope. Dating was not part of her plans.

And then she thought about Gina. In the six weeks James had spent at Grange House she had said little to Gina after that first day. But she had spent a great deal of time listening to her. James and Roddy were always so keen to talk and encourage everyone else to do the same. It had been her experience that listening was equally beneficial. It was Gina, gently asking Tom's mother how she felt about her son's drug addiction, who had shown the group that all the love in the world can't reform another person. It was Gina, commenting after Sandra had spoken that day in family group, who had said that there was no earthly reason why anyone who wasn't an alcoholic should expect to know how it feels to crave a drink more than anything else in the world. Gina had given her permission *not* to understand exactly how James felt and to realize that she never would. By the end she had grown to appreciate Gina's stillness and the calmness of her manner. She would find the time to write to her.

And then there was James.

James was behaving terribly well. It helped to divorce a man with very little interest in the material. James had mentioned that he had encountered Jasmine at Robert's wedding. For a while that knowledge had been painful. Just because she didn't want James it didn't mean she was happy for another woman to have him. For a short while she had had second thoughts. Should she try again? But then she ran the tape forward and knew that the outcome between them, the conflict arising from two people on diverging paths, would always be the same. If she were selfish it would be easier not to see him at all. But Matthew needed him. And so she behaved in a way that was more self-sacrificing and mature than she would have believed possible – by doing what was right and welcoming him at the Chapters. It was a revelation. There were times she could recall, screaming and shouting at him during the years of his drinking, when her behaviour had been as bad as his.

It was the final irony. It was time to do what she should have done years ago and embrace the biggest therapy cliché of them all – to find herself. To make her own security, allay her fears and realize that no one else could do that for her. Already she had begun to surprise herself. She had finally mastered poker. She was smarter than she had thought. She had bought a pair of trainers and gone running with Matthew. She was actually quite sporty. And Justin had secured her the guest slot on next Friday's Thames Radio lunchtime phone-in. She was billed as Susannah Agnew, property expert, advising listeners on how to find the home of their dreams. She had spent so many long, frustrating, wasted years first trying to change Steve and then trying to change James. But finally she had got it. The only person she could change was herself. It was a bloody shame it had taken her thirty-eight years to find that out – but then she told herself to stop beating herself up. Some people never find anything out about themselves, never follow their dreams, never even realize they need to change.

She closed the front door and double-locked it. Tomorrow she would make an offer. They would be able to move in before Christmas. All that remained was to persuade Cal to lend her his building team for a week.

The High Victorian setting of the Royal Courts of Justice would convince the most innocent person that they were guilty of some heinous crime. The Family Courts were at the back of the building, in a modern block that Natasha supposed was designed to be less intimidating, but first one had to walk through the vaulted Gothic main hall, the stone floor echoing to the footsteps of gowned barristers, harassed-looking solicitors and anxious litigants. She felt she was one step away from a prison cell. She sat with Tabitha and Barbara outside the court. It was nine thirty. Their case was scheduled for ten thirty. There was still no sign of Robert and occasionally neither Natasha nor Tabitha could stop themselves from looking up at the sound of a heavy footstep. All Natasha's efforts were directed at buoying up Tabitha's spirits – as she had done when she first met her at her cottage in Stokesham.

At the time, standing on Tabitha's doorstep, she had felt like one of the BBC's most hardened investigative reporters. It had taken all her skills of persuasion before Tabitha had even agreed to talk to her. She had stood in the drizzle while Tabitha decided whether to let her in.

Tabitha had held on tight to the aged oak front door. 'If this is some ploy of Robert's you can go away!'

'It's not!' Natasha had pleaded,. 'I know it must look that way but really it's not. I've left him. Look.' She held out her left hand. 'I'm not wearing a wedding ring. And think about it: he'd never run the risk of letting us talk to each other.'

Tabitha had hesitated. 'You're getting wet,' she said. 'You'd better come in.'

Natasha had gratefully entered the cottage and been still more thankful when Tabitha suggested that she sit by the fire.

Tabitha had brought them tea and her expression had softened. 'So why are you here?'

Natasha took a deep breath. 'I made a huge mistake marrying Robert. Two days later I realized it.'

Tabitha gave her a self-deprecating smile. 'Congratulations. It took me several years before I came to my senses.'

Natasha felt she was beginning to make progress. 'And I'm here to apologize for helping Robert with the court case and to say that I'm on your side and I'll do anything I can to help.'

Tabitha looked at her thoughtfully. 'I was so close to giving up. I actually told my solicitor to settle.'

'What?'

'Don't worry. She told me that she'd resign from my case rather than settle with Robert. She told me that lots of clients panic on the eve of the trial.'

Natasha reached out and touched her shoulder. 'You just have to hold your nerve.'

Now, in the surroundings of the High Court, Tabitha wore the same frightened expression that Natasha had seen on that afternoon in Stokesham. And Natasha repeated the same assurances she had employed then to reassure her.

'I got away. Jasmine got away. You can, too!'

Tabitha looked worn out. Her formal black suit, with a respectable below-the-knee skirt, served to make her fair skin appear deathly pale. 'Aren't you forgetting something? I have a child with him.'

'Yes,' interjected Barbara firmly. 'You will always be parents together, but that doesn't give him the right to run your life and veto your every decision for the rest of your days.'

'Look at me,' said Natasha urgently. 'Look at me and tell me this. Do you believe that you can beat him?'

Tabitha looked into the distance. 'That's a very good question. Of course the answer is yes. I know, on paper, I have a strong case.' She looked at Natasha. 'But inside me, deep down, I think that he will always win.'

Natasha took her hand. 'Then we'll believe for you. We'll fight for you. We'll do it.'

Tabitha's voice was empty. 'And how will you do that?'

'By telling the truth. About my marriage, about my wedding night . . .'

'And what about Lizzy?' Tabitha said despairingly.

'I'll deal with her,' cut in Barbara sharply.

'From what you've told me, she had her own reasons,' said Natasha. 'Maybe Robert paid her. Or maybe she just wanted the attention.'

'I feel so violated,' said Tabitha with anguish. 'My own friend, the person who knew so much about me, betraying me to join forces with Robert!'

'I know. It's awful.' Privately Natasha had her own thoughts about Lizzy and when exactly her dealings with Robert had taken place. 'Just tell the judge the truth. So will I.'

'And I'll speak too.'

Natasha swung round. Behind her stood Jasmine, holding up a press pass. 'It's my friend Rizzo's,' she said by way of explanation. 'The security here is lousy. They didn't even check my photo.' She stepped forward confidently. 'You must be Tabitha. I'm Jasmine. Natasha told me about the trouble you were having. I'm here to help.'

But before Tabitha could respond there was a commotion as Robert swept in with his legal team – a barrister, two solicitors and a porter wheeling three boxes of documents.

Barbara put on her glasses to take a closer look. 'I think Robert is preparing for a public inquiry. Something on the scale of Heathrow Terminal Six.'

Barbara turned to Tabitha. 'Stay calm. I will deal with Robert's barrister.' She pointed out a young, tall man speaking to Robert in hushed tones. 'He's got a reputation as a bruiser but that's nothing we can't handle. You have to remember,' she said to Tabitha, 'the law is on your side. You don't have to speak to Robert at all.'

But as Jasmine began talking to Tabitha, Barbara's assurances were disproved by Robert striding over to them. He radiated an arrogant confidence.

'What's this? The High Court Knitting Circle?' His gaze fell on Jasmine. 'You have no business being here. I'm calling security,' he snapped. 'You're being removed.'

'No,' countered Barbara, 'we're calling her as a witness.' She turned to Jasmine. 'Who are you?'

'His ex-girlfriend.'

'She's irrelevant,' insisted Robert.

Barbara glared at him. 'Let's leave that to the judge, shall we? We can certainly call her. Family courts are very flexible when it comes to evidence. And we would prefer to deal with your barrister. That's presumably why you have one?'

'I have one to speak for me, not instead of me,' Robert snarled. He jerked his head towards Jasmine. 'She knows nothing.'

Jasmine pushed forward. 'I know a great deal about Araminta and even more about you.'

'Fine. I have my own witnesses.' He threw a self-satisfied smile in Tabitha's direction. 'Including your best friend.'

Natasha put her hand on Tabitha's arm to indicate that she would handle this. 'Because you paid her.' It was a guess, but Natasha made the accusation with all the assurance that she could muster.

Robert flinched. 'You can't prove that. You have no evidence.'

Barbara cut in, 'No, but we can ask her when she gives evidence on your behalf. We'll get it out of her.'

Tabitha rallied. 'How much did you pay her, Robert?'

His colour rose very slightly. 'I'm not saying – or admitting – anything.'

Natasha gave him a hard stare. 'You slept with her, too, didn't you?'

He didn't even trouble to deny it. 'It's not a criminal offence, you know.'

It was still a shock to hear her suspicions so brazenly confirmed. 'What?'

'Before I married you, dear. So it's not adultery.'

Natasha instinctively retaliated. 'It doesn't matter whether we were married! We were in a committed relationship, for God's sake.'

He laughed. 'You may have been. I never said that I was. I have needs, like any man. You should ask yourself why you couldn't satisfy them.'

Natasha was temporarily thrown off course by this. It was incredible. He had a self-serving answer for everything.

Robert planted himself in front of them. 'I'm not backing down. I'm going into court and I'm going to have my say.' He addressed Barbara. 'It's a family court. All the proceedings are private. Whatever you say about me can't be reported without being in contempt of court. Even the editor of a British tabloid will fight shy of that. And besides, most of them are my friends.'

He turned to Natasha. 'So. You found my collection. Congratulations. What took you so long? If you're planning to blackmail me with it then let me save you the trouble. No one, absolutely no one could care less. Actually, most of my male associates will secretly admire me for assembling a collection they themselves would love to own.'

Natasha felt herself losing her cool. 'It's not a collection, you freak. It's an obsession.'

Barbara held up her hand to indicate that she wished to speak. 'Robert, I think you're running ahead of yourself. We're here today to decide your daughter's future place of residence. Faced with a loving mother in the USA, or a deeply dysfunctional, obsessive-compulsive pornographer father, I have no doubt which way the judge will rule. The only issue we will be deciding today is how much of my client's costs you will be paying. And that's before we reach the question of what I think I just understood to be the payment of witnesses. That is a very serious offence – and the criminal proceedings consequent upon it can be reported. I have no doubt they will be. You're not the only person with friends in the media.'

Robert was not giving up. 'Really? Can the *New Statesman* afford a legal correspondent?'

Natasha could see that Robert was shaken but not yet ready to fold. She had hoped, against all experience to the contrary, that he would be reasonable. She knew she had to play her strongest card.

'Yes, they can, actually,' Natasha answered. 'So can the *Financial Times*.'

'Oh?' His voice was sanguine but she could see the slight discomfiture in his eyes.

'Their legal correspondent will report your conviction on charges of tax evasion. And fraud.'

Robert moved towards her. 'What?'

She forced herself to remain seated. 'Your receipts, Robert. I took your receipts. And, as I suspected, when I compared them against your tax returns I saw you had claimed for an awful lot of expenses that even you are going to have trouble claiming are business-related.'

He had fallen silent.

She continued. 'Trips to exhibitions, dinners out – all claimed as corporate entertainment. Every taxi, every meal, some of your clothing even – all claimed next to some category of business expense. Except that's not true. It's personal expenditure.'

'It's trivial.'

Barbara cut in. 'It's the principle, Mr Agnew, not the amount. "It wasn't very much money, Your Honour" has yet to be accepted as a successful defence in a criminal case. You could try it.'

He was riled. 'Shut up!'

Natasha knew she had to keep the momentum going. 'I'm not so sure it is trivial. That's not the view of the accountant I consulted. There are some substantial sums involved. For example, a very expensive silkscreen print in your kitchen that you claimed as office furnishings.'

He could not keep the surprise from his voice. 'How do you know that?'

'I know it all, Robert. You kept what, in legal terms, is known as a paper trail.' She paused. 'Do you want it back?'

He hesitated. She could see his mind turning over. Eventually he said, 'How do I know I can trust you?'

'You don't. But you have no alternative. You're going to lose today,

Robert. The only question is whether you appear in another court in six months' time answering charges of tax evasion. The outcome would be irrelevant. You might get off – I've no doubt you would hire the most expensive lawyers. But the effect on your business would be catastrophic. Who wants a PR better known for his grubby tax affairs than his stellar client list? You've spent years perfecting your image, and that's precisely your problem. Your whole business is one of projecting the right front. What happens when the mask slips and the private face is revealed – the true, scheming, unpalatable face of Robert Agnew PR?'

'Settle it,' said Barbara. 'This is your best chance. Actually, it's your only chance.'

Robert looked from Natasha to Barbara. It was as if Tabitha no longer mattered to him. 'I want the files. I want a signed statement that you took them from me. I have a feeling that stolen documents are inadmissible.'

'Your signature first,' said Barbara, 'on an order consenting to Araminta's residence in the USA and six weeks holiday per year with you in the UK.'

'Eight,' countered Robert without hesitation.

'Seven,' said Barbara.

'Done.' Robert's voice was emotionless. It was as if Araminta was a lot in an auction.

Nothing more needed to be said. But Robert had to have the last word. He turned to Tabitha. 'I'll be watching your every move, waiting for you to trip up. And when you do I'll be there to see you never get up.'

As he began to walk away Tabitha stood up. Her voice rang out with dignity, causing him to stop and turn to face her. It was as if she held his attention against his will. 'No. It's over, Robert. You've lost and deep down you know it. Say what you want, threaten me all you like. You can't touch me now. I'm going – and I'm never coming back.'

'How did you know!' Tabitha and Natasha stood alone on the pavement, framed by the two Portland stone towers at the entrance to the Royal Courts. Barbara had gone back to her office to finalize the remaining paperwork and Jasmine had apologized and said that she really needed to get back to work.

'Hey,' Tabitha had called out as Jasmine pulled down the window of the cab to say goodbye. 'Come visit me in the USA!'

'I promise!'

Natasha laughed. 'I didn't know for sure. I noticed that last year's file was missing from the shelf and I knew that Robert was working on his tax return. So I put two and two together.'

'It makes perfect sense,' commented Tabitha. 'He was always tight with money.'

'He just couldn't resist saving the tax,' continued Natasha. 'I think Robert is one of those men who believes that they are above the law, anyway.'

'So there never was any accountant?'

'Nope. Or any tax barrister. I didn't have time. I just made it up.'

'Wow.'

'Hey, I work in television. It comes naturally. I don't feel good about lying – but sometimes you have to fight fire with fire.'

Tabitha reached out her hand. 'Thank you. Thanks for everything.'

'It was the least I could do. I'm only sorry Araminta has to come back for the holidays.'

'Oh, I've gone through that in my mind a thousand times. The bottom line is that I can't stop him seeing Araminta even if I wanted to. Besides, Robert isn't a paedophile. His issues are with grown women. No, any problems will start later, when Araminta gets a mind of her own – the day she answers back. But that's a few years away.'

'And if you do stop her she would probably resent you for it.'

'Do you think so? I often wonder about that.'

Natasha said sadly, 'Yes, she might even end up building a fantasy of a perfect father.'

They stood for a few seconds until Tabitha broke the silence. 'And you? What are you going to do now?'

Natasha shrugged. 'Find another agent. Start lunching some BBC execs.'

'That sounds daunting.'

'No. It will be exciting. For the first time in my entire life I will be in charge of my own career.'

They walked a few steps away from the courthouse. 'I'm going to walk to Waterloo station,' said Tabitha. 'I need to clear my head.'

It was time for them to part, but Tabitha hesitated.

'What is it?' Natasha asked worriedly. 'You're not thinking about Robert?'

Tabitha was clearly on the brink of saying something. 'Did Robert . . . did Robert ever run a bath for you? If you catch my meaning?'

Natasha wasn't sure that she did. Robert always took showers. She took a moment to think, though. 'Yes. Yes, he did! I'd forgotten that. It was on our wedding night, actually. Then his mobile phone rang and he answered it. He took for ever so I let the water out.' She laughed. 'Just as well. He'd forgotten to turn the hot tap on.'

Tabitha looked away at the slow buses and darting taxis and people hurrying to their appointments, and she seemed to be back in another place. 'Not necessarily.'

And suddenly, standing on a busy London street, Natasha could hear nothing. She could only feel a dreadful realization dawning.

She heard Tabitha's voice and as she listened she saw in her mind the marble bathroom at Cliveden. 'Natasha, he ran a bath for me once. He pushed me under the water. He held me there. And he told me, when he finally let me breathe, that he was in control.' Tabitha hesitated. 'I don't think, until today, that I ever stopped believing that. I think, with a man like that, you wonder if you will ever get away.'

Natasha knew it to be true. Another piece of the puzzle fell into place, another fact that she had explained away. 'But you have.'

'Yes. Yes. I have. And so have you. Please, Natasha, don't delay. Don't worry about money or possessions or anything at all other than being free of him. Walk away — as fast as you can.'

'You're right. Actually, I was thinking of asking Barbara to start divorce proceedings.'

'He'll hate that.'

Natasha spoke with determination. 'Never, ever, ever in my life have I wanted so much to be single. That's another thing they don't tell you — that a girl can yearn to be single more than she ever, ever wanted to be married.'

Jasmine saw Matthew first. He was standing by a photograph of Nastassja Kinski lying naked on the floor, a python wrapped around her, its head staring at hers and its tail by her toes. Jasmine edged forward through the packed exhibition until she was by his side. She felt ridiculously nervous. 'Matthew . . .'

'Hey, Jasmine. What are you doing here?' He was obviously not expecting her.

'Looking at the pictures?'

He grinned. He had the most disarming boy-band smile. 'Figures. We've been here for hours. Dad wants to look at everything.'

Involuntarily, her heart seemed to beat faster. If she looked apprehensive, Matthew did not seem to notice.

'Avedon was a cool guy,' he said, tilting his head at the photograph. 'Who was she?'

'She's an actress.'

Jasmine looked at the photograph with a professional eye. It was taken against a plain backdrop with no props or distractions, so that the viewer was drawn to the pattern and strength of the snake and the fragility and beauty of the girl.

Matthew read from the accompanying text. '"The photograph appeared in *Vogue* and was later made into a poster that sold two million copies." Hope they've got it in the shop.'

She tried to sound casual. 'Where's your dad?'

'Looking at Janis Joplin.' He mimed a yawn. 'Hey! This guy had an eye for the babes.' Matthew had taken off to the other side of the room. She followed him over to a photograph of Brooke Shields, photographed sitting on the floor, one leg extended in skintight jeans. The photograph was entitled 'Nothing Comes Between Me and My Calvins.' There was a throng around the picture. A group of Spanish teenagers clustered around, paying little attention to the photograph, jostling with each other and joking in Spanish until their teacher came up and began handing out questionnaires for them to fill in.

She felt rather than saw James's presence by her shoulder.

'You came. I was prepared to stay here all day if necessary.'

Relief flooded over her. She had tortured herself that his comment about the exhibition had been a throwaway remark, that he wouldn't be here or – worst of all – that he would be here and look aghast to see her.

She decided to tease him. 'It's a lucky coincidence.'

He was unruffled. 'No. Didn't anyone ever tell you there's no such thing as a coincidence?'

She was unsure how to counter. He took her arm. Matthew was engrossed in a series of pictures of Marilyn Monroe as they moved to one side of a picture of Jacques Cousteau.

Now James's voice was filled with urgency. 'I prayed you would come. I didn't know if you would and I wouldn't have blamed you for a moment if you hadn't. I'm sorry – really, very sorry – if anything I've done has hurt you. God.' He ran his hand through his hair. 'What a stupid thing to say. I should have said more last week. I'm sorry. I was distracted by the prospect of that damned wedding.'

She wondered how much James knew about subsequent events. He continued. 'It *must* have hurt you, sending you that letter from Grange House and disappearing from sight . . . but Jasmine, I swear to you I had to do it—'

'I understand.'

It was a direct appeal to her. 'I had to. There was no other choice—'

She sighed. 'Yes. I'm not saying I liked it and I'm not saying it wasn't hard. But you were – I mean are – married and you had to try to make it work. I know that.'

'You do?'

'Yes. Did you think I wanted to have an affair with a married man?'

'No. No, of course not. God, I don't deserve you . . . as a friend,' he added hastily. 'Hell, I've got so much to tell you, to explain. We've had an offer on the house. Matthew's staying with me most weekends. Susannah's frantic at work – that's when she has to do most of the viewings. And I'm thinking of setting up my own legal practice doing charity law.'

She laughed. 'It all sounds great.'

'It is. Oh, and there's one other thing. I'm going to start flying lessons.'

'Flying!'

'Well, gliding actually. I met a guy in AA who's a gliding instructor. Amazing story. He used to go up with a bottle of vodka wedged in his parachute.' He saw her expression. 'It's OK, he's been sober for yonks. Anyhow, he's offered to take me up. You could come.'

'I'd love to!'

He looked ridiculously pleased. 'There are some checks you have to go through first. Some health and safety questions.'

'No problem.'

'Actually, they're pretty thorough. And complex. You would need to have dinner with me to be sure you have made full disclosure.'

She laughed.

His expression was grave. 'I'm afraid I can't make any exceptions.'

'Well, in that case I'll have to accept.'

At this point Matthew found them and asked who Audrey Hepburn was and James said he felt so old that he would take them both for lunch at Brasserie St Quentin to recover. They left the V&A and walked into the tourist hustle of Exhibition Road. Matthew and James were talking simultaneously: Matthew about the latest film releases and James about a knotty legal case he was fighting, which had far-reaching implications for the rights of access in Wales. They turned the corner and stepped into the cold wind and the bright sun. It was natural for her to take James's arm as they crossed the Cromwell Road.